Illuminati

The Book of Life

Elizabeth Alsobrooks

Illuminati: The Book of Life

© 2015 Elizabeth Alsobrooks

Swartz Creek, MI 48737

Edition 2
Cover design by Clarissa Yeo

All rights reserved. No portion of this publication may be reproduced, stored in an electronic system, or transmitted in any form or by any means, electronic, mechanical, photocopy, recording, or otherwise, without the prior permission of Elizabeth Also-brooks. Brief quotations may be used in literary reviews.

Printed in United States of America

Printed by
Tell-Tale Publishing Group, LLC
5174 Peri St.
Swartz Creek, MI 48473
www.tell-talepublishing.com

Library of Congress Cataloging-in-Publication Data
Illuminati: The Book of Life / Elizabeth Alsobrooks

1. Urban Fantasy
2. Paranormal
3. Action Adventure

For my son, Thomas, who was proud of me.

For two remarkable people who define the word friendship, and whose professional and personal advice I have often sought and always valued: Nancy Gideon who endlessly offered a cheerful, "love to," as she grabbed a cup of coffee to read a revision with the eye of an award-winning, celebrated author; and for my favorite Renaissance man, Sully AKA "Pulitzer Nominated Author Thomas Sullivan," whose unwavering encouragement and praise warmed my heart and inspired my pen as only a Blarney Stone-kissing Irishman could. And finally, for Pat Lazarus, the world's best cover artist, for working her magic in my life, in a myriad of sincere and kindly ways.

I love you all.

The Nephilim were on the earth in those days, and also afterward, when the sons of God came in to the daughters of man and they bore children to them. These were the mighty men who were of old, the men of renown.

Genesis 6:4

Elizabeth Alsobrooks

Prologue

Persia, 2500 B.C.

Water.

The direction of ceaseless dripping was unclear, but its patterned echo and dampness enveloped them. The sound was secretive somehow in a moisture-starved land where water was prized more than gold.

It chilled her.

Nalini clung tighter to the warm, reassuring hand of her mother. She had learned at an early age the only safe place to seek salvation and unconditional love. Wrinkling her nose and opening her mouth she tried not to breathe in the earthy, long-buried smell of the subterranean passage. Even with her mother's sure grip, bravery was difficult. Why had they come to this strange place? The sense of urgency disturbed her as seemingly unconcerned with her daughter's reluctance, the queen moved swiftly through the sinister labyrinth of tunnels.

It grew cooler as they moved further into the underground passageway. Louder, too, as drips trickled into steady flows. An odd environment indeed for a desert. Nalini shivered.

She hurried.

Small for her age, at seven she seemed always to be running to keep up with those around her. Impatience overcoming caution, she strained to see past the flicker of her mother's torch. Shadows elongated, sharpening like monstrous teeth where jagged walls slivered the light. Shades of darkness loomed ever closer, so oppressive they felt like they might reach out and devour the flame, leaving mother and child at their mercy.

Absorbed in the imaginative threat, she didn't notice her mother's abrupt stillness and halted mere inches from her sandal-clad heels.

"Here, Nalini. Do you see?" her mother asked, raising her hand to illuminate a painted mural.

Nalini took a step back and let her gaze scan the rock-face as she studied the figures a moment. "Who are they?" she whispered, as if speaking too loudly would awaken the strange shapes to her presence. "Are they real, or is this a story, like the one you tell me about Gilgamesh?"

"This is the story of you and me, Nalini. It's a history of our people, of our heritage."

"Tell me about our people, mother," she begged, her irrepressible curiosity making her forget her earlier fears.

The queen knelt, drawing Nalini against her side. "Long ago, in ancient times so far in history most no longer remember," her mother explained in the soothing singsong voice of a sage revealing the past, "our people came here from a place known as Nibiru."

"Is it here in the picture?" Nalini asked, studying the designs and shapes on the wall before her. They resembled the sky.

"Here." Her mother pointed to a small circle among ten others of various sizes that surrounded a much larger circular object.

"Is this Rā?" Nalini guessed, pointing to the large globe in the center.

"Yes. Very good--"

"What are these swerving lines that look like snakes racing up a ladder?"

"The seed of life. From the woman came the seed of life that was crossed with the mortals by *Those Who Came Before*."

"What are mortals?"

"They were the ones who were here when *Those Who Came Before* arrived from the stars. They crossed the seed from their royal bloodline and then duplicated the new mixed people so they could have helpers in their new home."

"I think I understand, Mother. We are royal. Father is a king, so now they help us."

"Yes. But you must never forget, Nalini, that the people who help us have part of us in them as well." Her mother leaned closer and her lavender gaze stared solemnly into Nalini's. The wavering flame reflected off the near-sapphire highlights in her mother's ebony hair. It made the smooth paleness of her skin appear ghostly in the darkness. Shifting shadows made eyes so like Nalini's own look larger and almost frightened. "It is very, very important that you never forget," she added slowly, stressing each word to emphasize the seriousness of her message.

Nalini understood that her mother wanted her to be kind and treat the people who helped them with respect. She returned her hand from its exploration of the cold wall to the haven of her mother's warm palm. "Father doesn't like helper people very much, does he, mother? Do you think it's because they are not like us?"

"Who can say?" her mother said in the not-an-answer way Nalini had come to realize meant an adult didn't want her to know. Then, more directly, "Never speak of such things to Set. Ever. You must not tell him you were here, or what you know."

After an apprehensive search of the shadows, her mother turned and rushed them back the way in which they had come, practically dragging Nalini behind her as if fearing her mention of Set would make him suddenly appear.

"Mother, I can't keep up," Nalini protested.

"You must, child. He will be looking for us."

Nalini ran, then. The first thing she remembered knowing was that they must never, ever make her father angry. For some reason she was not yet sure of, what her mother had showed her today was very important, too. She would never let herself forget. After all, her mother had risked making her father angry to teach her this lesson.

It must be important.

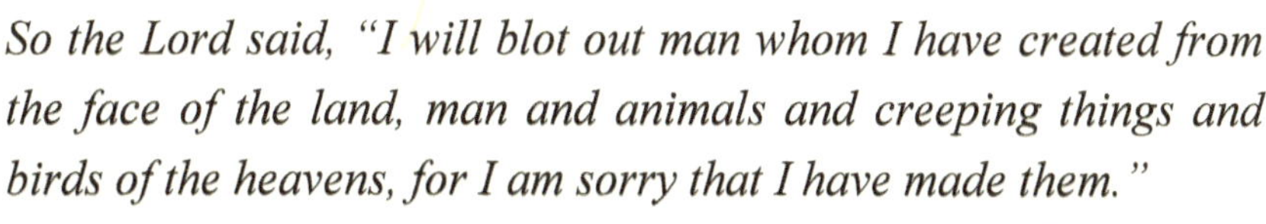

So the Lord said, "I will blot out man whom I have created from the face of the land, man and animals and creeping things and birds of the heavens, for I am sorry that I have made them."

Genesis 6: 7

Chapter One

Why was it always so damn hot whenever he was sent to kill someone?

At least it seemed that way to Luc. The heavy humidity matched his foul mood. It was sweltering and sticky even for D.C. in August. He dug a finger into the collar of his shirt and tugged. The air felt gritty, heavy with pollution and other less tangible remnants of a power base for the largest economy on the planet.

It was the kind of evening bound to produce high crime stats in tomorrow's news. Sensationalized stories, perhaps his, would trump summer closeout sales and free concerts in Lincoln Square.

His gaze scanned the sooty windows for nosey vagrants or addicts. Those in better neighborhoods sat in their controlled airflow high-rises listening to newscasters warn about a dangerously ignored and ever-growing population of disillusioned has-beens and wannabes whose fired-up tempers couldn't be cooled with tax breaks that never reached the sweaty tenements where they looked for lost hope in the bottom of a bottle or the end of a needle. What Luc saw was the inevitable decay of yet another civilization.

Which is why he didn't plan to linger in this back alley. Luc sighed softly, increasingly weary of the unending violence and secrecy.

A final survey confirmed empty brick-framed rows of darkened windows. Despite the filth, they still shimmered with obscured reflections of rising moonlight that might camouflage an unwary onlooker. Habit and a nagging whisper of something not quite right tightened his shoulders expectantly, and Luc again scanned the panes for a hint of rumpled curtain or a partially revealed face leaning curiously toward the glass.

No witnesses.

She knew he couldn't see her crouched in the shadow of the dumpster behind him. Yet as if his instincts screamed danger, he spun around and looked straight at her with a fierce, predatory stare. The hairs on the back of her neck tingled. He took a step forward and then stopped and shrugged the tenseness from his shoulders. She took a deep, slow breath and relaxed her own.

Instead of approaching the dumpster, Luc reassured himself that a mere ten feet separated him from the sedan he had parked near the rear exit. It was situated to the left of a dangerously neglected fire stairwell. He doubted the rust-welded tiers could still descend but no one lurked in the shadow of the landings and nothing blocked his path to the car. Yet something still made him pause.

Something's wrong. Where's the danger? Relax. I need to sense my surroundings. Deep breath. Yes. Better.

Premonition snapped his attention back to the alley. A near-undetectable footfall sounded behind him. As he spun around, a man lunged out of the shadows.

The man's fist, gloved in one-hundred degree weather, approached his face. Tilting his head aside, Luc barely avoided the blow. He stepped into the attacker's momentum. His own knuckles smashed into the man's stomach. The impact was reduced by what Luc assumed must be Kevlar. A quick turn. His arm flexed around the bulky, unprotected throat of his assailant. The brute was taller and outweighed him. Two-hundred and forty, maybe fifty pounds, plunged backward and shoved against his chest, repeatedly, the goal to break Luc's grip. Struggling to retain his hold, Luc almost missed the weapon.

Shit.

The man's arm slashed downward. When the assailant's hand came within reach, Luc snatched hold. He levered the blade it held forward, away from his own mid-section. A jerk of his wrist sent the thrust upward.

A burning sensation was followed by a spreading dampness. It was then he realized he'd been nicked. His shirt stuck to his side.

Extreme physical training and centuries of experience guided Luc's self defense. Reactive adrenaline added force to his actions. The long, surgical quality hunting weapon pushed through the assassin's body armor and into the man's chest. The knife skipped off a rib. Judging by the gurgling sound, it found a lung before protruding from his back. Luc relaxed his taut muscles.

It hit him then, full-strength. The scent of life flowing into death. Tantalizing. *Delicious.* Pulling at his senses. Hypnotic in its power. His spine stiffened and he froze.

What's wrong with me? Why am I having this reaction again? It's getting more frequent, at least half-a-dozen times now.

He clutched his side and fought to regain control as he released the body.

I can't let the family find out about this, at least not until I figure out what it is.

It occurred to him as he sprinted toward the car that he should have used the dumpster across the alley with social appropriateness, putting the trash who'd tried to kill him in its rightful place. But there was no time for delicacy. As the would-be killer's head hit the pavement with an unpleasant thud, Luc's hand was already jerking open the driver's side door.

Nalini's appreciative gaze shifted across the wide breadth of shoulders, and lowered to admire the cut of her target's highly tailored trousers. His legs were moving quickly, but she could still tell from their length that he was at least six-foot-five. Though lean, even covered in silk there was a sinewy tautness in those movements that hinted of well-honed muscle. She'd been following him for only a dozen hours, but already she had determined that he was much more of a threat than her arrogant brothers had suggested. When he turned to again survey the alley, she pressed herself against the filthy green metal and slid backward a few more inches until she could no longer see him.

Once the car sped forward, Nalini stepped from seclusion and leaned down to examine the fresh corpse. Her head tilted in concentration. She could smell the coppery aroma of blood that spread across his shirt where it had oozed from the confines of the Kevlar. Why had Ljluka Vargas bent toward the frontal wound, if only for a split second? He seemed entranced, almost as though the blood drew him against his will, like a hungry animal.

"Oh, he's dangerous, all right. Deadly so," Nalini muttered, as she turned to flee.

As he settled into the sedan, Luc unbuttoned his shirt and viewed his injury. The bleeding had already stopped. He jerked the arm rest compartment open. The small box held what he sought. It took only a moment for him to apply an adhesive bandage to the small cut on his side, just under his ribcage. He closed his shirt, buttoned his jacket and just before he steered the expensively-harnessed horsepower out of the alley glanced in the rear-view mirror.

His attention held.

She was glorious. A vision of beauty and grace.

Where had she come from?

The image lasted only a split-second as he sped away, but he would never forget the haunting impression she made upon him. Flowing fabric of gossamer spun gold caressed sleek, bronze limbs. Her fluid movements caused her layered skirts to float around her like a whispered rumor. The mirage rippled between his fallen victim and the corroded dumpster, as stimulating as any fleeting fantasy, and just as inaccessible. Then she was gone. He shook off his brief enchantment with a cold dash of reason. There wasn't enough time to look for her now--though he would have liked to see her face.

Ah, I'm too much like father used to be, letting my mind possess whatever pleases my eyes. Was the lissom apparition the presence he'd detected earlier? *Could the Usurper's minions be onto me so soon?* Letting out his breath, he sighed. *Back to business.*

His brow creased with concentration as he braked behind a city bus. A small group of twenty-something males filed out and loudly made their way toward what was, judging by the edgy music that drifted out as a couple exited, a local singles club.

In that moment's pause, his thoughts returned to the alley and the nagging feeling that the attack on him was a warning of more to come. He reviewed his movements. The sophisticated head of the subcommittee leaving the dingy hotel room, followed by the fulfillment of the first stage of his mission--insuring the

Usurper's minion would be permanently unavailable for future covert meetings with the quick flash of his blade. Then he'd gone out through the back alley where he encountered the would-be assassin. Judging from the shot-filled knuckles of the law enforcement-type glove the thug was wearing, he'd been no ordinary flunky.

So why attack me after the fact? I already carried out the hit. They never tried to prevent it. Revenge then?

From every angle, Luc arrived at the same conclusion, that the two events were completely unrelated. Either way, going back now just wasn't an option. It wasn't protocol. The mission came first.

The mission always came first.

A faint buzz sounded in his right ear. He reached up to tap the receiver. Amusement tugged at the corners of his mouth as Kirin's melodic voice teased him back to his present task. He was quick to reassure her.

"Just a momentary delay, nothing to concern yourself about."

"Oh, but I'm always concerned about you, Luc. Always," she responded playfully, using the affectionate nickname she'd christened him with when they were children. His given name, Ljluka, took too long to say, she'd assured him. He could imagine the teasing sparkle in his sister's emerald eyes.

"How long?" she questioned, her clipped, more professional tone alerting him that someone had joined her.

Finish it and return, commanded a voice used to instant obedience.

This message was transmitted without benefit of the earpiece. His mother needed only to think its delivery for him to receive it as if he were now standing in the room with them, rather than weaving in and out of late-night traffic. He was just a few cars back from one of several dark limousines ahead of him as he approached Pennsylvania Avenue.

Of course, he responded in like manner. He didn't bother signing off with Kirin. He knew she had disconnected even before the soft click sounded in his ear.

Pulling out his diplomatic identification, he extended it through the open window and waited for the guard to validate it.

The young Marine handed it back, saying, "Thank you. Have a nice evening, sir."

Electronics hummed while black wrought-iron gates swung open and an electrical impulse activated retractable bollards that receded into the asphalt before he was once again moving toward the limo now parked behind the White House.

Luc noticed without reaction the meaty secret service agent standing in the lee side shadow of an evergreen. Geared completely in black, starting with his seam-busting tight black t-shirt, Mr. White House Special Ops was packaged for delivery with Kevlar and Velcro, carrying some seriously fun party favors with plenty of popping power. Much had changed since 9-11—yet another reason his mother had no intention of letting up any time soon. She would never rest until the Usurper was destroyed.

The updated Rambo wannabe never moved, but even though all he could possibly see was another vehicle with tinted glass, his alert stare followed Luc's corporate- rented BMW until it rounded the curve in the driveway.

Pulling to a stop, Luc left the keys in the ignition and stepped onto the walkway. Careful to ensure his jacket was buttoned to hide his bloodstained shirt, he lifted his arms to shoulder-height, suppressing a grimace as the action caused a slight twinge in his side. A waiting agent swept his frame with a slow-beeping wand before signaling him toward yet another agent waiting to escort him to his destination.

Moments later he entered a high-ceilinged office filled with Chippendale period pieces and glanced across the room at the gray-haired, middle-aged cabinet member he had been sent to persuade. Shock, quickly masked, appeared in the man's watery blue eyes before he sprang up rather quickly for such an out of shape Boomer. Luc distrusted him on sight. The calculating gleam in the man's eyes disgusted him.

The door swung shut with a soft clack, the agent having remained in the outer office. "I-I was expecting someone else. Forgive me. No one . . . no one said they were sending you. I thought that--" He was already around the desk, motioning toward a more intimate grouping of furniture in the far corner.

The long-cherished gift from Kirin, the modified cufflink that bore the owl, symbol of his name, exquisitely carved in Etruscan gold had been slipped into Luc's jacket pocket. The cuff of his light blue silk shirt was pushed up just far enough to reveal the tattoo on his forearm. The cabinet member recognized the flaming sphere illuminating the cross within--the symbol identifying him as a member of the Illuminati's inner circle.

Luc moved forward with distaste. "I won't be here that long," he said softly, extending his hand.

The man gasped, but dutifully put his right hand out to be engulfed and squeezed within Luc's larger, firmer grip. Secret handshakes were supposedly only rumors, but in this case it confirmed Luc's superior status.

"As you can see for yourself," Luc continued more forcefully, "I am the message." He leaned down, closer, until he could smell the vile stench of stale cigar smoke emanating from the man. Directing the full force of his ice-blue stare at the man, he added,

"The cohort from your earlier meeting this evening won't have any objections if you wish to reconsider doing as you were instructed, I assure you. Don't forget that not so long ago others had to be reminded of what it means to be humbled. Not even the moneylenders are above our reach. We have toppled civilizations."

"I-I understand. I will call the committee together at once."

Luc straightened and flexed his shoulders. The man's pale face lost whatever color remained.

"It will be done. I swear it."

Desperation squeezed beads of sweat from the man's forehead. Luc grimaced and dropped the soggy hand. Without another word, he turned and left the room.

After he washed his hands, Luc had one more mission--somewhat more personal--to attend to before he flew back to Rome.

Even now no comparison can be made
With him and any other conqueror;
Before him the whole world
once quaked with dread.

Chivalry's and magnanimity's flower,
Fortune made him the sole heir of her honour,
And only wine or women could abate
His great designs and ambitious endeavour,
So like a lion's was his fighting spirit.

Chaucer, The Monk's Tale

Chapter Two

The stewardess stored the carefully wrapped gift box he'd handed her. It was not the gift Luc was watching, however. More enticing than the package were Sophia's well-formed curves as she bent to her task. Reluctantly, and with self-discipline, he redirected his thoughts to the purpose of his personal mission, the delicate crystal orchid he had obtained for his sister's name day— no, birthday. He would have to get used to buying presents now that Kirin had decided she liked colorfully wrapped gifts to celebrate her birth. The gift would never make up for the desecration of his sister's favorite flower, but at least she would know he cared.

He still remembered how her eyes glistened with unshed tears as she watched the news report that announced the extinction discovered by some university botanists. With each loss, she had cautioned them, came a greater chance that her research would never be completed. Research that could determine their very survival.

Their brother, Andrew, had used his influence with several environmental groups to pressure the Peruvian government. They had declared the ancient ruins a no fly zone. It should help, though it would have been easier to mask even the ancient ruins from public scrutiny. Their mother left the ruins visible now as a distraction to keep prying eyes from discovering their true secrets, far underground in Kirin's laboratory.

This gift was Luc's attempt to cheer Kirin, though he knew she wouldn't be truly happy until she was back in the Amazon with her plants and experiments—but none of them could predict when their mother would complete her business in Rome and let them all return home to Peru.

Until then, Rome was their temporary residence.

He flipped the lever and leaned back, stretching out as comfortably as a six-foot-four man could on an airplane. Even a private jet owned by the Vatican had its limitations. The pilot had informed him that they were not cleared to take off for a few more moments, so he settled back to wait.

"Your package looked fragile so I stowed it in the insulated cupboard, cushioned in blankets. Would you care for a drink, Don Vargas?"

"Please, I really do prefer it when you call me Luc. I'll have a bottle of water, Sophia." He could feel the tension packed into his shoulders already preparing to leave. "Is Valmont going to be ready for me after we take off?" he inquired.

"He's getting the massage table set up now." Sophia, in her light-gray skirt suit, as sleek, efficient, and unobtrusive as her service, already held a water bottle capped with an inverted glass in her right hand. She flipped the small tray next to his recliner up with her left hand. As she set down the glass and poured, he smiled his thanks, careful to keep his eyes on hers as she bent across his lap.

He got the distinct impression she brought her ample chest to his face level on purpose rather than by accident. Either way, it prompted him to close his eyes, dismissing her. She affirmed his suspicion of flirtation when he felt her gaze linger on him before she turned, sighed softly, and walked back to the galley. She was an asset to their organization, and he intended for her to remain just that. As usual, he would remain casual and polite, but distant.

He felt a slight tug at his manhood just the same. Perhaps Andrew was right. He was too predictable. Sighing to himself, he decided it suited him fine in this instance.

Stick to the plan. Hydration, a deep muscle relaxing massage and a mind refreshing nap. In that order. Yes, predictable. Predictable needs and predictable results—essential for someone with my lifestyle.

It was still raining when Luc stepped off the plane and hustled down the steps. His driver reached to position the umbrella over his head and rushed to keep up as they covered the short distance to the waiting vehicle. *It was raining when I left. Was that only two days ago?*

"I thought the plan was not to draw attention." He stooped to slide into the back of the limo.

"We're to rendezvous first, before you go to Vatican City," Antonio responded. He closed the door and quickly moved to the front of the car, collapsing the umbrella.

No one informed him that the others had failed to fulfill the preparations at the Vatican in his absence. The Usurper's spies from his latest takeover attempt should have already been eliminated, conveniently dying in their sleep or by some other undetectable means. Luc tapped his earpiece to find out if that was the case.

"I have no idea," Kirin stated, knowing before he spoke what his question was going to be. "But it's Head B on steroids around here. Something's definitely going on with Mother."

"Why didn't I get a heads-up?"

"Orders, Luc. *Monitored* orders. You know that." Her tone dropped, and he detected her indignation that he would question her loyalty.

"Of course. That's not what I meant, Kirin," he assured her quickly. "Where's An-"

"I don't know that, either. Apparently I don't *need* to know. He's on a private mission—something personal and top secret, I gather."

That explained why he'd been unable to reach his brother from the plane. "Can you at least tell me if everything has been handled in Vatican City?"

"Yes. The last one reported back over an hour ago. The Orac— I mean, the Holy Father will probably be expecting you."

The tension that Valmont had worked for an hour to loosen with an in-flight massage crept back into Luc's shoulders. Unlike his sister, he didn't like surprises as a rule—hazard of the trade. Antonio took the Via Aurelia exit from the Grand *Raccordo Anulare*. "Do you know who I'm meeting?"

"You know as much as I do," Kirin assured him, exasperation clear in her uncharacteristically harsh tone. She didn't like that her research work frequently left her in the dark about the intricacies of the financial and political work her brothers carried out for the family. Insatiable curiosity made her an excellent scientist, but sometimes a meddlesome sister.

"Okay, thanks. See you when I get back."

The car whizzed past the *Piazza degli Eroi* so fast he wondered why the pigeons pecking around the square didn't take to the air in fright. He now knew where Antonio was headed, if not why there was so much urgency.

They pulled alongside the curb in front of a small Bistro situated within a refurbished stone building that looked as if it could have occupied the same spot in the narrow lane since the Romans rode around in chariots instead of smart cars. Luc waved Antonio and his stalking umbrella aside and said, "Don't forget to take the package I left in the back seat to my room with the rest of the luggage. And be careful with it." Then he dashed toward the entrance.

The door opened before he reached it. Andrew filled the space it vacated, tailored, as usual, from his quick-slicked hair to his special order loafers. He had on black pants, deceptively casual, a blue polo-style shirt a shade lighter than his eyes—which he knew because Kirin had told him when she gave him an identical shirt--and an intricately stitched black leather jacket. He wondered at his brother's attire. Andrew usually spent his days in custom designer suits when in Rome on business. He looked up about six inches to gauge the seriousness of Andrew's expression.

His brother moved his hand to carelessly push a dark tuft of hair from his forehead and said, "Took you long enough." Then he snatched Luc into a one-armed hug. He pulled him along into the dim interior toward the back of the eatery and continued, "Welcome home, little brother. It's good to see you're still in one piece."

"Yes, including all my favorites," Luc quipped, laughing at their inside joke.

"Every little tidbit helps. Maybe you could try to make Sabina happy. She's been delightfully demanding lately." Andrew dropped his arm and moved ahead, the narrow aisle necessitating their single-file progression through the crowded yet somehow inviting table arrangement. The table tops were adorned with bottles filled with olive oil and the predictable flickering candle-topped empty wine bottle, complete with a variety of past dripping layers. The longevity of their possession made the eatery feel as much a home to the brothers as anywhere else they spent time.

"Surely you're not complaining," Luc said, feigning shock. He knew the high esteem with which Andrew held his current mistress and sometimes wondered how his brother would tell her goodbye when he inevitably didn't age and Sabina began to notice.

Andrew turned back, white teeth gleaming.

"Judging by the grin on your face, I gather I'd better give her a couple days to recover first," Luc countered, calling his bluff.

"You wish," Andrew chuckled.

"Hey, it was your idea," Luc teased.

"I think you'd better give your friend Magdalena a call, if she's still talking to you."

"You're right. I should," Luc admitted. "I do owe her a call."

How did I forget before leaving for America? Business always gets in the way. I could use a pleasant diversion. It's been far too long. Maybe that's what's been wrong with me lately. He'd call Maggie later that night, he decided.

His more flexible and casual relationship with Magdalena and previous, but equally independent women like her, kept his life a little less complicated, though sometimes through the centuries he had wished for the benefits of a more intimate relationship. It was an occupational hazard he had begun to resent.

"Listen, I really do need to talk to you about something," Andrew said, sobering. He motioned toward a table in the back, within easy access to the kitchen and cellar stairs. The establishment was closed so no other patrons would have intruded, but they never took any chances. A dozen or so of his brother's men waited respectfully at tables, guarding the front of the restaurant.

"Good," Luc said, pouring a glass of wine from the carafe on the table. "It's about time someone told me what's going on. Kirin's as cranky as mother gets whenever anyone mentions *his* name."

"Yes, I know. She's left a dozen messages on my phone. She even called to leave a message with Sabina."

Luc threw back his head and laughed, relaxing in his brother's company and the familiar surroundings. Only their little sister was audacious enough to call and leave a message with her brother's lover. He took a drink and waited to hear the real reason for all the secrecy.

"Did you encounter any problems in D.C.?"

"Just the usual." No need to mention the little nick he'd gotten. It had healed without trace within an hour.

"Are you sure? You didn't see anyone hanging around, get the sense of being followed?"

Luc turned the wine glass in his hand, remembering a pair of long, shapely legs, bared momentarily to the upper thigh. "Yes, there was a woman."

"I knew it. She disappeared about the time you left and she just returned."

"Who is she?" Luc leaned forward. "What's this about?"

Andrew met his gaze. His expression was now serious, reminding Luc that they could never fully let down their guard. "*She* knew. Mother knew and didn't tell me. What did the woman look like? Let's be sure we're talking about the same female."

"I only saw her for a moment. I felt her presence earlier, at the hotel. But it wasn't until I had completed the first part of my mission that I caught a glimpse of her." The image returned to tease him.

"Illusive little nymph, isn't she?"

"An understatement."

"Legs that go on forever. Spends a lot of time worshipping Rā."

"Yes. And long hair. I think she has long, ebony hair. I didn't get a good look at her face, but—"

"Oh, trust me, it's worth spending a couple lazy afternoons memorizing. But what's really striking about this woman is her eyes. I've never seen such lavender eyes. When the sunlight hits them they're almost a dark periwinkle, not blue, definitely lavender. It's startling."

Luc watched his brother's animated face.

So the woman has that effect on all men, not just me. I wish I had seen her face. "Sabina know about your latest infatuation?"

"I doubt she'd mind. I've been sent to kill our starry-eyed charmer. And I'm not supposed to mention her to either you or Kirin."

"Why? If she's following me then—"

"Exactly. Since she is following you, I can expect her to tail you to your meeting tonight. I think she knows we're onto her, so she probably won't be alone this time."

"Let me guess. I should hold a hook in my mouth?"

Andrew chuckled. "No, little brother. I'm the hook. You're the tidbit."

Luc stood and shrugged out of his raincoat. He tossed it over the back of his chair with resignation. "Let's get this over with," he said, loosening his tie and pulling it off to shove it into the pocket of his suit jacket. "I need to complete my mission as well."

Andrew glanced toward the front of the restaurant and nodded. Instantly the men who had appeared to be idly chatting rose as one, revealing that they had been alert and ready, covertly waiting for a signal.

They headed toward the cellar stairs. The catacombs would be the quickest route. It would also make it easier for them to clean up any messes they made along the way.

Luc ducked through an ancient stone archway, barely noting the faded religious symbols and mural remnants. They had played throughout these underground tunnels as children, back before the time of the Christian fugitives who defaced them.

"I'll go ahead," Luc said, turning toward his brother. "She's bound to be waiting in a side chamber up ahead. That is if she, as you believe, figured out I'd be here."

"Oh, she knows you're coming through here. I made sure of that," Andrew said. "I don't know how much more conspicuous I could have been than sending Antonio to pick you up, and having him drive that behemoth vehicle down this narrow little side-street."

Luc nodded his head in agreement. "She's had enough of a head start. Can I at least find out why she's following me before you kill her?"

Andrew shrugged. "Suit yourself. Just remember not to tell *her* I let you in on it."

Luc strode ahead. The flashlight he'd grabbed from the entrance illuminated a wide enough angle to avoid low rock formations and sudden twists in the tunnel, but in the complete darkness within the bowels of the earth, shadows swallowed even the air in his wake. The thrill of danger exhilarated him. He felt much more the hunter than the bait. Moist air, ripe with the scent of micro bacteria, pollen and fungus gave way at last to the less offensive odor of dust, ancient and forgotten.

Like them.

He continued downward, further still, and then stopped. He sensed her again. Inhaling deeply, he shut his eyes to savor the scent. Having expected the encounter, his instincts were alert and searching. Bergamot and coriander, with just a hint of lily. She smelled incredible, like a pheromone massage oil.

Damn, it seems a shame to kill her.

He knew she was there, up ahead in the tunnel to the left, just past the reach of his flashlight. She was no doubt pressed against the cold, damp stone, waiting, wondering why he'd stopped. She must hate it in this dark tunnel, being used to desert sands beneath her feet, an arid breeze wafting across her face, upturned to accept the warm caress of Ra.

It dawned on him then that the human assassin had been a test, or perhaps an exhibition so she could gauge his fighting ability and style. What was she thinking? Even to a grown man he was a formidable opponent. She had others crouching behind her. Out in front, though, she was the one who planned to attack him. But why?

Deciding it was time to find out, he rushed forward and reached into the tunnel, grabbing her by the waist. He lifted her off her feet easily, and tossed her over his shoulder. Something flew out of her hands—something that sounded like a gun by the heavy thunk it made against the packed earth. He turned and fled, his firm hold pinioning her arms to her sides, though it failed to prevent her legs from thrashing. His grip tightened until she yelped in outrage.

After their initial confusion, her companions ran behind them in pursuit. He might not like being surprised, but he sure loved being the surprise. His laughter was genuine.

Hearing warfare behind him, he realized it was Andrew's turn to have a little fun. This sort of fighting, the warrior-to-warrior combat, excited him. It was the subterfuge and deceit he hated, the assassination of an evil but physically vulnerable adversary.

He stopped. Unceremoniously, he dropped his cursing burden on the ground. She was up in an instant, pulling an unfriendly looking *shabriyyah* from a sheath strapped to her leg. Her stance proclaimed her a seasoned warrior. His admiration grew. Wearing jeans and a t-shirt this time, she was no less striking. The jeans snugged her trim figure and the tug of the shirt across her chest teased his senses. His first impression had been correct. His own chest tightened, and the reaction moved lower, to his groin.

Unconcerned with her aggressive pose, he raised his flashlight to look into her face. The vision blinked and angrily thrust her hand up to block the light, but not before he had seen her. His brother's raving had not done her justice. He had never had such an immediate and powerful reaction to a woman.

"Hold on. We can fight in a minute. But first, tell me who you are."

"Nalini," she spat out. Her chest heaved with her resentment. He noticed.

Nalini, it means lovely in Sanskrit, a lotus flower. It didn't do her justice either. Though, he reminded himself, she did want to kill him. He had read that in her eyes clearly enough. And what beautiful eyes they were. His brother had been right about that. Anger caused sapphire flames to darken the unusual lavender irises.

"So why are you following me?" He pictured her more as the type men followed around, waiting for her smallest attention.

"I'm not following you. I'm tracking you, like the animal that you are."

Said simply, matter of fact-like, as if it should have been obvious to him. That said, she rushed forward and sliced the air where he had been standing a moment before. He dodged and weaved, always dancing just out of reach of her blade. His opponent too kept moving, swiftly, with determination and cunning, countering both his trained and instinctive defenses. She round-kicked the flashlight out of his hand and it rolled on the ground, flipping shadows end over end on the stone walls as if they were dancing in a disco. Unfair he thought, and grinned. He was trying not to hurt her.

A rush of footfalls sounded behind him. Luc moved to get his back toward the wall and glanced to his left. It was all the distraction she needed. Nalini moved with him and sliced his chest open with a downward stroke. Watching her eyes in the diffused light from his fallen lamp, he realized she fully intended to catch his neck with her upward motion.

She's magnificent. Like a leopard closing in for the kill.

Her next motion was stopped by Andrew. He jumped past Luc's sagging body like the lethal beast she had accused his brother of being. "Babylonian whore!" he screamed. His arm came back and he ran her through with his dagger on the forward thrust.

...Then I inquired of one of the angels, who went with me, and who showed me every secret thing, concerning this Son of man; who he was; whence he was; and why he accompanied the Ancient of days.

The Book of Enoch 46: 1

Chapter Three

Luc's surprise matched the look on Nalini's face. As Andrew pulled his blade from her stomach, she clutched the place it had been and looked down. Then, she stumbled, dropped backward and crumpled into the ancient dust, and lay still.

"Always so dramatic," Luc complained to his brother. He fought to keep his knees locked. Failing. He slid down until he sat upon the earth now stained with blood. His. Hers. The crimson stain on the front of her t-shirt expanded outward, and reminded him of one of those tie-dye shirts from which the strings had come loose. The small hands that rested upon her stomach did little to stem the flow. Innately, he noticed a ring that looked too large dominating her slender index finger.

"What a waste. What did you do that for, Andrew?"

Chest pumping adrenaline, eyes sparkling with bloodlust, Andrew turned to glare at him. "Don't you mean, thank you?"

"I wasn't done questioning her," Luc objected. He clutched his chest. "Dammit! This hurts!"

"Stop complaining," admonished Andrew, but the concerned look in his eyes as he bent down softened his gruff tone. He pressed his hand to Luc's chest to slow the bleeding, and yelled into the darkness, "Bring me a medical bag!" Lifting his hand for a moment, he examined the wound. "It's deep."

Luc clenched his teeth together. "You don't say."

"I think she nicked bone," Andrew added, apparently impressed.

"Admirable. Just another female going for the heart you claim I don't have?"

"You whine like a mortal. Be thankful you're not or you would be dead by now."

Luc turned his head to study the prone form, made more visible by the battery operated floodlights being positioned on the ground around them. Bluish tints reflected off the spill of her hair where it obscured her face. She looked so small, suddenly, so regrettably vulnerable. Then he noticed something more, but kept quiet about it. He wasn't sure why, but he felt a sudden protectiveness for her.

He saw Andrew glance at the woman and said, "Get me out of this smelly tomb," to distract him. "It looks like you're going to have to deliver the message to the Pontiff."

Andrew grimaced with distaste, but stood up and motioned some men forward. "You're going to owe me again, little brother."

"Don't I always?"

Snatching the bag one of his men offered, Andrew pulled out some supplies. A quick tug at Luc's shirt revealed the gaping slice which he smeared with salve Kirin had prepared. Andrew then pressed on some butterfly bandages to hold the skin together and affixed a large adhesive bandage over the entire wound.

"Thanks," Luc managed as his brother helped him to his feet. He gasped, despite himself, the pain near-crippling. Taking a cautious breath, he dropped his arm around Gianni's neck. The shorter man gently helped him head back down the tunnel. "At least we hadn't gone too far, eh?" Luc said, grinning at his brother's most trusted servant.

"You always go too far, Don Vargas."

Further conversation was made impossible by Luc's tightly gripped jaw. He might be immortal, but that didn't protect him from feeling the pain of his wounds until they healed. To ease his suffering, he focused on the fact that though this wound was severe, by tomorrow morning he would be as good as new. So too, he now believed, would the lovely vixen who had given him this discomfort.

She has a lot to answer for. I'm going to take my time getting some answers.

In the meantime, a string of profanity that contained favorites from ancient Egyptian, Sanskrit, Latin, Greek and even a few choice Italian words--more for the benefit of the feigned pious frown on Gianni's face than himself--accompanied Luc over each bump in the path to the subterranean garage, through the elevator ride that took them further underground, to his quarters.

Here, at last, his weary companions lifted him to the bed. They shifted his weight to the plush cushions just as the door opened behind them. Upon seeing who entered, the men immediately let Luc go and bowed their heads respectfully.

"My queen," Luc began in surprise, tilting his head and maintaining a tight hold on his chest as he started to rise from the bed.

"Lay down at once." She made an impatient gesture for the rest of the room's occupants to depart and walked to the side of his bed as they scattered. "Well, my son, I see your brother listens with only half an ear as usual. I shall-"

"It's not Andrew's fault, Mother," he said softly. He seldom called her mother when in work mode and only did so now hoping to gain leniency for his brother.

"Let me see how badly you have damaged yourself," she said, uncommon tenderness adding a gentle quality to her lyrical voice.

He settled back into the cushions and moved his hand away from the wound. Her touch was light and skilled as she slipped a thin blade she wore tucked into her sash beneath the crude battlefield dressing Andrew had applied. Intent on her task, he studied her face, so close to his own. It was not just a son's pride that noted the flawless perfection of her skin drawn as youthfully as a twenty year olds across symmetrically pleasing bone structure. Feathery arched eyebrows, momentarily drawn together in concentration, framed expressive green eyes that were soft and approachable just now, but could become as cloudy as tourmaline when she wished to hide her thoughts, or as brilliant as priceless emeralds when she was amused or angry.

It was rather disconcerting at times to have the most beautiful mother in the universe, the woman from which all other beauty came and against which it was compared. She was a loving but somewhat temperamental mother who happened to be one of the first descendents of a royal bloodline so powerful they were once considered by mortals to be gods. Many still believed they were direct descendents. Was it any wonder she felt her word was law?

Whenever he questioned her about the first days, the days when his family openly ruled the world, his mother only smiled and refused to discuss such things. He wasn't sure what to believe of *Those Who Came Before,* which is what they had always called their ancestors.

He only knew there was much left unsaid. One had only to look into his mother's fathomless eyes to realize the vast knowledge she withheld. Which is why it took great effort on his part not to look away when she turned her head to gaze directly into his eyes. Even harder when she invaded his thoughts. Though mortals never detected her presence in their minds, he knew. And she knew he was aware of the quick intrusion.

Isis laughed, an indulgent maternal sound. Then she reached down and slid her hand across his chest, gently at first. As she repeated the movement, the pressure became more aggressive. She closed her eyes in deep concentration.

He tensed, expecting pain. Feeling none, he glanced down. She turned to pick up a cloth and dip it into the basin on the table beside the bed. The ragged edges of the wound had been smoothed down. She rung the excess water from the cloth and washed away the blood and medicinal salve. No trace of where the wound had been remained.

"Thank you," he said softly.

"I don't want you to suffer, Ljluka. I have never wanted that. No matter what happens, you must always remember that I have only wanted for you to be happy, and safe."

His face must have reflected his confusion, because she added, "Ah, my beloved Ljluka. You've always been the wisest of my children, but you still make some of the most regrettable mistakes." She glanced away as if considering something and continued gently, "It's not even your fault. But I'm not sure I can so easily save you from them all, my little owl. Come," she said, extending her hand. "Tend to your tenacious sister before I banish her to the Underworld with your father. She will give me no peace until she sees you up and well."

Luc stood and bowed his head, hands fisted, knuckles first to his forehead, then crossed wrists clasped against his now healed chest. Isis nodded her head in acknowledgement of his deep respect and glanced at his disheveled apparel, shaking her head at the blood and dirt encrusted on what was left of his shirt. "Go finish bathing and change into something more presentable first." Looking pointedly at the remnants of his suit coat, which had been cut from his body by Gianni, she added, "something more pleasing to me." She turned and moved toward the door, murmuring, "I know how you enjoy your bathing ritual. Just try not to linger too long, for your sister's sake."

No convincing was needed. The soiled clothing still on his body soon offended only the marble floor beside his bed. As he turned, naked, toward the bathing chamber, the doors to his suite burst open. "My lord, son of she who is fair as the moon and he who is more powerful than the blinding glory of the sun. He who-"

"Not now, Hassidim. It's been a long day. I need to be cleansed of it."

Ignoring--due to decades of practice--his servant's concern exaggerated to melodrama at his master's recent misfortunes, Luc followed him into the bathing chamber. Hassidim was painfully thin and a full eight inches shorter than Luc. Kirin had once commented that he was tightly wired for efficiency. Noting his current movements, Luc had to agree. The Arab busily pushed buttons and set out emollient cleansers that smelled of sandalwood and myrrh. His manservant then stacked the towel heater with thick linens and hurried out to remove all evidence of foul play from the outer chamber. Hassidim was one of the most efficient and loyal men Luc had ever employed, and he'd been with him for thirty years.

Grateful, even slightly amused, Luc stepped into the large granite enclosure and turned his head up appreciatively as a cloudburst of warm water descended from hundreds of spray holes in the ceiling. The experience was amplified by the sheets of patterned sprays that massaged his body at every angle from the walls. Luc raised his arms, slowly rotated, and sighed appreciatively. Now this, he had missed.

He was just rinsing the last of the soap from his hair when he heard, above the sound of the sprays, Kirin, in a heated debate with Hassidim. When it came to Luc's comfort and care, Hassidim could be as relentless as an eagle protecting its nest. Sighing, this time in resignation, Luc reached out to press a button and the water slowed to a drizzle and then stopped. Wrapping a towel around his waist, he strode through the steam into the bed chamber and demanded, "Can't I even wash the dust of the road from my body, Kirin?"

"You look clean enough to me. Now come on, I think this time mother is really going to kill him."

"Is that all?" Luc raised his arms to allow Hassidim to toss the robe over his head. Once it reached his knees, with a quick tug he stepped out of the towel. "She didn't seem angry any more when I last saw her."

"Well that was before she discovered that that she wolf who tried to cut out your heart got away. She is throwing weapons at him!"

Luc suppressed his delight at the news that the little she wolf, as Kirin called her, had escaped. He stared pointedly at Kirin, and then barely waited for her to turn around before stepping into the low-rise underwear Hassidim handed him. He pulled them up and let the robe fall. A quick kick slid each foot into a waiting sandal, before he moved past Kirin toward the door, pushing his fingers through his damp hair.

"I knew her maternal side wouldn't override her temper for long," he muttered.

43

And I have found both freedom of loneliness
and the safety from being understood,
for those who understand us
enslave something in us.

Kahlil Gibran, The Madman

44

Chapter Four

"Luc, say something. Try to reason with her," urged Andrew from behind a large urn a museum would have had to excavate to obtain. He cursed as it shattered, the victim of his mother's predictably good aim. Racing across the room, he ducked behind a marble pillar.

"Mother, please," Luc coaxed. "Thanks to your generosity and mercy I am fine. There is no permanent harm done."

"Yes, you see, he is fine," agreed Andrew.

Judging by the force of the stone splinters that pelted him from where the pillar deflected the arrow, it was not the right thing to say. "I swear to you, my queen. I killed the whore. With my own hands, I delivered a mortal blow."

"It's true. She would have severed my head if not for Andrew's quick intervention."

Ignoring Luc, Isis continued to vent her wrath on Andrew. "Did I not tell you to bring me that whore's body? If you killed her as you say, where is her body?"

"But why didn't you tell Andrew she was an immortal?" Luc asked.

That got her attention. He saw surprise at his knowledge before thick sooty lashes came down to veil her thoughts.

"Anubis! <u>Gana, lal uridim,</u>" she shouted in ancient Akkadian. Instantly Anubis, who she refused to call Andrew, responded.

They all knew the tone of her voice and what it meant when she yelled in the language of Mesopotamia. Her mood had just shifted from angry mother with a spoiled disobedient child to enraged queen whose servant had defied her. She seldom called her children names. Calling Andrew a dog meant he had acted in a beastly way, reacting rather than thinking.

Transformed as well, Andrew, their beloved sibling became Anubis, warrior, fearless general of his queen's armies. *No, not now, Andrew.* The fearless look of a soldier facing death shone from his eyes. She would see it instantly, and admire it. But she would shift from Andrew's mother to her general's queen. Andrew must be stopped before his pride summoned his death.

Too late.

Andrew jumped from behind the pillar and supplicated himself before his queen, face down on the cold marble, arms extended away from his body, palms and forehead resting on the floor, offering himself over to her will.

We must make her pause to think before she reacts.

Luc and then Kirin flanked Andrew, though they kneeled, bending at the waist until their foreheads touched the ground. They pressed their palms to the floor. The ancient rituals still lingered in their family culture, the familiarity usually comforting in a modern world so changed. Now was not one of those times.

Luc could feel her indecision. *It's working.* The very air was charged with her rage. *Remember who lays before you, mother.* He knew she was having a difficult time exacting punishment when her children had so obediently bowed to her will. She stalked across the floor to stand before them. *Please. Forgive him. It was my fault. I distracted him.* Would telling her shift her anger to him instead of his brother? He managed to chance a quick look by turning his head slightly. It was not just anger he saw in her face. There was pain there, too, a deep regret.

I must tell her.

Her decision made, she thrust the entire contents of her hand into Andrew's back just below his shoulder, all three or four arrows. They entered with enough force to chip the marble beneath him. Luc tensed at the sound of metal sparking on stone. It was as if she wanted Andrew to feel her pain, to realize what he had done by disobeying.

Andrew gasped, the substantial muscles in his shoulder and back convulsed involuntarily, but he managed to retain his subservient position, tensing his body in preparation for more blows, should they come.

Luc's own body, muscles still flexed to rise, quivered with his indecision. Andrew must have been working out with some of his warriors when she summoned him. He was wearing an Egyptian loincloth, his broad-shouldered back bare and vulnerable to her wrath. Anubis would not cry out, even if their mother killed him. It was he who had led legions. And he, too, was his mother's son.

Blood flowed from the wounds freely, obscuring the crimson plumes of the phoenix rising in rebirth with the dawn. Luc's back bore the same tattoo, a tribute to their great-grandfather, Rā, he who brought the first enlightenment, whose symbol was the sun—a sign of their heritage.

"You know not the cost of your carelessness. What you have set in motion cannot be undone. One day you may regret your mistake more than I, my son." Turning to look at Luc, she became still. Then she said quietly, "Ljluka, get your brother out of my sight before I follow my first instinct and disembowel him, slowly, each and every night until the full moon."

At this, Kirin reacted with her heart rather than her head. "No, no more, I beg of you," she cried as she jumped up to assist Luc with their brother, tears running down her face.

I should have been the one to cry out in his defense. I will not fail him again. Luc jumped up and reached down to his brother, ready to stand between him and any further danger.

Andrew shrugged him off. Again it was the warrior Anubis who pulled himself upright. He stepped from behind Luc and said softly, "Forgive me, my queen. I will not disappoint you again." He gazed unflinchingly into her eyes. "Thank you for sparing your worthless son from greater shame."

Isis responded with a slight nod of her head before turning to walk away. Andrew held his shoulders erect if somewhat stiffly as he walked toward the doors. Following closely behind him, Luc noted the look of terror in the eyes of the usually fearless guards as they hastily pulled back the heavy gold-plated doors to let them pass.

Once in his brother's chamber, Luc signaled for Kirin to get Gianni. As she left the room, Andrew turned his back and grabbed hold of the bed post. "Do it," he instructed.

Luc obeyed. He pushed the arrows through far enough to grasp the heads. Taking care not to jar them further, he snapped off the metal ends. Then he wrapped his hands around the shafts, paused while Andrew sucked in a mouthful of air, and jerked. The only indication Andrew gave that he felt their reverse motion from his ravaged flesh was the quick rush of air returning from his lungs and the blood pressed out of his whitened fingertips where they clutched the bed post. Luc let his own clenched jaw relax.

Gianni entered, and Andrew ordered, defiantly "Return them to their rightful owner. Apologize for the damage." Luc grabbed his waist and helped him to a stool. "It seems you are now returning that favor, little brother."

"She regretted it at once, you know," Luc said.

"I know." Said simply, meaning volumes. Andrew closed his eyes and lowered his head.

Kirin stepped forward, opening a drawer in a tall armoire. Finding what she needed, she placed the medicines and bandages on the table and began to treat Andrew's wounds. For once she was silent, respecting her brother's need to heal his pride as well as his body.

Having finished, Kirin busied herself putting away the supplies, then seeing that her brothers were still silent but watching her expectantly, she slipped from the room.

"She's pretty upset, I guess," said Andrew, raising his eyes to look at his brother in the mirror on the wall in front of them.

"Yes. She feels deeply."

"You're not going to let it go, are you? I mean the woman."

"No."

"But what if you should, for all our sakes? You heard what she said. You saw how upset it made her."

"She's keeping something from me, Andrew. She's hiding something big. Look what she did. Isis is afraid of something. I knew she was just trying to get me out of the country by sending me to America. Some flunky could have handled that mission. The man was a sniveling coward."

Luc pulled his hand through his hair and met his brother's gaze as he turned to look at him. "And then she sent my men to Giza? Why, Andrew? Father didn't need them there with the number of Illuminati operatives we have in Cairo. I think she was trying to keep me away from that woman, perhaps thought the woman would think I was with my men. Why? Who is she? I need to know." *I want to know her, in every sense.*

"What if it's for your own good?" Andrew persisted.

"When have I ever done anything for my own good?"

If she wasn't good for him, it would be quite an adventure finding that out.

"For mine then. Just wait for a while, until things cool down."

Looking at his brother's bandaged body, he nodded his head in agreement. "You're probably right." *She would still be around even centuries from now, if Isis didn't get her hands on her. He would have to make sure she didn't.*

They both turned toward the door as Gianni returned. "You are to pack," he informed them. "Tomorrow the household returns home." The brothers looked at each other knowingly, but said nothing.

Snapping her fingers, Isis waved her arm, dismissing her handmaidens. The sound of soothing waters drifted down to them from where it flowed over the top of a high wall. From there they gently cascaded down a series of rippled crevices in the granite-walled chamber.

The pillars surrounded a large pool that received and heated the cascading waters. Isis stood poised at the top of the stairs leading into the pool. She turned to her solitary companion and said, "He is my son. My heart. Have you ever known me to treat him differently?" The last said more softly, but just as earnestly. "And his siblings, would they not give their lives for him, willingly? He and Anubis are as one; each breath one takes, the other exhales."

Emerald eyes gleamed in the moonlight, artificially provided. A galaxy of stars, too, offered a sensual backdrop to gauzy linens blowing from marble pillars in an equally artificial evening breeze.

Her companion didn't notice. "No, I do not doubt your love. Never that. I owe you a debt that cannot be repaid. But do you not see, too, how much I love him? Do you not see how I suffer each time I am with him, to see him look at me with affection rather than love?"

"Recall that you do spend time with him. And he does love you, unlike the other."

"Please don't speak to me of the other, I beg of you."

"I will try one last time. We return tomorrow, as I promised. Do you go with us?"

"No, I need to monitor another situation."

"Yes, that is probably best." Isis turned, dropped her robe and walked down the stairs into the warm waters of her bathing pool. She had some hard decisions to make.

You ask me how I became a madman.
It happened thus: One day, long
before many gods were born,
I woke from a deep sleep and found all
my masks were stolen...
For the first time the sun
kissed my own naked face
and my soul was inflamed with love for
the sun, and I wanted my masks no more
Thus I became a madman...

Kahlil Gibran, The Madman

Chapter Five

Nalini shrugged off Utbah's hand, shoved him over the seat, and ducked out the open door, taking the aircraft's landing steps two at a time in her haste to rid herself of her brother, Typhon's, deviant scouts. She was certainly not grateful that they'd dragged her bloody body back to that seedy hotel. And she had no intention of letting them escort her back to Typhon like a Christian being tenderized for the lions. Seeing the waiting horses, she sprinted to her impatient Arabian, Mahdi, and snatched the reins from the young Bedouin in charge of his care.

Back across the small secluded airstrip she noted Utbah, fist raised, cursing in frustration as he tripped down the steps and hurried in her direction. It was all the incentive she needed to vault onto Mahdi's back.

All too soon she neared the palace. To those who didn't know, the sand plain seemed to continue on undisturbed for miles. It wasn't until she rode directly under the gateway, the gate having been opened for her by alert guards, that the palace transformed from a wavering dim mirage to a solid structure, the household of Set. She managed not to shudder as she returned home. Home. It seemed sacrilege when referring to the nightmare of her existence here. If not for her mother she wouldn't have returned.

Nalini rode across the courtyard, jumped from Mahdi's back and tossed the reins to the young stable boy who ran forward at her approach. "Take care to cool him down and brush him well, Kazim." He nodded. The coin she tossed flipped head over tail until he caught it deftly, and smiled his gratitude. She did her best to shield him from the rampant abuse in the palace. It was all she could do for her childhood friend's son. Since her death, he had been living in the servant's quarters. He was clothed and well fed, but Nalini knew he was lonely. Later she would try to find time to play some games with him, and would encourage his sister, Nalini's handmaiden, to spend more time with him.

Pride carried her to the antechamber of Typhon's suite. She wouldn't give him the satisfaction of sending guards to drag her before him. He couldn't be allowed to forget he was just her half-brother before Set put him in charge of this mission. The door ahead opened and Typhon's right-hand conspirator, Sirius, motioned her inside.

Typhon ignored her and continued to watch an American news channel. She noticed that his usual flat top haircut had been modified to a brush cut. The effect of softening the harsh lines on the sides of his military-type styling created an even harsher impression, without the comic relief of the squared off sides. A realization that would appeal to him, even if it had not been his intent. He was handsome, like his father, though his features were more severe and he had his mother to thank for the fiery tint of his auburn hair.

His eyebrows were arched and well formed, but came closer to meeting in the middle than Set's. Though aquiline, his nose was a bit longer, the nostrils more flared. His cheekbones were high and pronounced, which only emphasized the strong lines of his jaw. And the jaw line only hinted at the true inflexibility this focused and driven man had perfected. Nalini noted his desert camo uniform, and thrust her own chin up defiantly.

He increased the television volume, she realized, to get her attention. "In a surprise turnaround this morning, the Senate

Subcommittee on International Trade and Finance has rejected the--" He flipped the channel and she heard, "Stocks of the conglomerate holdings associated with the International Banking giant TCI, Ltd. plummeted this morning when--"

"We were so close!" Typhon yelled. "Now everything we have been working toward the past two years has been ruined. We've had to eliminate key players to keep this tied up. They've opened an entire investigation into fraudulent money laundering and illegal off shore drilling. Now we're going to have to bury that as well. The only ace we had left was The Vatican and the bitch's Illuminati Mafia have undermined that. How could you," he snapped, spinning around to spear her with his glare, "let that son of an Olympian whore get the best of you?"

Noting her stoic expression, he quickly covering the distance between them. "You had only to bring me his head or his heart, something vital. Once it was hidden away, even that slut couldn't put him together again!"

"She has done so before," Nalini reminded him.

His fist shot out with such force that even expecting it she couldn't hold her balance. She regained her feet quickly, and refused to let him watch her raise a hand to her cheek to stop the flow of blood his ring had caused, even knowing the sight of it would excite him and make him want to hurt her more. There were worse things he could do, if she didn't keep his mind off it-- or if he finally dared to defy Set. So far she had been able to manipulate him in order to leave herself with at least that dignity.

"You will learn to control your insolence!" he bellowed, slapping her face with his open hand. Her body shifted with the force of her head's reaction, but she managed to stay on her feet. He backhanded her for her trouble.

When would *he* learn she had no intention of kissing his ass? If only she dared to retaliate physically without ensuring she would never be allowed out of the harem again, never be allowed to act as a capable operative.

Frustrated with her emotionless endurance, Typhon grabbed her shoulders and shook her, screaming, "You arrogant little slut. Lower your eyes. I am the firstborn, and a male, your superior in every way!" The sleeve of her blouse tore. He looked down. His breathing rate increased between parted lips as he reached to twist his fingers around a handful of her blouse. She resisted then, unable to catch the quick flash of hatred that sparked straight from her soul.

He smiled triumphantly and yanked the entire front of her lightweight blouse from her body. Nalini grabbed for it, glanced at his face and froze. Disappointment tempered the open lust on his face. Attempting to get her to react again because fear and pain were his drugs of choice, he sneered, "I should have known you'd like it. You are your mother's daughter."

She saw her death then. Saw it and accepted it. Just as soon as she killed him, they would order it. Her mother would mourn, but she would get over it eventually. She reached down to pull the dagger from the sheath strapped to her leg, but a disturbance at the door stilled her motion.

"So, father was right. She's back. He wants to see her," Lucien stated, taking in her disheveled appearance. "I know some of those American women on the television dress in pretty trashy clothing, but did that really help you blend in?"

Typhon joined in his laughter.

Nalini crossed her arms over her chest and studied Lucien for a moment, wondering if he had the world's best timing or knew what their brother had been about to do and purposely interrupted. What did it matter? She took full advantage of her salvation, and ran out the door toward the women's quarters, their mocking laughter a hateful reminder of her precarious position in Set's household. And that position had just become more untenable. Survival should not have been a synonym for home.

Set, as her father, dictated her enemies. That meant she was the sworn enemy of Osiris and Isis and the entire Vargas family. So why did their family seem more appealing than hers? The wounded one's brother, Anubis, he had come to his defense as if he truly loved him and would willingly die for him. Ljluka. She remembered his name now, and she remembered *him* all too well.

Her heart had slammed against her chest when she saw him, and not from the shock of familiarity. His startling blue eyes had fastened on her with such intensity she had to will herself to breath. Forcing her attention away from his hypnotic stare, she had noted that his hair was a little longer on top than most conventional businessmen. It had that overpriced geometric grooming that resulted in a sophisticated tousle women longed to run their fingers through. She bet his golden locks were never out of place no matter where each strand landed. He probably rarely combed it with anything but his fingers. And for a moment she had longed to do the same. Not that it mattered. She knew what men were like. He could be nothing more than a target to her.

But then there was his face. His features were finely sculpted, strong and masculine yet sensual, as if carved from marble by a master. However handsome, he could be ruthless, too. She knew. When he had thrown her over his shoulder she felt his muscles move across that broad expanse and realized he was enormously strong. Though he laughed with amusement at her expense, she never forgot that he could be brutal, frightening in a very serious no nonsense way.

As handsome as a god, and as intimidating.

Centuries of battle victories were evident in the easy confidence of his carriage. The training of a warrior was evident too in the stiff brace of his shoulders and the grim set of his jaw when she slashed open his chest. A lesser man would have cried out or immediately slumped to the ground in agony. He had looked faintly amused at her lethal tenacity, even as his ancient blood flowed down his chest and spilled onto the equally ancient dust at his feet.

It made her want to know more about him and his family.

According to her mother, his father Osiris had decided to step down from involvement in everyday commerce. Her mother had been unable or unwilling to discuss what exactly he was now involved with. In fact, Astarte seemed very reluctant to speak of Osiris at all.

Having met two of the brothers, she was also curious about their other brother, Horus, who ran their Egyptian-based operations and a company named Orion that supposedly developed aerospace technology. Isis and the other Vargas sons had taken over their banking and financial interests. There was a daughter, too, a doctor or scientist. Nalini didn't remember which.

She wondered why their family no longer lived together. Her family shared the same roof even though most of them hated each other. She glanced up as she approached the closest thing to a real loving family she had in her own life.

Arai stepped from the shadow of a pillar and threw his cloak around her shoulders. She tugged it closer, grateful, overlapping it in the front. His dark eyes shone like polished mahogany. It was difficult to tell what her mother's bodyguard was thinking behind the somber depths, but they warmed reassuringly. A wide golden belt gleamed around his narrow waist, accentuating the chiseled stone-like muscles beneath his ribcage. It matched the tightly linked gold collar he wore that designated him a member of the royal family's personal staff.

She offered a word of thanks. His gleaming teeth broke through the dark contours of his face, much like his white loincloth contrasted with the ebony of his belly. He fell into step beside her. Though he stared down at her, he remained silent. His continued silence allowed her time alone with her troubled thoughts, to review in her mind the information Lucien had shared with her when he prepared her for her mission. Isis had created the Vatican to shield her faction's global involvement. But that was no surprise to her. For centuries, the organization that had once called its operatives the Knights Templar had secretly been referred to by those who knew or suspected its existence as the Illuminati. Nothing could be undeniably traced back to them, but much was attributed through rumor. Nalini wasn't convinced her brothers had found out as much about them as they should have.

"They didn't tell me all I needed," she said.

Knowing immediately to what she referred, Arai replied, "They have little reason to wish you success on your first solo mission. It would make them look bad."

"You don't think they would purposely--"

"Do you?"

She wasn't sure. It seemed illogical. Her failure would reflect badly on them, too. "All I had to do was take down Ljluka Vargas, Isis' primary enforcer. He can't be corrupted since he is her son, of course. It should have been simple. Ah, Arai, I failed miserably." Clutching the robe around her, she crossed her arms over her chest. Sometimes the battles within her family made the ones outside seem simple, even unimportant.

"You may be given another opportunity," was Arai's consolation. He knew well the demons that haunted her.

"If only they'd given me a picture so I knew what he looked like before I went."

Without probing for more details than she willingly offered, he responded, "They say he moves with the cunning of a jackal. They can't even get a photo of him from security cameras. Always he turns his face aside or runs his hand across his features or through his hair, blocking the view of the cameras."

Which meant, she realized, that he was constantly aware of his surroundings, knew where every camera was located, when it turned and on what it focused. "Well, I know what he looks like, now," she said softly. She was determined to find out more about this complicated man. There had to be a way to make sense of it, and until then she was not going to share her knowledge of who he resembled with anyone. If only she knew how it was possible. If only she knew why she responded to him so strongly. Her only reaction should have been her initial one.

Shock.

Had the Vargas family broken their own golden rule and stolen DNA for their research?

"You are the only one who knows what he looks like now, so you are the logical choice to carry out the assassination," Arai said, reassuring her that they still needed her help.

"Perhaps, but there will be retribution for my failure." The chill Nalini felt had nothing to do with the temperature or her altered attire. She feared her future, because each new day was filled with uncertain survival and repeated trials.

Nalini's past was an even bigger mystery. Once as a child so young she barely remembered, her mother had shown her hieroglyphics and faded drawings on the side of stone walls depicting, she said, their heritage. She wondered again if some percentage of her DNA was human, and what part truly came from the ancestors her mother called *Those Who Came Before*. Surely if her blood line was as pure as Typhon claimed, she wouldn't have failed. Something was wrong with her genetic makeup. Why else hadn't she inherited her mother's gift for seeing into the future? Why hadn't she sensed the Vargas duplicity in the catacombs?

She glanced at Arai. Nalini knew she should be grateful to Lucien for sparing her from Typhon's rage. He had saved Arai's life as well. But she knew Lucien's real mission had nothing to do with her. Saving her cost him nothing and didn't inconvenience him much, or she wouldn't be alive. She didn't have to ask to know her mother had sent Arai to save her from Typhon. It was hardly the first time.

"By the way, Arai, thank--"

"No need, small warrior. I knew you didn't need my help, but I saw no fault in accepting the blame for his demise in your stead should the need arise. Your mother would never survive your execution."

"So she didn't send you?"

The towering Nubian shrugged thick shoulders and looked down at her. "She was otherwise occupied."

Nalini considered his words. If Astarte was busy, it had to involve Set. Her mother's gift of sight was just another reason for Set's continued obsession with his third wife. She looked up at Arai, who now refused to meet her eyes.

His evasiveness confirmed her fears. Set--known only as the Usurper to those in the enemy camp she'd discovered with much amusement--knew she had failed. He had obviously taken his displeasure out on her mother. Or, more accurately, she thought, biting her lip, her mother had somehow insured once again that he didn't take it out on her daughter.

Knowing what it cost her mother to constantly run interference usually encouraged Nalini to do as she was told without complaint. She had tried. Remembrance of her failure and its probable consequences sent barely dormant adrenaline surging once again and she ran down the corridor, bursting through the doors to the women's quarters.

"Wait," Arai cautioned. "Look to your appearance."

She did look then, grimaced, and turned to take the corridor to the left of the antechamber. Making herself presentable for Set, which included getting her emotions under control again, would have to come first. Seeing into the future wasn't necessary to know another ugly scene was about to take place. If she wasn't so concerned about what Set would do to her mother, she would have turned around and run away.

Arai waited in the antechamber. Even Eunuchs rarely ventured further into the deeper recesses within. Nalini continued down the corridor, knowing she was watched by curious female onlookers, hidden from view by colorful, heavily embroidered draperies whose intricate details obscured the small slits which allowed the occupants of the cubical-riddled harem to observe without being seen.

Slipping into the small space allotted for her use whenever she was forced to spend time within the palace walls, she braced herself for her handmaiden's hysterical reaction to her appearance. To her relief, Amea rushed forward, took Arai's cloak without comment, tossed it onto the cushions and began the process of peeling her out of the dirty, travel worn clothing.

Once disrobed, Nalini motioned her aside and dipped her hands in the small basin of warm water on the stand against the wall—further indication that even Amea knew she had returned. She splashed water onto her face, reached to fill her hands with lather from a bar of her favorite lily, bergamot and coriander scented soap, and then scrubbed at the dirt and drying blood from her brother's assault. Blotting her face dry on the towel Amea handed her, she picked up a small mirror to examine her face. A bluish bruise showed faintly beneath the remains of the cut on her cheekbone. By the time she saw her mother she hoped it would fade.

As usual, she rejected the kohl and henna Amea offered. She knew she was considered beautiful. She looked much like her mother and Astarte had once turned the head of Osiris as well as Set, according to Lucien who used to talk to Nalini like a real brother when she was a little girl. Beauty had proven to be an unwelcome blessing for both mother and daughter.

Choosing only to dip her fingertip into some emollient balm made from royal bee jelly, she soothed her parched lips. Amea shook her head, but had learned not to comment on Nalini's refusal to use cosmetics. Instead she helped Nalini into an adaptation of the long, flowing layers favored by Bedouin women due to their overly modest body-masking qualities. Nalini wished she dared wear the headgear, a *rida'*, but she knew from past experience it would only make Set angrier.

Taking a deep breath, she lifted her chin and retraced her steps down the long corridor. Arai and her own bodyguard, Rashid, waited for her as she left the women's quarters. Rashid, a slightly shorter version of Arai, was assigned to her safety. He nodded his head in acknowledgement of her glance. His wide smile didn't contrast as sharply within his face as Arai's. His skin tone was lighter. The warm and genuine emotion, however, still reached his eyes. It welcomed her back without words.

Arai's continued presence, she realized, could only mean her mother had already been summoned to the throne room. "Why are you not with my mother, Arai?" she asked, hoping he wouldn't confirm what she suspected.

"I was sent away."

Nalini wondered why Set would have banished Arai. Realization came almost instantly. She increased her pace as she moved from one corridor to the next. Knowing her mother had made the choice to be with Set to ensure her safety was a burden she did not take lightly. Her shoulders pulled back automatically as she came to a stop in the antechamber of the throne room. The guards, knowing she was expected, opened the doors.

Arai remained banished by Set's orders, but Rashid followed her inside.

To where her uncertain fate awaited.

...Enoch was taken away so that he did not see death, "and was not found, because God had taken him"...[because] he pleased God.

Hebrews 11: 5

Chapter Six

The room in which Set handed down judgments or listened to appeals had few furnishings compared to some of the palace rooms. Stone pillars ran down either side of a long aisle that led to a raised dais upon which stood a large throne. Each arm of the solid gold chair was a seated lion with large rubies for eyes. The back depicted a phoenix with a crown on its head. It was presently empty.

To the right of it lounged Typhon, his shoulder against a pillar. Typhon chuckled when he saw her and Lucien stepped forward from behind the pillar, where he had apparently been distracted by a servant girl. She hurried away, chest heaving, straightening her bodice, looking annoyed by the interruption. Nalini rolled her eyes. Every female in the palace was moonstruck by Lucien. She supposed it was his blond good looks. His hair had been bleached nearly white by the desert sun. Only his closely trimmed beard retained a hint of his natural blond rather than the platinum that crowned his head. But even his facial hair stood out in contrast to his deeply tanned skin, as did his sapphire eyes. His coloring was rare among the desert people. She noticed with relief that his well manicured though more rugged looks left her completely unmoved and tucked the reassuring knowledge away to consider later.

She refused to acknowledge their presence as she strode past the guards and walked to the stairs that led up to the dais. There she stopped. Her wait was short. Set entered followed respectfully by her mother and a dozen soldiers. Dressed down in his favored loincloth—which showed off his muscled physique to advantage--and enough artistically crafted gold to satisfy a rapper like the one she had seen in America, including a wide gold collar, serpent coils wrapped around each bicep and a golden cuff at each wrist. To top off his finery, he was wearing a heavy blue war crown with a striking cobra centered above his forehead. The choice of crown was not lost on Nalini. She realized he meant to remind her that they were already engaged in battle with their enemies..

He strutted to the throne and glared at Nalini. "Your mother and I are disappointed in you, Nalini. You have let your mother down. She assured me that you would be of use for this mission and you failed miserably."

His mouth was crushed into a stern slit, which added to the harshness of his features. Though handsome, his volatile disposition had driven his normally highly arched brows downward, narrowing his blue eyes to piercing, ice cold darts that dominated his face and detracted from the otherwise aquiline appearance of his nose. His already strong chin was arrogantly raised, emphasizing the slant of high cheekbones.

A moment of silence satisfied him that Nalini was not going to answer. She knew better. He sat down and with a quick thrust of his hand on her shoulder her mother sat on the stool at his feet.

Her mother, whose golden gown shimmered as she brushed absently at an ebony curl that had fallen across her forehead, scanned her daughter's face. Her gaze paused as it reached the near imperceptible bruise on her cheekbone. Nalini noticed her mother's flushed cheeks and the way Set slid his hand down her shoulder, brushing his fingertips against the curve of her breast. He seemed well pleased with himself, his earlier glare tempered to a warm glow. His features softened and Nalini saw again the man whose concubines vied, albeit with limited success, for his attentions. Being a virgin in technicality only she didn't need a detailed explanation to know why his attention was so focused upon her mother. He had obviously just bedded her. The thought repulsed her.

Grinding salt in the wound, he said, "Your mother has been begging me all afternoon to forgive you. How can I resist such a beautiful and loving woman's tender pleas for mercy? I have promised not to kill you."

"Father, no!" Typhon blurted. "She has destroyed two year's work, work that was carried out by hundreds of operatives. She bungled a simple task she has trained for centuries to perform. As a soldier, she must be punished. If she insists on being treated like a man, refusing to take a husband or stay at home and bear sons, she should be punished like a man."

"He has a point, father," agreed Lucien. "At least that she should not be trusted with another mission by herself, as if she were a man."

Her mother reached up to place her hand beseechingly on Set's knee. He covered it with his own and sighed, "I'm afraid my sons do make a good argument. But I can't forget my promise to my beloved wife, either. A compromise, I think," Set declared. He smiled then, a smug, self-indulgent expression.

Nalini hid her terror. Set was more dangerous when quiet and calm than when ranting and raging, his usual behavior. She couldn't help wondering just exactly what her mother had done, or promised to do, to make him react this way. She sensed the presence of approaching disaster.

"A man would receive one hundred lashes, at the very least," goaded Typhon. Nalini tensed. Lashes. Could she bear them bravely? Surely he wouldn't let Typhon deliver them. One hundred though, that many would kill a man, whoever delivered them.

"No, please, my King, I beg of you," pleaded the queen.

"Would you be willing to negotiate a lesser sentence, Astarte?" he asked as he leaned down to stare into her eyes, so like her daughter's. He smiled again, and it was not a happy expression. Putting his hand to the back of her head, he forced her head forward and ravaged her lips with his own.

Nalini stifled a gasp at his public display. Her hands fisted at her sides, but she remained mute.

Set lifted his head and waited, his face inches from that of his wife, his expression expectant, his gaze intense. Her mother ran her tongue across her bruised lips and said softly, "Yes. Yes, I agree to your terms. Your every wish is my command, my king."

So Set had been manipulating her mother all along, using her love for her daughter, *his* daughter, to gain something he wanted. But what? What had her mother agreed to? she wondered. Set's smile widened and this time his delight was genuine, sending a shiver of fear down Nalini's back. He pulled Astarte to her feet and stared at Nalini.

She waited expectantly, unimpressed with his massive chest or the barely suppressed power in his near seven foot physic. Many women would find him attractive. But inside, she knew from painful experience, her father was a very ugly man. His heart, if he had one, beat only for complete control and possession of Astarte and an unquenchable thirst for power. As if he could read her thoughts, he reached to drag her mother closer, then turned and drew her back the way they had come.

"Thirty," Set said, nodding his head toward his sons.

She heard her mother's cry of protest as the doors closed behind them, whether from her sentence or something revolting

Set had done to her, Nalini didn't know. At the moment, she was concerned with convincing Rashid to allow the guards to take her captive. Her punishment must be carried out before he got himself killed for interfering with Set's will.

"Rashid, I order you to go back to the Harem and wait for me."

"I must witness the punishment. It is fitting."

"Very well, but only if you don't interfere." Her gaze was piercing, without compromise. He knew if he did not agree she would demand that he be removed.

"As you wish, princess," Rashid said slowly, grudgingly, stressing the "you". Swallowing, his fists too clenched at his sides.

She understood that he accepted her orders, but not Set's.

Nalini, arms quickly tied behind her back, turned to walk within the circle of guards who fell in around her. She didn't have to turn to know her brothers were at their heels, like dogs looking for a good bone to gnaw. They had been waiting centuries for such an opportunity.

They walked down several flights of stairs and down one long corridor after another. There was too much time to think about what was to come. When Nalini realized they were headed to the dungeons, she became angrier. Since the day she was born, her life had been a constant struggle to endure a life she hated. At least until now she had been able to pretend she mattered to her family, at least a little. With his judgment, her father no longer hid his contempt for her, even from his servants. All in the palace would know of her final humiliation before she reached her destination.

She had never fit in. The obvious answer was that she must have inferior DNA. Her mother's gift had not been passed to her.

And Set . . . how could he be her true father? Wouldn't she feel something besides hatred for him if he were? Typhon, like Set, was obsessed with maintaining the purity of their bloodline to ensure the success of his new world order. He insisted that Set give her to him in marriage. Set hadn't been persuaded yet, thanks to her mother, but would this present torture be enough to quench their desire to crush her spirit and possess her soul?

At last they stopped. A door was unlocked and released from the inside. They filed in and a huge Nubian guard grabbed her arm. She tried not to glance at Rashid, but needed one last look at his calm, steadying countenance to bolster her courage. It didn't help. He tried to appear supportive, but his face was riddled with deep shadows where his brow bunched anxiously. Nalini looked away and took a deep breath.

Could she be brave enough? A soldier in battle at least had a chance to fight back, to win. She felt completely helpless and vulnerable now, and it was not a feeling with which she was comfortable.

She forced herself to look away from the wretched, unconscious or even dead prisoners that were housed in this subterranean chamber of horrors. A young boy was tied to a ring in the wall, to her right. Too late she realized he was shackled at the elbows because his hands had been smashed to useless pulp. The young woman tied spread-eagle to a flat wooden table to her left had more chance of surviving, at least if they were done with her. She was groaning, bruised and bleeding, true, but women survived rape every day. Nalini had witnessed many things as a warrior who spent most of her life among adrenaline-pumped men. This evil she never got used to, and did what she could to interfere. She was in no position to help this woman now, but perhaps tomorrow she could arrange a bribe.

Nalini tried to distract herself as her arms were drawn over her head and tied to rings that hung from pillars placed what she figured to be about eleven hands apart, shorter than the distance to her horse's withers, surely. She could see a long corridor with rows of cages. No, that wasn't right. They were cells, for human captives, not animals.

The Nubian grabbed the back of her robe, and a small gasp of shock escaped her as he pulled it away from her body. He drew the long rope of her hair, tied with a piece of thin leather, to the front of her shoulder and then used a sharp knife to slice down the back of her gown. She tried not to shiver as cool damp air met bare skin.

Lucien appeared in front of her, his lips compressed into a hard line. She couldn't tell if it was from anticipation or commiseration. As she stared at him silently, he reached for the front of her robe and repeated the procedure the Nubian had performed on her back until she was naked to the waist, her sash the only thing saving her from total nudity. Was it for his personal pleasure or to prevent adding to Typhon's? She swallowed, but reacted with only a slight tilt to her chin. Lucien had become a complete mystery to her. But he too, she reminded herself, had learned to survive their father.

Then, for a brief moment he looked into her eyes the way the boy Lucien used to look at his little sister. He seemed embarrassed, or perhaps ashamed of what he had done, maybe even of what he'd become. She saw in that one look the young boy who bent down to help her up and brushed off her knees when she first learned to ride. Perhaps he saw in her that young girl who had struggled to maintain her dignity, but never gave up, because he sliced off a bit of fabric and held it up to her mouth.

"Here," he said quietly. "Bite down on this. It will help, Nalini."

It didn't though. He had barely stepped back when the first blow fell. She jerked against her bonds as her body convulsed in agony, biting into the fabric until it felt as if her teeth must all be loose. And that was after only one blow of thirty.

Six blows later, she could feel the blood begin to flow, could hear her brother, Typhon's, labored breathing, knew there were fifty-six bars on the first cell.

By twenty a sob of agony escaped her, despite her best efforts to capture it. Childbirth she was sure hurt as much. She had seen it once. Women survived that, too, every day. Women survived men every day of their lives, she reasoned. That's why they were the stronger sex. She spit out the rag. Breathing had become more important than the submission of pain.

Twenty-two and she sucked in her breath and remembered the deep timber of Ljluka's laugh as he ran with her on his shoulder as if she weighed nothing. She had never heard such unconditional humor. Twenty-three and she remembered the impossible blue of his eyes as she sliced into his chest.

At twenty-seven blows, she stared through tears into the equally blue and unwavering eyes of her brother, Lucien, and swore, "I will not fail again!"

By thirty blows, she was unconscious.

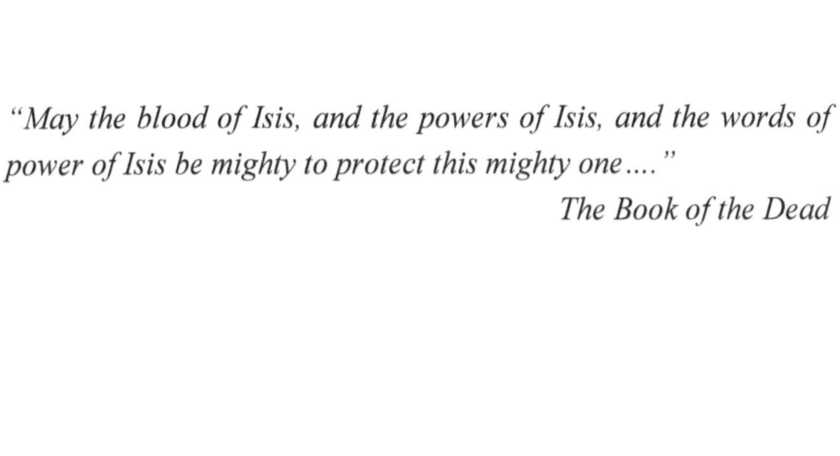

"May the blood of Isis, and the powers of Isis, and the words of power of Isis be mighty to protect this mighty one...."

The Book of the Dead

Elizabeth Alsobrooks

76

Chapter Seven

Thick vapor undulated through the canopy of the forest. Trees twisted and dwarfed by endlessly shifting winds crouched under the burden of countless bromeliads, orchids and other rare, unknown species of fauna and flora. Life, abundant and diverse pulsed across the moist ridges and valleys. Water collected in rivulets that became streams and rivers and plummeted from steep undercut moss-covered rock formations to ever deepening crevices below.

"There is nothing that compares with a cloud forest, Luc." Kirin, happier than he had seen her in months, sat perched upon a rock, dangling her foot off a citadel with an eight thousand foot drop.

"I think you mean nothing compares to a *yungas* forest. You have never cared about admiring elfin woods anywhere other than in the Andrea cloud forests of Peru." He sat down beside her and studied the drifting billows of clouds, or fog, or both, depending on the time of day or who you asked.

"Is it any wonder the mortals called us sky gods?" she asked softly.

Luc put his arm around her shoulder companionably. Kirin had inherited their parent's love for the earth's peoples and environment. Unlike Set who felt most humans had been created merely for the amusement of *Those Who Came Before*, to be enslaved and used or disposed of as he saw fit, they felt a sense of responsibility for the genetic intrusion their ancestors had foisted on the human race. It didn't matter that the tampering had been intended to improve and accelerate their evolutionary progress. Their father, Osiris, had abolished cannibalism as his first act as supreme ruler. Set had seen it as further proof that humans were no better than any other animal species.

"Look there," Kirin directed, pointing to a group of Howler monkeys in a wide multiple limbed tree on an outcropping to their right. A brazen blue and gold macaw had landed too close and they were determined that it should leave. Kirin laughed at their antics.

Luc heard rhythmic metallic clanking in the dense foliage behind them. He grinned as he stood up and turned to see Andrew and several of their men approaching.

"I heard you coming a mile off, Tin Man," he teased. "How many pitons you packing?"

Andrew tossed a harness, fully geared lumbar pack and a duffle with additional gear and clothing at the ground near Luc's feet. "Gear up, pretty boy. It's time to get you toughened. Up and down or down and up? Told the boss we'd help the boys out. You know how she worries when she's not here. The hydro power faucet needs adjusting or some such. We're to supervise, but after that we should have time for some real fun."

"The faucet, huh? Bring a wrench in that bag?"

"We've got a roll of duct tape and some chewing gum. You coming, or what?"

Luc needed no further encouragement. Home base in the middle of a cloud forest ran, by necessity, on hydroelectric power. Add to that fact the need for concealment and it made for a fun day of mountain climbing whenever regular maintenance or repairs were required. Racing halfway up or down the rock face beside a pulverizing waterfall to where they had to step onto a short slippery ledge and duck behind said waterfall seemed the most appealing part of the equation to Luc and Andrew. They often volunteered to supervise maintenance runs, as an excuse to spend the day enjoying one of their favorite activities. Most of their personal elite operatives readily agreed.

Except Roscoe, who feared no man, mortal or immortal, but still couldn't defeat vertigo. He happily volunteered to join Kirin's group as she trekked deeper into the jungle in search of new or short supply specimens.

A quick dash behind a tree and Luc was soon geared with enough strapped on, clipped on, plugged in and pouched or dangling metal carabiners, nuts, hexes, belays, camming, rappelling and ascending gear to spend a week on the mountain, though they would only be gone for most of the day.

He took off at a slow jog, waving goodbye to Kirin, who shook her head and laughed at her brothers' antics. Luc reached the rushing river in time to see Andrew swing over the side of the adjacent cliff face. His adrenaline pumped in anticipation, and he increased his pace. Looked like it was going to be down then up today. The surge of the water caused too much noise for even shouts to be heard, so he signaled to Rafael as he fastened his gloves, indicating that he wanted to go next.

Rafael nodded, drew out a foot of rope from the sling that had been rigged around a nearby tree, braced himself and held out a rope descender. Luc attached it to the locking beaner and snapped it onto his harness before backing up to the edge, bending his knees and pushing himself off.

He rappelled quickly, stepping off the ledge and landing behind the waterfall only a second or two behind Andrew. They unbuckled their harnesses, dropped them near the stone wall and grabbed some battery-operated floodlights before moving down the tunnel, glad to emerge a few moments later into the larger chamber where the deafening rush of the water wasn't as intense.

"Good to see you haven't forgotten how," Andrew teased.

"You don't call that rock climbing, do you?"

Their laughter ended as they turned to see their electrical tech rushing toward them.

"What is it?" Luc asked.

"You'd better come see this," he said, turning to hurry back toward the ladder that led down to the generator area.

They followed behind, climbing down past the pipes used to capture and redirect water that spun the wheels and powered the turbines.

Jumping the last few feet, Luc hurried over to where a group of their men stood clustered around one of the generators.

Andrew, already there, looked up at his approach. "This is your area of expertise, little brother. Anything you need us to get you?"

Luc's jaw tightened. Who could have done this? He swung down under the railing. A quick inspection revealed that a detonator was attached to the turbine with enough plastic explosive to make any other explosive devices redundant. "See if it has any relatives, just in case," he said.

"Already done. We reconnected the sensor and did a manual check as well. This one is it," the tech informed him.

"Then get everyone out. Emmanuel. Tools!"

The explosives expert nodded, already snapping on the belt of a zippered travel-tech pouch he was never without. It opened to reveal multilayered and compartmentalized pouches stuffed with technical and electrical tools. He reached in and pulled out some jumpers and a pair of wire cutters. "Looks like what we really need is more time," he said, indicating the thirteen minutes remaining on the bomb's timer.

Luc grasped the wire cutters, and looked up at Andrew. "They could still be—"

"Kirin!"

"Right!" He didn't know how Typhon's men got past the sensors, but figured their enemy must be trying to take out the security system so they could break the combination lockout codes on the computer system. It would only buy them about thirty seconds before the battery backup took over. He reached into an upper pocket, took out a cell phone for which they had their own satellite and tossed it to the closest operative. "Call Roscoe, and go protect Kirin, now."

Andrew was already halfway up the ladder. The rest of their men sprinted toward the metal stairs. Luc turned back to his task. He was too focused on the serious chore before him to try to figure out how this could have happened. One thing was quite clear, however. Obviously it was time to launch an offensive attack rather than run constant interference or damage control. The Usurper's organization had finally gained enough power to become a substantial threat.

In less than an hour, Luc, wet and anxious, strode into the security room where he found Kirin bandaging Roscoe's arm. Andrew stood at the console, scanning the camera readouts and orchestrating a near shoulder-to-shoulder search of the grounds by a full battalion of operatives. At his approach, Roscoe looked down as though embarrassed.

"You okay?" Luc asked Kirin, his relief at seeing her heartfelt, though he had already been notified of her location and rescue.

She reached up to rub her head. "Jerked a hunk of hair out, roots and all."

Andrew glanced over at him. It wasn't necessary to say aloud what they were both thinking. DNA.

"Never would have got that close to her, I swear it, if I didn't think it was you," Roscoe was saying.

"Who did you think was me?" Luc turned to him then, confused by Roscoe's strange claim.

"He looked just like you, Luc," interjected Kirin.

Luc glanced toward Kirin then. "Who looked like me?"

"The man who tried to take me, the one who grabbed my hair. Pay attention, Luc. He was your mirror image. It wasn't until he got up close that I knew. It was his eyes. I saw his eyes and instantly knew him for someone else. His eyes were so, so angry. No, they were more than that. They were cold and predatory, like someone who remains alert at all times and kills for survival."

"She speaks the truth. It was uncanny," confirmed Roscoe. "After we realized, of course, we noticed his combat gear, that his hair was longer, cut differently, more sun-bleached, his beard. His tan was deeper, too, but those aren't things one pays attention to immediately when you are watching the approach of someone you think you know, same height, same features, same--"

"You didn't notice I had suddenly grown a beard, grown my hair out, gotten more sun?" he demanded, his frustration growing. "It sounds like the only thing about him that *was* like me was your attitude of acceptance." Luc's forehead creased as he considered their story, despite his incredulity. He wondered if Set had managed to use his DNA to create some monstrous clone.

Knowing what his brother was thinking, Andrew said, "No way. We've been too careful. A cleaner goes through everything we handle when we're public, and there's no way they've gotten to any of the vehicles or residences. Besides, they're routinely swept for traces too."

"Until now he hasn't gotten any, that we know of," Luc cautioned. "Still, they didn't get Kirin," he said, unable to keep from grabbing her up into a big bear hug. "We're grateful for that, Roscoe." He nodded his thanks toward his best warrior above his sister's head, taking the sting from his earlier sensor. If Roscoe said it was so, it was so. He knew that.

"Hey," Kirin said, laughing. "You're all wet."

Luc grinned and released her.

"She was probably their target," said Andrew.

"Why me?" Kirin asked.

"Why do you think? You're the best scientist alive, Kirin," Luc said, adding his agreement to his brother's conclusion. Despite her protest, he gave her another quick squeeze, relief flooding through him. They definitely needed to get more aggressive.

"What good would that do them? I wouldn't do anything to help them."

"They don't know enough about you to realize that," their mother said, suddenly appearing in the doorway. It was the queen's voice that snapped, "Really, boys, I can't visit your father a single day without you letting the place go straight to Hades. Don't just stand here trying to figure out what to do. Andrew, take some men and go get back every hair from her head. Now. They haven't yet left the forest. They're trying to free their Jeeps from the bog."

She looked at Roscoe who had fallen to one knee and bowed his head at her entrance, despite Kirin's protest that she was not done with his bandage. "Were she not standing here, you would no longer benefit from those bandages."

As Andrew hurried to the door, she turned from her quick embrace of Kirin and said softly, "After today, there is to be no mention by anyone that Luc has a look-alike." Andrew nodded and kept moving. "And Anubis," she called after him. He stopped and turned to look at her. "Unless it means your own life, he is not to be taken down." Andrew glanced at Luc, then nodded his head in agreement and left the room.

Luc studied her. She hadn't been surprised. He was sure of it. "I should go with him," he suggested.

"No! They don't know about you, and it's best that they don't." She glanced at Kirin, sighed and looked back. "Come with me, Ljluka."

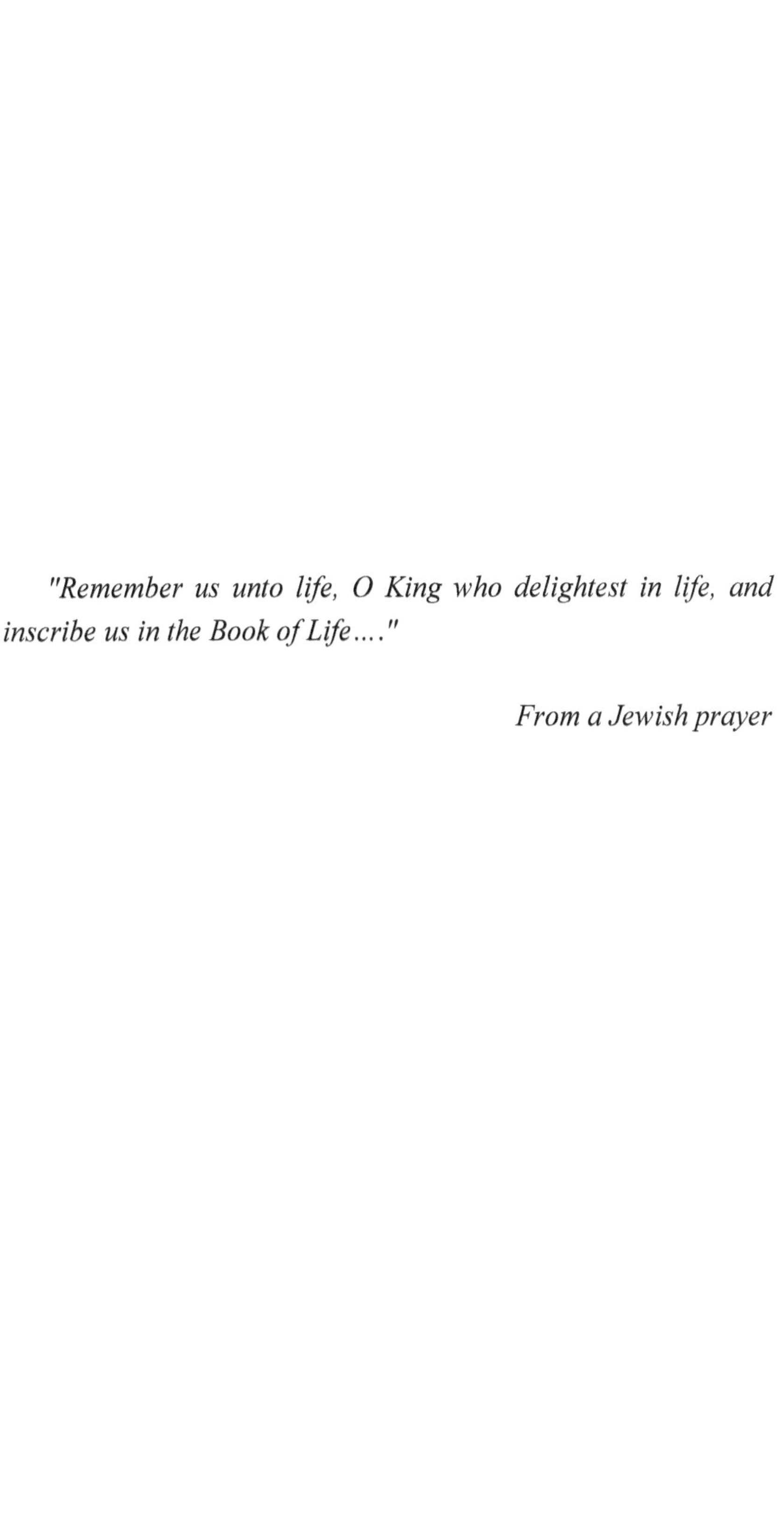

"Remember us unto life, O King who delightest in life, and inscribe us in the Book of Life...."

From a Jewish prayer

86

Chapter Eight

Luc stood in the center of the room, hands clasped lightly in front of him to mask his tension. He watched his mother silently stare out the large expanse of glass that allowed them to view most of the valley. Angled into the rock face, the glass wall was not visible from even the most inaccessible regions across the valley. If it were, it would look like a dark cave with only the black exterior of the glass visible. At twilight, a panel slid down over the glass to prevent light from exposing their location. It was yet daylight, so the valley lay visible below them.

The queen stood observing it, and her complete stillness heightened his tension. "Mother, please," he pleaded at last.

She interlocked her fingers and pressed them to her chin, as if making a difficult decision. Finally, she turned and indicated a small grouping of chairs to her right. "Sit down," she said and seated herself in the chair closest to the view.

Luc settled into an overstuffed arm chair, facing her, and bent his leg up to cross his right ankle over his opposite knee, and waited for her to speak.

"I knew this day would come," she began. "I have thought deeply and often about what I would say to you, and still I don't feel prepared."

She looked directly into his eyes and he was surprised by the anguish and what could only be fear that he saw there. Her pupils were dilated, nearly swallowing the irises. Dampness pooled and threatened to spill onto her cheeks. He tensed, suddenly afraid himself. To see fear in the eyes of a parent must be, he decided, the most terrifying experience of all, especially a parent as powerful and fearless as his mother. Another first.

"Ljluka, the man Kirin and the men mistook for you was not a clone. It was not some wild genetic accident or even a deliberate duplication." She paused, grasped her hands together in her lap, and seemed to collect herself before adding, "I guess there is no right or easy way to say this, other than to just tell you."

"What it is, my queen? What can be so terrible that you dare not disclose the truth to your own son?"

"Ah, my little owl," she said, turning to look out across the valley once more.

"Please, tell me. If not an accident or a deliberate act, who is that man who looks like me?"

"Your brother." Said quickly, as if the words had to be spit from her mouth to make her tongue act against her will.

"My brother?" He hadn't expected this. Why not? It explained everything and nothing at once. "But how can this be? Why isn't he here with us?"

She glanced down at her hands and twisted a large ring on her finger. "Set took him at birth."

"What? Why haven't you gotten him back? I should have gone with--" He stopped, remembering Kirin's words. He stared out the window, though he wasn't seeing anything. She had called the man, his brother, cold and predatory, like someone who killed for survival. Could they turn him back to the man he might have been if he hadn't been at the mercy of that monster? Did the man even want to leave Set's household? How could this have happened? Set wasn't powerful enough to get away with a crime of this magnitude. Not back then.

"It's not that simple," Isis said, interrupting his thoughts and drawing his attention. "The Usurper doesn't know about your existence. If he did, if he found out you were the firstborn, he wouldn't rest until he got his hands on you as well."

"I'm the firstborn? Even so, why would he want me?" Of course it wasn't simple, he thought irritably. Nothing was ever as it seemed with his mother.

"Who can know for sure? Probably for the purity of the bloodline." She was on her feet again, staring out at the horizon. Outside the sun blazed orange and red tinged on the outer edges with pink and yellow as it appeared to settle toward earth. The shutters levered downward.

Luc hesitated, realizing this one of thousands of sunsets was suddenly engrained in his memory. "I don't understand, mother." And for once he truly didn't have even an idea to explore or speculate about. "How could you and father have allowed him to just keep your son?" Their son. His brother. Then, randomly, his thoughts uncharacteristically scattered and fragmented, "What's his name?"

"Lucien," she said softly as if she found it painful to say the name aloud. "There just wasn't any other choice. We had to think of you. I can't tell you all the details, but it was during the time of the great battles, when the Usurper had, for a time, taken the throne from Osiris. Much was at stake."

And much was unsaid. She was either lying or not telling him the entire truth. Probably both. "I wish I'd known him. Do you think it might be possible to--"

"No. I'm sorry, Ljluka. He isn't who he might have become. If he knew of your existence, that you were the firstborn with the full measure of power, he would probably seek your life. You would be a threat to him, to his importance in Set's household."

Like someone who kills for survival. His mother might actually be right about this. It just seemed so strange. Kirin,

Andrew, Horus, they had another brother, too. How would they react? He was filled with so many conflicting feelings, but he didn't know what more to say. Time, he needed time to think about it. His mother had known for millenniums, and she hadn't known what to say. Why should he?

"I'm sorry I kept this from you. In truth I'd hoped you would never find out, since there was nothing that could be done."

"Is there no hope at all? Could we convince him, over time, how evil Set is, and how--"

"You are never to mention that name in my presence."

"Sorry. Yes, well, the Usurper, then. After being here, among us, after seeing how much different, how much better--"

"It's too late, Ljluka. It's always been too late. Consider. If the Usurper discovers your existence, he will probably kill Lucien, having no further need for the inferior DNA. Would you want to be responsible for that? Would you want to live with the Usurper for the rest of your life, if he were to kidnap and try to brainwash you?"

"Of course not."

"Then let it be, my son."

"But--"

"Your father and I have agonized over this since its occurrence. Do you think in one night you'll find some solution we haven't?"

He could hear frustration creeping into her voice, and the fear of losing him, or him not understanding how she had tried to protect him. Perhaps he was being too hard on her. What if it'd been as she said,? During the great war Set could have hidden the child away for years until it was indeed too late to rescue him.

"I'm sorry, mother," he said, standing and reaching to grasp her hands. "I'll try to be son enough for two. I hadn't considered how painful this must be for you, having lost a son. It was selfish of me to consider only my own feelings."

Isis closed her eyes, pulling his head down to her shoulder. "You have always been all a mother could hope for in a son, Ljluka."

She pulled back. "Don't apologize. You've only just found out. Of course you're upset. I'm relieved to have it out in the open at last."

Why didn't he believe that? "I'm surprised you felt you had to keep it from us for so long."

"Do you remember when I told you that everything I've done has been because I only want you to be happy and safe?" She look relieved, but cautiously so, watching him intently.

"Yes," he said slowly, wondering what more she might have to say.

"Good. Never forget," she said with unexpected finality. She glanced toward the door and called, "Come in," though Luc hadn't heard anyone approach.

Kirin entered. "I'm sorry to interrupt," she said, looking from her mother to Luc. "But Andrew and the men are returning."

"They were successful?" Luc asked.

Kirin nodded. "But they had to bury a lot of men, both good and bad."

"What of the one who looked like me?"

"Escaped. Andrew let him go though he killed the man's lieutenant, and his men killed many more."

Relief, unbidden, fluttered somewhere in the back corner of Luc's heart. Tomorrow he would learn to hate his brother, Lucien, if he must. He would think of him as another one of Set's minions, living happily among the enemy, thinking as they thought, doing as they did. He was now, as Kirin had seen, an evil man. But for today, just this one day, he would be his brother.

He turned and without a word went out the door to find Andrew. Only a brother could understand what he was going through. He needed to talk to the brother of his heart and soul, the brother who was far more a part of him than any other brother, no matter how identical, could ever be.

...Enoch walked with God three hundred years, and had sons and daughters.

Genesis 5: 22

Chapter Nine

They returned home to die. It showed in their dirty, sweat damp faces. There was no fear in their eyes, only exhaustion and resignation. Around fifteen men, camouflage clothing unable to disguise the dried mud and blood, theirs and others, stood at attention behind Lucien. On his right stood Typhon with around thirty of his own men, their tactical support team. In stark contrast that only emphasized the difference in their situations, Typhon and his men were dressed in unsoiled uniforms. As if aware of the negative connotation their outward appearance carried, their stature was even more rigid. On either side, no one spoke.

No one dared speak.

Set glared down at them, fists clenched at his hips. "Fools!" he shouted. His nostrils flared with the force of his quick intake of breath. "It's not enough that you failed to snatch her, even though you were close enough to drag her away kicking and screaming by her hair if you were not so weak and useless. But you let them take back even the DNA! Is there no end to your incompetence?"

Seeing the level of anger rise to death and mayhem, Lucien cried out, "Had our intelligence been of any use, we wouldn't have failed. They didn't even warn us that Isis had returned. It's the only way those bastards knew how to find us in the first place. And who but these idiots would have sent us through a bog as an escape route?"

"You would have failed even if they'd given you safe passage," Typhon shouted in defense. "They massacred half your men and you have nothing to show for it."

Set stalked over to one of his guards, snatched the spear out of his hand, brought it back over his right shoulder and flung it at one of Typhon's soldiers who was standing, by no mistake of Set's aim, between his sons. It passed through the man's chest with enough force to enter the chest of the soldier behind him. Needing no further persuasion, his sons' men prostrated themselves before the dead bodies hit the floor.

His rage unbridled, Set ran down the steps and reached to unsheathe a machete from one of Lucien's soldier's belt. The man shuddered. Ignoring him, Set crossed the demarcation between his sons and their men. He raised his arm, crouched, and brought the machete down on the neck of the first soldier he came to. The severed head rolled to its side. He stepped to the next prostrate soldier. Repeated his action. Again and again, though not always with such completion. He didn't stop until the room resembled a butcher's shop. He had killed roughly half of Typhon's men.

Dropping the machete at last, he walked over to Typhon, who had not dared to move during this retribution. Set kicked him and bellowed, "So now you have both lost half of your men and have nothing to show for it!"

His attention shifted to Lucien. He stepped over to him, reached down to grasp the back of his shirt and tugged him to his feet. "Your excuses are equally useless," he shouted, and struck his son in the jaw so hard Lucien's head snapped back and he flew several feet before landing in a heap. "Now both of you get out of my sight and don't return until you have a plan that will work!" Not waiting for them to move, Set spun on his heels and stalked out of the room without looking back.

Chaos erupted in his wake. Curses of the living mixed with groans of the dying. Nalini, hidden behind the hijab, the screen behind which women from the harem were sometimes allowed to observe special occasions, took a soft cleansing breath. She had discovered the outcome of her brother's mission, which was her goal. Now she fled toward the safety of the harem.

As a warrior and a resident of Set's perverse universe, she should have grown immune to the malicious slaughter of innocent men. But she never would. Like them, she dared not lift a finger in her own defense. There were worse ways to die, they all realized. Nalini was too intelligent to ever show it, but she was terrified of her own father. A sudden chill caused her to wrap her arms around herself.

Troubled and silent, she passed unnoticed down the corridors that led to the women's quarters. The palace's residents had other matters on their mind at the moment than what a mere woman might be up to.

Her mother rose anxiously at her entrance. "You should have let me send Arai, Nalini. Why do you insist on taking such chances?"

"His presence would have been noted. Besides, no one knows my brothers better than I, mother. Their body language tells me far more than their words. The same is true of your vile camel flea of a husband." Nalini moved to the table by her mother's chaise and poured herself a hot cup of tea.

Astarte glanced toward the door. "Use caution. I shouldn't have to remind you that the very walls have ears."

"Especially yours?" Nalini asked softly, sipping the warming beverage and letting its pleasant herbal essence relax her tense muscles.

Her mother gave her a warning look and moved back to the large chaise lounge, piled with plush pillows and luxurious fabrics. Astarte may have been only one of Set's three wives , but she was the only one in residence. Her quarters reflected his obsession for her. The rooms were spacious and filled with priceless artifacts, more like the men's quarters then the small spaces allotted to Nalini and Set's concubines. While they shared communal baths, Astarte had her own private bathing pool and an array of servants to attend her every whim.

What Astarte shared most happily was her husband. She encouraged his use of concubines, though he seemed unsatisfied with them. Nalini was annoyed at his constant acquisition, since he didn't seem to even know one by name.

"Do you ever feel guilty?" Nalini inquired, sinking into a deep cushion beside her mother, careful to keep her cup level.

"What have I done to feel--"

"Last night, Jasmine—he struck her so hard she will have a black eye a week from tomorrow. No one could help her of course. And we both know her only fault was that she was not you."

"I was afraid of this. It will only grow worse now that..."

Her mother turned aside, busying herself with filling a goblet with water. Nalini had not missed the way her mother stopped herself from revealing something she obviously didn't want her to know.

"I fear for whoever has the misfortune of warming his bed this night," Nalini said softly. "Pray don't let it be you, mother."

"Tell me what you saw," her mother said, changing the subject.

Nalini decided to let it go, for now. "What we expected, except that unfortunately he did not slice open the skull of that lecherous bastard brother of mine. A kick in the side was all he got for his stupidity. His men were less fortunate." She went on to describe in graphic detail Set's slaughter.

Astarte cried out and pressed her hands against her eyes as if willing herself not to visualize the scene Nalini had described. "Vile, senseless murders. Why has he learned nothing about being a ruler in all these endless years? Is he not powerful enough? Must he constantly strive to instill fear in his subjects? And in his children?" she added. Nalini studied her silently, amazed at her mother's ability to remain with a man she hated. Then, staring at something she saw beyond the confines of her gilded cage, Astarte whispered, "I wish Lucien had captured the woman, Kirin."

"Why? If as you say, you have seen that in the future Lucien takes her for his wife, surely it is only a matter of time."

"The future grows dim. It shimmers like a mirage, elusive, just beyond my sight. It may be too late."

"Too late for what?" Nalini sprang to her feet. "We must escape now. They are distracted. It's the best time."

"Where would we go, Nalini? Where could we hide from him? You know he would not rest until he brought me back. Then what? At least now we are able to survive, to escape much of the worst that…. Perhaps you can go. There must be a way."

"We must think of something soon," Nalini agreed.

Nalini knew her mother was still thinking of Jasmine as well as all the soldiers who had just died. She had spoken in annoyance, having grown fond of Jasmine. Her mother, she admitted to herself, did indeed feel guilty. Astarte did what she could to influence Set. She was the only one whose opinion or wishes he ever considered aside from his own. Nalini suddenly wished she had kept Jasmine's problems to herself. She knew Set only sent for one of his concubines when Astarte discouraged him from visiting her.

He sometimes grew frustrated with trying to please her, to gain her love. Not satisfied with possessing her, he wanted her willing capitulation. He had done his best to secure it since the day he kidnapped her from the court of Osiris, just nine months before her own birth.

Neither of them believed Set was capable of actual love. Both of them knew his already passionate fixation with Astarte was encouraged by herbs she placed in his wine and a secret love incantation she recited whenever he used the hidden passageway that ran within the palace walls and visited her chamber.

"What will your brothers do now?" her mother asked, breaking into her thoughts.

What now indeed, wondered Nalini. Understanding the question, she replied, "They are not to return to his exalted sight until they have a new plan that will work."

Set must be controlled if he was to be endured. Both of them despised him. Their survival depended on no one else realizing the depth of that hatred. The evils she endured were insignificant compared to what her mother suffered, Nalini realized. She had to find a way to save them both.

"Mother, I think there may be something we could use to our advantage."

"What?"

"Before, when I told you what happened on my mission, I didn't tell you everything."

"Nalini, what's wrong?" Astarte asked, leaning toward her. "What have you kept from me?"

"The Vargas I was sent to kill, Luc. Remember that I told you I was unable to get near him in Rome?

"Yes, which is why you had to go to America. I remember."

"Well, he always managed to stay one step ahead of me in Washington, so I only saw the back of his head as he exited the hotel and a shadowed view of his face as he ran to his vehicle in a dark alley." She hadn't mentioned the incompetent freelancer she'd hired to kill him. Seeing the moves she had heard so much about gave her an edge—or would have. She remembered the quick work he made of the poor fool. This Luc was slick and incredibly fast for such a large man.

"You must have seen his face in Rome, when you managed to injure him."

Though he was trim and athletic, much like Lucien, his economy of motion and modus operandi were superior. He was very good at his job. She needed to get better. He would not underestimate her again.

"Well, did you see his face?" Her mother touched her arm to regain her attention.

"What? Yes, I saw him. As I sliced open his chest, I looked him full in the face. I was going to finish the job by ripping through his jugular and—

"Nalini, please, just get to your point." Astarte's hand moved to cover her stomach as if Nalini's graphic story made her sick.

"And my point, mother," she said, dropping the gory details, "is that this man is an identical replica of Lucien. If I had not been so shocked, I might have finished the job before Anubis, who he called Andrew, stabbed me."

Astarte rose from the chaise. "Have you told this to anyone else?" She didn't move toward Nalini. Instead she lifted her hand, then dropped it. After glancing toward the securely locked door, she looked down at the floor, deep in thought. A slow smile appeared on her face and she whispered, "I knew I saw twins in Sekhmet's future, back when I was at the court of Osiris."

"Twins? He and Lucien are twins?" So obvious. Why hadn't it occurred to her?

As if she had momentarily forgotten Nalini was there, Astarte looked up at her and exclaimed, "Nalini!" She glanced toward the door from the passageway hidden in the wall. "You must say nothing about this. Go, Nalini. Set approaches." She hurried to the other room, muttering as she went. Nalini heard only, "Key to freedom. Won't want him to-- She'll do anything."

Nalini needed no encouragement to avoid Set. She fled to the confines of her own chamber. Amea looked up from a small cushion where she sat mending one of Nalini's shirts.

"Your rendezvous was successful?"

"Yes," she said softly, and dropped down onto her sleeping mat. She rested her elbows on her knees then propped her chin up with the steeple of her fingers. Knowing that Ljluka was Lucien's identical twin brother, and that their mother was Sekmet, beloved friend to Isis who was raising Ljluka as her own son, brought more questions than answers. *Who was the she to whom her mother referred?* Why all the secrecy? Was Set Ljluka's father too? She needed more information. Glancing at Amea, she said, "Do you have any more of that tonic mother gave me to heal bruising?"

Amea, who had fallen silent when she noticed her mistress's mood, now stood up and set down her needlework. "Yes, I put it in the cabinet. You did not get caught?" she asked, scanning Nalini's face for bruises.

"No, it's for my brother, Lucien."

"Why give it to him then?" Amea asked, scowling.

"Good question," Nalini said simply. "Sit down, Amea. I'll get it." She walked to the cupboard, took out the vile she was looking for, poured a small amount into a flask and added a double measure of wine. Shaking the flask, she headed for the door.

And if any man shall take away from the words of the book of this prophecy, God shall take away his part out of the book of life, and out of the holy city, and from the things which are written in this book.

Revelations 22: 19

106

Chapter Ten

Luc moved to where his brother stood watching a security tech check the firewall logs. "Saw Roscoe in the hall. He updated me on the casualties." He noticed the hard lines, etched deeply into the tender flesh around his brother's eyes, the dark soot-like smudges beneath his eyes, red-rimmed and heavy with self-blame, tempered anger and intense focus. "Stephen was a good man. Edward too. I'm sorry, Andrew."

"Thanks, Luc," Andrew replied, glancing up from the active computer screen. "I'm just glad we didn't lose any more of our men. I should have been more careful, taken everyone's safety more seriously instead of playing around. It's a good thing Roscoe was with Kirin."

Luc chose to let his brother's wrath run its course. Telling their head of security he wasn't to blame would likely start him on a tangent, and right now they had more important things to do.

"They breeched the first firewall, but never got any further than that," the surveillance expert informed them, looking up from a nearby terminal.

"We have to be sure," said Andrew. "Luc?"

Luc slid into a seat at an adjacent terminal and typed in his password. He logged into the firewall logs, affirmed Frederic's observation and typed in a short script to start Aurora, the program he had designed to run a full systems analysis. He wanted to ensure they hadn't managed to breech any of Kirin's genetic data files, or even worse, her research journals. He had individually encrypted them all, but with a good hacker one never knew. There weren't any government's files he himself hadn't managed to access when the need arose. It was one of his favorite mental activities. That and chess. He liked chess, though few would play against him.

"Everything seems intact. The alarms never went off, so I doubt any of the encryption was compromised. Aurora will tell us if there's a problem. I really think they came for Kirin, not her data," Luc said. He glanced up to make sure Andrew was listening. Seeing his intent gaze, he continued. "Once they discovered she was in the forest, they cut their connection to the main system."

"Or they stopped once they knew we were onto them. They had to be all through the forest. How else did they breech the firewall and nearly capture Kirin simultaneously?" Andrew insisted. He turned toward a half-dozen security techs and yelled, "How the hell did they make it this far without us knowing? It was only luck that Luc was in the right place at the right time and able to diffuse the bomb."

"Did you talk to the perimeter guards?" Luc interjected, trying to refocus his brother's fury.

"Yes, of course," Andrew said. "They didn't see anything."

"Anything on the camera tapes?"

"Nothing."

"Look, they could have gotten past the guards, but there's no way they got past the surveillance cameras without interrupting the sequencing," Luc persisted. "Let me look at them again, from before the firewall was breeched."

"Over there," Andrew said, pointing to where another security tech had numerous frames open on his terminal, scanning for irregularities. "Jacob's already on it."

Luc pushed back his chair and stood. "There's got to be something there." He walked over to stand behind Jacob's chair. "Mind starting the tapes over, from about thirty minutes before they breeched the firewall?"

"No problem." Jacob tapped the screen and stopped the forward progress of the tapes. He ran his finger down the time value bar on the bottom of the screen until it reached the desired frame. A tap of the play arrow and the videos began to run.

"Slow it down," Luc advised. There was no way the Usurper's agents were going to get the best of him. Not now. Not ever. He studied the feed with determination.

Ten minutes later, Andrew asked, "What is it you're looking for, Luc?"

"There's got to be a plug-in edit on here somewhere. They had to get to the feed somehow, had to insert a time offset. It—there, Jacob, freeze it." Luc bent down for a closer look. "Okay, run that bottom tape back a minute and really slow it down when you restart it," Luc instructed. He felt a rush of satisfaction. They may have snuck in the back door, but they were not breaching the inner sanctum any time soon.

He glanced at his brother, and pointed to the screen. "Watch right here when Jacob restarts it. Two tells, one the bird that starts to take off from that bottom branch but instead just remains immobile, and two, the slight waver in the video feed."

Jacob tapped the play button. The video moved forward in slow motion. Andrew pointed to the small bird, barely noticeable on the bottom branch of a tree and said, "I see it. So how did they manage to do this?"

"Shit. I can't believe I missed it," Jacob said.

"Probably mirrors and then a satellite hookup. The surveillance cameras can be rerouted and they need to incorporate multiple feed sources for various angles. They shouldn't be able to fool us so easily again."

"I'll take a crew and get right on the updates. It *won't* happen again," Jacob promised.

"Whoever did it was no amateur, Jacob," Luc reassured him. "Andrew. I need to speak to you. Privately."

"Sure. I'm glad you managed to find out how they breached the firewalls. Let's go to my office," he said, turning to walk out the door. "And you're right, Jacob. We can't let this happen again." Once in the hallway, he lowered his voice and said, "Luc, they're getting far too bold. We're going to have to stop them once and for all."

"I'll catch up to you in a little while, Jacob," Luc called out, before following his brother out the door and down the hall. "Andrew, I was thinking something similar about the Usurper earlier today."

He walked into Andrew's office, with its sleek titanium, leather and black marble décor. Without waiting for his brother to find a chair, he moved to the black leather sofa and threw himself down, head cushioned on a pillow, feet propped on the armrest.

"Is this to be a psychoanalyst session?" Andrew teased, settling into a gleaming metal chair with black leather cushions.

Consuela, a personal assistant Luc always warned Andrew was too good for him, sailed in bearing a tray with steaming espresso, fresh baked breads, assorted cheeses and fruits. As usual, she had also included Luc's favorite, dates and nuts.

"Ah, bless you. Impeccable timing, as usual. Just put it down here," Andrew said, indicating the smoky glass table beside his chair. Reaching for a cup he savored a sip despite its heat, waiting until she closed the door and left. He continued to wait, patiently studying his brother's face.

The phone rang. Andrew answered it. He held it out. "For you. London."

Luc took the phone, but didn't bother to sit up. "Talk to me," he snapped.

Robert, the head of a London-based Illuminati-owned corporation was on the phone, and he sounded angry. "So now they're dumping the stocks and buying them back at the reduced price under cover of a front company."

"Are you sure?" Luc asked, knowing the answer, but wanting a moment to decide what needed to be done.

"Yes. I rang up Spencer but he won't even take my call."

Spencer had gone over to the other side. Didn't he realize they would never protect him, were only using him, Luc wondered. "How much are we talking about?"

"Try one hundred million pounds."

They were getting their money's worth out of him, he thought wryly. "I'll make a couple calls," he said, trying not to take his irritation out on Robert. The man had been right to call him.

"Thank you. Sorry to bother you with it, but I knew you'd want to know right away." The phone went dead. Their best Italian operative never wasted his time unnecessarily. It was one of his best characteristics.

He turned to Andrew. "The Usurper's trying another tactic. I thought I cleared it up in D.C., but apparently he's trying the European market--trying to undermine stocks from companies he knows are affiliated with or owned outright by the Illuminati. He's messing with us, basically. We need to find out why he is doing this now."

"How much?" Andrew asked.

"One hundred million pounds."

"Shit. That's heavy," Andrew said, grinning.

Luc shook his head at Andrew's foolish pun, but it did the trick and momentarily lifted his dark spirits, as his brother had intended. "I should call father and have him let you clean this mess up," he threatened.

"Ha-ha. You're the enforcer. So enforce. I'll clean up your sloppy leftovers."

Sighing, Luc pulled out his cell and pushed a button. He spoke in fluent and fast Italian and ordered a personal Illuminati visit—also known as a hit--to the appropriate brokerage personnel. They worked diligently to be sure there were plenty of dangerously capable men to execute backup plans when family business took precedence, as it always did. The Illuminati existed to make the family enterprises run efficiently, not the other way around.

He hung up and pressed another number and told the recipient of his call to get on the Internet and make some interesting number switches to various accounts he provided numbers for. Luc pressed the off button and handed the phone to Andrew. Luc knew his brother needed to hear only one side the conversation to know what was occurring in Europe.

Luc let him wait a while longer for the reason he wanted to speak to him, collecting his thoughts. Sitting up, he said, "Mother had some rather surprising news." His brother, as he had assumed, took the subject shift in stride. Luc, the Illuminati's chief enforcer, had quickly handled the problem in Britain. There was now more important business, family business, to discuss.

"Judging from your present demeanor it was not good news," Andrew commented.

"Honestly, I have not had time to decide what I think about it. I-I was hoping to discuss it with you." Luc ran his hand through his hair and sighed, feeling heavy with weariness, both mental and physical.

Andrew reached to hand him a cup of espresso. "Here, you look as if you could use this. And you know I will do whatever I can to help, no matter what it is you need, Luc. You have only to ask."

Luc accepted the cup, took a swallow and set it down on the table to his left. "The guy, the one they said looked like me."

"Yeah, I figured it might have something to do with that. Kirin said you were hauled off for a private chat."

"Well, the thing is, she said he's my twin brother." He waited for the reaction.

Andrew's hand stopped, midway to his mouth. He lowered the cup, looked as if he was going to say something, but then lifted the cup back up and drained it. After he set it back down on the table, he said softly, "What else did she tell you?"

"Set stole him at birth. They couldn't get him back because they would have found out about me. She thinks they took him for the DNA and they'd rather have mine if they knew I existed because I was the firstborn."

"Damn. Why the hell are we just finding this out? She didn't even tell us we had another brother. She didn't think it mattered? And a twin, an identical twin." Andrew shook his head. "Damn," he said again.

"There's got to be more to it," they both said at once. Then they were both silent, each considering the magnitude of the secret their mother had kept all these years.

"Should we even think of him as our brother, this Lucien? Kirin said he's evil, little better than an animal, a predator. He's been living with those savages all this time," Luc said, breaking their mutual silence.

"Lucien, huh? Shit, I don't know. This is too much to take in." Andrew crossed his arms over his chest and leaned back, stretching out his legs.

"Look, maybe it's because he's supposed to be my identical twin, but I feel like I need to know more about him," Luc said softly.

"More than she'll ever tell us," Andrew agreed.

Luc had known Andrew would understand. They seldom disagreed when it came to family matters. And this was a family matter, whether their mother had seen fit to include them in her decisions or not.

"Do you have any ideas about how you can find out more information?"

Standing, Luc walked over to the windows. Andrew's office faced another direction and the blinds had not yet lowered. He looked out across the valley, shrouded in mist and deepening shadows.

Hidden in mystery, like their past.

"Anyone who might know anything would never dare to tell," Luc said.

"Obviously."

He could feel his brother's gaze resting on him, waiting to hear what help he could be in whatever plan Luc came up with. It warmed him, strengthened his resolve. "There might be one way to find out more information, about a lot of things."

"How?" Andrew asked cautiously.

"*The Book of Life*," Luc said, turning to look at his brother, to see his reaction.

Andrew stood and walked toward him. Unspoken, the question he asked was there in his eyes, measuring his brother's seriousness for himself. Then, "She'll never let us go, never let us look for it. Hell, she may keep it in the bottom of her jewel chest."

Luc chuckled. "We can't both go. Too obvious. I need you to run interference, to keep her from finding out what I'm really up to. We need to come up with a cover story, too,," he added, already formulating a plan of action.

Andrew knew better than to try to dissuade him, and immediately began to assist him instead. "It'll be dangerous, especially if either of our parents get wind of it. Who will you take?"

"Only a couple dozen of our best men."

"Where will you start looking? Do you have any idea where it might be, assuming it actually exists?"

"It must. She thinks it exists, so I know it does. And where else would I go to rummage through the cellar of *the old ones*? I'm going to Syria."

Andrew nodded. "The Bedouins will be available. Abdul has probably been itching for some action. Damn. We need to figure out a way for me to go, too," he said, warming to the sense of adventure.

"I hope it's not as much fun as you envision," Luc cautioned. Then, more seriously, "If what I suspect is true, this could change everything I thought I knew to be real. I've never wanted to be wrong about something so much in my entire life."

Those living on earth, whose names were not written in the Book of Life from the foundation of the world, will be surprised when they see the beast because it was, is no longer, and will come again.

Revelations 17: 8

Chapter Eleven

Nalini walked across the lapis lazuli tiles in the antechamber of Lucien's suite. Several of her brother's servants came racing through the door to his bedchamber, the last one pulling it shut behind himself. She heard something smash against the door from the inside. Undaunted, she pulled it open and strode boldly into his bedchamber.

"What the fuck do you want?" Lucien managed to blurt out without moving his mouth.

"Is that any way to speak to a sister who has come bearing gifts?" Nalini asked. She stepped over broken shards of blue glass as she continuing toward Lucien, despite his ill- tempered and obviously painful greeting. She almost felt sorry for him.

Yes, it did have to hurt. She was certain his jaw was broken, in at least one place. The entire left side of his face was swollen. His eye was half closed. From beneath his tan and blond whiskers, the bruising had begun to turn green. "Hmm, you couldn't even suck on a straw about now. Do you think if you tilt your head back I could pour this into your mouth?"

"Huh?" Only his complete confusion at her behavior kept him from throwing her out at once.

"No, don't try to speak. This is one of Astarte's tonics, for bruising and pain. Trust me, it works almost at once. And who would know better than I?" Nalini knew enough to quickly provide her peace offering if she hoped to get any information from him.

"How come?" He was rightly suspicious. She had never before offered to help him recover from one of their father's frequent assaults.

"For what you did for me, in the dungeon," Nalini said simply. And she meant it, she realized.

Lucien walked over to a low stool and sat down so Nalini could reach him more easily. He tipped his head back by slow degrees, and she poured the tonic into his mouth, one mouthful at a time. Swallowing hurt too, she realized as she noticed him press his hand against the edge of the stool. He would never have admitted it, of course. Besides, they both knew Astarte's tonics would make the the healing time shorter and the interim more bearable. Her knowledge of magic and herbs, and her ability to see into the future made most in the palace fear her nearly as much as they feared Set.

Nalini watched him swallow the last of the drugged wine and sat down across from him on the chair for which the stool was intended. "You want an ice pack until you enter the warm heating pad stage?" One didn't grow up in Set's household without knowing how to manage severe injuries, even if they were guaranteed to heal by the next day.

Lucien pointed to the ice maker beneath a granite countertop situated to the left of the doorway. Nalini stood up and walked over to the bar to pick up a small towel. After filling it with ice, she returned to Lucien and gently pressed it to his mandible. He reached up to take the ice pack and studied her. She could tell he was curious, wondering what she really wanted.

He took a deep breath, and from his appreciative release of it, she realized the tonic had taken effect. "Good. You see? I told you it was worth it."

"Ah-huh."

"I realize it's difficult for you to speak. Give it another minute or two and it will be greatly improved. I was wondering about something. What can you tell me about this Kirin?"

"Huh?" She could tell this mono-syllable conversation was going to be difficult.

"The woman, Kirin. What can you tell me about her?" He looked away, downward, but not before she had seen a reaction far greater than just regret that he hadn't managed to bring her back. Or was that it, but for a much more personal reason than Set's orders?

"Astarte has had one of her visions."

His attention now riveted to her face, his narrowed eyes flashed like blue ice. *So I'm right*, Nalini thought. He already wanted this woman that Astarte had seen as his future wife. Should she tell him?

"And?"

"And what did you think of her? Is she as beautiful as the soldiers are saying?"

"What soldiers?" He actually sat forward on the stool, aggressively.

She recognized the possessive, jealous reaction--he was more like his father than he knew. "I'm not sure. Rashid told me. What was your impression?"

A shrug. No words. A tough nut to crack. Could she be wrong? Was he just angry that his men had discussed any aspect of the mission as fodder for the palace gossip mill? But no, there it was again. He looked away, remembering. A swallow, his Adam's apple bobbing. Yes, he was infatuated at the very least. How to get an honest response?

"I wonder if Set will give her to Typhon? They are both so obsessed with the purity of the bloodline."

That did it. Rage simmered in the back of his eyes, though he refused to say a word. He returned her gaze steadily.

"Or, what of you? Why do you not take her as your wife?"

Again nothing. Ah, he was onto her. Fine. "Astarte has seen your wedding."

"To her?" The response was immediately, anxious.

"Yes."

Silence. He studied her intently, trying to gauge her sincerity. His unbidden hopefulness touched her and she said, "For Typhon I wish only broken ribs and a ruptured spleen. For you, Lucien, I wish this union if it pleases you."

She could sense his confusion at her words. The fact that she meant them confused her as well. But she did want him to be happy, she realized. Lucien, unlike Typhon, had done little to antagonize her or make her life more unbearable. Though he also did little to openly defend her, she was convinced he had done what he could to protect her from Typhon at least. "Will you go for her again?"

"Yes."

Said with determination. She almost felt sorry for this Kirin. Lucien would not fail a second time. "You should rest now. Soon the damage will be completely healed, but the healing is hastened by rest."

He nodded. Then, softly, "Thank you." For more than the tonic.

As she left his suite and walked down the corridor, she noted the nervous scurrying of servants rushing in and out of Typhon's quarters. Too bad he wouldn't be foolish enough to accept a tonic from her, she mused. For him she would have provided a slow, agonizing death potion. She hurried down the corridor, unwilling to take a chance of running into him.

Arriving in time to see Arai emerge from the women's quarters, she realized her mother was alone again. She must have sent him on an errand. Somewhat surprised by this, she went to her mother's chamber.

"Good, you're back," Astarte said. Her cheerful greeting was also surprising, considering she was seldom anything but irritated after one of Set's visits. "How did your visit with Lucien go?"

"I never told you I was going to see him."

"Right. So how did it go?"

Nalini rolled her eyes and went over to lounge on her favorite cushion. "He's into it deep for that Kirin woman."

"Excellent. That'll work out in our favor. I've put the wheels of my plan in motion."

"What plan?"

"The plan to get you out of here for good, Nalini. While there's breathe in my body, Typhon won't have you." Her brow worried into uncharacteristic wrinkles, reflecting the struggle within her. "You've been keeping things from me, Lini."

"You know of my punishment, mother. You know what he did to me."

"I'm not talking about that. I'm talking about what he did to you before that, while I was with Set convincing him that it was not your fault." She twisted the edge of her silk robe and knotted it within her hands, then paced toward the door and back again. "I honestly thought you'd be safe. I saw you defeat Ljluka. Saw him fall by your blade," she said softly, as if to herself. "I thought you would return in glory and be treated with respect at last."

"But you didn't see that Luc's brother, Andrew, stabbed me, mother, and then managed to save his brother. That's the problem. Sometimes you don't see enough."

Her attention once again on her daughter, Astarte said, "Yes, I can see that I haven't," but she was no longer referring to what went on *outside* the palace.

"I can take care of myself," Nalini insisted, sitting cross-legged.

"No, you most certainly can't. It's no longer safe for you here. I'll not have Typhon turn you into what his father has made of me."

Nalini heard the iron inflexibility behind those words. Alarmed by her mother's uncharacteristic determination she said, "Mother, you must come with me."

Astarte sighed, then walked over to sit in the chaise next to her cushion. "It's no longer possible, Nalini."

A sick feeling started in the pit of Nalini's stomach. She didn't want to hear what her mother was about to reveal. Her arms went around her knees and she braced herself. "Why?" she asked softly.

"Because I'm fulfilling my bargain with Set".

"What did you promise him, mother? That you wouldn't leave?" But she knew even as she said it that nothing that simple would have dissuaded Set from harsher punishment for her failure. Astarte could never escape him, or so he probably thought. A promise to stay held no value.

"No," Astarte said. Then quieter, and more troubled, as if she were remembering, she added, "He was much angrier than that. I had to promise him a son."

Nalini squeezed her eyes shut. A son? He would never stop looking for them if Astarte tried to run away with his son. She must change her mother's mind. "Mother, no! That's insane. Look at what he has done with the sons he already has. He can't make you do this. It doesn't matter anyway. He can't make you fulfill the bargain if we are gone." She couldn't fathom this new development. Why would her mother agree to such a stupid plan? "Now you *must* go with me."

"But I told you, Nalini. It's too late. I'm already with child."

No! This couldn't be happening. Not now, not when they were finally going to be free! But she saw the truth of it in her mother's eyes. "Dammit! How could you have done this to us?" Nalini covered her face with her hands, thoughts spiraling out of control.

"Nalini, please understand--"

"No! No, no, no, no…." she crooned, tightening the grip on her knees and rocking back on her heels. What would they do now? They were doomed to this never-ending hell for eternity.

"I did it for you, Nalini." Her mother reached out to her, tears glistening in her eyes.

Nalini jumped up, clutching her fists at her sides. "Don't you dare blame me for this, mother. I won't live with that kind of guilt." She couldn't endure watching Set ruin the life of a young child. How could her mother place another victim into Set's vile clutches?

"Nalini, please." Her mother stood and reached out to grasp her hands. She resisted, but her mother held tight, forcing her to acquiesce. "Don't think of it as something terrible. Did you turn out to be evil? Won't you love this brother who grows within me, who'll be nurtured by me?"

"But will Set allow you to raise the child, mother? It is a male."

"It was a condition of my agreement."

Since when had Set kept an agreement if it didn't suit him, she thought, angry at Astarte's naiveté. Then, seeing the near panic in her mother's eyes and remembering her new condition, she stilled the sharp words that came to her. "Okay," she said with resignation. "So we stay. For now."

"Oh no, *we* don't stay. You're going, Nalini. Once we get our hands on the proof, she'll do anything we ask. But we need Set's help to obtain it."

"Who'll do *anything*? What are you talking about?" This pregnancy must be clouding her mother's mind more than she realized.

"Lucien's twin. Their names and parentage will appear in the book. I told Set that I had a vision, that I saw *our* son's name appear in *The Book of Life* so he'll help us find its location. I told him that you held the book in your hand, that it was your destiny to find and return with it."

"Why would you tell him that? He'll know it for a lie." Even she could have come up with a better cover story than that, given time.

"But it's not a lie, Nalini. It's the truth. I've seen it."

A vice gripped her heart and squeezed until she could barely breathe. "What have you done, mother?" she whispered, stumbling to her feet.

"I have seen the truth of Ljluka and Lucien's parentage. It is a truth Isis would do anything to keep hidden. With the book in our possession, we will bend Isis to our will. It contains the names of all who descended from *the ancients*, including their genetic heritage."

"These are the secret words which Jesus spoke, and which the twin, Judas Thomas, wrote down."

The Gospel of Thomas

128

Chapter Twelve

Luc felt like he'd been chewing pumice. He turned his head and spit. Running his tongue across his teeth, he repeated the gesture. A tilt of the goatskin flask he pulled from his saddle did little to remove the feel of grit from his mouth. He tugged the corner of his *kaffiyeh* across his face, first to wipe off the sweat and help block the sun and blowing sand. Then he tucked in the ends of the *agal* with the crescent moon and star he used to secure the black fabric to his head. A snort interrupted his private grousing. Abdul, who was riding the camel behind him, was apparently amused by his discomfort.

"You have forgotten the *Badiyat Ash Sham.*"

"I've not been here since I was an infant, Abdul. But I won't deny you're right. I'm not used to the Syrian Desert."

"It has made you soft, the gentle sun in your new home. Rā is strong and powerful. You should take off your *kaffiyeh* and put on the ball sport cap of a tourist. Maybe your *gallabia* is not meant to protect you from the desert heat, but is really a dress you stole from a female tourist?"

"Abdul, I don't have any objection to the comfort and practicality of my clothing. And I haven't forgotten it's the best disguise I could wear this close to the war zone just across the border. I just wish I could've been on horseback."

"My prince, your noble beast could carry you for a week or more without food or water. He can move nearly as quickly as a horse, and an Arabian beauty of the type that would honor you equally would have drawn too much attention"

Luc muttered to himself, wondering perversely if his mother's surprising and sudden demand that he retrieve the book, along with her orchestration of the entire mission, had been some sort of punishment for his having plotted to do so without her permission. He would never have found it without her knowledge, of course. They would have wasted a lot of time thinking it was hidden closer to *Tell Hamoukar* in the upper *Khabur* river basin.

A few minutes later, he said, "Look, just keep talking to me to keep me awake. I feel like I'm being rocked to sleep. And the smell! The first chance I get, I'm headed straight to a *hammām*. What I wouldn't give for a Turkish steam bath, freezing plunge and a massage right now."

"Soft, like a woman," Abdul laughed.

"I can see I need to visit Horus more often," Luc sighed. "I guess I am soft. My ass has gone numb," he conceded.

Abdul turned to share the joke with members from his tribe, the *Hassana*, who joined in his laughter. Luc, who assumed he would find it funnier once this desert ship he was sailing took to grazing instead of cresting waves of sand, yelled up ahead at Roscoe to throw him a sports drink. He wasn't an archaeologist and he was not on an exciting adventure to study an ancient culture. This was his life and the artifact he was after held the secret of his birthright.

At long last, the Bedouins signaled that they would stop for the night. Their women had fared much better than Luc and the other men who had accompanied him. They quickly erected tents made from panels of goats' hair that would keep out the cold night winds and sand and keep in the warmth of the fires they would soon build to cook the evening meal. The men tended the animals and ran some security scouting around their perimeter.

Luc took the opportunity to pull out his satellite phone and check in with Cairo. Though the Illuminati was a well known faction in the Middle East, there were still palms to grease in order to get instant obedience. Most of their operatives were from families who had been with them for many generations, despite the political unrest. Some of that unrest was their doing, like the call he was now making.

Once satisfied that his previous orders had been carried out, he hung up and noticed Abdul motioning him to come inside. Soon enough they were drinking welcome if bitter coffee and listening to young men tell old stories as they smoked their *chibouques*. Tired but sated, Luc shook his cup, indicating that he was finished, stood and walked outside. He nodded to Mosheim and Emmanuel, standing guard outside the main tent. Walking toward one of the smaller tents to the left, he flipped open his phone and waited for the satellite bars to fill.

"It's me," he said needlessly, a moment later.

"And who else would call me when I was with Sabina?"

"Kirin."

"I stand corrected," Andrew said, laughing. "Any trouble?"

Luc wondered if staying awake atop a smelly beast counted, but said, "The men found a couple buried mines. Emmanuel removed them."

"How the men holding up?

Luc reflected dryly, "About as well as me. I'm at least amusing the Bedouins. What's mother doing? She hasn't been in contact with me yet, which makes me nervous."

"She's interviewing members of the Sacred Congregation for Extraordinary Ecclesiastical Affairs, personally. Apparently she doesn't think they are interpreting Code of Canon Law appropriately. As you might imagine, she also has some ideas about who should be appointed as Bishop to certain dioceses. You can also imagine how well they're taking that."

That should take some time, Luc mused. As flexible as his mother was about such things, the arguments could go on for weeks. "So business as usual," he concluded. "And what riveting chores has she assigned you?" His brother hadn't been separated from his mission long enough to start complaining that he should have accompanied him. He'd give that another day or two.

"Let's see. Today I had the thrilling job of pointing out to Giovanni that racketeering was not the same thing as tithing. We're still monitoring your route via stealth satellites, of course, though Horus and his people are supervising this one. Oh and mother told me that when you asked tonight, I was to inform you that she would give you more specific directions once you arrive."

"She's one scary broad, you know it?"

"Who you telling?"

Luc heard Sabina in the background, urging his brother to hurry. "Hey, gotta go. I'll talk to you tomorrow, little brother."

Flipping the phone shut, Luc hunched his shoulders against the chill night air. As hot as it was during the day, it got quite cold at night. He walked to his tent where he knew a fire already awaited him.

He was in no mood for any more surprises. Last night, the Bedouins had enacted a longstanding custom and sent him a young virginal bondswoman to *add to his harem*, as Abdul had put it. A woman fit for a Prince, Abdul had tried to reassure him when he had politely refused--though he had provided the rather insulted young lady with enough dowry to become truly free for life. He had no intention of deflowering or becoming responsible for any clinging, dependent females. That was more Andrew's style. Well, maybe not the virgin part, but he liked the familiar exclusivity and continuity of his otherwise informal relationship with Sabina.

His own relationship with Magdalena was more casual. They were friends with benefits, a mutual understanding. She was an independent sole proprietor, by choice, of a string of global luxury spas, and nearly as busy as he. Still, he should have called her before he left. They could have gotten together, had dinner. He missed her sense of humor. Unfortunately, his mind had been too preoccupied with someone else. A call sounded outside his tent and he responded with permission to enter.

Abdul ducked through the goatskin flap and rushed forward. "How long?"

"Let the men and animals rest four hours and then we have to move." Luc turned to a nearby stand and motioned Abdul forward. Tapping the pad to wake up his laptop, he pointed to a location on the satellite map that should take them them six hours to reach and said, "This is the closest point I can give you for now. By tomorrow morning my mother will give me the exact location of the dig." *Which is the only good reason she read the truth of where I was going in my thoughts*, he reflected. He must figure out why she had decided to help him, because it nagged at his intuition in a chilling way.

"That should work," Abdul replied. "We'll meet up with the rest of our caravan here," he added, indicating a point about five hours away. "They scouted ahead as you ordered and will report to us there unless they need to send a message sooner."

"Good." Luc opened a minimized screen and indicated a small blip. "There's a group of traders here, under a dozen, moving toward Iraq. My brothers have found no one else in the area via satellite surveillance." He switched off his laptop, handing it to Hassidim who had appeared at his elbow. "Let's get going. I feel uneasy, and I'm seldom mistaken about such things."

"What's wrong?"

"I wish I knew," Luc muttered.

Osiris in the Underworld is clothed in white and he goeth to the great lake in the midst of the Field of Offerings whereon the great gods sit; and these great and never-failing gods give unto him [to eat] of the tree of life of which they themselves do eat that he likewise may live.

The Book of the Dead

Chapter Thirteen

They'd nearly reached their destination when Abdul rode alongside Luc and said, *"Simoom."* He pointed to the south.

Luc turned to look. "Great, the last thing we need," he said. "How long?"

"Maybe ten minutes."

"How long do you think it will last?"

"Who can say? I think not long this one. Hopefully not more than ten or fifteen minutes," said Abdul.

Luc's phone rang. He listened a moment. "Right, we see it," he said, flipping it closed. "Roscoe! Rafael! Stop the others," Luc yelled. "There's a sandstorm coming. Have Hassidim get the masks and goggles out of the duffle. Get grouped together. Hurry!"

They rode ahead to help group their caravan into a tight cluster rather than a long line. Once his men were organized, Luc turned his camel so that its right side faced the coming sands. *"Soeg! Soeg!"* he commanded. His camel folded downward, first his rear and then his front legs. Luc jumped off on the left side, and accepted the goggles and mask that Hassidim held out. Then he motioned him away. "Get yourself sheltered. I'm fine," Luc assured him. He quickly donned the safety equipment his brother had insisted upon to protect their eyes and lungs from the fine dust particles and blasted sand and reached up to grab the rolled goatskin blanket from his camel's back. Just as the sandstorm reached them, he pulled it over his head and tucked his body against the leeward side of Sarib to wait out the storm.

Soon sand vibrated across the ground and escalated the frantic dance of destruction. The velocity increased. Sand stung his fingers where he grasped the edge of the goatskin. He turned his hands and folded the edges of the blanket to draw his fingers within the covering. Static raised the hair on his arms, and the forced confinement took on a surreal quality.

Outside his tight cocoon the wailing of the wind muffled the moan of camels and the bleat of goats. He heard the occasional tinkling of metallic objects brought together only to be separated again and again as they were tossed about in the unforgiving clutches of the storm. Then thunder announced the elevation of the static to the role of lightening.

Eventually the wind quieted, the sand slowed and fell to again lie still upon the landscape. Luc sat up and drew the blanket backward from his head. Several inches of sand slid to the ground. He stood and shook out the covering. The lenses of his goggles were dull with dust, so he grabbed his sleeve and rubbed them. Minute particles hung thick in the air and he was glad for the mask that filtered it from his breathing. He looked around, relieved to see his men reappearing from under their own sandy blankets.

The Bedouins, being Bedouins, were already gathering scattered supplies and rounding up livestock. Luc's camel groaned without pain and unfolded his legs, first back, locked in place, then front. Sand dripped from him like water. He regurgitated his last meal and began to complacently eat it again. The gas that came up with this second helping did little to improve his already unsavory scent and Luc burst out laughing at his complete nonchalance. The dromedary was beginning to grow on him, belches and all.

Why is it I'm glad I don't smell you right now, Ljluka?

Be nice, mother. He chuckled despite himself.

Aren't I always? I see that you've felt their presence.

Switching to more serious thoughts, he agreed. He held his hand up for silence as Hassidim approached. Understanding at once, Hassidim turned and stood still to run interference should anyone else seek to disturb his prince while he was deep in thought.

I've felt something unsettling, but I can't determine what. Can you elucidate it for me, mother?

The storm interfered with standard surveillance of course, and the enemy used it as cover. Even now they approach. The traders you saw were a preliminary scouting party. They're but a fraction of the force sent against you. It's now a matter of time and skill as well as power.

What's the plan, mother?

Horus comes to help you, my son. He brings more forces. We're no longer able to hide our presence, but we must protect the location of the dig. The Syrians know. They will not interfere. But you must hurry, Ljluka. The Usurper cannot be allowed to get his hands on The Book of Life.

Tell me what I must do.

Andrew has sent you a satellite image. There's a rock formation ahead. Pitch a large tent before it as cover from above, to hide the entrance I'll reveal to you. Go now.

Luc sprang into action. "Hassidim, my laptop! Emmanuel! Roscoe! Abdul! Come here, quickly!"

Hassidim raced toward the pack camels and his lieutenants ran to his side. "We have trouble coming at us and I don't know if help will arrive in time. Abdul, how long before the scouts should report back?"

"They are arriving now, my prince," Abdul informed him, nodding toward the north where the first of the scouts appeared through the hazy remains of the storm.

"Unfortunately, they're going to have to go right back out again. The traders from earlier aren't traders."

Hassidim arrived with the laptop. He popped up a small wooden stand, pulled the computer out of a padded leather case, still encased in the specially designed plastic bag necessary to protect the electronics from the elements. "This weather, these conditions, it is so unreasonable, so dreadful for you, my prince. How can you be expected to function like this?" He opened the lid and pressed the power button, setting the computer on the small stand.

"It's fully charged, my prince. I only wish it was easier to read the screen through this necessary but evil plastic. This was the best I could do. I am so unworthy to serve your exalted greatness." Luc barely noticed Hassidim's bended knee and exaggerated reverence.

As he waited for the computer to boot, he did notice Abdul staring at Hassidim. So used to ignoring his theatrics, he sometimes forgot the wiry Arab was a walking hyperbole. He shrugged a shoulder indulgently.

The screen finished running its boot sequence and he clicked on the satellite program, downloading the map Andrew had just sent him. His men stepped closer, taking off their goggles to peer intently.

"I know this place. It's very near here," Abdul said. "If not for the dust, we could see it from here."

"Good. Get us there." Luc no sooner shut the laptop than Hassidim had it snapped into the case. He tucked it under his arm, collapsed the small stand before snatching it up and ran off toward the pack camels.

Their entire caravan was moving within five minutes, the camels urged to speeds horses would not have been able to maintain in the still heavy dust. Before long, a large rock formation appeared.

This is the place, Ljluka. Beneath that large outcropping near the bottom of the bluff is a sealed entrance. You can't see it, but it's there beneath the sand. It opens to a complex tunnel system. Pitch a tent to cover your work. Have the men dig down and find the entrance. From there you must read the signs and follow the clues left by the old ones. I don't know the exact location of the book. I only know this is where it was hidden. It's up to you to find it, and you must not fail.

Anyone whose name was not found written in the Book of Life was thrown into the lake of fire.

Revelations 20: 15

Chapter Fourteen

Their entire camp was all but invisible until one was within a hundred yards of it, situated as it was at the bottom of a huge sand hill within the shadows of the bluff. Once noticed, all one saw was a large Bedouin encampment, complete with penned goats and corralled camels. The smell of coffee and *zaarp*, a goat cooking in a makeshift underground oven made from rocks, emanated from the cluster of black tents.

Masking their activity required a series of these tents to be strung together. One, the largest, was necessary for covering the dig site itself. Others were used to move the sand they were shoveling into buckets away from the deepening trench near the rock face. Everyone, including the women they had not left behind at their base camp with the children and older members of their tribe, had a job to do and was diligently performing these tasks. A young woman sat on a small stool milking a goat. Another plucked a chicken. Their very presence enhanced the ordinary tribal community persona.

No one would suspect that a cluster of soldiers surrounded the camp, huddled in goatskin and sand-covered trenches. Still others were further away, bellied atop sand hills, binoculars focused on the horizon. These Bedouin were not goat herders by trade. For centuries they had been trained from father to son to be members of an elite desert fighting force able to be called up at a moment's notice by the descendants of *Those Who Came Before*. The legends were told over and over around their campfires. Proud, fiercely brave and faithful though still independent, they followed this tradition by choice and with honor.

Luc never questioned their loyalty. There was no need. He knew they were prepared. It was now up to him to retrieve what he came for. He'd changed into clothing more practical to his current activity. Bareheaded and bare-chested, he was wearing only a pair of wicking socks, high-tech mid-shin leather desert Ops boots and a pair of desert camo pants issued by multiple military units. The matching shirt lay flung over a pile of supplies up above him, despite Hassidim's protests.

Having filled another bucket, Luc stooped to lift it and hand it over his head to Emmanuel, who took it before handing him back its replacement. The hard manual labor helped quiet his mounting tension. A sense of urgency emanated from him to his men. The six of them had dug around twelve cubic meters of sand in the past hour. Luc figured they probably had twelve to twenty more to go before they reached the entrance. They couldn't move any faster just yet. More men would mean a wider hole, not a deeper one. Several of the Bedouin had begun shoveling a slope at the far side of their trench, to enable easier access to the site and faster removal of the sand. Luc and his men continued to add depth to the trench.

He stopped for a moment, wiping the sweat from his forehead with his arm. Hassidim appeared with a light head wrap to absorb sweat and a water bottle to prevent dehydration from what was lost. "You're a genie, aren't you, Hassidim?"

"If only I were so worthy, my prince. It is the least you deserve."

"These men deserve it too. See they get water, whatever else you can think of," he said. Hassidim bowed, then hurried to comply.

Abdul appeared above him, leaning over the pit. "A scout has returned."

Luc speared the sand with his shovel and hurried up the sloped access to ground level. He noticed with approval that Roscoe passed him to take up his shovel in his absence. The men were more than proficient. They understood the urgency. Taking turns was more efficient, keeping everyone fresher.

Luc, answer your phone.

"Hassidim! My phone, get me satellite bars!" Hassidim appeared and Luc tossed his phone. He caught it deftly and dashed from under the tent to acquire a signal.

Seeing the scout next to Abdul, Luc approached them. "What did you see?"

"Their scouts have rejoined them. They don't have a full battalion, but there is more than a platoon, more like a company at least."

"My prince, it's your esteemed brother!" Hassidim called from the edge of the tent.

"I'll be right back," Luc said, turning toward Hassidim.

"Wait, my prince!" called Abdul. He reached down and picked up Luc's shirt, handing it to him.

Luc glanced at the young Bedouin beside Abdul who had dropped to the ground and prostrated himself as realization of Luc's identity was revealed by the tattoo on his back.

Nodding his thanks to Abdul, Luc looked down at the young scout, little more than a boy. "Rise up, son," he said, resting his hand on the boy's shoulder. "I call on you to face death itself without flinching. It's I who should honor you." As the scout regained his feet, Luc slipped his shirt on and rushed toward Hassidim. He grabbed the phone and said, "It's me."

"Shit, where have you been? I tried to send you a satellite feed, but you must be in a dead zone. Look, the trouble that's coming? It's Typhon and his special forces. I'm sure of it. I zoomed in and recognized Sirius."

"How far?"

"You still have at least two days. Mother is sending them a pagan holiday that will make that little dust bowl you just experienced seem like a breath of fresh air. The new technology Horus's guys invented really works."

"You still have one more problem over there."

"I should have known," Luc said, running his hand through his hair.

"There's a strange group of nomads, a ragamuffin array of small clusters really, that seem about to converge and rendezvous on the opposite side of that bluff you've seized."

Luc tossed his phone to Hassidim and hurried back inside. The young scout now stood proudly beside Abdul, but he still seemed nervous at Luc's approach, awed to be standing before a living subject of the incredible stories he had believed only legends since he was a child.

"You did well," said Luc. "I need you to do something more."

Stepping closer to Abdul he told them the news and directed Abdul to send the scouts back out to discover what was happening on the other side of the bluff.

Abdul drew the scout toward the exit, calling out to more of his men so that he could organize the operation. Luc hurried down the slope to where his own men had just uncovered what looked to be the top of a large stone covered with cuneiform.

Luc leaned forward. Boldly across the top, written in cuneiform, it announced *Words to be Spoken*. He had feared as much. An incantation of the type that was picked up in Egypt was needed to open the entrance.

The majority of the sand was quickly moved and Luc helped Roscoe finish brushing off the stone. "You can read it?" Roscoe asked.

Luc nodded. "Yes. I need everyone to clear the tent."

Roscoe nodded, unsurprised, and motioned for the men to accompany him above. A few moments later, he appeared above Luc. "They're out. I'll join them. Call when you're done," he said, before turning to leave.

"Words to be Spoken," Luc read aloud. He read through the rest of the message silently once, then aloud, "It is I, Ljluka, whose blood is the blood of the ancients, whose royal birth appears in *The Book of Life*. I, Ljluka, beseech you to grant me entrance into your sacred vault. I offer you this tribute, this proof of my claim to your bloodline." He pulled a knife from his boot and slashed open his palm, pressing it against the stone. The cut, angled wide though not too deep, still bled enough to quickly fill the cavity beneath his hand. The blood disappeared as if absorbed within the stone.

A moment later, he heard the sound he'd been waiting for and stood back. The shifting of colossal weight, of stone grinding against stone sounded from within the now trembling wall. A swoosh as though a vacuum seal had broken was followed by the inward motion of the massive door. It swung back two feet before sliding to the right, revealing a dark passage.

Luc turned and ran back up the slope, wrapping a bandana around his hand. "Roscoe, bring the men and the floodlights," he shouted. Watching until Roscoe appeared toting a duffle with supplies, he turned and hurried back down the ramp. Time was running out. He could feel it.

Something was going to happen.

"Grant thou my soul be brought unto me
from any place wherein it may be.
Thou findest the Eye of Horus standing by thee
like unto those beings who resemble
Osiris, who never lie down in death."

The Book of the Dead

Chapter Fifteen

Nalini wrapped her arms over her head and hunkered down. Rashid, kneeling beside her, bent his large frame across her protectively. A large explosion erupted, followed by an avalanche of falling stone and sand. Once the debris settled, Rashid stood and pulled Nalini to her feet. She was surprised by the size of the crater that appeared next to the bluff after this latest explosion.

They had first dug down about twenty meters, and then set the charge to create an opening in the rock. Now they were nearly fifty meters into the rock formation. Their intent was to come up from underneath one of the existing tunnels.

If those already inside the tunnels were killed, so much the better. She should have known Typhon wouldn't stop them. He lost an entire day insisting he needed to escort her to within a half-day's ride. Now they were stalled by a sandstorm.

"You are uninjured?" Rashid bent down toward her, putting his hand on her shoulder.

"Yes. Let's go see how close we got this time," said Nalini. She grabbed the electromagnetic gradiometer, and followed Rashid into the trench. The men were hand passing the larger stones and shoveling the smaller debris into buckets. She pulled what her mother claimed looked like a sniper scarf over her face to protect her nose and lungs from the dust, drew the brow fold forward like a visor until only a slit remained for vision. In truth, Nalini wore it because along with the baggy Arabic pants and long shirt she wore under her outer robe while in the desert it was comfortable, practical and disguised her gender without hampering her movement.

They waited until enough rubble had been moved to allow them to make their way to the detonation site. Then Nalini stepped under the rock face to the end of the indentation that had been formed with the explosion. She held up the machine that should show her existing tunnels by signaling underground anomalies. "Hold the light closer, Rashid," she directed.

She had to read it again, but then grinned up at Rashid. "We are directly below one of the tunnels at last."

"You chose the spot well, princess. We will yet beat them," he said, encouragingly.

"Hakim, get the equipment. You need to drill here," she said, pointing above her head. "Not far, maybe eighteen or twenty centimeters."

It took only twenty minutes for them to erect the portable scaffolding. Anticipating her next command, one of the men hurried forward with a generator feed, which he placed off to the side. Three more men stepped forward, carrying rock drills. Once they were plugged into the generator feed, they shouted toward the entrance. The gas powered generator could be heard running in the distance. They started the rock drills. Nalini wedged earplugs into her ears. The echoing of the drills was deafening in the cave-like space.

An hour later, they shouted down their success. Once inside the tunnels, Nalini managed to decipher numerous clues that led them safely through the labyrinth with only one casualty. Unable to stop him in time, Nalini had watched in dismay as Hussein was sliced nearly in half by a mammoth pendulum that swung out of the wall without warning. If only he had waited for her to press the hidden lever in the rock wall. The other men had learned immediately not to venture ahead of Nalini. They waited patiently for her to interpret the clues and warnings, moving forward only when she directed them to do so.

Nalini contemplated the various symbols on the stones widely spaced on the floor of the chamber, seeking a pattern or possible connection between them.

"Can you read it, princess?" asked Hakim, expectantly. He seemed genuinely enthusiastic, his eyes sparkling with anticipation. Apparently he had acquired a sense of adventure working with her to find the relic. Reporting her progress to Typhon didn't require him to enjoy himself or to try so hard to help her solve the clues. She had always known he was one of her brother's spies. Rashid had informed her of his identity. But she favored his help over Sirius's constant criticism and thinly veiled hatred, so kept quiet about his true mission.

"Yes, Hakim. I can read it, but it doesn't make any sense. There are no words or patterns that I can decipher." She pulled her head scarf down and rubbed the perspiration from her dirt-smudged face.

"Perhaps there is no message here," offered Hakim.

Planting her hands on her hips, she continued to study the symbols. "Then why bother hand-setting all these stones and carving the symbols on them in the first place?" Nalini reasoned.

"We could try to cross," Hakim suggested. "Send some of the men out."

"Yes, if we want to watch them die," Nalini confirmed. "This is...no, wait. I think I know what it is." Why hadn't she seen it sooner? She was getting tired. "We're closer than I thought. If I'm right, we're at the very threshold of the inner sanctum."

"How do you know?"

"I just know. I need to get some information first. We need to go back to camp," she said, turning to hurry back down the tunnel toward the entrance. She knew she was right, and it made her so angry she ground her teeth to keep from cursing. What she needed was the secret name of *The One Who Came Before All*, from whom all *Those Who Came Before* were descended. The problem was, she didn't know. Set wouldn't have told this even to Typhon. He wouldn't trust anyone with that much power, which wouldn't stop him from holding her responsible if she didn't come back with *The Book of Life.*

If she couldn't move forward, the only alternative was to go up and over. They would need to blast another hole in the ceiling, and if they killed some of Vargas' men who from time to time they had heard in a tunnel above them, so much the better. It would only help ensure they got to the book first.

She cautioned her men to drill at an angle and stand well back from falling fragments. Worried that descending rock might collapse the scaffolding, she had ordered it positioned beyond the drill point.

They made progress quickly.

Several meters in, however, she heard what she had feared. A loud cracking sound was their only warning when an eighteen meter sheet of rock above them decided to give way.

About to shout a warning, she instead found herself sprawling in the sand where Rashid had shoved her, bruised but unhurt. Scrambling to her feet, she rushed back past the rising Nubian to assess the damage and injuries. Her precautions paid off. No one was hurt. The rock had collapsed in front of the scaffolding, crushing only cables.

They would no longer need them she realized as she noticed a man's legs dangling through the hole that had been created in the ceiling.

Rashid now dashed past her and grabbed the kicking legs. He pulled. Nalini ran to assist him.

"Abdul!" Thick blond hair, hanging in precision cut layers even when upside down, appeared atop a dirt-smudged face and Luc Vargas's fist shot downward. He punched Rashid in the face so hard the huge Nubian actually fell backward in the dust. Then the bastard grabbed hold of the flailing Bedouin who was trying to hoist himself back through the hole. Vargas tried to jerk him upward to safety.

Nalini used a toehold in the scaffold to launch herself high enough to wrap her arms around the man's waist. She tugged and thrashed, pulling downward.

"Help me!" she shouted in Arabic. If Luc Vargas valued this man, she intended to take him away. Feeling a pistol tucked into his belt digging into her side, she moved her hand to grab it.

Luc's face appeared above her again. "You," he said with obvious recognition--though all that he could have seen were her eyes. Then, he noticed her intention and let go of the Bedouin and grabbed hold of her by the back of her pants intending to haul her upward.

Arai arrived to aid Rashid. They focused on keeping Nalini on their side of the hole. The Nubians won. Nalini tumbled downward and Rashid caught her easily, slowing her descent. Something fell past her, bumping into the side of her head. She glanced down, gingerly massaging her head.

Her pain forgotten, she gasped. "It can't be. I think it's the *Book of Life*," she cried.

Two large male forms, Vargas and the Bedouin, literally dove through the hole after the book. Nalini was knocked to the ground and all three of them sprawled in a tangled lump of grasping hands and kicking feet, mostly hers.

"Get off me! You smell like the backside of a camel," she screamed. Sharp shattered rock fragments ground into her back, igniting her temper. "Move, before I blow your head off," she warned, clutching the gun. She hoped for their sake they knew she meant it. Her temper flared as they ignored her and continued to struggle for possession of the book.

The click of the gun as she pulled back the hammer and pressed the barrel against his head finally got Ljluka's attention. Instead of a normal reaction, however, he grinned down at her if only for a moment before he was yanked, roughly, to his feet. Rashid, himself already enraged from the blow to his pride if not his jaw, had him in a headlock and would have snapped his neck if Nalini had not shouted, "No, not yet, Rashid."

Hakim offered his hand, which she took. He hauled her to her feet and she focused on slowing her breathing, accepting the book he extended toward her.

Next to him, the Bedouin called Abdul struggled in the vice-like grasp of Arai, glaring eminent death in her direction. His pistol in her hand, she raised it and smiled without warmth.

"Nice of you to drop by," she said. "Which one of you was clumsy enough to hand over the book?" Neither man responded, but she saw a spark of anger in Luc's eyes and rightly guessed the culprit. She actually admired the instant plunge the two had taken to retrieve it, even knowing it was unlikely they would escape with their lives or the book.

The shots she fired, taking care that they went through the hole to avoid ricochet down below, were intended to discourage foolish rescue attempts, but managed to still the Bedouin's struggles as well.

"Put some guards on this area, and get these two secured," she said. Then, looking at Arai and Rashid, she added, "Don't leave them alone. I need to make a call."

Luc and Abdul apparently didn't plan to go meekly. Their struggles were useless. The Nubians had their arms secured behind them, but Nalini added, "Kill the Bedouin if Vargas refuses to cooperate." She noticed with satisfaction that Luc calmed himself at her words.

She followed them outside, but moved past them to climb the hill in search of a phone signal. Pushing a number, she lifted the phone to her ear. "We had a rewarding accident. We've got Ljluka Vargas and one of his sidekicks. They were nice enough to present me with the book. Yes. They are? So what's Set planning to do about it? Okay." She snapped the phone shut and headed toward the tent now guarded by two heavily armed nomads.

A few moments later, she entered the tent to find Luc and Abdul tied back to back against the center tent post, wrists roped and secured to rings above their heads. Her gaze lingered there a moment, remembering. She would never have been whipped if he were not still standing here. Swallowing, she pushed the memory away.

Their ankles were tied and fastened around the post. Apparently Rashid and Arai had taken her at her word. She had also noticed the rough fabric that had been jammed in their mouths and fastened around their heads and decided Rashid had warned them only once to stop talking.

Each bound and gagged man faced a highly alert and slightly irritated near seven foot Nubian warrior. The warriors stood with their arms folded across their massive chests, pistols shoved in their waistband and a scimitar within a scabbard hanging from a loop attached to their belt and strapped to an upper thigh. She noticed sapphire sparks flying from Luc's eyes and suppressed a smile.

She paused, walked over to him and reached into his shirt pocket to take possession of his cell phone, which was vibrating, probably alerting him that he had a message waiting. Then she began a thorough search of his person, ignoring Rashid's assertion that they had already taken his weapons. She started with his other shirt pockets and ended with the half-dozen pockets on his pants, glad he was gagged when she glanced up and noted his lifted eyebrows. Running her fingers around the inside of his boot tops, she stopped to fish a folded pocket blade from his left boot. He failed to react.

Standing, she stood observing him for a moment, irritated by his intense study of her. On impulse, she reached up on tiptoe, leaning against his chest to reach behind his neck. Slowly, she ran her hand around the collar of his shirt pressing the fabric between her fingertips. His eyes, so close to her own for the moment, were no longer angry. He was enjoying himself, she realized.

Finding what she sought, she raised the now sprung blade she had filched from his boot, moved it past his face suggestively and down to his neck where she hesitated before cutting the tiny tracking device from his shirt collar. Again he didn't react.

She dropped from her toes, which caused her to slide down his chest as she arrived at her flat-footed height of just under two meters. His nostrils flared ever so slightly as he sucked in air. She studied him as she unwrapped her scarf and pulled back her headgear, shaking out her hair and revealing her face. Unabashed, he stared back at her, then moved his gaze slowly across her face, as if memorizing her features. His chest increased its in and out movement. She might have known, she thought, more disappointed than angry.

Her smile, though inviting, never reached her eyes. She could tell he was wondering what it would look like if it had. Or maybe he wasn't. But no, he was just the same as every other man, after all, she thought and stopped just short of telling him that he would never know.

She held the electronic chip up to Rashid and said, "Strip him. Everything. Find him something less aromatic to wear. Have him scrubbed down first. His smell is offensive."

Flipping open his cell phone, she walked outside and watched for a signal. Finding one, she pressed a button to dial the last call received.

"Luc, where the hell—"

"You must be the big dark-haired one. Andrew, he called you." She heard his quick intake of breath.

Surprised by her interruption, he exploded, "Listen you Babylonian whore, I killed you once and I'll kill you again, but this time I'll make it stick if you so much as--"

"Since you so nicely pointed out why I already don't like you, I'd say you're in no position to be making threats, big brother. So just shut up and listen."

"I'm listening." The frustrated rage was still in his voice, but he held it rigidly in check. His obvious love for his brother took priority.

"Better. Now go call off your other brother. You know, there really are too many of you Vargas boys. Tell Horus that if he doesn't back off *my* brother, his little brother, Ljluka, dies. For keeps, since you're so fond of going all the way."

She heard his deep inhalation as if he'd like nothing better than to reach through the phone and choke the life from her. "The call's being made. Tell Typhon to stop moving forward and leave Luc's men alone and Horus won't attack."

So they cared for their operatives, too, she thought, marveling at their compassion for the mortals who worked for them. Though her mother had taught her to respect mortals, she was surprised that these warriors had such consideration. "I got what I wanted. Just relax and let us leave."

"I told you, we're cooperating," he ground out, emphasizing each syllable. She could almost visualize his clenched teeth.

"Good," she said, hanging up the phone. She took out her own phone and hit a number. "You back off his brother's men, Horus backs off yours. They will let me leave with what I came here for." She listened a moment, then snapped, "Look, do you want to be the one to tell Set that I wasn't able to bring it home after finally getting my hands on it?" She flipped the phone shut. "Stupid lecherous pig. Arai, the testosterone is simmering. It's getting dark, so tell the men we leave at first light and double the guard."

Nalini turned toward her tent. She needed to take a look at the book before anyone else got their hands on it.

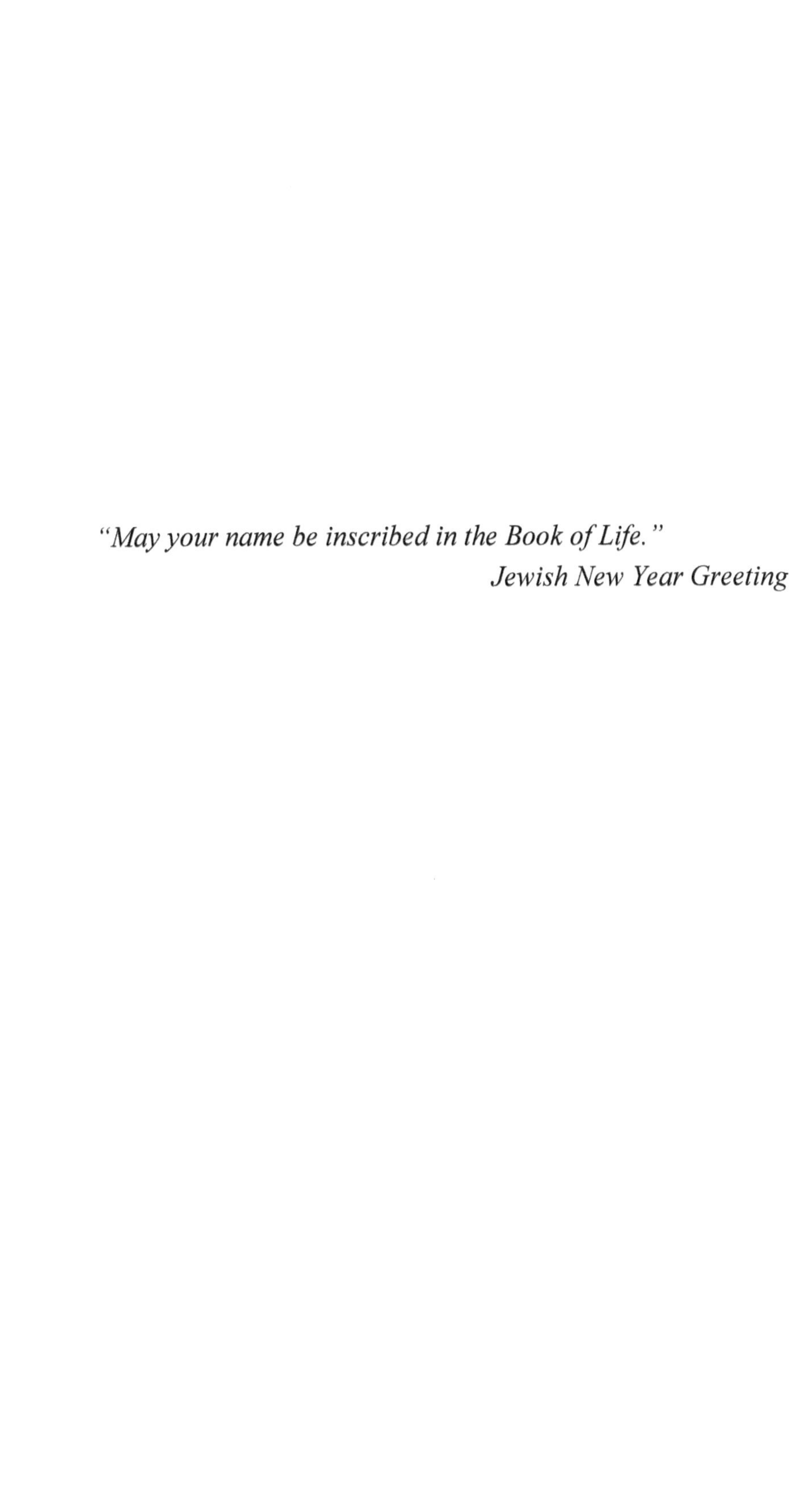

"May your name be inscribed in the Book of Life."
Jewish New Year Greeting

164

Chapter Sixteen

"Princess. I'm afraid you're too late. A young lad they called Kazim already scrubbed me down with sand and wasted buckets of water over my head. And now I smell like a flower. I hope you like it. I wonder whose soap he used? Now if you still want to look for wires in my collar, I sure wouldn't mind. In fact—ugh! Shit! What'd you do that for? I was just being friendly."

"You will address the princess only if she asks you a question, savage dog," Rashid informed him, preparing to punch him in the gut again.

"I'll take it from here, Rashid. Thank you. You may be needing your scimitar though, so stay handy."

"With pleasure, princess," he said, grinning for the first time, and she was sure Vargas realized he was even more frightening when his face was in such an unnatural position.

"I need some information, Vargas. Give it to me or I start convincing Abdul here that you're not a very caring master."

"I'm not Abdul's master. He's his own man."

"Nevertheless, unless you tell me what I want to know, I will have Rashid pile him at your feet, one piece at a time." She watched him carefully, but not a muscle twitched in reaction to her threat. Though he had sobered, acknowledging her seriousness, he remained mute and expressionless, watching her watch him, gazing deeply into her eyes.

Rashid pulled his scimitar from its sheath and walked to stand in front of Abdul, who also remained mute, though he too had his gag removed.

"Tell me how to decipher it," she said softly, knowing he knew to what she referred. A flash of satisfaction showed in his eyes, though he quickly looked down to mask his thoughts. Not quickly enough, however. So he had known she wouldn't be able to read it. "Tell me, and only me," she directed, standing on tiptoe again and resting her hand on his chest to bring her ear next to his mouth.

He turned his head and nuzzled her neck until the scarf she had knotted at her neck was pushed away so he could kiss the soft skin just behind her ear. "Mm, it smells better on you," he said, once more jocular at her expense. She jerked her head away and stepped back, raising her hand to strike him. Arai reacted more quickly, slamming his fist into Vargas's no longer grinning face.

She clenched her own fists at her sides and gazed at Rashid, who awaited her orders. Breathing deeply to calm herself, she moved to his side and said, "He must tell me." He bent to hear her softly spoken words. "If he doesn't, my mother must coerce Set an--"

"He will beg to tell you, princess," Rashid assured her. Then he crossed the tent, bent down to retrieve something and walked back. Clutching the front of Vargas's clean Arabic cotton shirt, he ripped it from his body. Stepping back, he held the whip out and raised his arm. "How many? The thirty you withstood because of him seems a good place to start."

She drew her bottom lip into her mouth, considering. Vargas was looking at her in a strange way, his gaze focused, probing, as he considering Rashid's words. She wished Rashid had not revealed so much to this stranger. What must he think of a father who would allow his daughter to be whipped? She could just imagine what he would think of a father who had ordered it done. He didn't say a word, but just kept staring at her as though it had just occurred to him that she might have problems and obligations to equal his own. Why did she care what he thought?

Honesty, she decided, would work better than torture with him. "Rashid, Arai, take the Bedouin. I wish to speak to Vargas alone," she announced.

"Princess, no!" they both cried.

"Do it."

"He will try to deceive you. Believe nothing he says," Rashid urged, untying the Bedouin and dragging him from the tent. Arai followed, holding out a pistol. She shook her head, motioned to her waistband and turned back to Vargas.

"You must tell me what I need to know. Please. I-I will find out anyway, but you would save someone from terrible shame if you would simply tell me now." She had gotten very good at reading men by their reactions and actions, even when they were very good at hiding them. Though she knew he still desired her, he had now learned to respect her.

He didn't mock her, didn't grin suggestively. Then, quite intently, he finally spoke. "You were whipped? Thirty lashes? Who would do such a thing to you, such a fragile creature as you?"

"I'm hardly fragile. It's none of your business anyway. Rashid spoke out of turn because in his mind you're already dead and it doesn't matter what he says in front of you." Why was he so concerned about her? she wondered. Perhaps she could use it to her advantage. She'd already realized she couldn't torture him into revealing what he chose to keep hidden.

"Was it because you didn't kill me?" He obviously didn't miss much. His eyes were an intense, icy blue, like Lucien's, but with something more. He had compassion, the ability to wonder at the existentialism of others. She looked away first, angry at herself for the weakness, but afraid of what she might reveal.

"You're changing the subject."

"I'm sorry, princess. Nalini, isn't it? You know I can't tell you. If you kill Abdul--which I hope you won't as it's not his fault and he was only following orders--or even if you threaten to kill me, again I can't tell you. It's not my secret to tell. Besides, you're mistaken. That's not what you need in order to decipher the book."

"Don't lie to me," she pleaded, thinking of her mother, now with child, supplicating herself to Set to convince him to tell her. She would do it, without question. All she did, Nalini knew, was for her.

"I'm sorry. I really wish I could help you. Surely you understand that my duty is to my own family. I have gladly vowed to protect them, and I never break my word. Ever."

"Not even if you were to swear something to me?"

Surprised, he paused to consider her strange question, but then answered softly, "Not even then, Nalini. If I made you a promise, I would keep it."

She loved the way he said her name. A slight accent--clearly European but too blurred by centuries of well-known languages to be distinguishable--added a stronger emphasis to the third syllable. It made her heart flutter softly. Made her believe him, too. She didn't know how yet, but this information would be very useful in the future. Forcing herself to focus on the issue, she admitted defeat.

For now, she must reach her mother. It was clear he wouldn't tell her anything, no matter what they did. She turned to leave and he called her back. Hesitating, she turned her head to look up at him.

"Why didn't you torture Abdul or have Rashid whip me as he so obviously wanted to?" He seemed confused by her decisions, as if they were not the ones he expected of her.

"Honestly?"

"Of course."

"Because I don't find pleasure in the pain of others, as some cowards that I know. I do only what I must to survive and protect those that I love. Which is why, Vargas, if you knew even for a moment what it's like to be me, you'd be very certain that what I say, I mean."

"Beauty is eternity gazing at itself in a mirror."

Kahlil Gibran

Elizabeth Alsobrooks

Chapter Seventeen

Her eyes were hypnotic. They could burn into a man's soul. For a brief moment, her sincerity was apparent in the desperate depth of her eyes. They contained a haunted hunger to believe in a world where hope existed. It made him want to give her whatever she needed. Anything to brighten the dark realities she so obviously hid from behind her gruff, business-like demeanor.

He wondered if she knew how expressive her eyes were. But she must. Anyone could see how every emotion she felt, every thought she had was instantly reflected in those lilac orbs. She'd looked away, refusing to meet his probing gaze—hiding her true thoughts.

Too late, after she'd left him, Luc realized his easy flirtation had been seen by her as just another attempt by a physically advantaged male to dominate her. How arrogant he must have seemed, challenging her even when he was bound and restrained. Before the anger he had seen hurt in her eyes or perhaps it was disappointment. Her opinion was never asked, her feelings never considered. What men in her world wanted, they took.

Why wasn't she married? She was the most breathtakingly beautiful little waif. Every man she knew must want to hold her close, to bury his face in her hair and inhale, to shield her from whatever pain lurked behind her brave facade. The desire to protect her was very apparent in those two giants whose attention never left her. Yet here she was, on a very dangerous mission in charge of a large number of equally dangerous men. She was a complicated woman, and he hadn't figured her out. Not yet.

And you are by far too intrigued by this woman who tried to kill you and now holds you captive. Explain away that foolishness.

Just an idle observation, mother. It's not like I have anything else to do with my time.

They are coming for you.

And the book.

Of course. She will be unable to read it anyway.

As long as Horus doesn't attack her brother, we should be safe until they get here.

He felt a sense of relief that a rescue party was en route. Set, no matter what arrangements Nalini made, would never let him go after he laid eyes on him. They'd all seen him and reacted with predictable shock. Set probably now knew Lucien had a look-alike.

It was imperative that he get the book from her as soon as his men arrived. Nalini had given up trying to make him to tell her what he knew, so she probably thought her mother could decipher it. They knew her mother had mastered botanical and incantation magic. Isis had once raged about it, claiming the woman acted above her station, and that she was nothing more than a weak imitation in all things and all ways. They never did figure out why Isis hated her—though Luc had his suspicions, knowing his father's lust for beautiful women.

Ljluka. Anubis comes for you within the hour. Be ready.

He felt elated but not surprised to discover it would be Andrew. No way his brother would miss out on an adventure. What did surprise him was that just before nightfall the Nubian they called Arai returned, took he and Abdul outside to relieve themselves, and then let them lie down on a rug, chaining their ankles to the post. Only one nomad remained on duty. The others lay down on the far end of the tent. Obviously they were going to pull guard duty in shifts. So much the better.

The camp soon fell quiet. Finally, a slight noise sounded. The nomad who stood guard glanced at the prisoners. As they appeared to be sleeping, he moved to the entrance, pulling the flap aside to look out. Luc watched as the man disappeared without a sound. The goatskin parted again, and Andrew appeared, quickly followed by several of their men. They hurried to the sleeping nomads and with a swift blow on the back of their skulls insured that they would slumber without dreams the remainder of the night.

"Nice to see you, little brother," Andrew whispered as he motioned to Raphael. He noted Luc's swollen eye and added, "Something you said, or something you wouldn't say?"

"Probably both," Luc admitted, amused by his brother's habitual dry humor.

A lanky Italian hurried over after tying up one of the unconscious guards. A quick look at the shackles on Luc's leg and he reached into his pocket and pulled out a torsion wrench. He made quick use of it and Luc pulled his ankles out of the shackles. Abdul was next.

"She has the book in her tent. I doubt anyone is inside with her except perhaps a small boy, but two hulking Nubians are likely planted right outside. Come to think of it, I wouldn't doubt it if that bigger one isn't lying across the foot of her sleeping mat like a dog."

"Do you know which is hers?"

"I saw her go to her tent once. It's near this one, a little behind, further up the hill."

"Okay, so we slip over there and go in from the back. The men will take care of any guards. We already took out their sentries."

Luc nodded. They slipped from the tent and headed up the hill, crouched low to snag shadows. Spreading out they soon surrounded her tent. Luc noted the presence of only one Nubian, standing to the left of her tent's entrance. The other one must be inside as he'd predicted. That complicated matters, but wasn't insurmountable. If he could get his hands on her the Nubian wouldn't make a move. He would easily give up the book.

He watched three of their men belly down into the sand and squirm toward the Nubian. Andrew followed his lead and headed around to the back of the tent. Once there, Andrew pulled out a stiletto Luc knew could have been used for precision surgery and silently sliced through the goat's hair tent like it was silk.

He held the edge of the gap open and Luc ducked inside, looking around. Coals still glowed from a small fire, lending enough light for him to see the boy they'd called Kazim curled up next to its warmth. Flowing dark tresses identified Nalini. She lay on a narrow pallet covered with goatskin her back to Luc. He didn't see the Nubian called Rashid. That might be a problem.

Ducking into the tent, he hurried to Nalini's pallet. Andrew moved past him, toward the boy. He reached down and covered her mouth and simultaneously threw his leg across her lower body. He pinioned her arms, straddling her as he flipped her onto her back. She was awake the instant he touched her, and was still struggling to reach the weapon on the pallet close to where her hand had rested.

To still her struggles, he whispered in her ear, "Have a care for the boy," and hoped she didn't realize it for the lie it was.

She stopped and turned her head to where Andrew had already gagged and was currently binding Kazim. Glancing over at them, Andrew finished his task and rushed over to tie a scarf around her mouth. Once she was silenced, Luc was able to free his hand to grasp her wrist, and pull both arms over her head. "Look for the book," he whispered to Andrew. Then he leaned forward to run his hand under the cushion beneath her head. "It's here." He slid the book from under the cushion, and with it came a cell phone. His. He shoved it in his pocket and tossed the book to Andrew.

His brother stuffed it under his shirt and pulled a scarf from the floor by her pallet. Luc pulled her arms down and held them while Andrew tied them in front of her. Andrew dove through the slit in the tent, reaching back to take her as Luc shoved her head-first through the opening. He joined them quickly, and grabbed her, throwing her over his shoulder with enough force to knock the wind out of her, which stilled her attempts to scream through the gag. The squirming, kicking and uncontrolled rage had been expected. In truth, he would have been disappointed with anything less from her.

He followed Andrew up the sand hill. Just before they reached the top, he saw the rest of their men. Then the first shots sounded behind them. Running faster, they topped the hill and he was relieved to see the horses.

Andrew ran up to a prancing stallion and held his hands out for Nalini. Luc handed her over, threw himself into the saddle and reached down to pull her onto the saddle in front of him. An arm on each side of her, he grabbed the reins and followed Raphael, who was already leaned over the back of an Arabian heading toward the moon as it rose above the hills of sand.

His horse shortened its stride as it climbed the next hill. He glanced back and saw camels just cresting the first hill in pursuit. They had enough head start. Soon they would leave them behind. The horses wouldn't falter in the cool evening breezes. Andrew pulled alongside, his teeth gleaming. He too loved the thrill of the chase. Luc chuckled and reached with his left arm to draw his captive closer so that he could lean forward, urging the horse onward.

They raced to the bottom of the next hill, and she began to struggle again in earnest, forcing him to warn, "I will have to render you unconscious for your own safety if you don't still yourself, Nalini."

He felt her stiffen, and try to say something against her gag. Reaching up, he pulled it down. She could scream all she wanted now. Their secret was out.

"Let me go," she cried. "You have what you want, why have you taken me?"

He leaned down and said truthfully against her ear, "Because I don't want you to be whipped, ever again, and never because of me."

She fell silent then, and reached with her bound hand to clutch the stallion's mane, leaning over his neck. He wondered what she was thinking.

But not for long.

As they reached the next summit, a platoon of Arab's appeared about two kilometers away. The tall Nubian was among them. Seeing them, she chose that moment to fling herself under his arm and off the horse onto the ground, though they were at full gallop. He immediately pulled on the reins and turned back. Rolling to her feet, she sprinted toward the Arabs. No, not fragile at all.

Andrew was on her in an instant. He launched himself through the air and brought her to ground. Luc rode up and swiftly grabbed his horse's reins. Her own people probably wouldn't chance shooting her, but who knew how stupid they were?

Andrew already had her in the air and shoved her atop his horse. He had one toe in the stirrup when she reached out to kick him in the chest. She was off, again, with Andrew's horse and *The Book of Life* in the saddle bag. Luc kicked his heels against his horse. Illusive, Andrew had once called her. That didn't come close to describing it. Holding her was like trying to grasp pure mercury.

"Hiyah! Hiyah!" Luc yelled, flattening himself across his horse's neck. He was there, almost on her. If he didn't get her soon they would be too close to the Arabs to safely retrieve her. Then, he reached out and grabbed her arm and jerked. Hampered by her restraints, she was unable to catch her balance and tumbled to the ground, rolling over and over down the hill until she managed to dig in her bare feet and stop herself. She struggled to rise, arms held in front of her and swayed a moment, turning to see Andrew's horse race past her, having been spooked once too often.

Before Luc could go after her, another horse dashed in front of him, and an arm scooped downward, hand extended toward Nalini. She didn't resist, but instead reached her wrist-tied hands toward the rider. Once lifted and seated in front of him, she grabbed hold of the pummel and stared defiantly back at Luc. The rider turned to look as well. The moon, now at its zenith, provided ample light. The rider froze, glanced down at Nalini's head before looking back again. Luc met his questioning stare with his own startled response, and felt an undeniable spark of primal recognition.

The bearded man drew Nalini against himself protectively, possessively. Then he turned his back on his twin brother before riding toward the Arabs now waiting at the top of the next rise.

...he looked back, not of desire to return,
but to see, by the light of day, what hazards
he had gone through in the dark...
he saw the Hobgoblins and Satyrs,
and Dragons of the Pit, but all afar off;
for after break of day, they came not nigh;
yet they were discovered to him,
according to that which is written...
John Bunyan, The Pilgrim's Progress

182

Chapter Eighteen

Luc stopped his horse and watched as the Nubian appeared over the adjacent hill, the reins of Andrew's captured horse in hand. His brows buckled under the weight of his thoughts, enhancing an uncharacteristic scowl. Then he too turned, and rode toward his brother, Andrew. Andrew accepted an arm up and settled behind him. Their silence was mutual. Luc didn't know what to say or how he felt. Andrew understood his habit of thinking things through before confiding in him.

He pointed Luc in the right direction and then Luc noticed the group of Andrew's men who had apparently arrived just moments ago. They were a few meters behind them, watching, poised to defend them if the need arose. He now knew why the Arabs had decided to merely observe as Lucien snatched Nalini, willing and grateful, to return to a life she must surely hate.

He'd gotten a glimpse of her life and didn't want to imagine for even a moment what it was like. Dysfunctional didn't come close to describing what must be going on in that family. There was no clinical term for that kind of chaos. He'd wanted to take her away from it. Why the hell would she jump from his horse to go back? The evil she knew opposed to the unknown theory just didn't make sense to him, especially when that evil would never end, not even in the welcome peacefulness of death.

Pressing his heels against the stallion's sides, he galloped up the hill and soon found Abdul and some of the Bedouin who'd been keeping vigilant watch over the camp that held their leader captive. Scouting the enemy as was their custom, they were now waiting on the shadow side of a sand hill. They fell in behind them and rode back to Horus's camp in silence.

Half an hour later, Luc looked down at the elaborate makeshift base camp from a rise about a kilometer away. Made visible by the full moon, he scanned the familiar sight. He brought his men around once a year for PT with Horus's army. The unit he had with him now spread out across the desert floor for only five acres or so. What looked to be around fifty tents were pitched in symmetrical rows that mimicked the rippled sandscape beneath his brother's camp. Corralled horses, camels, sheep and goats formed the nucleus of their portable village.

Positioned in various locations were more modern modes of transportation and battle readiness, including Humvees, and at least one of them, knowing their enemy, had to be a *rat rig*, geared with wireless toxic gas detection.

There was a mobile command center outside the largest tent, which is where Luc headed. The guards, wearing full desert camo, including *shemaghs* under their helmets and wrapped around their necks to help keep the sand from finding its way down their shirts, were fully armed for combat. They let them pass without comment. Their approach would have been common knowledge to the guards for some time.

He pulled the reins, waiting for Andrew to jump down. They dismounted in front of Horus's tent. A young Bedouin ran up to take Luc's horse and he was soon wrapped in a heartfelt embrace. Though they had spoken he hadn't seen his eldest brother for nearly a year, not since the last PT. When Horus pulled back, he studied Luc's eye, tilting his head and quirking an eyebrow.

Luc grinned. "I did try to beat their platoon single-handedly."

"I'd ask if the other guy looks worse, but I heard it was a woman, a petite and beautiful woman." He smiled then, the amusement making his hazel eyes sparkle with mischief. The warmth softened the dangerous and imposing impression his size alone often conveyed to those who first met him.

Even taller than Andrew by about an inch, he was bulkier, broader in the shoulders. His eldest brother's mass was solid muscle. Luc knew just how solid from experience. They often stripped to loincloths to fight during their PT games. Though neither as red nor as blond as Kirin's, Horus too had crimson highlights in his dark blond hair. He had their father's nose, but the fullness of his lips, he had inherited from their mother.

Throwing his arm over Luc's shoulder, he added, "And I heard it's not the first time she's kicked your ass, little brother. So do you like it or something? You kinky?"

Luc laughed, but didn't respond further to the bait. He walked within the wrap of his eldest brother's arm as they entered the tent..

Andrew, following behind them said, "In all fairness, she did have some help this time. That big bastard stole my horse and made away with the book. Mother's going--"

"Knock it off, Horus," Luc snapped suddenly, pulling away from his brother. "Stay out of my head." Sometimes he was as controlling as their mother, Luc thought with irritation.

"I'm sorry. Really," Horus said, holding his hands up in a gesture of surrender. "I am, truly. It's just a habit. I was worried about you, wondering about what you're not saying." He looked genuinely upset, worried even.

"I'm not saying the obvious, that we have to get that book back," he said sarcastically, only slightly mollified.

"You do seem to be playing musical tents," Horus noted , raising his eyebrows.

Luc sighed and ran his hand through his hair, deliberately calming himself after his brother's unusual and thus startling breach of trust. They all had an agreement that Horus wouldn't enter their mind unless it was an absolute emergency. As the only sibling, he being the firstborn, who shared their parents' mind-reading ability, Horus carefully respected their wishes most of the time.

They all knew better than to even suggest that it was too intrusive, or violated their privacy, to their mother. Their father didn't communicate with them as often, and had a more subtle approach than their mother, who seemed to like to listen in on their private thoughts before she intruded. Andrew joked that they should just keep diaries and hide them under their mattress for her.

Taking a deep breath, Luc looked up at his brother, regretting his overreaction. He realized he was afraid to admit his thoughts even to himself just now. He wasn't sure how he felt about either his newly found brother or Nalini. "What I seem to be doing is making an ass out of myself whenever Nalini's involved. Look, I'm not oblivious to it. But thank you, thank you both for rescuing me, even if you were just rescuing me from myself," he said, glancing at Andrew to include him in the apology. Luc realized Horus' explanation was sincere, and also had to admit that his uncharacteristic moodiness was the cause of his sibling's concern.

"It's not like you haven't pulled our butts out of jams," Andrew reassured him.

"You don't actually think we would resent rescuing you from whatever trouble you have, do you, Luc?" Horus asked, looking relieved that his little brother had apparently forgiven him.

"No, but I want you to know how much I appreciate it. Lately, well lately I'm just really glad I have the two of you, the relationship we've always had. I'm sorry I took your head off, Horus." And he was. He needed to figure out how he felt, what he needed to do about it, and who would be affected by his decision.

Horus pulled him into a bear hug.

"I feel like I'm about to weep, little brother." Andrew chuckled, slapping him on the back.

"Yeah, I know," he said, laughing as he stepped back to grin at Andrew. "It's just that now that the Usurper knows about me, and I think we can assume that he does since I was just face to face with my identical twin brother—and don't think that wasn't spooky--I am even less inclined to be at Set's mercy."

"Yet all the more reason he will want you," Horus predicted, instantly sober.

Luc had spoken to Horus about his twin brother only once, over the phone. Horus, being a teenager when Luc was born, had always known. Isis had, of course, forbidden him to speak of it. Both Andrew and Luc had forgiven him for not telling them, and then browbeat him to disclose any other family secrets he possessed. They were still unsure despite his pleas of innocence that they'd been given full disclosure.

"You need to leave until this is over," Andrew suggested.

"Not a bad idea," added Horus. "We can take it from here. You're probably needed in Rome anyway. Monsignor Lisante has been calling for you."

"Thanks for telling me," Luc muttered. He reached out to grab up a phone and dialed a long string of numbers. "Monsignor Lisante. Saluti. Giovanni? Ha trovato una miniera d'oro. Ti fa bene, è un sant'uomo. Fondo fiduciario. Ringraziamento. Arrivederci."

He hung up, looked at Andrew and said, "Giovanni did something right for a change. He's setting up the trust fund for those charities so the Illuminati can launder some money legitimately. Now, about Set. If he wants to harm me, why is he raising my twin as his own son? He doesn't seem inclined to seek me out —at least now that he knows what I look like."

"A reasonable point," Horus conceded. "The Usurper obviously no longer wishes the woman to kill you, or she would have done so." He turned to walk to a group of manned tables set across the back of the tent. They were functioning as a portable communication headquarters. A half-dozen laptops were set up with satellite feeds rolling. Each one was monitored by an alert soldier. Luc wasn't surprised to see that Horus had the mobile headquarters forwarding their feeds to his tent. He hated the confines of the armored vehicle and didn't enter one until absolutely necessary.

One screen displayed a live feed using night vision equipment with enhanced motion detection. Luc studied the screen a moment before realizing it was a zoomed image of Typhon's camp. The group of Arabs who had apparently been sent too late to stop the rescue was just returning. "They've reached Typhon's camp, your highness," the Arab said, addressing Horus.

Horus joined Luc behind the man's chair just in time to notice that Nalini was sitting atop Andrew's horse. "I gave that horse to you personally, Andrew," Horus complained. "It's a magnificent beast, from Shalimar's bloodline."

Andrew angled in against Luc's other side and looked at the screen. "Yeah, he is a beauty. Sorry. I'll try to get him back," Andrew promised.

"Well, don't risk your life on it," Horus said, placated.

Luc, more interested in the female beauty, watched as she stopped and jumped down, and then reached into the saddlebags to pull out the book before hurrying into the larger tent in the center, on the heels of--he supposed it was her brother as far as she was concerned--Lucien. What must she think when she looked at him, Luc wondered. Did she think of him only in a brotherly way? The thought, unbidden, displeased him. Some inner sense told him that was not a barrier. His instincts were seldom wrong.

He hesitated, and then pulled his phone out of his pants pocket. "Hey, gorgeous. Behaving yourself?"

"Better than you, obviously. It's so good to hear your voice. Promise you will never scare me like that again," Kirin begged.

"I'll promise to try," Luc said, chuckling. He continued to watch the computer monitor.

"Seriously, Luc. Don't you realize how much we love you?" He could hear the tension in her voice and realized she had been distraught the entire time he was incarcerated by Nalini, not knowing as the rest of them had, that he was in no real danger.

He opened his mouth to respond, glanced up at a movement in front of him, and said, "Mother." Interrupting whatever else Kirin was going to say, he spoke quickly, "Listen, Kirin, I'll talk to you later. Love you," and snapped his phone shut.

"You've caused quite a commotion the last few days, Ljluka." Though said lightly, the tempered fire in her eyes, the slight upward tilt to her chin and the tenseness of her shoulders illustrated her anger. Isis liked to be in charge, and she didn't like it when things went wrong, especially if one of her children was put in danger.

"I'm sorry. It was a stupid mistake, I admit it," he blurted, moving around Horus to cross behind the table so he could be pulled into her outstretched arms.

"It was my fault. He was trying to save me," Abdul insisted, walking over from where he had been studying a satellite feed with Roscoe. He bent on one knee and bowed his head.

"Leader of the <u>Hassana</u>, Sheikh Abdul Kummel al-Rahman," acknowledged Isis, stepping back from her youngest son. "Please, rise. You have been a great friend to us." Abdul rose, brought his wrists to his forehead then crossed them and pressed his hands to his heart in recognition of her praise and in reverence to her position and power.

Luc looked at Horus, who looked back at him and grinned. Horus might be a king, but that, like Isis's true identity, had not been public knowledge since ancient times. All he had received from Abdul, though he was aware of Horus's status, was the ancient version of the genuflection, a weak obeisance at best. Though polite and indicating recognition of Horus's authority and power, it did not signify subservience or submission. Apparently even the Bedouin knew who the head bitch in charge—as Andrew liked to call her whenever he was angry-- really was. Luc returned Horus's amused grin.

Ignoring them, Isis nodded her approval and said, "We have been in contact with your son, Mukhtar. He is a fine warrior. You should be proud. In your absence he has gathered the rest of your warriors, at our request. They are arriving now. You probably wish to join them to prepare for the coming battle. If you wouldn't mind returning when you have seen to their readiness, we can discuss strategy." He nodded and left the tent. Luc, surprised by the revelation that the young scout he had spoken to earlier was actually Abdul's son, made a mental note to add his praise to that of Isis.

Her smooth dismissal of Abdul completed, she turned her attention to her sons. Glancing at Luc, she turned to one of the soldiers by the entrance, "Get him a shirt." Then she turned back and said, "Where is that crazy Arab that constantly hovers around you? You are forever ruining your clothes. You've done so since you were a child."

Luc shrugged, lifted his hands helplessly, and gave her a crooked smile. She made a motherly sound of impatience, air forced across the top of her mouth in a fake sigh, but it no longer sounded convincing. She was glad to see him unharmed, of that there was no question.

All business again, she said, "Let's get this started. I want the book back." Staring meaningfully first at Luc and then at Andrew, she added "now."

It ignited them into action. Andrew hurried out the door to see to the organization of the men, animals and machines. Luc took off the tattered cotton Arabic shirt and traded it for the desert camo the young Arab soldier held out to him. Shoving his arms into the sleeves, he moved back to the computer screens as he fastened the buttons. He would help Horus and his mother strategize their attack plan. Duty dictated that he plot against his twin and Nalini. His heart, however, felt rebellious.

Thou shalt not have power over me, for I live by reason of the words of power which I have with me…. Heaven hath power over its seasons, and the words of power have dominion over that which they possess…I am clothed and am wholly provided with thy magical words, O Rā….

The Book of the Dead

194

Chapter Nineteen

"Do you think we'll be able to intercept before they reach Set?" Luc asked.

"I don't know. Their Intel knows we're coming," Andrew replied loudly, to be heard above the roar of the Humvee he was driving. "They're on horseback, mostly, but they had a head start and these things won't crank out any faster than 65 mph."

"How far, Roscoe?"

"They're still about six klicks away," he shouted from the back, monitoring the movement of the small cluster of blips on the portable tracking device he held in his hand. "We're steady on, closing in," he added.

The Bedouins and the rest of the men in the cavalry couldn't keep up, Luc realized. He only hoped they were able to cut off their escape route in time. Their goal was always to use the least amount of force possible. A skirmish was always best, always easier to cover up. The Syrians were used to turning a blind eye, their very existence depended on the generosity of grateful benefactors and oil rich nations sympathetic to their religious cause.

The Coalition Forces were a more delicate matter. So close to the border, their presence in Iraq could present a problem, and problems tended to get complicated. Luc, as his mother's primary problem solver, was the one most often relied on to finesse, negotiate or outright eliminate loose ends. He was the front-end cleaner.

"Just two klicks ahead!" Roscoe shouted.

Luc tapped his earpiece. "They'll be in sight soon. This is going to be tricky. We don't want to get sandwiched in between Set and Typhon with no way out and the support team too far away. They could wipe out the entire convoy and take home both Andrew and I for their trophy wall."

"One klick ahead," Roscoe yelled.

"Your call," Andrew offered, turning his head to look at Luc.

"How far away is Set?" Luc shouted to Roscoe, adrenaline already starting to pump through his veins.

Roscoe tapped his screen, looked up and said, "Not even on the kill grid yet."

"Let's do it," Luc shouted. "Hey, you hear that?" he asked Horus through his headset. "Okay, yes, okay," he responded, leaving his headset on.

Roscoe bellowed into his own headset, "It's a go. Get a cannon cocker up here." He paused to listen, and then shouted, "That's the word, per the actual. Assholes and

elbows! Double time!"

Another Humvee with an add-on stinger air defense system hurtled past them and took the lead. Roscoe stood up and shimmied through the gunner's hatch in the roof. They heard him lock and load the Bravo machine gun. Luc preferred a quieter, more deadly weapon. He picked up a small high-powered laser that could cut a man in half from a mile away. It was made from technology known only to humans in science fiction movies. Horus had been trying to get his hands on one for centuries. Pointing to another, he offered it to Andrew.

"Any minute now," said Andrew, his mounting excitement evident in his voice and the tight grip he had on the steering wheel.

And then there they were. Up ahead of them to the north, headed south, maybe fifty riders on horseback and a couple of Humvees that looked more like they were being used for supplies and ammo than combat.

The Humvee they were now following fired a rocket over the heads of the approaching riders, as a warning. They didn't slow. Instead they increased their speed, trying to outdistance the approaching enemy before their escape route was completely cut off.

They arrived in time to block their exit, so spun around and forced the approaching unit to stand and fight or flee. Roscoe fired the machine gun in front of the riders, showering them with sand, avoiding direct hits but getting progressively closer to signal an escalation of force. Luc fired at the tires of the Humvees, halting their forward motion, but not their return fire. He doubted they would capitulate, but Luc hoped they could avoid undue bloodshed, especially that of his brother or Nalini.

Andrew stopped the vehicle and jumped out. Luc ran around to the driver side of the vehicle, using it for cover. The six vehicle convoy followed their lead and formed a blockade.

Some of the enemy riders stopped and dismounted to huddle behind the disabled Humvees and return fire. Others continued forward from between the vehicles. These riders were shot down by Roscoe and the other gunners who were protected by steel shields atop the vehicles, or those using the vehicles themselves for cover. It didn't take the enemy long to figure out that they were outgunned. The majority of them turned to flee. Just then the Bedouins arrived, removing that option.

From their elevated advantage point upon camels they were better able to fire upon those on horseback, but the Arabian stallions were fleeter and allowed for greater mobility, darting in and out among the less agile camels. Here and there hand to hand combat broke out as riders of both species were knocked from their mounts.

The Bedouins blocked their escape route from the rear, but that meant the gunners had to avoid casualties caused by friendly fire. They abandoned the Bravos. Hand to hand combat increased. They were forced to depend on swords, knives and pistols rather than rifles or machine guns. What began as an escalation of artillery became a chaotic mass of fighting where knowledge of martial arts and swordplay rather than artillery use meant survival. Their night vision equipment had given them an additional advantage when they were using the artillery, but the full moon was ample illumination for hand to hand combat.

Luc noticed several riders breaking off from the main group to make a wide sweep around them. He saw a riderless horse approaching, reached out to grab the reins and pulled it to a stop.

That's when he saw her.

She fired her rifle at a Bedouin who fell from his camel, and then used its butt to knock an Arab from his horse. As the Arab jumped up and ran toward her, she dropped the rifle and re-armed herself from her belt. A scimitar in one hand and a pistol in the other, she was apparently ready to hack her way through his army single-handedly. Fragile had nothing to do with this angel of death. She sliced through the sleeve of the young Arab's shirt, deeply cutting his arm and forcing him to drop his sword and clutch at the wound. Without hesitation she then shot another of Horus's soldiers before spinning around to clash swords with another Bedouin. He parried her thrust and she brought her arm up, shaving her sword against his. When he forced her sword downward, she backed up to avoid losing control of her weapon.

He thrust and she sidestepped the blow, twisted away and responded with a thrust of her own.

Luc had seen enough. There was no way he was going to let her kill any more of his men and like it or not, and he didn't, there was no way he could stand by and watch her die. He jumped on the horse and raced toward her. The bigger Nubian, seeing his approach, rushed forward and reached out, intending to pull him from the horse. Luc slashed his arm and kept riding. In order to grab Nalini, he had to sheath his sword. At the moment he approached her, she was busy landing from a jump kick she'd just delivered to the Bedouin she was fighting. She heard the horse approach and turned her head slightly, but the Bedouin having recovered was coming at her with his sword raised. As she parried, Luc grabbed her from behind and lifted her off the ground. Having few options, he threw her face down across the saddle in front of him, and knocked her scimitar from her hand before digging his heels in and racing toward base camp.

He plowed the horse straight into the chest of the other Nubian who rushed to block him. Taking advantage of the man's backward stagger, he grabbed a handful of her hair to keep her from pushing herself backward from the horse, and once again urged the horse into a gallop.

They managed to clear the battlefield, but in frustration he was forced to shove the laser gun against the back of her neck to keep her still. He would think about the consequences of this decision later. For now he had all he could manage just keeping hold of this tiger's tail.

"I'm headed back with a prisoner," he said into his headset.

He heard a horse behind and turned his head. Cursing, he pushed his mount harder. The damn Nubian was still gaining. He's probably fueling his horse with a portion of his own adrenalin, Luc thought dryly. Sighing, he turned and fired his laser pistol. He shoved her head back down, hard, before again pressing the weapon into the nape of her neck to keep her from flinging herself from the horse. When he looked back again, the Nubian had fallen to the ground.

He ran his horse past several Humvees and additional cavalry, bringing up the rear of their forces. As he approached the portable command post, which was currently parked just two klicks away from the conflict, he pulled on the reins. He jumped down, pulling her with him. When she moved, he immediately snatched her wrists behind her back and repositioned his pistol against the back of her neck. Now irritated, wrestling this hell cat was not on his agenda.

Apparently she didn't care what his plans were. She elbowed him in the side, managing to free her wrists, then spun around and drew back her arm to--from the position of her hand and the way she had curled in her fingertips--push the cartilage from his nose into his brain. He used her own body for leverage as he shoved his knee into her upper thigh and thrust her under his arm, twisting in time to grab her wrist. Pulling her arm up behind her back, painfully though not excruciatingly so, he shoved the laser under her chin, and pressed his face against her cheek.

"Surely someone cares if you live," he growled. "Stop this nonsense. Now."

The door to the command center opened and Horus reached down to snatch a handful of hair and scarf and drag her tripping backward up the stairs. He quickly pulled her pistol from her waistband and shoved her at Luc, as he entered the command center behind them. "Search her. You know she's packing an arsenal." He nodded to two soldiers standing behind Luc. "Hold her for him and watch she doesn't bite you. She may be rabid." Nalini glared.

The soldiers each grabbed an arm and held her, a difficult task as she was angrier than Luc had yet seen her. "Watch her legs. She kicks like a mule," he advised. He wondered at Horus's anger, but moved to run his hands down her arms, across her back and over her hips, down the outside of her legs and then the inside. She stilled her struggles, probably worried at where it would send his hands, but her eyes fired complete hatred at him. She was wise to be offended, he thought. In truth it was not a difficult task to discover the enticing body beneath the bulky layers. He wished for a brief moment he were not the gentleman that his powerful mother had raised to respect all women.

So far he had found two folding knives, a handcuff key and a cell phone. He paused, but then ran his fingers between her breasts, and pressed against the underside of her bra, careful not to be too unnecessarily intimate. This time the respect was for his sake as well as hers. It was difficult to think of anything but her curvaceous allure when his hands were on her. His earlier anger had shifted to a different but no less emotional instinct. He was unreasonably glad it was him instead of one of the guards who searched her when he was forced to reach down her shirt and fish a folded scimitar, his, from the bottom of her already overly full left bra cup.

Blood rose slightly in her cheeks at the humiliation, but she covered her embarrassment by snapping, "Enjoying the show, boys? What's next, a full cavity search?"

"If you like," bellowed Horus. Luc was grateful for the interruption. His own discomfort went unnoticed. He stepped away from her. Resumed breathing.

Realizing his rage for the first time, Nalini studied Horus a moment. "That won't be necessary," she conceded wisely.

Seeing his mother at the other end of the mobile unit, Luc said softly, "My queen."

You have something to tell me?

Her brothers got away with the book. I was unable to go after them all, so decided to bring her. He was still angry with them for leaving her behind, even with the Nubians to guard her. Clearly the book was more important to them than her safety.

After everything I have done to try to keep you away from her, this is the ultimate irony. I had hoped never to lay eyes on her.

Mother, what are you talking about?

It doesn't matter. You did what you felt in your heart you had to do, and I suppose you had no choice.

I felt her father would trade the book for her.

We shall soon see.

Luc looked at Nalini and wondered again why she struggled so hard to go home rather than take the escape he had offered her. That escape was no longer an option. She was now being held for ransom, and that ransom was *The Book of Life.* One of the soldiers snapped a pair of handcuffs on her. Horus indicated that they should put her down the hallway in a stationary chair at the table that was also attached to the floor. They moved to comply.

"Let's get this thing turned around. Call them all back. We're leaving," Isis said.

Everyone in the room looked at her in surprise. "We need to start negotiations," she said simply.

Luc watched Nalini to gauge her reaction. There was none. Defeated, for now, she had ceased her struggles and silently surveyed her surroundings. Her gaze was thorough and calculating. He realized she was searching for any possible escape route or means to sabotage them.

Sensing hostility, he looked over at his mother and froze. She was staring at Nalini and her eyes were stormy with a suppressed anger the present situation didn't justify. Remembering her earlier comments, he wondered again what further secrets his mother concealed.

Come, weigh me the weight of the fire
or measure me the measure of the wind
or recall me the day that is past.
                    Ezra, IV

Elizabeth Alsobrooks

Chapter Twenty

Nalini looked around the crowded command center, memorizing the location of personnel and equipment. Her actions were reflexive, from years of training and discipline. Her thoughts, however, were on Rashid. She'd barely been able to keep from bringing up the remnants of a quick supper with the way her head had been slamming into the side of the horse whenever her arms got too tired to support herself. but still managed to lift her head enough to see past that Vargas's leg. As soon as he twisted in the saddle, she knew someone was coming to rescue her, either Rashid or Arai. Perhaps even Lucien, she had thought. If her mother had sent him to her rescue once, why not again?

But then Vargas had lifted the metal barrel of the laser from her neck, turned and fired. A warning, surely, she had thought, rising up again. For just a moment she had been allowed to look, to see Rashid fall from his horse and lay unmoving in the sand. Then the bastard had shoved her head down with enough force to send her face into the sweaty side of the horse.

All she had been able to think about was that Rashid didn't move. He would have moved if he were not dead. She knew that. He would have continued to run after her, with his last breath. She would have done the same for him. That's why she fought Vargas so earnestly, until he shoved the weapon into her neck and asked if anyone cared if she died. Her thoughts had turned instantly to her mother, alone with that monster. Her mother, had she seen this coming? Had she seen that Nalini would lose her best friend in the entire world?

Her only friend.

Her temper flared again, and she struggled against the cuffs. An intrusion, sudden and powerful caused her to suck in her breath. Quickly she began to recite an incantation, over and over the way her mother had taught her.

You can't possibly think your pathetic magical spell can protect you from me.

"Get out of my head, you pathetic old hag!" Nalini screamed.

A quick intake of breath could be heard from several locations in the room. All heads turned in her direction. Expressions of shock and bewilderment were seen on the faces of soldiers. Horus and Luc knew exactly what was happening. Luc looked like he'd been expecting but dreading it. Isis was livid. Nalini had sensed her as soon as she felt the intrusion into her thoughts, but she would not be humbled by the haughty queen. It could get as ugly as they wanted. She wasn't going anywhere, at least not yet.

"Ljluka, did you kill some woman? Some best friend person of this woman?"

"Her body guard? Unavoidable." He looked surprised that she would care for her servant. It was probably beneath him to care about someone less important than himself, Nalini decided.

Isis nodded and turned back toward Nalini.

Nalini watched Luc tap his earpiece and turn his back, walking to the other end of the command vehicle. Complete disregard that he had killed someone she cared about, she thought. Then she cried, "Damn it, stop!" She put her hands over her ears, uselessly, and noticed the Vargas boys move toward them, like schoolyard children expecting a fight she thought angrily.

I have a few questions.

"Ask someone who gives a shit!" Nalini yelled, refusing to reply to Isis's conversation in her head. Again she chanted, over and over, thinking of nothing but the words she was saying.

You are no match for me, little one. If your mother was unable to resist my will, what makes you think you can? And just that suddenly Nalini finally knew the person responsible for condemning her mother to be Set's whore, third wife or no wife. She was up and on top of the table in less than a minute and launched toward Isis, hands cuffed but outstretched in less than that.

Both Horus and the other Vargas dove from opposite directions, hurtling their bodies between the two women. Isis never moved. Nalini felt an explosion in her head as Horus's palm connected with her cheek, snapping her head to the side and tilting the trajectory of her body toward Luc, who caught her and jerked her up against himself to still her movement.

"Of course you would come to her rescue," Nalini sneered. "You're all a bunch of mama's boys."

Isis threw back her head and laughed. The bitch had a truly enticing laugh, too. That irritated Nalini even more. Did the wretch have to be so breathtakingly beautiful, so youthful and seductive, so completely aware and yet unconcerned about it all?

"Are you nuts?" Luc was yelling at her. "Do you know what she will do to you if you ever manage to even come within a foot of her?"

"Bring it, mommy dearest!" Nalini taunted, struggling against his chest. "Do you think you can scare me? What more can you do? You've already condemned me to a living hell for all eternity! Haven't you? It was you, wasn't it? Wasn't it, you selfish b-bitch!" Her voice broke on a sob, despite herself. She shrugged out of Vargas's grasp and threw herself back into the seat, staring down at the table. Silent. Without hope. If this was the evil hag her mother thought could save them, there truly was nowhere for them to go.

She glanced up as she heard the whir of a helicopter overhead. Luc was staring silently at his mother and they looked to be deep in conversation. Then he glanced once at her, meeting her gaze steadily before he turned and moved toward the door, opened it and ducked through the hatch.

Isis, for the moment, had decided to leave her alone with her thoughts. As regal and unhurried as the queen she was, the woman turned toward a monitor on the back wall. Horus, equally impassive, moved to stand beside her. They were not speaking aloud, but Nalini was sure they too were communicating.

Two guards, stationed to either side of her, watched her intently. Apparently she was a rogue entity. She supposed she was. Survival in her world had turned her into someone incapable of letting her guard down. Her cheek hurt, but it didn't feel like the bone was broken. She could tell, from experience.

It was first broken when she was twelve. Set was not even angry. She remembered because it surprised her that he could be so violent without cause or intent. He was just mildly annoyed at her constant curiosity and questioning, and had hit her with the back of his hand so hard that she had flown across the room and hit the wall. When she was carried from the room by Rashid she had screamed in agony until tears of anguish ran down Rashid's face as well. Her loving father had broken twelve of her bones, one for every year he had suffered her presence, she had told herself at the time.

He had then given her a beautiful stallion, the first horse that was hers alone, as a peace offering. He had seemed genuinely dismayed, almost as if it really had been an accident. But it wasn't an accident. She knew that now. Nothing he did was an accident.

He and later Typhon hurt her occasionally, but not often since she had learned better ways to protect herself. What was it those American warriors said? Pain is just weakness leaving the body. Yes, that made sense. Once the pain was survived, one realized what could be endured. Each release of weakness made her stronger. Yes, she was strong, she told herself.

She kept telling herself that as Luc came to reach out his hand and said, "Let's go, Nalini. Please don't try anything." He gently ran his finger across her cheek and added, "I can't keep you from getting hurt if you insist on acting foolishly."

Standing, she let him lead her toward the door. She noticed that he was now wearing a kaffiyeh, the edge drawn across his face, and then realized the rest of the vehicle's occupants, her guards excluded, had already departed and wondered vaguely how she had missed that, missed a chance to escape.

"No one here," Luc was saying, "takes any pleasure from your pain. If you don't try to escape and don't use force against us, none will be used against you. Horus could quite literally have caved in your face with his fist. He used his open hand on you, to push you away. We did not approach you once you defied her because we feared for her safety, Nalini. We were trying to protect you from yourself." His tone was soft, almost gentle as if he was trying to keep her calm.

He pulled her scarf over her head and wrapped it around her face, leaving only a slit for her eyes. One of the guards opened the door and Luc moved down the steps, and then pulled her behind him. He slipped his hand under her elbow and escorted her to the military transport helicopter that she had heard land a few minutes ago. It was kicking up enough dust to create a sandstorm. He reached up to duck her head down and hurried her to the helicopter. When he reached the open side door, he lifted her up to a soldier who stood ready to assist them. The older man lifted her into the helicopter and then set her on her feet and motioned her to a seat in the rear, next to a tall dark man who was not Arab, though he was dressed like one.

She sat down, edging away from him when his arm brushed against her shoulder. Luc took the seat to the other side of her and she leaned in and asked, "Where are you taking me?"

He shook his head, indicating that he couldn't tell her, and she settled back, trying to see out the window once the door slid shut. The helicopter lifted, hovered momentarily and then rushed upward and forward, leaving the desert sands, and Rashid, behind.

But he knoweth not that the dead are there; and that her guests are in the depths of hell.

Proverbs 9:18

Elizabeth Alsobrooks

Chapter Twenty-One

Luc inhaled, trying not to move as she snuggled against him. A faint sound of contentment passed her lips and he suppressed a groan of frustration. She curled her fingers into his shirt and tugged as if trying to pull up the covers. Her cuffs clinked together, but she didn't notice, just burrowed deeper into her dreams.

Raphael glanced over. His eyes widened and he grinned. Luc held his look long enough to make him turn his attention back out the window.

"Nalini?" He said softly. When she didn't respond, he leaned down and whispered into her ear, "Nalini, we are nearly at the landing strip."

She bolted upright. Startled awake, she dropped his shirt and turned to face forward with her arms in front of her, laying her hands in her lap.

To ease her embarrassment, he said, "We'll be landing at the airstrip soon. From there we'll be catching a jet."

Her sleep-heavy stare moved to the window, her expression surprised. She remained silent.

The helicopter slowed and began to descend. It moved forward, but increased its descent until it hovered, listed slightly, went stationary for a moment, and then landed. Roscoe slid open the side door and jumped down, turning to wait for Luc to hand Nalini to him. Standing, he reached to grasp her upper arm and helped her to her feet. She followed quietly. He wondered idly why he hadn't noticed how petite she was. She had to be nearly a foot shorter than he was. When she wasn't so tired, or distressed, she seemed much larger, certainly more animated.

Luc put his hands around her waist and handed her down to Roscoe, then jumped down beside her. He put one hand behind her elbow and another to press her head down as they ran from under the blades. A jet sat waiting a short distance away and he led her there, and up the steps. Once inside, he noted that his mother and Andrew were already seated on the couch behind the cockpit, having exited the helicopter through the front door. He led Nalini toward the back of the jet, indicating a recliner. Still silent, she sat down and didn't resist when he reached to press a button that set the chair to recline. He grabbed a blanket, tossing it over her. This time she wouldn't have to go looking for one that wasn't there.

She regarded him soberly for a long moment, then closed her eyes and sighed as if she had seen enough of the world. Roscoe settled in across from her. He didn't like surprises either, and apparently he felt she was full of them.

Walking to the rear cabin, he opened the door and stepped in, closing it behind him. "How is he doing?"

"Doc just stepped out to use the head. He said it was a bit hairy for a while there, but he thinks he'll live. He gave him a sedative that should last until we get him where he's going. Personally, I think he'll live if only so he can kill you," Emmanuel said. "He has been asking for you. No, wait, he was cursing you. Not the same, I suppose."

"Funny," Luc said without humor. He turned and left the cabin, hanging a right to stop by the row of facilities. As he stepped out, Sophia pointed to a phone.

He picked it up, listened to Muhammad complain about the board of the museum. Softly, in Arabic, he said, "Only those on the list I personally gave to you are to be allowed access to the archives. Anyone else must get permission only from a member of the inner circle."

"My prince, he is making threats, trying to force me to comply."

Luc sighed. "I'll take care of it, Muhammad."

He hung up, then picked the phone up and dialed. "Morey? Ljluka Vargas. Would you like a member of the inner circle to come and personally escort you through the archives? It seems odd, since we have already done so once. However, as you know, you can gain access no other way. What in particular did you wish to see?"

The phone was silent for a moment, as though Morey were making a decision. Then, "Forgive me, Don Vargas. They have threatened my daughter. I don't know who they are, but they said if I didn't get them in to see the collection of Coptic Papyri, they would kill her." The explanation was about what he'd expected.

Angry that someone had threatened the family of one of their most faithful operatives, he forced the muscles in his shoulders and biceps to relax, loosened his grip on the phone. "I am sending someone to see you at once, Morey. They will handle this. Do nothing and tell no one. You will know them by my symbol tattooed on their forearm." He took a deep breath and then said, "And Morey, don't worry. We will not let them harm Aneesa. If you ever have any more problems, call me personally. You have the number." Relief sounded in the heavy sigh he heard over the phone, and Morey thanked him effusively.

He made one last phone call, gave specific directions, which included continuous updates, and decided he needed another personal assistant.

A moment later, Nalini was still as he had left her, eyes shut, though he doubted she was asleep. Raphael had taken up a position to her right again, so Luc slipped into the seat to her left. He flipped up his foot rest and put his arm behind his head. As long as he had the watchers present, it was time to catch some shuteye. The time change alone would kill him.

He managed to make good use of a few hours before the sound of food trays woke him. Thirst was his first thought. Coffee his second. Which is probably why Sophia was standing in front of him with a bottle of water.

"I need to use the, um…"

Luc turned to look at Nalini, knowing without asking what she wanted. Nodding, he stood and said, "I'll be back in a minute, Sophia, but that is exactly what I needed. Thank you. Coffee next?" She nodded and he reached up to pull his weapon from where it again resided in a shoulder holster. He handed it to Roscoe. Reaching into his shirt pocket, he filched out a key and moved to reposition Nalini's recliner and unlock her cuffs.

"Do us all a favor and just take care of business. There's nowhere to go."

She managed to make a smile look like revulsion, but stood and lifted her hands. When he removed the cuffs he noticed the lacerations, but said nothing. They were created by her struggles and would soon heal. She flexed her wrists, and then raised her arms to stretch. He tensed, but she merely looked at him inquiringly.

"Back there, to the left," he directed. This time he followed behind her and when she went inside, he leaned against the adjacent wall, waiting.

He was relieved when she reappeared a short time later. By the time they returned to their seats, the stewardess, Sophia, was waiting. She had already flipped up the trays attached to each of their chairs. Nalini sat down and Sophia swiveled her tray to a position across her lap. It already had a bottle of water and a cup of steaming coffee on it. His too.

"Would you like steak, honey chicken, lasagna or *Ruz bil-loz wa bil-tamar?* Perhaps a salad or fruit plate?"

Nalini shook her head.

"Maybe you would rather have breakfast?"

Again she indicated she wanted nothing, so Luc insisted. "Nalini, you need to eat. And you definitely need to drink something. You're probably already dehydrated. You're only halfway through your second long flight."

"Nuts. Fruit," she said simply, apparently too tired to argue with him. He watched as she chugged half the water bottle. She didn't touch the coffee.

"Would you prefer tea?"

She looked over at him, studied him as if his consideration were some kind of trick. Then she nodded her preference. When Sophia returned with her food, he informed her of Nalini's choice, and she removed the coffee without comment.

By the time his food arrived--Sophia already knowing he would be ready for some red meat about now--Roscoe was already finished. He stepped over to him and handed his weapon back, staring at Nalini until Luc had secured it.

Perhaps it was the water that refueled her energy, but her spirit was returning if the glaring defiance she offered Roscoe was any indication. He upped his alert level.

By the time they arrived in Rome, the tension had exhausted him, but he placated himself with the thoughts of a long hot steam shower. He had returned her cuffs, so he leveled her seat and helped her to stand. Slipping a jacket off a hanger by the door, he tossed it over her handcuffs. Roscoe went first, and he moved down the stairs behind her, leaning in to grasp her waist. Once they reached the bottom, he and Roscoe each grabbed an elbow and hurried her into the back of the second vehicle.

Antonio closed the door, and the dark windows secured them from any curious stares. He took the coat off her arms, then accepted the scarf Roscoe handed him and blindfolded her. She might know they were in Rome, and he was sure she did by the way she had quickly scanned the area as they rushed her from the plane, but she didn't need to know the particulars of how to access their headquarters.

An experienced driver in all sorts of conditions and circumstances, Antonio used caution but urgency to arrive quickly without drawing undue attention. They glided past the impressive entrance of the five star resort hotel with its valet parking and ready staff. They instead entered the garage. Circling downward, Antonio stopped just long enough to insert a card into a machine which triggered the upward swing of the barrier that protected their exclusive base level parking. He drove down a ramp and circled to the other end of the subterranean lot and stopped beside an apparently solid stone wall.

Andrew and his mother, already out of the first vehicle, approached the wall and waited as Emmanuel pressed his hand against a particular stone. It slid open, revealing what looked like a fuse box, secured with a push button code. He typed in a code and pulled open the small metal door. A screen appeared, with another key code pad. He typed in another code and then leaned forward for the retinal scan. The soft metallic slide of greased metal against metal sounded, then the stone wall separated and an elevator door appeared. This time a simple card key slide opened the elevator doors and they stepped inside and took the elevator down to their personal residence. To the outside world, they were occupying the penthouse suite, which, by other hidden elevator systems they could also access from their subterranean location.

Antonio opened the car and Luc pulled Nalini toward him. She slid across the seat and he positioned his hand between the door frame and her head as she exited the vehicle. Soon they too were moving downward.

As they stepped from the elevators, Kirin ran toward him from down the corridor. Ignoring their unwilling guest, she threw her arms around him. "At last. I am so glad to see you."

He chuckled at her enthusiasm, and returned her hug. "I've missed you too."

Then she pulled away and studied the woman at his side. She reached out to snatch off the scarf to reveal Nalini's face. Nalini studied her coolly. Kirin glared. Nalini, still indifferent, ran her tongue across her lips as if she were thirsty. Before he suspected her intent, Kirin slapped Nalini in the face and said, "That's for slicing open my brother's chest. And this--"

He grabbed Kirin's downward swinging backhand and slammed his arm down on his harnessed weapon, knowing Nalini's habit of borrowing pistols whenever the mood struck her. Andrew rushed up to grab Kirin, pulling her back and allowing Luc to contain the explosion that had just gone off beside him.

"You're lucky you're handcuffed," Kirin yelled. "Take them off her," she demanded of Luc.

Hearing his mother's chuckle in the background did little to lighten his mood as Nalini lifted her knee, fully intending to groin him. He swiveled his hips, deflecting the blow with the side of his raised leg. Spinning around, he stepped behind her and lifted her off the ground, immobilizing her arms. She continued to struggle, violently cursing in Arabic. The handcuffs apparently didn't inhibit her movement.

Kirin returned her compliment for compliment. Andrew and Luc exchanged looks, as they realized that she was cursing in Akkadian. "I wonder where she gets that from?" Andrew asked, laughing, which only made Kirin angrier.

Roscoe unsnapped the holster and took possession of Luc's pistol, yet again. Luc tossed Nalini over his shoulder, yet again, carrying her down the hall to pass through a door held open by Emmanuel, and down a flight of stairs.

"Wow, that went well. How do you like my little sister, sweetheart?" Luc snapped. He soon regretted his show of irritation, however, as she twisted sideways and clonked him on the head with the handcuffs as she grabbed hold of his hair and began yanking. At the bottom of the stairs, he reached up and slammed her hand with the flat of his palm. She released his hair and he released his hold of her, dumping her onto the hard stone tiles.

Instantly on her feet, he didn't give her time to react before grabbing her arm and pulling her down the corridor. At the end, he opened a metal door, shoved her inside and slammed it shut again. Tossing the cuff key through the small barred opening, he said, "Welcome to Rome," and turned to walk away.

"You're going to regret bringing me here, Vargas!"

"I already do, Nalini," he said too softly for her to hear. "I already do." Running his hand through his hair, he headed toward a hot steamy shower.

The gods shook like beaten dogs,
hiding in the far corners of heaven,
Ishtar screamed and wailed:
The days of old have turned to stone:
We have decided evil things in our Assembly!
Why did we decide those evil things in
 our Assembly?

Why did we decide to destroy our people?
We have only just now created our beloved humans;
We now destroy them in the sea!"
All the gods wept and wailed along with her,
All the gods sat trembling, and wept.

Shin-eqi-unninni, Gilgamesh

224

Chapter Twenty-Two

Luc walked into his bed chamber and shrugged into a t-shirt. Picking up a pair of denim jeans, he quickly stepped into them. He pulled them up and fastened them, lifting his arms as he realized Hassidim was lacing a belt through the loops. Slashing his hands around the ends of his shirt inside his waistband, to tuck it in, he grabbed the belt buckle and fastened it. Hassidim laid out a leather designer jacket. The distressed leather he liked. Comfort mattered. The style looked like something Kirin or Hassidim--who had his own ideas about how a prince should look even in casual attire--would have chosen.

"They fit well," he said.

"Oh, it is my greatest honor to serve you, my worthy prince. I was so happy that this small task could be completed before your arrival when our most awful and awesomely powerful queen commanded me to come home and await your arrival."

"Awful, huh?" Sometimes it paid to actually listen to what Hassidim was saying. It was pretty amusing, especially until he realized someone *was* listening.

"No, no, I meant no disrespect. I was so grateful to honor the slightest wish of she who is fair as the moon, mother of all who are righteous, and--"

"Luc," said Kirin, sticking her head in the door. "Do I dare enter?"

"Depends. You carrying any weapons?"

Ignoring his comment, she came in to sit down in the chair beside him. "You certainly look and smell much better than when you arrived."

"Thanks, I guess."

"You planning to go out?" She asked, glancing at his jacket laid out on the bed.'

"I was thinking about it. I'm due a little liberty."

"Magdalena?"

"You pull sentry duty tonight?" Her insatiable curiosity was about to get her in trouble, he thought irritably.

"Sorry." She recognized his mood, he realized, and instantly regretted his harshness. He knew she was only trying to defend him. Family was everything to her. She was unfailingly nurturing and always concerned, possessing huge portions of Isis's more often suppressed maternal side.

"Kinda surprised you're not working on all those new specimens you were collecting," he said, trying to turn the conversation to safer territory.

"Well," she said, looking down at a perfectly manicured nail as if it needed attention. "I had to see for myself that you were alright. I guess I messed up our greeting."

"It was a surprise." His lips turned up at the corners.

"And we both know how you hate those." She lifted her head and looked up at him then, from under her lashes, grinning. It was a trick she used to pull when she was a little girl.

He completed his smile, shaking his head. "You have us all wrapped around your little finger, don't you? How can I stay angry with you when you so obviously don't have a mean thought in your head? That said, why did you do it, Kirin? I've never seen you act like that."

"It was you. I didn't plan to do it. I hate her, yes, for what she did to you, but it wasn't until I, until I saw how you looked at her that I wanted to--"

"Me? Kirin, please. I was looking at her because you had pulled her scarf off. Shit, the woman was in handcuffs." What was she saying? How could she blame this on something he had done? His irritation returned.

"I know. Don't you think I feel bad about that?" She stood up and moved forward until she was in front of him as if she needed the physical advantage of being taller. Her hands were thrust against her hips defiantly.

"Your behavior didn't support that theory."

"Listen, I asked about Magdalena because I was hoping you were going there. You need to stay away from that other woman. Let Andrew and the others deal with her."

Now she was going too far, trying to tell him how to do his job. "You're not making any sense, Kirin. Not that this has anything to do with you, but I'd love to have them deal with that she-devil. They don't want anything to do with her either. She's a pain in the ass, but I'm the one who kidnapped her. That makes me responsible. Do I think I need a break? Yes. Why do you think I was planning to go out tonight?"

"Are you really that naïve, Luc? Why is it, do you suppose, that mother claims the woman is only calm and cooperative when you ask her to do something? She's playing you, and it's working. You should have seen how you were looking at her."

"I wasn't looking at her in any particular way. This is nuts," he said, standing up and walking over to pick up his coat.

"You looked as if you wanted to kiss her and you were staring at her lips, Luc. At the very least you desire her."

She had noticed that? "Okay, let's say I give you that one, Kirin. You may not be aware of this, but every man who has seen her finds her desirable. Since you've seen her, you must understand why. Even dirty and travel weary she is one of the most beautiful women alive."

"It's not just lust with you, Luc. You're protective of her. Your immediate response to my attack was to protect her."

"I repeat, she was wearing handcuffs, Kirin. Given your defense training, that hardly seems like fair odds." Now she was way off base. He had to defend her. She was his responsibility.

"From what I've heard, she can kick even your ass. It didn't look as if those cuffs were going to get in her way!" She was angry now, frustrated, close to tears. "And that doesn't explain why I just finished changing the bandages on a giant Nubian who is apparently her lifelong friend and bodyguard. You had the men risk encountering the enemy to go get her bodyguard, Luc. Had a specialist meet him at the plane for treatment. It was because she cares about him, wasn't it? You don't see that you want to protect her, to keep her from feeling pain? And you don't see that as unusual or erratic behavior?" She had warmed to her subject and her voice rose with her temper.

He sighed, sitting back in the chair. Wasn't it he who had admitted to his brothers that he knew he was making an ass out of himself around her? And since he was admitting things, he *had* been wondering what it would be like to kiss her just then, when she ran her tongue across her lips, and again when her eyes flashed with the violence of her reaction to Kirin's assault. He found her fire and energy intoxicating.

Even when she annoyed him or got him angry it was such a rush, like the extreme sports he and Andrew loved so much. She was exciting. Well, he found her exciting. Shit. Was Kirin right?

He stood up again, and grabbed his coat. "I won't be back until tomorrow," he said. "I've got my cell, if anything comes up."

"Luc?"

He sighed, bracing himself. "Yes?"

"You know it's only because I care about you, don't want you to be hurt. You do realize there's no way you could ever be with her?"

"It hadn't even occurred to me one way or the other. We're ransoming her back to the devil himself." Sending her straight back to the hell she so obviously craves.

"It's just that--"

"I know I don't feel as much animosity toward her as you think I should. I probably never will. Try to understand, Kirin." He put his hand on her shoulder and stared into her eyes. "For one thing, little sister, she was already given thirty lashes with a whip because she failed to kill me, an attempt for which you slapped her in the face."

Kirin drew her breath in, shocked at his revelation. Her hands balled into fists and she drew them into her chest. "That's barbaric," she muttered.

"She didn't just wake up one morning and decide to kill me. She was ordered to do so. And never forget, Kirin. She isn't Set. She's just another one of his victims. Try to imagine what it is like to grow up in Set's household."

"It's not even conceivable. Look, I understand now. But I still can't condone what she did to you. All she has done to you. Just promise me you'll be careful."

"I promise I'll try," he said, smiling at their little ritual.

"And I promise I won't beat up your kidnap victim unless she first attacks me."

"A done deal," Luc said, picking her up into a big bear hug. He set her back down and said, "See you in the morning, slugger," and walked to the door, opened it, glanced back once, winked and hurried to the elevator.

He wondered if Magdalena would have those massage oils ready by the time he got a quick haircut. She'd better, he decided. He had more stress than a political candidate on Election Day, and more restless tension than a pubescent boy.

A dungeon horrible, on all sides round
As one great furnace flamed, yet from those flames
No light, but rather darkness visible
Served only to discover sights of woe,
Regions of sorrow, doleful shades, where peace
And rest can never dwell, hope never comes…

John Milton, Paradise Lost

232

Chapter Twenty-Three

Nalini sat on the floor of the bathing room, leaning against the tiled wall that separated the shower from the rest of the area. She was actually impressed with the thoughtfulness that had gone into the design of her upscale dungeon. There was no mistaking it for what it was, but it was the most comfortable prison money and modern technology could provide.

There was no tub. No possibility of drowning herself. Not even the high efficiency lavatory had enough water for that. She couldn't hang herself with strips of sheet or towel from the curtain rod or showerhead. The shower consisted of numerous holes in the ceiling through which water sprayed out when one turned a chrome dial. There was no glass door, from which she might have tried to grab a hunk of glass to kill herself or anyone else. Water was contained by the wide tiled wall upon which she leaned. The mirror, rather small for the size of the room, was slightly opaque, distorting her reflection just enough for her to notice that the mirror itself was covered with the type of plastic laminate, about ten times thicker than real glass, they used in bullet resistant glass.

They had supplied their unwanted guest with the same requirements for personal hygiene one might expect in a luxury hotel penthouse, with even a blow dryer that resided in a recessed cavity of the tiled wall—no cords to use for strangulation--and plenty of fresh towels, even a plush robe. The well furnished bathing room was her choice of occupancy not because of the amenities, however, but because it was also the only one of the two rooms without security cameras. A veritable paradise.

Every other angle in the entire suite was under surveillance. They had zoom capability, night vision in case she managed to break the all but bullet proof—hell, it probably was bullet proof-- glass over the lights recessed and inaccessible in the vaulted ceiling. The cameras too were merely black dots in minute holes in the ceiling and upper walls. They could even listen to her snore, assuming she did snore. No one had ever told her that she did, though who would know or care, she asked herself.

A complete investigation of her suite had provided her with all the information she needed to realize she was up against some savvy adversaries and they were surprisingly generous if overly cautious with their prisoners. Unfortunately, she had found nothing that could aid her in an escape attempt.

Realizing that, she decided to at least feel better on the outside, since she was a mess otherwise. She had already taken two showers, one last night and one this morning. Though she knew her brothers and Set had them, the women's quarters didn't boast showers, only bathing pools and Jacuzzi tubs. The Jacuzzi tubs had been a recent renovation, one suggested by her mother. These were the first showers Nalini had taken since her last hotel stay, and she was convinced more than ever that she needed to find a way to talk her mother into getting Set to put one in her suite.

The clean clothes the guard had slipped through a grid that opened in the door were comfortable, Egyptian cotton that smelled faintly of lavender. She wondered if they were trying to keep her calm. If so, it wasn't working. Hugging her knees into her chest, she folded her hands across them and rested her chin on her hands.

What was her mother doing now? she wondered. Surely she must know about Rashid. Of course she would know about Nalini. Hopefully it wouldn't make her too upset in her condition. She had begun to show, which elated Set. He had been even more solicitous and generous with Astarte lately. For now her mother was safe, at least from Set. But Typhon was not as pleased about the upcoming birth of a new son from the wife Set so adored. Nalini had been watching him closely. His attention moved to her mother's stomach whenever she entered a room. What was he planning? Hopefully Aria had made it home safely, to look after her mother in her absence. She'd been gone for weeks on a mission that should have taken days.

She was worried about how Astarte would deal with Set's refusal to part with the book to save her. There was no question in her mind that he would refuse. Had they but asked her, she could have told them their folly. Set wouldn't even have traded the book to save a son. If only Rashid were here to help her think of a way to escape. He never gave up. He always helped her devise some plan to overcome every plot of Typhon's making, or some irrational decision made by Set, and there were many. She would miss, too, Rashid's slow smile. Genuine smiles, he reserved only for her and even then they were rare.

He was such an extension of herself that now she felt as if a limb had been severed. Set would replace him with some stranger and then she would be forced to be always in the presence of someone who didn't know when to leave her alone, or when to drop an arm across her shoulder for comfort, though only when they were alone could Rashid, closer than any brother or sister, touch her even in that way. She suppressed a sob that stuck in her throat and made it difficult to breath.

Swallowing, she forced herself to think of her present situation. Unfortunately, even if she escaped her cell, she had no idea where she was. And now only one other person alive cared, and she could do nothing about it. Was she even now bargaining with Set? What more could her mother promise him?

The outer door opened. She scrambled to her feet. A soft tap sounded on the door of the bathing chamber. She walked over to open it. It's wasn't as if they didn't know where she was.

"Are you alright? They said you've been in here for hours." Luc studied her face as if looking for signs of distress or illness.

She shrugged. "I wanted a little privacy," she said simply.

He nodded, understanding. "Listen, I need to talk to you about   something."

Tensing, she said, "If you want to tell me that my father thinks you're welcome to keep me, don't bother. I already know about how useful he thinks I am, especially for a girl."

"No, that's not true, Nalini," he said softly. "I know you want to go home. We're still negotiating. He did offer to pay us millions of dollars, so he does care if he gets you back. We're just having some misunderstanding about what it is we're willing to accept in trade."

A misunderstanding? He meant an impasse. Why not admit it? The way he looked at her was so penetrating, as if he were trying to read her mind the way his mother had. He glanced at her mouth, his expression changing, the sapphire of his eyes glittering with splashes of molten silver. Shocked by her reflexive impulse to move forward, she stepped back. His usual intensity, though, and she was not as immune to it as she pretended even to herself, was even more evident this morning. Why? What was different about him? Something.

She stepped back once more and studied him, silently. He returned her gaze and her heartbeat increased, despite her attempts to remind herself that he looked just like her brother, Lucien. But he was nothing like Lucien, not in his mannerisms, the timber of his voice, or the too easy way in which he seemed always to know what she was thinking.

"You need to understand," she said, breaking whatever spell he was trying to cast over her. "My father will never, ever give up the book. Not for anyone or anything. Don't you think I know him better than you? Why don't you just let me go?"

He glanced away then, and she could tell he already knew exactly what Set was like. They all did. He was trying to make her feel better, but would never let her go until Set agreed to their terms. Knowing Set would not make a trade, why was he keeping her here?

Living among men and studying their reactions and actions for her own survival, she had learned to pick up the signs. His usual intensity, the tension he exuded whenever he was with her, the part that was more than just the prisoner versus guard relationship, the man versus woman part, that was the part that had changed.

It had intensified by a thousand fold, and he was battling himself to resist it, to resist her.

Why did she care? "I don't need your pity, Vargas," she snipped, suddenly angry, angry with herself for her own unwanted feelings. "Just tell me one thing. Since you obviously do know what my father is like, why did you take me? You had to already know he wouldn't trade the book for me."

"Who can say what your father will or won't do?" he said almost defensively. "Not even you can claim to know that."

She glared at him for being right and for more than that. "Who can say what any man will or won't do?" she said in a way that could not be taken as anything but derogatory.

He didn't answer her, but he moved forward into the room. "Who indeed," he muttered before he lowered his head and kissed her. His lips were full and soft and gentle against hers, and then more insistent, more possessive, more consuming. Her shocked immobility disappeared and she surrendered unwittingly to her escalating reaction. It was her first kiss. Her only kiss. He smelled of sandalwood and reminded her of the desert and the sun on her face. She thought of the comical way his face suddenly appeared upside down from the hole in the ceiling, and the way he smiled at her.

He reached down to lift her up and hold her against himself, slipping his tongue into her mouth. Her initial surprise melted as he teased his tongue across her bottom lip, then traced the line of her upper lip before plunging between them to massage her tongue and coax it into an ageless dance of passion and desire.

He was kissing her again, and his lips trailed across her face and against her throat as his head turned so he could nuzzle against her and he again found that sensitive spot beneath her ear. Backing up, he moved toward the tiled wall she had previously leaned against, and she felt its cool pressure against the warmth of her back as he used it for leverage so that he could press more intimately against her. She lifted her head and sighed, and he continued plundering her senses. Her lids opened dreamily and she saw them in the mirror. But it wasn't her. It was Ljluka and some stranger, some wonton whore, opening for him like a twenty-four-hour diner.

She shoved against him, still breathing heavily, and cried, "No! Stop! Let me go."

Her release was instantaneous. She nearly collapsed, had to grab the wall to catch herself. He hadn't just released her as he had when they'd fought on the stairway. At her angry words, he lifted his head to stare at her in surprise, then lowered her gently to the ground, stepping away, quickly, as if she were fire and he was getting burned.

"I-I'm sorry. But you weren't struggling, Nalini," he said, his spasmodic chest a visible reflection of his surging hormones. His pupils were still dilated, still smoldering with desire.

"Would it have mattered? I think you got out of bed too early this morning, Ljluka. Apparently your woman, and I can smell her on you, couldn't give you the satisfaction you sought. How is that my fault? What now? You take me in the next room so your men can watch?"

That doused the flames. Her first comment shocked him and she saw the truth of it cross his face, briefly, before he shuttered it away. He was angry now. She watched it move from his eyes to his shoulders. Better. This Vargas she could control. This was the kind of man she knew and understood. This kind of man didn't terrify her, not like that other did. That man that made her want him, too.

"Of course not. You don't believe it either. My kissing you is unforgivable, an uncharacteristic abuse of power, I admit it. I-I'm not sure why I did it. It is so unlike me I hardly know where it came from. You can't know that. It is true though, I swear it. But how far it went, how intimate it became…Rā help me, that was me responding to you, Nalini. I've been with enough women to know when the response is real. But last night I sat and drank with one of my men, because you confuse and bewilder me, and I can't seem to stay away from you. And if you must know, if it will ease your feeling that I wanted you as nothing more than a quick toss, I did see a woman. I saw her this morning. I saw her long enough to break it off with her, because I had to admit to myself that if I stayed with her, it would only be a substitute for you, to help me forget you."

No, no, no, she needed that other man back, that angry reactive man, not this reasoning and honest man who could see into her soul. "Should I be expecting a visit from your brother now?"

She watched as his emotions shut down behind the impenetrable guard of the man she sought, but did not like very much. Here was Ljluka Vargas, enforcer, front-end cleaner for the Vargas Dynasty, the deadly power behind the Illuminati.

"Don't think less of yourself than I do, Nalini." Cold. Rigid. "Again, I apologize for kissing you. If it ever happens again, it will be your initiation so that there will be no question as to intent." So formal, no remnant of the passionate man from a moment ago.

He turned then, unhurried, deceptively calm and relaxed, and left the room. She didn't move until she heard the outer door click shut. Not even by a slam did he display a hint of emotion. She'd seen him angry before, but perhaps he only shut off his emotions when he chose to.

The woman in the mirror before her was a stranger. Her cheeks were still flushed, her hair still rumpled from his fingers weaving through it. Already full, her lips looked bruised, swollen from his plundering.

Swearing in Arabic, she grabbed a brush and threw it against the mirror. As she had known in the back of her mind, it didn't shatter but instead bounced off, hit the carved marble countertop and clattered to the floor. She moved back to her earlier harbor and slumped on the floor, wrapping her arms around her draw up knees. And then she did something she had not done in centuries. She cried, with complete abandon and self-indulgence. Rashid, home, her mother, all these things she cried for, but mostly she cried for she knew not what, so great was her confusion and frustration.

A few minutes later, she pulled herself from her uncharacteristic selfpity. She walked to the sink and splashed cold water on her face, grimacing as she noted that now her eyes were puffy and swollen.

A sigh escaped her and she went back to sit on the floor. Let them wonder what she was doing, at all times. She wanted only two things at the moment, her mother, and something that would break with loud satisfaction when she hurtled it across the room.

Sing, O goddess, the anger of Achilles
son of Peleus, that brought
countless ills upon the Achaeans.
Many a brave soul did it send hurrying
down to Hades, and many a hero did it yield
a prey to dogs and vultures,
for so were the counsels of Jove fulfilled
from the day on which the son of Atreus,
king of men, and great Achilles,
first fell out with one another.

Homer, The Iliad

Chapter Twenty-Four

He put down the pen and reread the letter. *Nalini, Having time to think, I realize what you must have thought. I am sorry. Your Rashid however is spared. I would have told you sooner, but wanted to be assured by the doctor that he would make a full recovery. Anubis, who will be seeing to your needs, is not as insensitive as he will probably seem. He's rough around the edges. Give him a break. He's just following orders. That's something you understand too.* He had signed it simply, *Vargas,* which is what she most often called him. Though he could still remember the sound of his given name on her lips for the first time…could still remember her lips.

What he could not imagine was how she so quickly knew he had been with Magdalena. The woman had only hugged him and kissed him on the check. He had held her for a moment until she no longer had tears in her eyes. She would miss him, she said and he knew, because he would miss her, too. But his heart had not been in it any longer and he didn't want to make her a whore with deceit or misunderstandings. Until his sister's ranting, and his beer-tipping talk with Roscoe last night, he had not admitted his true feelings to himself. Hell, what were his true feelings anyway? He was drawn to her like a lifeline, but he also knew they could never be together. It would be impossible for him to resist her if she were constantly in his presence, and it would be a disservice to her if he let a relationship form.

He sighed and ran his fingers through his hair. Glancing down at the letter, he considered his decision. The letter was short and sometimes cryptic, but he felt it said what he wanted. He hadn't told her he was leaving, but he knew she would understand why. Folding the parchment, he reached for the candle on his desk, held the flame to the wedge of wax. Once enough red paraffin had fallen to seal the letter, he put down the candle and sealer, picked up his signet ring and pressed it against the cooling puddle.

A quick tap on his door and Andrew appeared.

"Thanks for coming right away. I need you to take this letter to Nalini."

Andrew, being his brother and his best friend, looked at him with question and concern in his eyes, but said nothing, just nodded. He accepted it from Luc's outstretched hand, noted the symbol of the tree of life containing a solitary owl on one of its branches, and said, "I wouldn't have read it, Luc. You should have known that."

"It's not sealed for your benefit. It's for her, so she'll be able to decide if she wants to read it."

"Oh." Simple affirmation of understanding, no judgment in the tone, no questions about why he wasn't just taking it to her himself.

"Here you two are," Kirin said, sailing into the room. "So what's with all the rush? Hassidim made it seem like a matter of life and death."

"Doesn't he always?" Luc asked.

"True. So what's up?" She moved to the desk and sat on the corner, waiting for his response.

"You need to get packed. I'm giving you a personal escort home so that you can get back to work."

"Why the sudden—are you taking my advice?"

Yes, I'm running like a coward, he told himself. "Sure, why not. Let's get going. I need to go find mother and let her know the change in plans." He stood up and ignored the look that crossed between his siblings.

"Luc, come on. Are you sure that's the right thing for you to do right now? I mean, you're the one who usually negotiates this stuff, and—"

"In all fairness, he can negotiate from anywhere, Andrew."

"I know but--"

"Am I invisible? Look, I've got this one. I'll see you both in a few minutes. Kirin, I suggest you be packed in an hour."

He walked out and left them to argue it further without him. His mother would not be ignored, though he didn't think she would object. Typing in his code, he pressed his hand against the metal imprint and leaned into the retinal scan, waited for the buzzer to sound, and opened the door to the communication center.

Standing in the middle of the room, three steps up above the lower deck with its manned semicircle of terminals, levers, buttons and satellite readouts, Isis was watching instead the dozens of televisions that curved around the far wall. Her business attire was a soft gossamer gown of emerald green. Sleeveless, with an empire waist and a deep neckline, it fell in generous folds to the floor where it swirled around her legs with her every movement. It reminded Luc of the golden gown Nalini had worn when he first saw her.

His gaze swept the stations quickly, from habit, but though he instantly knew what information she sought, he did not have her ability to actually ingest the minute details of the information from them all, simultaneously, or use the complicated remote to flash quickly through the channels on multiple televisions understanding and noticing everything, also concurrently.

Apparently done with her task, she stopped flicking the channels and said, without turning, "So when are you leaving?"

"About an hour," he said, unsurprised that she knew.

I may have to send her there, too. Less complicated in other ways. You cannot run from yourself, Ljluka. You know what you must do and what is forbidden.

I'll think of it as a reprieve then, and better prepare myself for the battles ahead.

Yes. I should have better armed you.

Mother?

She turned to look at him then. *Yes, my little owl.*

Please don't take it out on her, whatever it is that makes you so angry.

She walked over, lifting her arms up so that he could embrace her before he left. "I will see you soon. Take care of your sister," she said aloud.

He nodded, bent down to kiss her on the cheek and then looked into her eyes and said so softly the men working three steps below them were unable to hear, "I love you, mother," before turning to leave the room.

When he returned to his suite, Hassidim was singing Egyptian hymns, praising Isis and thanking her for her benevolent wisdom. Clearly she had returned to his good graces, since Luc had agreed to let him accompany him to Peru. He knew if she objected, no one would be going.

"How long?" Luc asked.

"In less time than it takes a camel to pass through the eye of a needle, oh great prince," Hassidim said, grinning widely.

"So is that less time than it takes me to change my mind about taking you with me?"

"In a brief instant, I swear oh kind and generous prince. Forgive me, your most worthless and undeserving servant. How can I make it up to you, my venerable prince, he who is beloved of Isis, high queen of all the--"

"So ten minutes?"

"Yes, five, most certain."

Andrew walked in and scowled at him. He waited until he was standing in front of him to accuse, "Luc, what did you do to her? I mean, I know there's no way you—"

"What are you talking about? I thought you said you wouldn't read it?"

"Read what? The letter? I didn't, but why has she been crying?"

"Crying?" Nalini, crying? Surely not.

"Come on, little brother. I know enough about women to know that when you have one as tough as this one, one who fights like a man and probably doesn't even know how to talk to another woman she spends so much time around men, and her eyes are all swollen and puffy from crying, it's more than just because she's homesick and being held hostage and feeling all sorry for herself."

"Shit. Crying. I'm such a bastard." She had responded. He didn't just imagine her tongue plunging into his mouth, entwined with his, or the way she pressed against him. Her soft moan of rising desire. Still, he should have resisted her allure in the first place, suspecting how innocent, inexperienced and vulnerable she was. There was no denying that he wanted to seduce her, even now.

"What did you do?"

"Nothing. Nearly nothing. I kissed her. That's all." All she allowed him to do, not all he wanted from her. He wished Andrew would stop looking at him like that. He felt guilty enough without his brother's condemning glower.

"Did you force her to kiss you?" Andrew looked confused, as if trying to figure out why the woman was so upset. He'd like that information too. What if she were upset because she wanted him as much as he wanted her and she was as angry about it as he was? No, that wasn't true. If it were, she wouldn't have pushed him away.

"I would never force a woman, Andrew." How low did his brother think he would stoop?

"I didn't mean it like that. When did she start to like you?"

As if it were so unbelievable that she might like him, too. But hadn't she made that perfectly clear? Fed up with defending himself when he felt the sting of his own self-incrimination so strongly, he snapped, "Shut up, Andrew. I'll be in the car, Hassidim. It you're there with the luggage in five, you can go too."

He turned and headed for the door.

"Look, little brother, come on. I didn't. Shit. I didn't mean to imply you could or even would hurt that Babylonian whore just by--"

Luc spun on his heels, "And Andrew?"

"Yes?" Andrew stared at him soberly, as if trying to understand his brother's sudden moodiness. Or perhaps he did understand and was worried.

His brother's expression calmed the tone of his voice. Quietly he asked, "Do me a favor and don't call her that any more. Though I seem to recall you having a particular fondness for Babylonian whores, Nalini isn't one of them. It was my fault, not hers. It won't happen again. I've already apologized, thus the letter, okay? Try to be nice to her. She's had a lot happen to her lately that isn't her fault." An understatement, he thought. It was his fault, so he was going to remove himself from the situation so as not to make it worse. He didn't yet trust himself to resist his near uncontrollable impulses where she was concerned. He'd never been so drawn to a woman. Even now as he was leaving he felt a compulsion to stay, to be near her.

"Sure, I mean, no problem. She's been kidnapped and we have all the power, I get that. I wasn't planning to rough her up or anything. I mean, she is a woman, even if she can kick ass like a man. I get how you might have, that is, well, I guess I can understand why you might, not that you…shit, do you think I'm blind? I can see how you like her."

"Thanks, Andrew," he said dryly. Luc laughed, shook his head, and walked out the door.

Kirin was just approaching, and he raised his eyebrows at her timely arrival.

"Don't look too impressed. I just got here a couple days ago and I keep essentials in both places. I didn't need to grab much, just some things I bought when I went shopping on Monday."

"Great," he said, heading with her toward the elevator. "The jet's already fueled, and I bet Hassidim knocks us over in his haste to beat us to the limo."

She chuckled and reached out to slip her hand around his elbow. "I'm glad you decided to take a breather, Luc."

"I know," he said simply.

With her usual sensitivity, she let the subject drop and began to regale him with the latest advancement in her research. As the elevator doors swooshed softly shut behind them, he nodded at something Kirin said and wondered if Nalini had read his letter.

The Emperor of Rome has seen you in a dream,
And now life and being and existence have
all left him.

Celtic Tale, White Book of Rhydderch

254

Chapter Twenty-Five

"I haven't been much company, have I?" Luc glanced sideways at Kirin.

"Sure, just not great company," Kirin said, smiling indulgently.

He turned the Land Rover onto the track and waved at Jacob, knowing he would be manning the surveillance cameras. Even over the sound of the SUV the screams of Howler monkeys and screeching parrots could be heard. An anaconda hung from a tree and nearly brushed against Kirin's window.

"It's so good to be home," she enthused, "where the wildlife consists of more than sewer rats, drug dealers, prostitutes and pick pockets."

"Getting just a touch cynical there, sis? Bit of a motley crew. Since when have you ever come into contact with any of that wildlife, as you call it?"

"I believe that was my point. Who would want to?"

Luc drove between two large trees and put the vehicle in park. The Land Rover began to lower into the ground. A few minutes later, the automobile elevator, the surface of which was completely hidden beneath vines, ferns and lush greenery, stopped and Luc shifted and drove over the jam signaling the elevator's return to the surface, and pulled the vehicle into the garage. They got out and he grabbed Kirin's bag from the back. Hassidim had already begun gathering the rest of their luggage.

He noted that the use indicator light had gone out as they passed the elevator on their way into what he always referred to as Kirin's lab facility. The main entrance slid open and Luc glanced toward the surveillance camera and nodded his thanks.

Once they reached her suite and he had deposited Kirin's bag on the floor, he said, "I think I'm going to get a couple of the boys and do a little cliff diving. I have a few business things to take care of first, but I should be done in thirty minutes. Care to join us?"

"Illuminati business?"

He nodded, but refused to elaborate.

"Hmm, and then you and the hole in the head gang, up and downing the canyon. Tempting, but I think I'll pass," she said, laughing.

A few hours later, he and his men entered the facility amid exuberant joking and laughing, fully charged and animated. Hassidim ran up and grabbed his bag, which made him raise his eyebrows, but for once the Arab wasn't talking. Then he noticed Kirin signaling him from down the hall.

"Hey, I'll see you guys later. Thanks. We need to do that more often," Luc said, heading toward his sister.

"What's up? You manage to run Mandu out of the kitchen and burn dinner?"

Just as he reached her, Andrew stuck his head out of the security center down the hall and said, "I wish I'd been here a few hours earlier. Don't know the last time I went cliff diving."

"What are you--"

"That's what I was trying to tell you, Luc. Not Andrew, but who he brought with him," Kirin said in a rush.

Realization hit Luc full in the face. He had actually managed to stop thinking about her for a few hours, and now they had brought her right back to him. How far did he have to run?

He hadn't had enough time away from her.

"Hey, little brother. Before you object, we didn't have any choice. There was an attempt to infiltrate the penthouse in Rome. We can't risk something like this there with all those wealthy tourists, celebrities and dignitaries in house."

He knew his brother was right, but he had thought he'd have longer. His head wasn't on straight yet. "Mother with you?" he asked.

"No, she went to Egypt."

"That explains why she said I wasn't to continue negotiations until tomorrow. Where's the Nubian?"

"On site, feeling healthy and cranky. Mother figured she'd solve that problem before she left, too."

"Great, another complication." He took a deep breath and let it out. Complications were supposed to be his specialty. "Shit." There went his great mood. "When do we eat?" he asked Kirin. He would deal with this mess later, but not on an empty stomach.

*Behold a watcher and an holy one
came down from heaven.*

Daniel 4:13

Chapter Twenty-Six

Luc's decision was uncomplicated. He intended to stay away from her. Nalini didn't know where she was, so had no way of knowing he was here. He swallowed a mouthful of Mandu's famous spicy omelet. He had no idea what all was in it, but it had just the right amount of fire to get his engine started. Between that and the coffee he was feeling better about both the day and his newest decision.

"She's demanding exercise," Andrew said, apparently determined to give him indigestion before breakfast was over. No one bothered to ask who he was talking about.

"Give her a treadmill." He didn't want to do this. Not yet. Didn't want to be involved in her welfare or supervision.

"She wants to go outside to feel Rā's glory on her face, or so she claims."

"Get her a tanning bed." Why was Andrew doing this? His brother knew he didn't want to deal with her.

"She is from a climate that boasts heat and sunlight nearly every day," Kirin said. "I suppose the lack of--"

"Enough!" His sister too? Was this a conspiracy? "How can either of you think we could allow her to leave the facility? It's too dangerous. If as you say they already tried to get to her in Rome, having doubled security here is not reason enough to chance having her seen on the grounds. It's going to have to wait anyway. I have a conference call this afternoon with Set. I need to get these negotiations moving."

"Of course we don't think you should take her outside. It's an insane idea. I'm just saying she's cranky and complaining and you seem to be the only one that can handle her. As far as the negotiations are concerned, what angle can you use that you haven't already?" Andrew snapped back, clearly annoyed as he moved to the counter to refill his coffee.

Ignoring his brother's irritation, he said, "By now they know they can't read the book. I hope to make Set realize it is useless to him." It sounded weak even to him.

Turning back to look at him, Andrew defied Luc's attempt to change the subject and said, "Look, I know you don't want to see her, but she really wants to go home. Maybe you could get her to tell you something that would be helpful in the negotiations."

"The only thing she has told me so far is that there was no one or nothing Set would ever exchange for that book." She had also told him to leave her alone.

"I was afraid of that. Still, it couldn't hurt to talk to her about it."

"I take it you've already tried." That better be the reason Andrew was trying to force him to see her again so soon.

"She won't even talk to me except to complain about her confinement and the lack of sunlight. Demands to see the Nubian, of course. She was cold, too. Kirin had to send her an athletic suit. We turned up the heat." Cold? She was not cold, Luc thought.

"Luc, you don't need to talk to her. Andrew can try again. Or perhaps I could apologize and try to talk to her," Kirin offered.

"Have someone get her some clothes." Heavy, bulky clothes that completely concealed her curves. A parka might work, and one of those ski masks.

"It's already being done," Kirin said. Great, Kirin chose her clothes. In that case they would be trendy and that meant they would leave little to his overactive imagination.

"There's no chance she'd talk to me either," Luc insisted, trying to think of a way out.

"I feel she would. She seems pretty disappointed to be dealing with me, but Kirin's probably right and you should stay away for now. I just thought that before your conference with the Usurper you might need more information." Was Andrew goading him? It sounded like a dare. He was being unreasonable. Why wouldn't he be the one to interrogate a prisoner? It was what normally occurred.

"Fine. I get it. I'm going." So much for my great day, Luc thought. He pushed back from the table and headed toward the elevator.

"Luc, wait. I could--"

He spun around and snapped, "You could what, Kirin? Get your nose broken? You two aren't exactly shopping and lunch buddies, remember?" Kirin didn't respond as he turned and continued to the elevator.

Pushing the button, he took a deep breath. The doors opened, the elevator apparently having been on his floor. As he stepped in, he turned to see Kirin and Andrew standing in the corridor talking. They both watched as the doors closed. He couldn't help wondering how they would look if he were going to his execution.

He stepped from the corridor and pressed the key code of the surveillance room, which was only manned when they had unwilling guests present. Cisco glanced up, but Quando continued to watch the terminal in front of him.

"That giant muscle machine has been at this for almost two hours," he said.

Luc walked over and glanced down at the screens that were open on Quando's terminal. One displayed the corridor he himself had just walked down and the rest were of Rashid's accommodations, from various angles and distances. The Nubian was presently using the door to the bathing chamber as exercise equipment. It was halfway open. His hand cupped over the top, just past the outer corner, he was doing one arm pull-ups, the muscles in his shoulder and arm bulging and flexing with each movement.

"Great. I wouldn't want him to hit me with any less force next time," Luc said. "Although, that's his left arm and he is right-handed."

"He switches arms every half hour," Quando offered, laughing.

Luc grinned and glanced over at Cisco's screen. He quickly realized Nalini was in her favorite spot again.

"She only comes out of the head to eat. Drags a pillow and blanket to the head at night. That's what Emmanuel told me she did in Rome, too," Cisco said.

"She gets creeped out by people watching her," Luc said. Probably too much like home, was what he thought.

"Well, first the lion's den," Luc said, walking toward the door. Cisco stood up to accompany him, reaching to grab a tazer capable of administering 5000 volts from around four and a half meters away. "That won't be necessary. I don't think you even need to come. I doubt he'll give me any trouble while we've got her," he said. Knowing that triggered his next decision, a possible way to avoid seeing her after all.

A few moments later, he momentarily wondered at his decision. Upon entering, the Nubian unbent his knees and stood up to face the door. When he saw who it was, his entire body tensed as though readying to spring, like the lion Luc had suggested. "Come to finish the job, duplicate castoff?"

"If I wanted you dead, I wouldn't have sent them back to dig your sorry ass out of that giant cat litter box," Luc replied softly. He decided to ignore the second half of his comment, for now.

The Nubian didn't respond. "I need to speak to you about Nalini," Luc said. If anything, the man's body became as rigid as steel at his last comment.

"We are done speaking then," said Rashid.

"Would you like to see her?"

A slight movement under his cheeks that revealed his jaw being clenched alerted Luc to the fact that the Nubian was very smart. Rashid was aware of the manipulation coming and resented it. His desire to see her and ascertain her wellbeing warred with his near-manic tendency to refuse disclosure of whatever information Luc was after. The anger flashing in his eyes had less to do with the fact that Luc had shot him in the chest and kidnapped his charge and more to do with the fact that he doubted he would be able to do either one of the things Luc was suggesting. Both were factors in the fists that formed at his sides.

"Yes," said quickly, with cautious resignation.

Luc appreciated the man's self-restraint. He also understood his present turmoil. His reaction would have been the same. Unfortunately, time was not on their side. He needed some solid leverage and quickly if he was to convince Set to change his mind.

Honesty seemed the quickest route, so he said, "I need information, some way to convince Set that he should exchange the book for his only daughter. She seems convinced that he would rather she not return. Is there no one and no way to convince Set to change his mind?"

Rashid didn't move. Luc realized he was probably weighing what Luc had said, considering what was currently transpiring, what he already knew, what he now knew Nalini had disclosed.

"The mother." Rashid's eyes never wavered. He stared unflinchingly into Luc's—quite a feat, considering most men had difficulty doing so when he purposely leveled them with the full force of his stare.

"Nalini's mother?"

"Yes."

There had to be a catch. Rashid wasn't going to give him anything willingly. "Can we get to her?"

"No."

There was the catch. "A message?"

"Perhaps, from the princess. She will never write it."

Did he want Luc to let Nalini send a message? Did they have a code? They must have. How else would they survive in Set's palace? He looked down, considering his next move.

"He will not trade the book for her unless her mother can convince Set to do so. But I do not want her to go back."

Luc's attention flew back to the stoic Nubian in surprise, though he managed to mask it with casual interest.

"Why would you want her to remain a prisoner?"

"I don't wish her to be a prisoner. I wish you to rescue her. Her mother, too."

"Rescue her?"

"She is safer with you than with them. But you already know that, don't you?"

Luc refused to respond, forcing the Nubian to reveal more information. He saw the toll the internal struggle cost the man in the continued rigidity of his frame and in his angry glare.

"I fear for her life. Though I would give my own to save her, I cannot ensure her safety within her father's palace. What must I do to turn her from your prisoner to your ward?"

Luc admired the man's courage in admitting his inability to protect the one person for whom he cared most. He recognized the sincerity in Rashid's eyes and said, "Tell me how to get a message to her mother. You know she will never agree to leave her there. We must arrange for her mother to join her."

Luc saw a flicker of surprise followed by grudging admiration in Rashid's eyes. His accurate assessment of the situation was winning the Nubian over. Though surprised at the turn his negotiations had taken, he found himself disturbingly excited at the fleeting idea of having Nalini as his family's ward. He felt keen regret that he would be unable to do as the Nubian suggested. His present mission was to get the book, and that was what he intended to do.

"There's a young stable boy. He can deliver a message to his sister, Nalini's handmaiden, who could get it to Arai, the other Nubian of your acquaintance. He is Astarte's bodyguard." Rashid looked at him with hopeful expectation.

Luc nodded. "I'll arrange a meeting between you and Nalini later," Luc said on his way to the door.

He stood in the corridor, considering his options. The Nubian had not lied. Luc was unerring in his ability to detect deceit. The facts, Luc knew from centuries of negotiating and manipulation, masked the real truth. Truth, at least in the minds of those who believed it, generated motivation. Manipulating the motivation of key players was the way to control the power. They had been playing that game quite successfully for millenniums. And Nalini had been keeping herself safe in her father's household for centuries. There was no reason to believe she would not continue to do so, he assured himself.

From what Rashid had said, Luc realized Set's Achilles heel was Astarte, not Nalini. That had never occurred to him. He had a hard time believing Set considered any woman as more than a means to his own ends, existing solely for whatever use Set imagined or desired. That was certainly the impression Nephthys, Set's first wife, had given them when she fled from Set to their protection.

If Astarte was the means to getting Set to trade the book, Luc needed to convince Astarte that Nalini's life depended upon it. Unfortunately, to do that he did need to send her a message. This also meant he couldn't avoid speaking to Nalini. He took a deep breath, walked down the corridor and pressed in the key code.

Once inside, he went to the bathing room and knocked on the door. It opened shortly, and he saw surprise register on her face. She masked it quickly behind a cool unemotional facade.

It was probably the one she most often presented to the world, he thought idly. She was less successful masking the emotion in her expressive eyes. At present they reminded him of irises that bloomed in the early spring. He stepped back and indicated the small table and chairs in the bed chamber with a sweep of his arm.

"I need to speak with you," he said. She moved without argument to the small table and took a seat. He sat across from her. "I'm sorry to hear you are unhappy with your accommodations."

"Apparently I will be spending the rest of my life in captivity. I saw no reason for eternal suffering, since you seemed fairly generous in your housing of prisoners. Is that what you wished to speak to me about?"

"No, but a treadmill will be delivered later today, and should help alleviate the boredom." The thought came unbidden that he wondered if she liked to play chess, and he decided she would be very good at it. "Also some books. If you have any preferences, just let one of the guards know. They can send out for whatever you like. I came to speak to you about Astarte."

She studied his eyes, looking for more information. The overhead light flashed off her hair in blue iridescent shimmers. Her pupils constricted where previously they had been so dilated her eyes seemed almost cerulean. His attention moved despite himself to her lips. He glanced up and noted the slight blush to her cheeks beneath her slowly fading tan.

His brief indiscretion caught, he jerked himself to the present and said, "Rashid seems to think she might be…overly worried about you." He watched her closely, this time waiting to judge her reaction. There was no wait time.

"What are you talking about? He has spoken to her? Is she okay? She's not ill or…." She trailed off, realizing that she had said too much. The bond between them was stronger than he first imagined.

If Set would allow, perhaps even order Nalini's whipping, he must surely be evil beyond imagining. The mother and daughter must have become fiercely protective of each other in such an environment. Horus, who hated Set with a passion that as times nearly consumed him, often called him a defiler of women. He claimed Set had once attacked Isis and tried to rape her as well. They all had a hard time imagining anyone trying to force their mother to do anything, let alone that. None of them were surprised that Set had been unsuccessful.

Horus insisted it was true. It was this act that turned them all, finally, against Set for all eternity. It wasn't just his greed and dark, evil ways, as if they were not enough. It was his continued near-hatred and complete disregard for all women, his degrading subjugation of all those he could possess. How had Nalini escaped his vile attentions, Luc wondered. He knew, having kissed her,that she was still innocent in that way.

"Could I talk to her, if only for a moment? I wouldn't tell her anything, I swear. I don't even know where I am. Do this one thing for me. Ljluka, please."

He cursed, silently, at her use of his given name. She was hard to resist. Rising from his chair, he walked to the far wall, turning to retrace his steps and burn off enough surging energy to be able to speak. How the hell could he do this? he wondered. He stopped, and without looking at her, he said, "A phone call would leave a traceable signature. You know that."

"What about a note, a letter?"

"It would be intercepted by Set."

"No. No, there's--" She stopped herself, but not before she had confirmed for Luc that Rashid's suggested method was tried and true. "You're probably right," she conceded.

She had revealed enough to assure him that she and her mother had worked out elaborate schemes to exist in that hellhole. They had a complete network of liaisons. It was how she had avoided being violated. Rape was Set's favorite way to conquer women. It's how he convinced Nephthys to become his first wife. He had raped her, impregnating her with Typhon. Nephthys had tolerated Set until the final Great War. Unable to rescue her son, she had escaped to the protection of Horus, which is where she still resided. Why hadn't Nalini's mother managed to flee with her before now, he wondered. It didn't occur to him that she might not want to. He suppressed a twinge of conscience for the way in which he was forced to deceive them both. They were his only way into Set's palace where he intended to get the book, not Astarte.

"Could I perhaps see Rashid? We would not even speak if you wish, but if only I could see him."

"It will be arranged for this afternoon. Anything else?"

She stood up and gazed into his eyes, obviously grateful. "Do you think you could take me outside, for just a brief while? I-I can hardly breath it is so, so dark and…I am used to being outside and unconfined. Active. I find that I am not very good at continual inactivity. I feel like I am buried alive. That must sound like the ravings of a spoiled woman, but I assure you I am sincere."

Nalini reached out and placed her hand on his chest, and he could barely restrain the desire to step away from the scorching agony. Surely she felt the way his heart threatened to burst from his body. Her gaze was as pleading as her voice had been and he was undone. He found himself unable to deny her this one small pleasure. Besides, he told himself, it would be easier to pressure her to write a note to her mother, one that he would later add to, if she were in a better frame of mind from the fresh air.

"I'll try. I do not see how it will be possible, so don't hope for it too much."

"Don't worry," she said softly, pulling her hand from his chest, which he then instantly missed. "I never hope any more."

And he knew she spoke what she believed to be the truth.

"O Lord of Amentet,
I am in thy presence.
There is no sin in me.
I have not lied wittingly.
have not done aught with a false heart."
-   The Book of the Dead

274

Chapter Twenty-Seven

"Okay, now, take off the blindfold," Luc said loudly, close to her ear. His hand slid around her waist and he pulled her around until she stood before him, and then drew her against himself. She hesitated. His solid presence behind her, so intimately close and protective, held her entire attention, and caused a sudden tightening in her lower abdomen. Resuming her movement, she reached up to tug at the scarf, the metal clink of her cuffs unable to be heard above the roar of the water. The scarf came down and hung around her neck, freeing her vision. Air rasped in her throat as she sucked in her breath and held it.

Survival reminded her to release it and take another and another to restart the natural sequence. "It's so-so green," she shouted in amazement. "Everything is so alive." Turning her head, she found the waterfall whose thunderous power she had heard for some time. It plunged over the precipice and disappeared into a cloudy vapor of mist and fog and magic that prevented her from seeing where it filled the hungry belly of the river below. Nalini had never seen such plush plant life or so much rushing water.

She could detect the flow, separate the crashing liquid collision of water into the canyon below from the sound of the powerful surging here at the top. It was a long way off, echoing through the canyon. They were standing near the edge, which explained why he held her so firmly, so closely. Though it occurred to her momentarily that he might have positioned her here to prevent any attempt to disarm him and flee. Could he know she had requested this outdoor visit to evaluate her situation, scout the logistics and plan an escape?

He pointed and she followed the direction of his finger to where loud monkeys of a variety she couldn't name leapt and swung and groomed, completely oblivious to their presence. It was paradise. Surely the tree of life sprang from this soil.

Dragging her thoughts back to her responsibilities, she thought of Rashid, wanting him in on any strategic planning and shouted above the roar of water, "Please, can I not share this with Rashid? When would he ever have the opportunity to see this again?" The thought genuinely pleased her, despite her duplicitous request, and she turned in Luc's arms and looked up at him pleadingly. He stepped back and drew her from the edge.

His hand again on her waist, he continued moving away and she noticed the men surrounding them in the unusual forest, visible and then not visible. This strange land had lush foliage and hanging mosses and flowers that grew from trees. Here too there was a shifting fog, wafting through the trees, rising and falling away and undulating around them. All she knew so far was that she must be miles from any civilization. Would survival be possible even if she were to escape?

"How can you guarantee that he would not try to escape and take you with him, or harm one of my men?" He was stalling and she knew it, but held out hope that he was going to agree. Or was he letting her know that he already knew what she was trying to do?

"Because I will give you my word, and will tell him that I have done so."

Their negotiations were interrupted by Kirin. Nalini watched her approach through the mist like an apparition. She was astonished at the surreal beauty and elegance of this woman who not so long ago had attacked her like an angry market vendor. Kirin resembled her mother, she noticed, but where Isis was statuesque, Kirin, though slender and long limbed, was only a few inches taller than Nalini. Moving through the forest, the earth-bound clouds made her appear to float rather than walk, a graceful forest nymph. Her hair, thick and layered, fell in soft waves to her waist and gleamed like molten bronze with flashes of red as fiery as Rā's glory. It radiated around her like a beacon. Though not as small as Nalini, she seemed even more diminutive with that dark, brooding, muscle-bound brother, Anubis, in tow. If nothing else, Nalini now knew the direction of the waterfall from the holding site.

The approaching siblings stopped in front of them, and the woman, Kirin, yelled, "So what do you think of the landscape?"

Just like that, as if the last time they met she had not been held back like a mad woman who wanted to claw her eyes out. "It is very beautiful and very different from my home," Nalini replied loudly, noting that Kirin's eyes were deep green, an earthy yet somehow icy color compared to the fire of her hair.

"I'm sorry we got off to such a bad start. You must understand that I am rather protective of my brothers."

The woman's tone and the sincere look in her eye made Nalini believe her. But of course she didn't understand. She also didn't understand how fanatically the woman's brothers protected their sister. However, the woman was making an effort to be sensitive. Why? "Thank you for the loan of your clothing." She knew it had been borrowed from Kirin. The pants were cuffed at the bottom, but otherwise the fit was not too bad. The warm-up suit was much cozier than the other clothing they had provided.

"You're welcome." The woman was now studying her brother, Luc. Perhaps they had some prearranged agenda.

"She wants the Nubian to see the forest, Andrew. Would you explain why this is not possible."

"What? It's not bad enough that you have her out here? When we saw you in the security cameras, we--are you nuts?" he asked, abruptly turning his attention to Nalini.

Nalini's heart stopped. Would the dark one persuade Luc to keep Rashid from coming outside? She needed to see him, to make eye contact and somehow signal him. In their only brief meeting she had managed to make him agree that they would strategize an escape.

He looked back at Luc and snapped, "I came to make you bring her back inside. You know damned well it's too dangerous. What were you thinking?"

"I was thinking how much I would hate being confined day after day."

"Here," Nalini said, slipping off the large purple gemstone from the first digit of her left hand. "Show this to Rashid and tell him I said to do nothing, only obey, that you will bring him to me for some fresh air too. He will understand."

Luc took the ring and studied the intricate ancient setting, the beauty of the diluvium tanzanite, mined long before the modern world even knew of its existence. The fact that the color closely resembled her eyes didn't escape him. He handed it to Andrew, who took it and examined it briefly.

"A pretty bauble, but I fail to see how you think it would make me believe anything you have to say."

"I do not lie," Nalini said indignantly. Then, she shivered as if someone had walked on her grave and said, "It is cold here." In truth it was at least twenty degrees colder than what she was used to, but she reacted to a premonition not the temperature.

"Once you get used to it, it's fairly mild. The temperature is around 68 degrees year round," Kirin informed her.

"Like living underground," Nalini said. She thought of the dark tunnels her mother had taken her to as a child.

Luc exchanged a look with Kirin and shook his head slightly. Nalini pretended not to notice and wondered what she was not to know, but instead asked, "What is the name for those monkeys I saw?"

"Howlers."

"It is fitting," Nalini said, laughing.

Kirin pointed above her head, toward something behind her and Nalini turned to see a bright red and black bird squawking in a nearby tree.

"It's a *Rupicola peruviana*," explained Kirin.

Nalini turned back to look at Kirin and saw Anubis arguing with Luc.

"Okay, you win," she called out. "Just let me see the waterfall once more and I will go back to my cell." She turned toward the falls, hesitated and glanced up at Luc. He nodded approval and she walked back the way they had just come. Sooner or later the cloud cover must surely lift and she would be able to see if she could make a jump. She and Rashid had once jumped from a cliff in Africa, escaping from some of Horus's flunkeys. She recalled the incident well.

This time she didn't go as close and Luc didn't touch her, though he came to stand beside her. Kirin stepped to her other side and she pointed to the monkeys across the canyon, laughing at their antics.

"Does the mist ever clear so you can see to the bottom?" she asked Kirin. Anubis, she noted stood behind her, well away from the edge. He was not very trusting, and incredibly strong and deadly with his hands. She had seen him in action and realized he was a formidable enemy. His brother, Luc, on the other hand was even more dangerous. He was good at communicating ideas and convincing people of his logic. He was also good at manipulating her emotions.

She had to get away from them, and soon.

"Sure. You can frequently see the entire valley from here," said Kirin. Instantly Anubis was at her side, whispering in her ear. Clearly she was unused to the intricacies of espionage or subtle unwritten laws of warfare. They must keep her sheltered from the ugliness of the world outside her nuclear family, Nalini decided. Anubis was having difficulty controlling his growing impatience with his brother, she thought, seeing the look of irritation he darted toward her.

Luc apparently saw it too because he said, "I think it best that we return now." Then he paused, tilted his head as if listening, though what he could hear through the blast of the water would not be much. Suddenly he said, "No, no, something is not right. Back! Back, now!"

Without question, Kirin and Anubis turned to comply. Nalini, confused, glanced up at Luc. He had the strangest look of disbelief on his face. Clutching his chest, he stumbled backward. A crimson stain spread outward from under his hand. She heard Kirin scream, and Anubis rushed to Luc's side. Then his back arched and he flew forward, into Luc.

Nalini instinctively reached out toward Luc, realizing too late that he had been shot. He looked directly into her eyes and then she watched in horror as the brothers tumbled over the side of the precipice.

This explained the feeling of premonition she had experienced earlier. She looked toward Kirin, who had stopped screaming, because Lucien had punched her jaw hard enough to knock her unconscious. "Run, you fool!" Lucien yelled at Nalini, throwing Kirin over his shoulder. He took off into the forest, the opposite way in which she had come. She watched, shocked into momentary immobility.

She thought fleetingly of Rashid, but having no choice at the moment she regained control of her limbs and sprinted after Lucien.

I can't let him take her, she thought. He might have good intentions, might actually think she'd make him a good wife. But he was so very wrong. Kirin would never survive in Set's house of dementia. She would kill herself, nightly, rather than submit to Lucien's lust. And her brothers would never, ever stop trying to save her—if they were able to recover their bodies. Where would Lucien even keep Kirin if they made it home? The dungeon? Oh, this was going to get very, very ugly, Nalini thought, feeling fear like a vice squeezing her heart. She knew with sudden clarity that their lives would never be the same. Though she did not know how it could get any worse, she still dreaded the unknown.

Just ahead of her, Lucien was tossing Kirin into the back of a jeep. Lucien got in beside Kirin, sliding her into the middle. Nalini got into the front passenger side. She no sooner shut the door than the vehicle took off. They were far enough away from the water for her to hear the shouts and gunfire coming from behind them. A row of jeeps, she saw, were lined up behind this one, which had left them behind for now.

The man driving was one of Lucien's, an Arab whose name escaped her at the moment. He was talking through an earpiece to someone. She reached to pull out the seatbelt after the jeep went over a dip hard enough to bump her head against the roof. When she looked into the back, Kirin was just waking.

Nalini stopped what she was doing to watch. Kirin's eyes focus by degree, and at first when she saw Lucien she looked relieved. Then just as suddenly she was angry, having realized it was Lucien and not Luc who leaned toward her.

"You son of a bitch!" she screamed. Lucien reached into the back of Nalini's seat and pulled out a roll of duct tape. It didn't help him when Kirin decided to punch him in the eye the moment he turned toward her. She elbowed him in the gut, and then managed to punch him again before he grabbed her wrist. He wrapped duct tape around one wrist, then snatched the other as it approached his face, brought it down and bound it to its mate. She continued to struggle. Nalini was quite impressed, realizing that Kirin's brothers had seen to it that her keen instincts for survival were coupled with at least a minimum of self-defense tactics.

"Hold still or I will have to hurt you!" Lucien yelled. It was disturbingly familiar to Nalini. She found herself silently rooting for Kirin, the weaker female being overpowered by the brute force of a physically stronger male.

Her brother bent down to tape Kirin's ankles together. The entire time, Kirin was swearing at him, now in ancient Akkadian. Lucien sat up, stared into Kirin's eyes for a moment, and reached out to grasp a handful of her hair. He looked at it as if fascinated by the color, rubbing it between his fingers to feel the fine texture. Then he drew it to his nose and inhaled. The intrusive intimacy of the gesture sent Kirin into a ballistic rage. She swung her bound hands at him and tried to bash him on the side of the face. He easily grabbed her hands and leaned against them in her lap. Then he stilled her tirade with a kiss. It was not gentle and probing like Luc had been with her. Instead it was aggressive and demanding, invasive. Kirin struggled to pull her mouth away.

Lucien finally lifted his head and before Kirin could respond, he slapped a line of duct tape over her mouth.

"You have to let her go," Nalini said.

Lucien, surprised, turned to look at her. "Why? I thought you said you hoped for my marriage to her."

"That was before I knew anything about her, Lucien. She's not for you. She will make you miserable. A spoiled, pampered child, prone to temper tantrums. This cold wet, damp place is the only place she ever wants to live. She will hate the desert."

"Her brother and father live in the desert. She must visit them."

"Yes, she visits, but she lives here."

"She will adapt."

"There is no way she will ever agree to be a true wife to you, Lucien."

He understood her meaning. Looking again at Kirin, he said, "I will change her mind about that, too. I will not care how long it may take to do so." Kirin tried to strike him again. He caught her hands and chuckled.

"She will hate you, Lucien."

"She has fire, but I will tame her. It's a challenge I will enjoy." He was studying Kirin as he spoke.

Nalini rolled her eyes, and turned around. She fastened her seat belt and crossed her arms. He would do well to recognize what was in Kirin's eyes. Lucien refused to see the violent hatred in those emerald depths. Why should he? All they had been raised around was fear and anger. He would not understand the deep unconditional love Kirin's family had for each other. Nor would he understand the vindictive revenge this woman was now capable of. As far as Kirin was concerned, Lucien had just killed two of her brothers. Regardless of whether or not they would recover, they had suffered terribly and she would want her pound of flesh. Nalini had seen enough to realize Kirin was capable of getting it.

All is not lost; the unconquerable will,
And study of revenge, immortal hate,
And courage never to submit or yield:
And what is else not to be overcome?
                    John Milton, Paradise Lost

Chapter Twenty-Eight

"We know you can uplink telepathically to mommy dearest and already have. But Kirin, Mommy can't help you right now. You have to start using your own brain, because Set is going to want to suck it dry."

Kirin looked at her soberly and nodded.

Glancing across the plane, Nalini watched the Arab who had driven their jeep grab hold of the stewardess's ass. As the young girl tried to sidestep him, he grabbed her arm and continued to fondle her.

"Not here and not now!" Nalini shouted in Arabic. "I am trying to eat, you flea from a camel's backside!"

The soldier let the woman go, but she faintly heard him mutter <u>sharmoota</u>, bitch, under his breath. Before Nalini could react, Lucien was out of his seat, tray on the floor, and across the plane. The knife from his belt already in his hand, he drove it into the man's throat. "You dare speak to a daughter of the royal bloodline in such a manner?" he yelled in Arabic, twisting the blade. Spitting at the man whose blood first spurt and then slowed to a steady drain, he added, "Worthless dog! Son of a whore!"

His first lieutenant was standing behind him, though Nalini had not noticed him move. Lucien said, "This bloodline and all memory of it and its ties to the royal bloodline shall be wiped from the face of the earth for all eternity!" He glanced at his lieutenant, who was already moving. Jerking a man out of a seat just behind the cockpit, the officer threw him to the floor. The man cried out for mercy as the lieutenant extended his hand toward the man next to him, accepted his offered scimitar and raised his arm.

Kirin was spellbound with horror. Nalini as warned, "Look away, Kirin!"

But it was too late.

The officer swung his arm downward and beheaded the cowering man with a single stroke.

"His brother," Nalini said softly. Kirin clenched her eyes shut. "By the time we return his entire family will no longer exist and all reference to their names will have been removed from all data bases as if they never did. It is the ultimate punishment and mandatory for insulting a member of the royal bloodline."

Kirin chanced another look at Lucien. He was nodding to another of his officers. The man tapped his earpiece and began speaking in Arabic. "Like I said, it'll be over before we arrive," Nalini explained.

Pulling up the shirt of the man who bled out before him, Lucien found the edge and wiped off his knife on a dry spot. He then sheathed his weapon, pointed to the man next to the corpse and said, "Remove this abomination from my sight." Turning, he casually walked back over, stepping around the stewardess who was busily cleaning up his spilled tray, and said, "Bring me another."

Nalini forced herself to continue eating, wondering how Lucien could have mistaken the man's comment to the stewardess to have been directed toward his sister. But more likely it was a disciplinary demonstration for his men more than an act of justified outrage. She handed Lucien a pear as a diplomatic expression of thanks, and glanced at Kirin, who looked as if she might throw up, and said softly, "Remember, we're the nice ones."

*"There are a thousand forms of evil;
there will be a thousand remedies."*
                    Ovid, Metamorphosis

Chapter Twenty-Nine

They laid each body on a long, narrow table.

"Get them undressed. Quickly!" Isis commanded. The men, themselves dressed in preserve ranger uniforms, were visibly nervous as they entered the subterranean chamber bearing the bodies of their sacred leaders.

"They must be bathed and anointed with sacred oils," she instructed, indicating clothes and basins of herb scented water and the oils she had placed on a nearby service table. She moved to Anubis, softly brushed his damp hair from his forehead and said, "Turn him."

Once on his stomach, she placed her hand over the deep wound on his now naked back. She closed her eyes in deep concentration. The men rubbed heavily fragrant oils into his chill, bruised flesh. She lifted her hand and dropped the collapsed bullet onto the table. The men watched in solemn awe and fascination. She knew they had heard the secret legends, passed down through the generations of their families, but for most it was the first time they had actually seen the wonder of immortality.

"Now, wrap him with these bindings, completely," she commanded.

She moved to the table on which Luc's body was laid out, already anointed with oils. Placing her hand upon the wound on his chest, she repeated the procedure. Turning to see that they had moved Anubis onto his back and had just begun winding the bindings that covered his face, she moved to stand at the head of the table. They finished fastening the last wrap and she held her arms out across Anubis' mummy-wrapped body. She spoke a secret incantation in a language none of the men understood. *"Sāhu, I call thee back to thy worldly realm. I, Isis, daughter of Rā, wife of Osiris the anointed head of the royal bloodline call forth from the arms of Rā, Sāhu. Sāhu, say ye unto Rā, ye who shall sprout like plants: My flesh flourisheth. I exist, I exist, I live, I live, I flourish, I flourish, thy soul liveth, thy body flourisheth by the command of Rā himself without diminution, and without defect, like unto Rā, for ever and ever."*

Again she moved to the head of the table upon which Luc's body rested, and repeated the incantation. Just as she finished, the men surrounding Anubis gasped, and stepped back from the table. Anubis rose to a seated position. Then his body collapsed. An unearthly shriek sounded, and then another and another, agony upon agony, terrifying to hear. The men stood wild-eyed and distraught, unsure of what to do. Isis stiffened, stealing herself against the audible anguish of beloved son.

"Unwrap the bindings," Isis commanded. They rushed to remove the bindings from his face as if that would ease his suffering. Then they began the unwrapping his torso and limbs. All the while, he trashed and screamed as his body gave birth to his soul.

She didn't have to give directions to those who stood sentinel over Luc's body. Though shaking with fear, as soon as he moved upon the table and started to scream they began unwrapping his bindings.

Luc threw back his head and took a deep breath, shuddering, arching his back and throwing wide his arms. A loud, low moan escaped him and he writhed beneath the sudden agony of rebirth. It felt as if his life force would erupt through the wall of his chest cavity, and his back bowed again and again against the strain, his hands fisting and opening, seeking some small moment of pain-free solitude. He turned his head from side to side, gasping, and cried out, "Rā!"

Too slow and gradual was the relief, and too lingering was the pain, but at last Luc could think beyond the torture that lessened finally to an ache where suffering had been. He stood with the aid of helping hands, and raised his arms, allowing the men to drop a robe over his head. They bowed their own heads, touched their hands to their foreheads, then, wrists crossed, they moved their hands to cover their hearts. "Ljluka, royal prince of the true royal bloodline, honored and beloved of Rā," they said in unison.

He looked across the room at Andrew, scattered images tumbling through his mind: Nalini laughing, animated, Kirin, emerging from the forest as though part of it. Pain, hot and searing, Andrew, shouting his name, Nalini reaching toward him, tenderness and disbelief in her eyes, Kirin screaming, Andrew rushing forward, falling, pain, falling, nothing.

Mother? What has happened?

Calm yourself, my little owl. You need to eat and drink, refresh yourself. Then we will discuss what needs to be done. Come, join your brother, Anubis.

Obeying, instinctively, Luc walked across the room. He fell into step beside his brother and followed his mother toward the door. Glancing at the twin tables and the mummy-type wrappings on the floor, he realized that Isis had performed an eternal life ceremony and wondered vaguely how their bodies got so damaged, or why she wanted them to recover so quickly.

He reached up to feel the golden ankh that hung from a chain around his neck. It had been placed there by Osiris when he reached manhood. A strong tug on the bottom of the icon and it separated from the upper portion, becoming a small but deadly dagger. Life and death must always be equally balanced, his father had said. They were but different phases of an eternal cycle.

"What must we do, mother?"

"Since the Usurper will want Kirin to work in his research labs, there is only one thing he wants above all others. He needs the incantation if the Book of Life is to be read."

"Where is it? We'll fetch it at once," said Andrew.

"In the Underworld," said Isis. Her gaze shifted away.

"What? Then no one can get it! What else can we do?" Andrew demanded.

"It is our only option," she insisted. "And it not impossible. Ljluka can do it."

Luc, shocked to think his mother believed he could survive a trip to the Underworld, stood up and said, "I have no choice then. We must save Kirin,"

"If there were any other way, you know I would not ask this of you."

"I must go too, mother. You must find a way." Andrew's voice sounded desperate.

"You will accompany him there, but he must make the decision to take the journey alone." Luc thought he saw tears in his mother's eyes. Regret too. She refused to meet his gaze and added softly, "If he survives, he too will be forever changed."

If he survived, Luc repeated to himself. Even Isis doubted his success. "So be it," he said without hesitation. "My love for Kirin has already made the decision. She would do the same for me, without question."

"Yes," Isis said softly, "she undoubtedly would."

"No! This is suicide, a death from which you cannot return, little brother! We wouldn't be able to retrieve your body! Mother, you cannot refuse to let me accompany him. It doesn't make sense." Anger sounded in Andrew's voice, and not just annoyance that he would miss out on an adventure.

"Anubis! You yourself know that if he does not go alone he can never return from the bowels of the Underworld. And you know why."

"Then let me go. I am stronger. It should be me."

"Do you think this is what I want?" she said, her voice breaking as she wiped away a tear. She reached out to draw Luc into her arms, resting her cheek against his chest. "Ljluka has a different kind of strength, Anubis." She stepped back and cupped his face in her hands, finally meeting his gaze so he could see the raw anguish in her eyes. "This time, it is his cunning and wisdom that are needed, along with his courage and inner strength. He may be the only one capable of retrieving it and bringing Kirin home to us."

She fell silent then, as they all thought about the fact that should Luc fail, she would lose two of her children forever.

Luc shivered, feeling a footfall upon his grave.

Through Me Pass into the Painful City,
Through Me Pass into Eternal Grief,
Through Me Pass among the Lost People.

Justice Moved My Master-Builder:
Heavenly Power First Fashioned Me
With Highest Wisdom and with Primal Love.

Before Me Nothing Was Created That
Was Not Eternal, and I Last Eternally.
All Hope Abandon, Ye Who Enter Here.
Dante Alighieri, The Divine Comedy

Elizabeth Alsobrooks

298

Chapter Thirty

They drove through sand that looked more like shallow rust-filled water that rippled outward like a puddle stirred by a breeze, but onward for endless miles like an ocean. Displacing the wind-regulated ripples, the spray of it splashed up behind the Land Rover creating a mist of impenetrable soot. For hours their visibility was limited. In truth the small caravan produced a sandstorm of minor proportions.

"You didn't get much sleep," Andrew commented, glancing sideways at Luc.

"Not much," Luc agreed.

"Been a while since we saw father."

"Too long." Luc tensed. Andrew didn't make small talk. He was leading up to insisting that Luc allow him to take over the mission, and Luc had no intention of doing so. This journey called to him. It was meant to be, fated as their mother decreed.

"I'm not comfortable with this," said Andrew.

"Yeah, I'm sick of this gritty shit, too," agreed Luc, purposely feigning confusion.

"You know what I'm talking about."

"Yes," he admitted, hoping Andrew would drop it.

"New color. More orange in it than the last grit." Andrew said idly, deep in thought.

"Yes," Luc said again, gazing out at the horizon and watching the sun surrender at last and fall from the sky to splash like molten lava against the scorched sands in the Valley of the Blazing Sun.

"Dammit, Luc!"

"Let's just wait until we talk to father, Andrew." His tone indicated no compromise. Andrew would know the subject was to be dropped.

"I'll wait that long," he said, indicating his reluctant acceptance. "We'll be there in about twenty minutes. It'll be about an hour trek. Pretty damn hot today."

"It'll be cooler by the time we arrive. Sun's setting now."

"Finally, yes. Gorgeous display. Ironic really."

"Looks like Kirin's hair," Luc commented.

"I was thinking the same thing," Andrew said softly.

"I wonder what she's doing right now?" Or what's being done to her, he thought but didn't dare put into words. To say it aloud would be to admit it might actually happen. He couldn't face that possibility.

"We'll get her back, Luc. Mother said she'd be coming home."

"Yes. I won't fail, Andrew. I can't, there's too much at stake."

Andrew slammed his hand against the steering wheel. "I can't stand feeling helpless. I should be doing something. Anything."

"You are doing something, Andrew. I couldn't do this without your support."

"Seems like that's all I do lately," Andrew said, his voice thick with frustration.

"You're not whining, are you?" Luc asked, teasing him out of his foul mood.

"Fuck you, little brother." He glanced over and grinning, acknowledging his brother's intentional manipulation.

"There, you see how supportive you are?"

Andrew laughed, giving him a friendly punch in the arm. "I do what I can," he said. Pulling up to a rock formation, he parked the SUV and switched off the engine. Several more vehicles lined up beside them.

Luc swung open the door and reached for his water bottle. It was attached to a strap that clipped to his waist. He also grabbed a headlamp like those used by sports enthusiasts. It was lightweight and halogen, attached to an elastic adjustable strap that fastened around his forehead and freed his hands for the rough climb ahead in the near dark. He stood up, shut the door, checked the pistol in his holster, the knife in his boot and the other one strapped to his belt.

"All set?" he asked Andrew.

"Fine by me. Everyone else ready to go?"

Roscoe walked over and said, "Sure. It's dark so I can't see down. I'll be fine."

Luc laughed and started up the mountain. They wouldn't need any climbing gear, just a good pair of gloves and tough hiking boots, which they had. He switched on his headlight and focused the beam downward, a little ahead of himself.

For nearly half the trek they were able to walk, stepping up from stone to stone, using their hands to stabilize themselves. Then it became a little more complicated and they needed to pull themselves up, climb onto a ledge, then stand and pull themselves up again to the next level.

An hour after they started, as Andrew had predicted, they arrived at the narrow indentation. Siding up to the wall, Luc stepped into the crevice and reached his hand out to press on the stone in the correct location. It swung open and he stepped into the chamber beyond and waiting for the rest of the men to join him.

Andrew entered next and said, "I wonder how long it's going to take them to fix the entrance below? Trekking up this mountain is a pain in the dark."

"I imagine father will have it done soon. He can't expect mother to come up here this way."

Andrew laughed, nodding his head in agreement. The men having all arrived, Andrew pulled a lever and the wall shut behind them. Luc moved across the rock chamber, found the panel that opened and pressed his finger against the scanner. Soon they walked into a modern, well lit lobby, boasting doors with symbolic pharaohs and queens behind which were modern lavatory facilities. To the right was a small café from which reasonably pleasant aromas drifted. Several groupings of comfortable seating were scattered strategically around the lobby, tables stocked with current magazines and newspapers from around the world.

Ahmed, who was all but an extension of their father, stepped off an elevator and hurried forward. A distant relative, he was immortal like them. His warm greeting was genuine, having known them all their lives. "Your father has awaited your arrival with happy anticipation. He wonders though at the sudden arrangements. His understandable frustration with the workers due to their unfortunate inability to finish the renovations on the lower entrance before your arrival has escalated to some less than satisfactory communications."

Andrew and Luc laughed at Ahmed's customary capacity to make their father's ceaseless, often frenetic energy and belief in perfection--and therefore sometimes unrealistic demands on his staff--seem like normal, even admirable qualities.

"Then let's don't keep him anticipating any longer. His people may not survive all that escalating communication," Luc suggested, walking toward the elevator. Andrew opted to stroll over to the café, point to some meat mixture wrapped in a flat bread, and then to the espresso machine behind the waitress. He glanced at Luc, who indicated he would take the espresso but not the food.

Ahmed turned to the men loitering near the entrance and said, "Please, avail yourselves of anything you desire at the café. If there is anything else you require you have only to ask and it will be provided." Then, he quickly crossed the lobby to join Luc and watch as Andrew wandered over, trying to juggle two espressos in paper cups in one hand while biting into the meat wrap held in his other hand.

The doors opened and Luc took charge of his espresso before Andrew could spill it. They stepped into the elevator and Ahmed pressed the ground level button. Almost at once the elevator sped downward. "More modifications," Luc observed, chuckling as Andrew jerked back and quickly lowered the steaming cup from his mouth.

'Father has no patience for slow machinery," Andrew said, joining in his brother's amusement, even if it was at his expense.

The doors opened to reveal another lobby, but this one didn't bear a resemblance to an airport waiting area. Noticeable before they even stepped from the elevator were breathtaking mosaic murals and splashing fountains. They headed to the left, toward the far side of the spacious lobby, with its vaulted ceilings and masterpiece sculptures, including an unknown free-standing bronze by Donatello. Luc thought the more youthful and less exaggerated figure of Mary Magdalene may have inspired Donatello's later wood-carving of the aged Mary Magdalene, but never had the chance to ask him.

"The place is beginning to resemble a museum," Luc observed.

"Looks more like a mausoleum to me," Andrew offered facetiously.

"A modern pyramid!" They said together, laughing out loud.

Ahmed gave them a shocked look that hinted at the displeasure their father would feel at such blasphemy. He then opened one of the intricately carved gilded doors that led to their father's inner sanctum and stepped back to allow them to enter.

Their father was pacing back and forth across the black marble floor before a wall of monitors. He wasn't paying the slightest attention to them.

"Looks like we don't need a receptionist to announce us," Luc whispered.

"Her timing is impeccable as always," Andrew said.

Luc walked over to a couch and took a seat. Andrew chose a leather chair adjacent, throwing his feet up on a coffee table while he finished his snack. They watched their father continue to talk, or what looked more like argue, judging from the way he came to a stop and folded his arms across his massive chest.

Nearly seven feet tall, like Anubis his hair was thick and dark. He wore it long by today's style standards, just to his chin, though he tucked it behind his ears. His eyes, blue like his sons', were a startling contrast to his dark hair and complexion. Though he now dwelled in this underground mausoleum, as Andrew now apparently called it, he went out riding nearly every day and often moved secretly through the Valley of the Kings after sunset, or visited Thebes. He disliked the tourist element immensely, so rarely traveled to Luxor. Horus's corporate headquarters near Cairo was a frequently visited site, Luc knew, but Osiris never left the Underworld guardianship for long, and never left Egypt, ever.

Seeing his father run his hand through his hair, Luc decided his mother had won. Personally, he had never doubted her. Knowing he would be allowed to undertake the task, he braced himself for the upcoming revelation of just how treacherous an endeavor it would be. From what little his mother had told him—and he had learned to glean more from what she withheld than what she revealed—it would be a near impossible feat, but one he must nevertheless achieve, and quickly.

Osiris turned and looked at his guests. "I'm happy to see you, my sons, but I wish it were under more auspicious circumstances. Excuse me a moment, won't you?" They watched him, silently, as he walked over to a desk, picked up a crystal vase and hurtled it across the room to where it smashed into tiny fragments against the stone wall.

Luc and Andrew both jumped to their feet, and stood watching their father warily, though it was their mother's and not their father's temper they most feared.

"There, that's settled then," he said. Walking over to greet them, he pulled first Andrew and then Luc into a near-painful bear hug. "I'm sorry to keep you waiting. Your mother and I had a few loose ends to tie up," he said simply, as if he had just finished tying his shoelaces. "Please, have a seat. Apparently we need to talk."

Ahmed, who had stepped from the room for a moment, returned with a young Arab who was toting a whisk and dustpan. He quickly cleaned up the mess Osiris had made and rushed from the room. Luc picked up his espresso and took a long swallow. Osiris took the chair opposite Anubis. He wasn't even mildly angry, so Luc wondered at his uncharacteristic display of temper.

"Where to begin? First, Anubis, your mother is right about one thing, this is a trial Ljluka must undertake alone. Eventually, my son, you will discover the truth behind my decision, which I assure you is not taken lightly. But then there is my little Kirin, more lovely than a desert sunset, so sweet, so innocent in all of this. How can I not save her from the clutches of that vile bastard?"

He jumped up from his seat and snatched the limestone bust of Horus--as the Egyptians had depicted him--from the side table and hurtled it through one of the screens across the room. "Did I mention that your mother would have come, but that my incompetent workers have not yet finished--" The brass horse statue followed. Another surveillance screen shattered. "--the renovations to the entrance." Then the lamp took out yet another screen.

"Come, boys. We will go down to the Underworld termination deck and I will explain on the way," he said, his voice calm but his shoulders now taunt. Walking toward the door, he turned aside to say, "Ahmed, you will have to call the technicians in to repair my screens again. They seem to always be going out. If only the workers would finish the renovations perhaps we could get back to normal and my wife would visit me more often." He held the door open and turned to confirm that Luc and Andrew were at his heels. Luc now realized his father was having some dispute with Ahmed—apparently about the completion of the entry--and his twisted sense of humor rather than his temper was to blame for his uncharacteristic behavior.

Not to be outdone, Ahmed fell to his knees and said with Shakespearean dramatics, "Oh great king, beloved of Amon, all shall be as you desire. Please forgive your humble servants for their clumsy mortal ways." He brought his hands to his head, then with wrists crossed, his hands moved to his chest. Osiris stopped, glanced sideways at Ahmed, and said, "Are you auditioning for a job as Ljluka's valet?"

"I wish only to please you in all things, my king, rightfully appointed ruler of the true royal bloodline." The comically exaggerated look of abject subservience on his otherwise classically handsome face made his words farfetched.

"As well you should," Osiris said, refusing to take the bait. "Are you coming with us? Because we're moving."

Rushing, in order to keep up with their father, Andrew and Luc hurried toward the elevator, Ahmed in their wake. The elevator arrived and they stepped inside. Luc cast a quick glance at Andrew and then looked away from the amusement he saw mirrored in his brother's eyes. He realized they were both struggling to contain their laughter.

"Luc, this is your last chance to change your mind, so before you answer with a lot of sentimental reasons for accepting, you need to know what you're up against." His father's words sobered them instantly.

The elevator shot downward.

Luc remained silent. Too soon they reached the lowest floor, ten levels below ground. The doors opened immediately and they moved into a small foyer with a security booth in the far right corner. Another elevator that looked more like a freight elevator was centered in the wall across from them.

"I'm sure Kirin would be better at explaining how the anti-metabolites in the access tunnels have a toxic effect on healthy cells. They are used the same way in chemotherapy to treat cancer, except then they attack mutated cells."

"I've heard of the scientific security methods used to contain the victims of the first experiments, the unfortunate gene mutations which resulted in calamitous mistakes. Everyone knows the ancients created grotesque beings devoid of human emotion or conscience. I know that you use anti-metabolites to block their escape. As Kirin explained it to me, should they break through the barrier and reach the escape tunnel, the anti-metabolites would attack their cells, killing them very quickly."

"Yes, my son. They would eat them from the inside out almost instantly at the genetic level."

"What you are telling me, if I understand you correctly, is that they don't just attack and kill the mutants, but will kill any living organism they come into contact with."

"Yes, now you understand the stakes. Though we have no anecdote yet, we do have a method for keeping the metabolites from attacking a particular DNA strand. But it is only temporary, lasting six hours. An injection has been set to your personal DNA fingerprint. It can't be reset until you have returned. Until then, no one else can come to get you or assist."

"Will I be able to communicate with you?" Luc asked.

His father shook his head. "Because of the metabolic shield we will not be able to communicate with you. You will be entirely on your own, my son. Are you absolutely sure you want to do this?" He realized his father already knew the answer, but was making one last effort to dissuade him. Apparently even his father feared for his survival. Luc swallowed, straightening his spine.

He met his father's troubled look steadily, and said, "Yes, father, I am sure."

Pride shown from his father's eyes, along with concern. He nodded. "I expected no less, my son."

"I need to know how I can find the incantation." Was that hesitation? Luc braced himself.

"It is in the possession of Brontes."

"Brontes!" cried Andrew. "The Cyclops? Wasn't that a legend, father,told to scare young children? If not, what else will Luc encounter? He needs more artillery!"

"He needs only his wits and his bravery, the magic words his mother has taught him, and this." Osiris took something from Ahmed and held out his hand to offer Luc an ancient relic, a long, narrow metallic rectangle bearing an image of a falcon.

"I need to carry Horus' symbol, father?" He turned the hefty rectangle in his hand, studying it. Then, he pulled on one side and as it separated from the larger side, a blade centered in what now appeared to be a handle slipped from the fitted center of its mate.

"They fear Horus," Osiris explained. "It was he who defeated them, and imprisoned them here. But more importantly, it also has that." He pointed to the knife Luc held. "You knew instinctively what it contained," he said softly, as if surprised. Then, "Yes, I see you are thinking of this," he continued, tapping the ankh hanging around Luc's neck. "But this blade is unique. It was forged by the fiery eye of Rā from a metal not found on earth. It fell from the heavens. It will protect you. Only you will know when you must use it."

Osiris placed his hands on Luc's shoulders and gazed soberly into his eyes. "This sense you have, Ljluka, what you call premonition, it is only the edge of your true power. On this quest hold true to your instincts and you will find your destiny even if that destiny is never to return."

"Yes," Luc agreed. It was this sense of inescapable destiny that he had felt all along. "I know I must go, father. This quest is mine alone. As you say, I have an instinct for what will be. I feel as if I have been moving toward this moment for centuries."

"And so you have. Rā be with you, Ljluka, son of my heart."

Andrew stepped forward, and turned Luc to face him. He placed his hands on either side of his face and stared into his eyes. Luc did the same, memorizing, perhaps for all time, his beloved brother's face. Andrew straightened and held his hand over his heart. He then rested it over Luc's, and said, "With you, you take my heart. May it beat in harmony with yours, giving you the courage and strength of a thousand armies. It beats for you, little brother. Bring it back to me."

Luc nodded. Ahmed stepped forward and said, "I will come down one level with you and give you the injection. I can go no further. From there, we cannot tell you where to go. We do not know where Brontes is at any given moment. But be careful, Ljluka. There are all manner of creatures in the Underworld, including cannibals."

Stepping up to the elevator, the mystical blade in his hand, Luc took a deep breath. The doors slid open and he followed Ahmed inside. As he turned, he looked at Andrew's anguished face and said, "I'll see you in less than six hours, big brother."

Where thou shalt hear despairing shrieks,
and see Spirits of old tormented, who invoke
A second death...

Dante Alighieri, The Divine Comedy

312

Chapter Thirty-One

Ahmed reached out and placed a syringe against Luc's neck. "Ready?" Seeing Luc nod, he pulled the trigger and administered the injection that had been calibrated to Luc's DNA. Then, he strapped on a watch with a large digital timer that read six hours. Pressing the button on the bottom of the watch, he saw the readout move to five hours fifty-nine minutes and fifty-nine seconds and said, "A warning will vibrate against your wrist once each fifteen minutes. A sound would alert others to your presence, perhaps at a dangerous time. Take this elevator down. Once it stops you will enter the tunnels and the anti-metabolites will permeate the air." Ahmed fell silent and Luc could detect the apprehension behind his serious expression. "Be careful," Ahmed cautioned. "Remember that as soon as you exit you will be without additional help, but you will also no longer be alone. May Rā bless and protect you."

Luc nodded and typed in the key code his father had given him for the elevator. Not even Ahmed knew this code. The elevator shot downward immediately.

It felt as if he had been going down forever, but according to his watch, it had only been five minutes. Still, it was five minutes of plunging into the bowels of the earth. Five minutes of anticipatory mental damage control.

The elevator stopped.

Complete silence.

He waited, listening.

Then the doors swished open, startling him.

On a *Here I go this is it* level, he said, "Shit. Here goes everything," and stepped through the elevator doors, vaguely wondering if saying it aloud were for his own benefit or to alert anything lurking outside the elevator doors. He switched on the night vision goggles Ahmed had given him, happy that he had extra batteries, though he doubted he'd need them.

The corridor ahead was empty.

He moved cautiously forward, and decided that if anti-metabolites had a scent it must be dust or mildew. The tunnel wound through limestone the color of the desert sands far above. As he turned the first corner, he realized why the corridor was empty. There was a large wooden door blocking the passage, bolted from his side. He read the inscription, *"All Hope Abandon, Ye Who Enter Here"* and smiled at Horus's sense of humor.

Pistol in hand, he reached out to pull back the bolt, and cautiously opened the door.

Something darted around the corner ahead in the corridor too quickly for him to see clearly. He swallowed and took a step forward, wondering if it was waiting for him just around the bend in the tunnel. It had looked like a man in that it ran on two feet, but didn't move like a man. It had been hunched over, its movements slouchy, swinging forward and back from the shoulders, almost like a primitive form of hominid.

Perhaps it was more afraid of him than he was of it. He moved more quickly ahead and encountered his first problem. The tunnel split off and moved in two directions. He stood indecisive for a moment. Then, having an impulse to move to the left, he did.

The tunnels were consistent, nothing but darkness. It was fine by him. He walked for only three minutes before he saw another turn in the passageway. This time the choice of direction was easier. One of the tunnels seemed brighter, greener with his night vision. He slipped up the goggles and confirmed that there was a distant light.

Moments later, he suddenly emerged into a large cavern. He realized he was standing on a ledge that circled downward to the floor of the cavern, and crept closer to the edge to look over. Several meters below him, a fire burned. Around it were creatures such as he had seen when he first entered the Underworld. Stationary and made more visible by the light, he now saw that they were indeed hominids. It seemed impossible that humans had evolved from such creatures.

Turning his attention to the fire, he watched for a moment and discovered how they came by it. A surge of hissing gas ignited by volcanic pressure from a fissure somewhere in the rock below flared on the other side of the cavern--which also explained why it was so much warmer here. He looked more closely. Their fuel at first glance appeared to be wood, but on inspection turned out to be bones. Unfortunately, this also explained what they were eating--the cannibals Ahmed had warned him about.

Luc scanned the outer walls for exits, deciding there must be more than one way in and out of such a large cavern. He saw one. About halfway around the fissure, on the same ledge path upon which he now crouched, there was what appeared to be another opening in the wall. Slowly, staying low, he made his way along the narrow pathway, making sure not to dislodge any rocks to drop below and alert the local residents.

Nearly there, he sensed a presence behind him and spun around in time to encounter one of the inhabitants who had apparently been out grocery shopping. The creature dropped the body he dragged behind him and screeched in rage, lurching toward Luc.

A quick glance below confirmed that the pack was up and screaming, racing to give their support. His decision made quickly, Luc shot the creature in the chest, then turned and sprinted through the exit. Another creature loping toward the opening attacked him with a bone. He averted it with his arm, and managed to hit the creature on the side of its head with his gun. Its thick skull deflected the blow, and it relentlessly attacked again. Luc kicked it in the knee cap and like modern man, it went down.

Hearing the screech of its approaching family members, Luc didn't stick around to finish the job, but instead ran as fast as he could down the corridor, alert for oncoming late arrivals.

Fortunately the creatures were not very coordinated or swift. The sound of their pursuit gradually faded, then stopped. Apparently they had given up or didn't stray too far from their territory.

His watch vibrated for the third time, and Luc glanced down. Calmer, though still anxious, he reached to pull the water bottle from his belt, took a small swallow and returned it. One more glance behind him to assure he was alone, and he continued forward. The tunnel was moving downward, yet the temperature was increasing. Ahead he saw light again, but this time he also heard the hiss and sputter of ignited gases.

Cautiously approaching a narrow opening, he saw that it was another cavern, filled with flame-spurting fissures. There was no access from the slit through which he peered. The room instantly dropped away from the opening by at least twenty meters, so he moved on down the tunnel, seeking an entrance.

There was a split in the tunnel up ahead. It moved in all four directions. Great, Luc thought. Again he hesitated, and then took the tunnel that appeared to run parallel to the cavern. The air smelled gaseous and the temperature rose again. The tunnel turned and then opened immediately into the cavern. He entered cautiously. No creatures were visible so Luc rushed down the pathway. Sensing movement, he turned, but saw nothing. He increased his pace.

The trail moved inward, away from the outer wall and dipped toward the base. He looked upward, toward the rockier sides, seeking another exit to indicate the direction he should take across the cavern, then jumped to his left. A slight rumble had been his only warming before a fissure erupted with flames right where he had previously been standing.

The distraction cost him.

From above, something swooped out of the air and gouged the side of his face with talon-like claws, narrowly missing his eye. He ducked, then dropped and rolled onto his back, raising his gun, searching for a target.

The creature swooped down, arching toward him and he shot it in the head. It fell like a stone. Before he could get up to see what it was, he saw another one enter his peripheral vision from the right. He rolled to his feet and fired, then turned and fired again as another creature attacked from the left. Slow-turning a three-sixty, once, twice, he paused and listened intently, and then relaxed his arm, lowering his gun. While keeping his attention keenly alert for further attacks, he approached the winged fiend that had fallen closest to him and leaned down to examine it.

The eyes, now closed, once glowed as red as the molten lava. Those eyes were the obvious and helpful target he had used for his defense. Sharp incisors curved down over the lower jaw. Four legs with feet that resembled a lizard ended in razor sharp claws. The right front claws gleamed red with his blood. He lightly touched the burning gash across the left side of his face, wiping away a rivulet of blood that pooled beneath his eye, annoying him and threatening to obscure his vision. The creature's skin too, he noted, was lizard-like. They looked, Luc decided, most like the gargoyles on cathedrals, though those had faces like dogs, and these creatures definitely looked more like lizards.

Abdul had not exaggerated. For the first time he allowed himself to wonder if he would make it out in time. He forced a knot down his throat as he thought of his beloved sister, the sister who had always looked up to her big brothers, trusting them to keep her safe. What would happen to Kirin if he failed? And then, as if in a natural progression his thoughts turned to a pair of lavender eyes. They sparkled with delight at the beauty of the cloud forest. His heart fluttered even in remembrance. He wanted more than anything to hear the joy of her laughter. And wanted, too, to feel her respond to his kiss.

Thoughts of Nalini turned his attention from the glowing inner fire of the demon birds. More determined than ever, and not wanting to encounter any more without being prepared, he took a swig of water, then set off at a jog across the floor of the cavern, toward an indentation in the rocks he spotted during his continual scan of the area for additional danger.

Nearly there, he heard thrashing to his left and then a scream of terror. As he drew nearer he saw another of the creatures, attacking a small man. He shot the creature, who fell over and flapped its wings briefly, before dying. The small man, for man he appeared in all but stature, was painfully thin. His arms seemed long for his height and his shoulders a bit too wide. His hands and feet were also big, mainly due to the long length of his boney toes and fingers. Thin as he was, his torso seemed thicker than his limbs and as he ambled toward him, Luc noticed that they continued to sling back and forth with rhythmic motion that was directed by some inner music only he could hear.

"Thank you, human. And as such, how came you to be here in this purgatory of unending misery and despair?"

Shocked, it took Luc a moment to realize that the rag-covered little man who scarcely came up to his waist had actually spoken to him. "I seek Brontes."

Horror stretched the creature's sharply angled features into a distorted mask of grim drama, the image advanced by the solid ebony color of his smallish eyes. "So you have come here to die. Yes, many die here, but still there is Legion. How can this be so?" He turned and began to run toward the opening Luc had seen. He was surprisingly fast for such a small man.

"Wait! I can give you food."

The man stopped, instantly, as Luc had hoped. He spun around. "Food, did you say? You have food? Give it to me? You will give it to us?"

"What is your name?" Luc inquired, wondering at the strange little man's constant use of plural pronouns when speaking of himself.

"I am called Legion. Shut up, fool! No, he asked, I but told him. He has food."

Now the man was arguing with himself. Hoping this Legion was only mildly psychotic, Luc moved forward and said, "If you can take me to Brontes, I will give you food."

"Show me first. No, fool, it is a trick. Brontes will kill us. Brontes will kill us all."

Reaching into a pocket in the side of his pant leg, Luc produced a protein bar. "Look. If you take me to Brontes I will give you this. Do you know where he is?"

Gazing at the protein bar, Legion licked his lips and smiled, revealing sharp, pointed teeth. He reached up to grab at his greasy hair, pulling it straight up, again and again, which explained its troll-like appearance. "Legion knows. No, shut up fool. We will die. Yes, we can take you. No, we will all die! We can take you now. Come, we go now," he said, waving him forward, smiling encouragement.

Luc studied him a moment, felt his watch vibrate, glanced down to see that he had already been gone two and a half hours, and moved forward to follow Legion.

I was not dead nor living. Think thyself,
If quick conception work in thee at all,
How I did feel.

Dante Alighieri, The Divine Comedy

Chapter Thirty-Two

Ambling toward the exit in his unique loose-jointed fashion, Legion turned to see that Luc still followed and darted out into the corridor. He turned right, downward, and Luc kept him always within armslength. The tunnel divided, and it was Legion who without hesitation made the decision to move right.

Luc made the decision to follow.

A slight scraping sounded behind them, like a stick being dragged intermittently across the rock wall. Without turning back, Legion increased his pace, and Luc, unwilling to investigate the source of the noise without cause, joined him. They came to a place where two tunnels intersected, then merged with another, going forth in three directions. The forward and ever downward choice made by Legion was a tunnel in which the ceiling was higher and Luc was not required to dodge and duck beneath low-hanging rock formations.

He wiped at his forehead with the back of his sleeve, and tucked his gun in the front of his waistband while he unbuttoned the top few buttons of his shirt. Up ahead he saw that the tunnel broadened and it appeared to be illuminated. Legion increased his pace as if anxious to arrive.

As they drew nearer, Luc realized that the passage broadened into an enormous foyer-like room, with tunnels intersecting it at odd angles.

The size of the cavern and the height of the ceiling gave the impression of stepping outside from the close confines of a tunnel. This illusion was further emphasized by the star-like glow of florescent minerals deposited in the walls and ceilings.

Far below an active lava flow snaked along the farthest side of the cavern. He glanced down at Legion expectantly, but the man shook his head until his wild hair gyrated. "No, Legion can't go. They kill us. Kill us all. You give us food. Give it to us now."

"I told you after you showed me Brontes." Luc held firm, but began to fear the little man was having a complete mental breakdown. Perhaps he had been lying all along.

"I have brought you. There," he said, pointing to the center path. "Straight down. Brontes will find you. Kill you. You give food now. Not a trick. Fool, I told you to shut up! Give food to us," he said, holding out his hand.

The ground trembled, and Luc glanced down at the glowing river, expecting to see an eruption of molten rock squirting out from the lava tube from where it first entered the cavern before disappearing from sight again further underground. Nothing he could see explained the continued rumble.

"Fool! They kill. They kill us all," screamed Legion and turned to flee.

Seeking the danger, Luc spun around and then jumped aside. The sledge hammer like fist of the ten foot giant he faced missed his head. The thing's body mass was so dense--his muscles rippling in grotesque bunches down his arms and bare chest and torso--that his shoeless feet running down the corridor had actually made the ground tremble.

Legion didn't so easily escape the giant's bull-like charge. The huge creature's attention had turned toward him, and his left fist caught Legion on the shoulder. The force continued downward smashing flesh and crushing thin fragile bones. Legion flopped down, writhing and withering like a ruptured balloon.

Luc jerked the gun from his waistband, glad he had reloaded. He aimed for the great head and let loose three rounds. The side of the monster's head splayed open. Brain matter was exposed and dripping. The beast still turned in his direction.

"Shit, you've got to be kidding me!" Luc shouted, adrenalin pumping. He jumped back and emptied the gun into the broad forehead of the freak. That brought him down, at last, first to his knees and then finally it flopped over and lay still. Swallowing, Luc pulled a bullet from his belt and began the reloading process which was slowed only a little by the slight tremor of his fingers. Dropping a bullet, he retrieved it and pushed his breath forcefully out of his mouth. Then, he clamped his teeth together, finished loading his gun and looked toward Legion. Sudden clarity made him appreciate what fear of the unknown was all about.

He kept the gun in his hand and approached the little man, though he was fairly sure he, too, was dead. Lifting his night vision goggles, he switched them off, now able to see in the light from the cavern. The man's black eyes, like dilated pupils, were still open, but gradually faded to a dull, filmy gray. Then, almost simultaneously, Legion seemed to float above himself like an opaque spiritual replica and came to rest beside his now dead body. Confused, Luc watched as the replica grew still, then slowly solidified, as if taking the place of the now fading original body.

The old Legion disappeared and as quickly the new Legion opened his eyes. He sat up, stared at Luc and said, "Yes, many die here, but still there is Legion. How can this be so?" How indeed, Luc thought in wonder. Legion could only be an example of the regenerative cell structure of the ancient immortals gone horribly wrong.

Luc shook his head and handed Legion the coveted protein bar. So much for split personalities, he thought.

"Food, you give us food!" Legion held it against his chest and pointed to the middle pathway. "There Brontes, like promised." And he turned and ran back the way they had come.

His watch vibrated and Luc looked at the readout. He had only three hours left. If he did not find the incantation soon he wouldn't have enough time to make the journey back, even assuming he managed to obtain it from Brontes.

He took a deep drink of water, and then jogged down the middle pathway. The heat went up with his proximity to the lava flow. Fortunately the center path veered away from it toward the left and narrowed until it intersected with a wider tunnel, with vaulted ceilings. It was a much more comfortable height than the previous tunnel, and Luc was grateful that he was able to keep up his brisk pace without ducking under jagged rocks. He was also able to keep using the natural light since the tunnel was studded with florescent minerals.

Five minutes later, he began to worry that he had indeed been misled by Legion. He noticed that the tunnel leveled out and the temperature began to drop. "No more than five more minutes," he said to himself.

Then, up ahead he saw the tunnel begin to widen again as if he approached another cavern. He inhaled, deeply, deciding that he must be mistaken because the air smelled moist and fertile rather than dusty and decomposed. Opening onto a broad cavern, the pathway dipped quickly downward. Luc halted at the entrance.

Before him was the source of the scents he detected. A pool of water, gurgling in the center as though fed by an unseen stream shimmered near the far wall. From that wall rivulets of moisture trickled down to help maintain the life-giving wetness. Hearing a familiar sound, Luc's head turned to see goats, dozens of them, ranging on coarse but ample plant life. The source of the plants' survival was positioned in the ceiling, a minute but powerful facsimile of the sun, no doubt a gift from Rā. Sunlight, water, plant life, animals, all that the creatures sentenced to dwell here for the safety and sanity of mankind needed to be self-sustaining, he thought in wonder.

He again felt tremors, and turning toward his right he saw the reason. Below him, a giant with one eye centered in the middle of his forehead chased down a goat, caught it, and then turned around and lumbered back toward a cave-like opening that Luc had not noticed.

"Brontes," he whispered.

Checking his watch to discover that he had only two hours and fifty minutes remaining, he ran his hand through his hair and took a deep breath. Gun clutched securely, he ran down the pathway into the valley below.

As he reached the bottom, he moved toward the cave. Back pressed to the rock wall, he inched toward the opening, listening intently. He heard the goat bleat, and then suddenly go silent. Crouching down to give himself a smaller profile, he slowly turned to face the rock wall, and then cautiously positioned his head around the edge of the opening. The Cyclops sat down, heavily, and pulled a leg from the goat. He munched on it happily, still oblivious to Luc's presence. A small fire burned beside him, but it was apparently to chase away the slight chill so far from the active lava flow. He seemed to relish his meat raw.

Scanning the large cave, all he saw was a small stack of bones, and a pile of pelts used as a pallet for sleeping. He didn't see any obvious place for the monster to have stashed the incantation. Dressed in skins he had somehow managed to fasten together, perhaps with a crude bone needle and leather lacings, there seemed nowhere on his person where he could be concealing a papyrus.

With little time to spare, Luc stood up and walked into the cave, raising his arm and pointing the gun at Bronte's head. "I have come for the incantation given to you for safekeeping by my father, Osiris."

Bronte leaped to his feet, growling in anger. He tossed the goat against the cave wall and shouted, "Who dares come to me here, asking for favors?"

"It is I, Ljluka, prince of the true bloodline, beloved by Rā."

"Look around you. Do you see any princes? Rā can't help you here, pup."

"The incantation."

"I have no such magic."

Holding the relic above his head, so that the Cyclops could see the symbol, Luc chanted, "My hiding place is opened. The Spirits fall headlong in the darkness, but the Eye of Horus hath made me holy. I am not a man to whom violence can be done. I shall not die a second time. I am he who cannot be known. I am he who knoweth thee!"

"No. Go away. Leave me in peace!" roared the great beast.

"I come for the incantation. My father has sent me to take it back from you. My brother, Horus has sent me," he added, tucking his gun in his waistband and pulling the blade from the falcon embellished case.

The monster's eyes, widened, and he pointed toward the pile of pelts beside him. "It is there. Take it. It is cursed, as are all who dwell here."

"Give it to me," Luc insisted, raising the knife.

Brontes moved to dig through the pelts and turned back with a rolled leather casing in his hand. "Behold, it lies within," he said, holding it out toward Luc.

Luc slid the knife back into its cover and reached to take the leather casing. As he grasped it, the beast swung his fist and connected with his jaw, sending him flying back toward the entrance. He held fast to the case, but dropped the relic. Before he could pull the gun from his waistband, the Cyclops had reached him. He picked him up like a rag doll and sent him flying back in the other direction.

Luc scrambled to his feet, shook his head to clear his vision, and saw that the beast was nearly upon him. He ran in the opposite direction, fast enough to carry him several steps straight up the wall and then vaulted himself upside down and over the monster's head, landing on his feet behind him. The creature spun around and Luc pulled the gun from his waistband.

The monster was upon him.

Brontes slapped the gun from his hand and crushed it underfoot like an empty aluminum can. Luc cursed in ancient Babylonian, which actually made the creature chuckle. The low grumble reverberated around the chamber. It was not a pleasant sound.

Luc pulled his arm back and delivered a swift martial arts blow to the giant's solar plexus. It all but bounced off, but Brontes was no longer amused. He backhanded Luc like an irritating insect. Luc flew across the cave and slammed into the wall. What had once been his undamaged cheek rubbed against the wall as he slid to the earth, scraping away skin until it nearly exposed the broken bone beneath. He landed in a heap and groaned despite himself.

Though he didn't move quickly, Brontes had Luc by the back of his shirt before he managed to pull himself upright. Again he went sailing, but this time landed short of the opposite wall. He sprang to his feet with supreme willpower and searched quickly for a weapon, realizing he could never match Brontes' physical strength. His attention fell on the fire, and he sprinted forward to grab a smoldering log. Just as he reached down, Brontes, who had been closer than he realized, clutched him from behind and lifted him off his feet, applying increasing pressure to his ribcage.

He tried to free himself by pushing downward against Brontes' arms. His efforts only made Brontes tighten his grip. Luc's breath rushed out and he felt a rib crack. Struggling to stay conscious and think through the pain, he raised a leg and kicked backward with all the force he could muster. Thankfully Brontes didn't have balls of steel. He grunted and dropped to his knees. His grasp loosened just enough to allow Luc a recovering breath of air and the slight leverage he needed to reach out and grasp a log, now within reach. Holding it with both hands, he thrust it backward over his head. It entered Brontes' eye and Luc shoved harder, pushing it into the gray matter of Brontes' brain. The monster swayed for a moment, and then released his grip on Luc. Luc scrambled away.

Brontes toppled like a redwood.

The ground shuddered as it absorbed the force. Luc gingerly turned and noted the log still protruding from Brontes' now lifeless face. He clutched his ribs and calmed his breathing to ease the pressure on his broken bones. The pain dulled to a manageable ache. He held his breath as he regained his feet.

Luc felt his watch vibrate and despite the discomfort, he raced around the cave, retrieving the relic and the leather casing, which he quickly unrolled to ensure it contained the incantation.

It did.

He then sprinted back up the pathway, realizing by the time he reached the entrance above the valley that he now had to retrace his steps in less time, but uphill, and despite his injuries which now included at least two broken bones.

Time and his energy were running out.

Woe to you, wicked spirits! Hope not
Ever to see the sky again. I come
To take you to the other shore across,
Into eternal darkness, there to dwell
In fierce heat and in ice. And thou, who there
Standest, live spirit! Get thee hence, and leave
These who are dead."

Dante Alighieri, The Devine Comedy

Chapter Thirty-Three

Only two hours remained. He still hadn't reached the cavern in which he first encountered Legion. His watch had a tracking device, and he thought he had backtracked accurately. It still seemed like he should have arrived at the third cavern by now. What if the watch wasn't working properly so far underground,?. It had taken him almost two hours to reach the cavern on the way down.

He watched the blinking arrow and moved forward. It was still blinking, indicating that he had not taken a wrong turn. Assuming it was functioning properly. Half an hour later, he finally saw an opening up ahead and realized he had found the cavern at last.

In his excitement, he ran until he reached the opening. Looking in, more cautiously, he searched for flying or roosting creatures. Seeing none, though he doubted he had killed them all, he jogged down the pathway and across the base of the cavern, hoping to reach the pathway across from him that led upward, to freedom.

The upward pathway now directly ahead of him, he heard a voice call out, "Ljluka, why do you rush away?"

Slowing, he glanced to his right, and saw Legion sitting on a small boulder. "You have water, human? Shut up, fool. Do not speak to him. Something for us to drink?"

Luc stopped and checked his bottle. It was empty, though he was sure it had been about a quarter of the way full last drink he took. He wished he had filled it at the pond. "No. No water," he said, realizing he was thirsty too.

"Legion has water. Give you some?"

"There's water here?" he asked, moving closer.

"You have water. Take some. We will."

"No, I have none left. I thought you had some?"

Even for Legion he was making no sense. Instinctively Luc reached for his pistol, remembered that he no longer had it, and instead pulled out the relic. Premonition sending shivers up his spine, he followed instinct now as he slid the blade from the symbolic cover.

Legion stood up, eying the blade. He drew his hand from behind his back and revealed a blade of his own, serpentine and gleaming black, like his eyes. His grin was not a pleasant expression. The pointed teeth opened in a wide smirk to reveal a forked tongue as black, Luc's pulsing instincts told him, as Legion's heart.

He advanced a step and Legion appeared to move around him in a flash of motion. Focusing intently, Luc saw that Legion was actually multiplying over and over until duplicate versions of him crowded the cavern, surrounding him. Only centuries of training kept him from turning to run. The odds had become seemingly impossible, especially given the disadvantage his injuries already provided. But warriors were not trained to accept defeat when to do so would mean death to themselves or others. If he were to die down here, he would not die alone, and he would not die easily.

"We are Legion, for we are many," they said in unison, laughing hysterically, the hideous sounds echoing throughout the cavern.

Luc didn't wait to hear more. He spun around, slicing the throat of those closest to him, nearly severing their heads. The blade was sharper than any he had used. From all sides, they kept coming. He slashed and thrust and jumped and clashed Legion's steel against his superior metal. They stabbed at him and one even managed to bite him on his forearm.

His breath came in heaving gasps that shot waves of pain through his ribcage, and still they came and still he killed them. He let the pain fuel his anger and used the adrenaline to sustain his energy. Another one managed to sneak past his defenses and nicked his arm, just under the shoulder.

The smell. The salty metallic scent he had ignored by habit from the fallen Legions now assaulted his senses, its presence so near and undeniable he surrendered to it. Blood. For the first time, he drew the power inward and then directed it outward toward his enemy. He let it surge his adrenaline to preternatural heights, and fire his fury like the birth of Hades.

He killed.

One, two hundred, three, four hundred he killed.

He reveled in it.

They no longer reached him, bled him, bit him. He was too fast, too angry, too lethal.

He lusted for their blood. Euphoria exalted him, and he slaughtered yet another and another Legion. The need to massacre them all overwhelmed him. He killed and killed and it only wet his appetite for more.

Luc jumped over a pile of bodies and headed toward the upward pathway. Cutting his way through dozens of Legions, his bloodlust fed on their now-desperate frenzy for survival. No longer on the defensive, they fell before his offensive fury like toy soldiers. Their fighting too intensified. All knew there could be only one winner.

Despite his continual annihilation, still they came, still he stepped upon and over the bodies of the fallen. And then, finally, he could see his enemy, could distinguish the forms of the few, the dying and then the conquered. Having reached the top of the pathway, Luc looked back at the carnage in his wake. Hundreds of dead bodies lay sprawled across the floor of the great cave, the cavern running red with their blood.

How was it possible?

It no longer was possible. This time they did not regenerate and drift into another incarnation of themselves. They had used up their reserves. His chest ached with its constant heaving. Thirst burned in his throat.

His thirst was unquenchable, for now.

The watch vibrated on his wrist and he realized he had only thirty minutes to reach the exit, and it had taken him twice that to come this far on the way down. He breathed deeply of the blood, blood that covered his own body from head to toe until he must surely look mortally wounded.

Again the scent invaded his senses and carried him forward with the fierce passion of his intent. Victory at all costs. He ran faster than he had ever run, pumping adrenaline to every cell in his body. He ran with the ferocious zeal of his earlier slaughter.

He didn't slow when he reached the final cavern. Creatures stirred at his passage. One moved toward him as he exited the upward entrance. A closer look at Luc's bloody countenance and frantic expression and the creature quickly pulled back in alarm.

His watch vibrated on his arm.

Fifteen minutes.

His feet barely disturbed the dust below him and he ducked and weaved like a maniacal dancer wound too tight and released without benefit of a tune.

The door.

He raced through it, slammed it behind him and bolted it.

Six minutes only remained.

He sprinted for the elevator, pressed the button. It was there, waiting, and opened on the instant. Inside, he pressed the button and it rushed upward. The doors opened. The watch vibrated, and he fell, a bloody, wounded, exhausted slump.

Andrew caught him in his arms, lifted him up and rushed with him, Ahmed at his side, to the opposite elevator. They stepped in and the doors swooshed shut. Luc could barely hear them. They sounded a long way off.

"I got it, Andrew," he muttered, and lost consciousness.

He awoke what he felt was a short time later, when Andrew pressed a cup of water to his mouth. He gulped it completely and Osiris handed Andrew another. Luc clutched his chest and sat up on the examining table upon which Andrew had placed him. The small clinical room housed drawers and cupboards with glass fronts through which he could see medical supplies. Above the sink to the right of him, he looked in the mirror.

He stared in shock at the sweat and blood spattered face staring back at him. Wide gouges sliced deeply down one side of his face, from the talons of the winged monster. The cheek on the opposite side of his face was all but missing. Even his hair was caked with blood, though little of it his. His eyes looked wild and confused.

"I made it. I made it out in time?" He tensed, uncertain.

"Yes, my son, only just," Osiris reassured him. But his voice was tense with emotion.

"What happened to me, father?" Shaken and past exhaustion, Luc felt disoriented and fearful. He turned from the stranger in the mirror and sought Andrew's reassuring gaze. Finding it, he focused on the constant and reassuring warmth in the steely blue eyes and the tightly wound tension began slowly to uncoil in his stomach.

"What I spoke of," Osiris was saying. "Now you will need to learn to control your power rather than just suppressing it as you have been doing for all these years."

"Now is not the time to speak of such things," said Isis, sailing into the room. He turned his head to the left. She paused when she saw him, as if startled by his appearance. Recovering quickly, she continued across the room.

"We have examined him. It is not his blood. Well, mostly not his, mother," said Andrew reassuringly, though it was unlikely necessary. "He has only broken two bones, a rib and his cheek."

Isis disregarded his hideous appearance and leaned forward to press her cheek against his forehead and said, "You are safe now, my little owl." And with the tender contact and those few words, he felt safe. This was the loving mother who had nurtured him from childhood, soothing away nighttime fears and the first terrible trauma of rebirth when he had fallen from a cliff as a young boy. He trusted her unconditionally with his life, knowing she would do anything, yes, unfortunate or not, anything, to keep him safe. If she said he was safe, it was true.

She stood back and said to Andrew, "Bring him. An herbal, healing bath has been prepared. Have a care for his rib."

Despite Luc's weak protests, Andrew easily albeit gingerly scooped him up again and followed their mother. She entered the elevator and it moved up several floors before stopping. Once it did, she walked across a marble foyer to a set of double doors which opened as she approached.

Hassidim emerged, studying him intently. Genuine tears glistened in his eyes. Terrified of Isis, he said little, but indicated with a sweep of his hand that the bath awaited. Luc vaguely wondered if he would be able to keep from slipping down from a sitting position and drowning, he was so exhausted. His teeth chattered, and Andrew glanced at him, concern drawing his eyebrows downward. He was so cold. Shock, he realized.

"You will be warm again soon, little brother," Andrew said softly.

Quickly ensconced in a nearly unbearable hot tub, he felt immense pleasure and accepted, for once, Hassidim's help. After plunging his face into the soothingly warm water, and tensing as it stung the gouges and abrasions, he allowed Hassidim to smooth away all remaining traces of blood. Hassidim lathered his hair and pulled up the long-hosed rain-shower nozzle Luc had never used before, and rinsed his hair. He then set down the cloth and handed him a steaming cup.

"Orders from the queen," Hassidim informed him. "You must drink it all. At least you look cleaner now, my prince. Your face is still quite terrifying to behold."

"It reflects the terror I beheld, Hassidim."

Luc stood and waited while Hassidim rinsed him off with the sprayer. Smelling like sandalwood rather than blood, Luc then stepped from the tub into the thick absorbent towel Hassidim held out. He walked with assistance from the bathing chamber to the bed chamber and Hassidim quickly rushed forward to pick up a robe and slip it over his head. The sheets had already been turned down. He slipped gratefully between them, easing to a reclining position to pamper his rib and let his head sink into the pillow. The herbs Isis had sent him in the drink relaxed his mind as well as his body, allowing the exhaustion to pull him into a deep, dreamless slumber.

What nightmares remained would catch up to him soon enough.

Now that she dwells across that stream of evil,
She can no longer move me, by that law
Which was imposed when I emerged from there.
Dante Alighieri, The Divine Comedy

Chapter Thirty-Four

Luc leaned back, still weary though he had slept ten hours. Hassidim hummed, stroking the shaving cream from Luc's upturned face with a small dagger, which this morning didn't even make Luc nervous. Hassidim was happy not to have his usual *I'll do it myself* response to everything. This morning Luc accepted the help without complaint. A knock sounded, and Andrew strolled in.

Walking across the room, he stood next to Luc and extended a steaming cup. This is from mother. She said to drink it all, now. Using the warm towel Hassidim had laid across his face to wipe off the last traces of shaving cream, Luc handed the towel to Hassidim and took the cup from Andrew.

"How do you feel?" Andrew asked, hesitantly, apparently unsure of how much he could or should talk about.

"Like I couldn't have survived another moment in that hell hole," Luc responded honestly.

"Another moment and you wouldn't have," Andrew said, resting his hand on Luc's shoulder, as if reassuring himself that his little brother was indeed there and well.

Luc dutifully drained the herbal tea his mother had sent. "Why can't she learn to put this stuff in coffee?" he asked, handing the cup to Hassidim. Remembering something, he said, "You'll never guess what our big brother had engraved above a large wooden door across the last threshold."

"Do I want to know?"

"Sure, it's funny. It said *All hope abandon, ye who enter here,"* Luc quoted, chuckling.

"Only you, and yes, probably Horus, would find that funny," Andrew said.

"You may be right," Luc agreed.

"Am I allowed to ask what you encountered? It had to be pretty bad, judging from the look of you last night." Andrew grasped Luc's chin and turned his face. The gouges were now healed, of course, and smooth skin also covered the opposite cheek. The broken bones were healed, all bruises gone.

"Worse than we even imagined when we were children," Luc muttered, remembrance causing him to close his eyes and shrug his shoulders, one at a time, before turning his head to crack his neck.

"Ugh, stop that," Andrew said.

Luc opened his eyes and looked at him, seeing the warrior's curiosity tempered by concern for his brother. Deciding that openly sharing his experience would be a good way to release it, and already knowing it would reassure his brother that he was indeed safe and pushing the trauma behind him, he began the retelling, finding Andrew a rapt audience.

"A forked tongue?"

Luc couldn't resist a grin at his brother's appreciation for the horror he had witnessed. It made it seem more like an adventure than a never-ending nightmare to him as well. He was glad he had decided to share with his brother. "Did I mention that those gargoyle type things had red glowing eyes, like fire?"

"No, really," said Andrew, leaning forward with enthusiasm. "Do you think they were demons? Tell me more about this Legion."

Hassidim, wide-eyed and terrified had left the room when Luc first mentioned the savage humanoid creatures. He returned and said, "Your mother requests that you join them in Osiris' office."

Luc stood up, somewhat surprised at how refreshed he now felt. Then he remembered his mother's morning prescription. "Thanks, Hassidim," he said. To Andrew he said, 'Come on, I'll tell you about Legion on the way down."

A few minutes later they walked into Osiris' office and Andrew said, "So what do you think gave you the power to do that?"

"That is something your mother would like to discuss with you, my sons," Osiris said, motioning for them to enter and be seated.

Sekhmet was seated next to their mother. She rose as they approached. Pleasantly surprised, Luc moved to embrace her. "Dearest aunt, it has been far too long," he said with genuine warmth and affection.

"Yes, much too long," she agreed, kissing the cheek he lowered toward her.

Andrew picked her up into a great bear hug and spun her around. "Why have you not been to see us sooner?"

"I have been busy, of course. Now put me down," she said, laughing.

He complied, grinning mischievously.

"Sit," Isis commanded. Luc glanced over at her, wondering at her sharp tone. She was very serious, and seemed agitated.

Sekhmet chose a leather chair across from Osiris. Luc and Andrew positioned themselves on either side of the couch. They looked from their father to their mother curiously.

Osiris looked at Isis, who stared at Sekhmet. No one said anything. Then, Iris said, "Sekhmet has something to tell you. It is her secret to tell."

All eyes turned to Sekhmet. Luc felt premonition settle in his spine, stiffening his posture until he wondered if others could sense his tension. He didn't want to hear what Sekhmet had to say. She didn't want to say it. Hesitating, she stood up as if nervous and began to pace, as was their father's custom when agitated. Osiris stood up and walked over to her. He stood before her and she was forced to stop. "The time has come, Sekhmet. He has earned the right to know, and probably already suspects."

She nodded. "Yes, I know you are right."

They glanced at Luc, and he felt the tension work its way into his chest and turn to fear. He too stood and looked at his mother for guidance, as she had trained all her children to do in her presence whenever they sensed fear or danger. She met his eyes steadily, but remained silent.

"What's going on?" Andrew, the less patient of the two brothers demanded.

"We've been keeping a secret from you both. It is now time for us to tell you the truth."

"The truth," said Luc. "Does this mean rather than just not telling us something you have been lying to us? Does it concern Lucien?" He could tell by their snap attention that it did. Sitting down, he admitted, "I think I already know."

"What is it you think you know, my son?" asked Isis.

"You're not my birth mother are you, my queen?"

Andrew gasped. "What are you saying? Of course she's your mother. You're her little owl, the wise one, remember? What did happen to you down there in the Underworld?"

"Father," said Luc. "You slept with Sekhmet, didn't you?"

"No!" Isis was now on her feet, bristling with anger. "Everyone sit down, and Sekhmet, tell the entire story, from the very beginning. Do it, now."

Sekhmet and Osiris returned to sit down in their original seats. Again Andrew and Luc looked at her expectantly. "It began three thousand years ago, before the last great war," she said. "At that time, I worked in the job you now hold, Luc. I was the enforcer. It was still complicated, even then. Before the creatures were sent to the Underworld, they were held above ground, and often escaped or found a way to overcome their jailers. There was also a lot of infighting, tension and distrust. Set had not yet become the Usurper."

Luc glanced at Isis, surprised she didn't comment about Sekhmet's mention of Set by name. He was startled to see her intently studying him rather than looking toward Sekhmet. His attention returned to his aunt with reluctance. Though she was about to tell him what he had longed to know, he also feared the truth. The feeling of premonition that had moved up his spine and then settled in his heart began to squeeze.

"Anubis had just been born, and Isis was busy caring for him. He was a beautiful but demanding infant," said Sekhmet, smiling at Anubis. "I was often gone for long periods of time, so didn't see them as often as I would have liked. During my absence, Set became more obsessed with Isis. He married her twin, Nephthys. I'm sure you have heard the story of how he raped and impregnated her in order to shame her into the union."

She stopped speaking as the wine glass in Isis' hand shattered. Since she had only been reaching for it when her fingers projected her anger over her sister's fate, it shattered over the table beside her. Osirisfound her a towel and returned. "Go on, Sekhmet," he said.

"Yes, continue," agreed Isis.

"You know I am not your real aunt, but because Isis and I have always been close, like sisters, you have called me aunt."

"Because you are our aunt, to us," Andrew assured her.

"Yes, we love you as if you were," Luc agreed.

"Well, because of this bond, Set waited for me to return from visiting Isis one evening and raped me." She glanced away, obviously distraught.

"Please," Luc said, moving to kneel beside her chair and grasp her hand. "Must you continue? It is so very personal and obviously causes you a great deal of pain. Is it something you feel you must share with us?" In truth he willed her to stop. He now realized the truly grim details in his heart, and didn't think he could survive the reality of hearing it out loud.

She clutched his hand, and took a deep breath. "Yes, you know I must say it. I should have told you long ago, but I have been a coward. Isis and Osiris have kept my secret all these years, but they are right and though it is mine to tell, now is the time it must be told." Bringing his hand to her lips, she kissed it and smiled. "I am better now. Please, be more comfortable in your seat." Her insistence could not be denied. Apparently she was unable to go on with him so near to her.

He released her hand with reluctance and returned to the couch and sat down. Isis, he noted, was still staring at him intently, watching his reaction. It made him mildly uncomfortable, but he focused on Sekhmet.

"When I became pregnant," she continued, "Set tried to force me to marry him, but I refused. He finally tried to force his attentions on Isis and the feud between Osiris and Set erupted into full blown war yet again. Set ambushed Osiris and killed him-

"What!" Andrew exploded from his chair, his fists clenched in anger.

"Sit down, Anubus. It was thousands of years ago. Go on, Sekhmet," Isis commanded.

Andrew sat down, but his brow was creased with continued irritation.

Sekhmet said, "Isis was busy finding and restoring Osiris to life. For a time, it looked like Set had won, but I still refused him. Then, Horus was able to defeat Set for good. It was at that time that I was taken to bed, and delivered my sons."

Luc stood up, gazing from Isis to Sekhmet. He saw the truth in their eyes. It was the truth he had suspected since his experience in the underworld. "As the firstborn, I inherited your vampirism, your thirst for blood," Luc said, his fears realized. "And as if that were not curse enough, I am the bastard spawn of that evil monster?" His shoulders slumped in defeat. Everything he knew, everyone he felt connected to, his whole life had been a lie.

He turned to confront the woman so beloved who he had always thought of as his mother and cried, "Mother, Isis, Queen, whoever you may be or not be to me, how could *you* have kept this from me?" Turning from the pain in her eyes, feeling little sympathy for her through his personal anguish and feelings of betrayal, he turned to Osiris.

He opened his mouth to speak, then paused and clutched at his chest. His broken heart became a physical pain. He could barely breathe. "Father no more?" he whispered. His chest heaved with his struggle to draw air. "You taught me to ride, to hunt, to fight, to become a man. I have looked up to you all my life." He drew a deep breath, suppressing the primal rage that struggled to rise to the surface. Taking a few deep cleansing breaths, he calmed himself and continued.

"Your bravery I sought to be my bravery. Your wisdom and kindness to your family, I have always sought to be my wisdom and kindness. How can this lie have so easily tripped from such noble, truthful lips?" His voice grated on his own ears, and he realized he had begun to yell, something he rarely did. To calm himself, he exploded into fast strides, spun on his heel and turned.

Grabbed his hair, he jerked his fingers through it. "You once told me so earnestly that the truth will always try to be heard, and can never be silenced forever. It was how I learned to be truthful." He closed his eyes to contain the indignation of tears, squeezing them shut against the torrent that gathered. "I guess you were right, weren't you?" he murmured harshly. When he opened his eyes, he turned away from the sight of them, of the parents he suddenly felt he'd never known. He focused on Andrew, Andrew who obviously had known no part of this.

Andrew stood up, wide-eyed, tears streaming unchecked down his face. Luc vaguely realized he had never seen Andrew cry. Instinctively he stepped toward him and reached out his hand. But then he pulled it back, realizing that the person he most loved in the world he no longer had the right to call brother.

"Damn it, no!" Andrew cried, seeing Luc's withdrawal. "This is some vile, evil lie. And I don't care, damn you all. He *is* my brother. He is the brother of my heart." And he stepped forward to put his arm around Luc and said, "You will always be my brother, do you hear me? Always."

"I love you the same today…as every day of my life," Luc agreed brokenly.

"Come. We need to talk," Andrew said, and pulled Luc with him toward the door.

"Sons," Osiris said, holding out his hands.

"No!" Andrew yelled. "Not now. Not yet. This is too much. Too much to know. Too much to bear. Hasn't he been through enough?" He jerked open the door and shoved Luc through it, and then followed him from the room.

Sin alone can rob them of their birthright
And render them unlike the highest Good
So that they beam less brightly in its light.

They never can recoup their innocence
Unless they fill up what faults emptied out
By paying for bad pleasures with just pains.
Dante Alighieri, The Divine Comedy

Chapter Thirty-Five

Andrew nudged Luc into an overstuffed chair and walked to the bar. Numb, Luc idly watched as he grabbed a couple of glasses and filled each with four fingers from a twenty-nine year old cask-strength bottling of Port Ellen, a rare find from a distillery that had been closed for decades. He'd been very pleased by the small gift Luc had managed to find him in America.

The significance of the choice didn't escape Luc and he accepted the glass, clinked it against Andrew's and let the smooth single-malt slide down his throat and ease the tension of rigidly suppressed tears.

Setting the bottle down on the table between them, Andrew settled into the chair across from him, and said, "Is there really any reason that anything has to change, Luc? I mean, aside from the knowing, what has really changed?"

"It feels like everything has changed because of the knowing, and especially the not knowing for so long. I don't even know who I am now. Can we believe anything they tell us any more? You remember what I told you, about how I was in the Underworld, so out of control?"

Andrew reached over to refill his glass. "Father said you can learn to control it instead of suppressing it. So there must be a difference."

Luc nodded thoughtfully. He thought about what Osiris had said, drank the last of his whiskey and held the glass out toward Andrew so he could refill it.

"A lot to take in, huh?"

"Yeah, you were right, bro. Too much."

"Hey, you called me bro. That mean you don't mind staying my brother?" Andrew asked.

"Not so long as you don't mind."

"Didn't plan to let you leave the room until you agreed anyway."

"What do you think Horus and K—shit," Luc said, suddenly remembering why they were there in the first place. Feeling guilty about it. Feeling self-centered. In that respect Andrew was right. Nothing had changed. He didn't risk the Underworld for nothing, and time was still a factor if he was to get Kirin back unharmed.

A knock sounded, and Andrew walked to the door. He opened it a crack. "We're talking. It's private. You had your say. Fine. Luc, do you wish to speak to Mother?"

"Whose?"

Andrew staggered back, encouraged to do so by a less than gentle shove from outside the door, and quickly righted his glass so he wouldn't spill any. Luc rose as Isis entered. Without asking, she moved to take the chair Andrew had vacated.

"I think you need to remember something, Ljluka. Even though you feel overwhelmed right now, you need to understand that we love you. All of us. Osiris and I chose to adopt you. That means we chose you for our son. We weren't stuck with you. We didn't just get whatever child happened to arrive after nine months. And we didn't just save you from Set. We adopted you as our very own son. Our *real* son. We raised you with our other *real* children." She was suppressing frustration, unusual for her. He saw the evidence of her very real concern about his feelings and understanding of the decisions they had made.

"I know. I appreciate that. But surely you can see how betrayed I feel about the deception. If I had always known this, as if it were nothing rather than some dirty little secret, I would not feel so ashamed. How can I not feel horrified when you found my parentage so objectionable you kept it from me for three thousand years?"

"He has a point, mother."

She fired a heated look at Andrew intended to shut him up. Andrew's hand flew to his forehead as if she had yelled the command into his thoughts as well.

"Ljluka," she said, leaning forward to grasp his hand. "From the time you were placed in my arms, moments after your birth, when you looked up into my face with those big round blue eyes, so wise, so trusting, so precious, I have loved you as if you were my very own." Her tone was compelling. The urgency and pleading real. Her eyes glistened with unshed tears. But he sensed something more remained hidden, some other truth still struggled to reveal itself. He believed she loved him, but he also knew she was capable of fearful things to protect and hold onto those she loved. It was both a blessing and a curse to those within her family's inner circle.

"I have loved you all my life as well. Surely you know that. It's not just that I mind being lied to—though of course I do. It's the feeling that I can never believe anything else again." The feeling, too, he thought, that they would all soon know how deep her duplicity ran.

She lowered her head and looked down at her feet. "Would it help if I explained that we were trying to keep Set from knowing about you so that he would not kidnap you? Too many people knowing a secret can only ensure it will not remain a secret."

"I get all that. It does help, some."

"Would it help if we also felt you would react as you have, knowing Set fathered you by raping your mother?"

"I can understand your reasoning." Her logic was always flawless, so convincing. He learned the art of diplomacy from her. But the problem with Isis was that she didn't always follow her own advice. She sometimes acted impulsively, as if no act was too extreme if the reasons behind it were good enough.

"Your birth mother loves you, too, you know. It doesn't matter to her how you came to be here. She still loves you--loves you both, actually. I have no such feelings for the other." She looked into his eyes then, expecting his next question.

"What happened that Set managed to get Lucien?"

"He had spies. They told him when she was taken to bed with the pains of birth. He came to take the child away. He came with a strong force of men and muscled his way in. The nursemaid had only placed you in my hands when I sensed his presence and immediately fled to ensure your safety."

"So when he arrived, there was only Lucien, and he didn't know there were twins?"

"Yes."

"Does Lucien know who his mother was?"

"Yes. But he, like Set, did not know of your existence. He found out when he first saw you."

Andrew was seated on the edge of the table. "Besides, I'm your brother, not him. And I'm so much better looking than he is, too," Andrew said, smiling. He had consumed enough alcohol, quality beverage or not, Luc noticed. He had managed to break the tension though.

"Hm, I think I resemble that remark. I wonder what he thinks, having no one to explain what's going on. He has no one to talk to about it." Now more than ever he wished to speak to his twin.

"I am more concerned about what Set thinks," said Isis. "We can't let him get you. Ever. He would have you chained to a table in a genetic engineering lab."

"Which is probably where he has Kirin right now, though she's the one being forced to do all the experiments," Andrew reminded them.

"Can we move past this until we get your sister? And have no doubt that she will still be your little sister, Ljluka, no matter what. You are part of our family and we will protect our family. All we have done has been an attempt to protect you, too. Sometimes we make mistakes. I hope you can trust us, Ljluka. We never meant you to feel shame or feel the circumstances of your birth somehow made us love you less."

"I know. I just need a little time, mother," he said softly. He saw the way her eyes, still glistened with unshed tears, began to pool over when he called her mother. Standing and turning slightly away to wipe them away, she said, "Are you up to starting negotiations?"

"We can't let him have the incantation, mother."

"No, but we can let him have a forgery that is off just enough to keep him from understanding the book," she explained. Warming to the change in topic and the thought of tricking Set, she let her lips turn up slightly.

"Great! Let's get her home," Andrew urged.

They stood up and followed their mother toward the door, headed back toward Osiris' office. Luc realized a conference call was the only way to continue the negotiations. His father would not channel Set. He would not allow his wife to do so. Horus was not there, so the easiest way was to simplify and use the old fashioned means.

A few minutes later, Osiris had Set on the phone. Luc, as usual, was handling the negotiations. "What guarantee do we have that Kirin is safe?" Luc insisted.

"What guarantee do I have that you are in possession of the incantation?" Set thundered.

Luc hesitated, and then said, "If you put Kirin on a satellite phone for two minutes, we will uplink the papyrus via satellite simultaneously."

"Done. Fifteen minutes," said Set brusquely.

"Confirmed," said Luc, hanging up. Taking a deep cleansing breath, he tried to push back the knowledge that Set was his father, tried to forget it until later, after Kirin was home safely. He could think about it more then. "Okay," he said. "We have fifteen minutes. Do you dare put the original up there, my queen? Will the forgery be close enough that he will not be able to compare the two and see it for the lie?"

"He will not expect the actual incantation. We can show him the outer edge, the edge that names it. I don't think it's a large enough portion for him to be able to zoom close enough from his saved and downloaded pictures," Isis explained.

Osiris walked over to the desk, unlocked a drawer and pulled out the papyrus. He gave it to Isis, who looked for an innocuous spot in the room in which to display it for the camera. It certainly couldn't be near the monitors or near any of the recognizable artifacts. There was no reason to alert him to their whereabouts.

"Anubis. Bring me that plant," she said, pointing to a large potted palm near the door. He clenched his jaw to balance its weight, but brought it over and set it next to her.

"Now pull out the tree and dump that earth on the floor over here. We will place the papyrus on the earth and he will think it's in a climate with rich black soil. Grab some of those philodendrons from that plant on the table over there. Make them look as if they're growing out of the soil on the floor."

"Here, let me help you," said Luc. "We only have five minutes. Ahmed, get that satellite lens over here."

They rushed around and got the uplink ready. Nothing could go wrong. Set would see it as a deliberate attempt at subterfuge. "Two minutes," called Luc, suddenly reminded of the last time he was worried about each moment.

"We're ready," said Ahmed.

"Good. And five, four, three, two, one, start the feed."

Kirin, anxious but unharmed, at least from what they could tell in the slightly grainy feed, sat at a table, her handcuffed hands before her, wearing a blindfold. "Kirin, it's me, Luc," he said softly. "Have you been harmed?"

"Luc? It's really you? Please don't do anything stupid. They haven't hurt me, I swear it." How like her, he thought, to think of his safety rather than her own even as she sat there blindfolded, handcuffed, and at the mercy of kidnappers.

"We're going to get you back, soon, Kirin," Andrew said, reassuringly.

"Andrew is that you? Listen to Luc and don't get mad and get carried away, okay? I love you both so much. Stay safe."

"You're the boss, little sis. Whatever you say. We all love you."

The feed cut out.

Ten minutes later, the conference call phone rang.

"Okay, you've got it. I want it. When and where?"

"Kirin must not be harmed, in any way."

"You saw she was fine."

"In *any* way," insisted Luc, relieved that he sensed Kirin had not yet been raped. Somehow he felt he would have known by some sign in her carriage or demeanor if one of those animals had violated her.

"Agreed."

"The trade will be made at the *Naguib Mahfouz* Coffee Shop in the middle of the *Khan El-Khalili* market in Cairo, at twelve-hundred hours on Friday," Luc said firmly.

Hesitation. Luc figured he was trying to find a way to slant it to his advantage. He knew the public forum thwarted bushwhacking.

"Done." Disconnection.

"We've got three days," Luc needlessly repeated to the room's occupants.

It was his brother Andrew, the one who never picked up on emotional nuances who said, "That had to be hard for you, Luc. I'm sorry you had to speak to him. It would have been rather odd if after all this time one of us did the negotiations. He would have wondered. Besides, you're the best. I never would have thought of Cairo. It's brilliant."

"You did well, son," Osiris said. He was a gruff but loving father with his boys, and Luc almost felt sorry for him. He was trying to make amends, but didn't know how.

Sekhmet wasn't present. He looked at his mother.

In her room, Luc. It would be nice if you could go speak to her. Maybe later if you're not ready yet.

He nodded.

"Let's wash that drink down with lunch. Whataya say?" Andrew asked. "You've got a stack of business calls to return anyway. I can't do all your cleaning up."

"Sounds fair to me," Luc agreed and followed his brother, his real brother, out of the room.

In power of others, never in my own;
Scarce half I seem to live,
 dead more then half.
O dark, dark, dark, dark, dark,
amid the blaze of noon,
Irrecoverably dark, total Eclipse
Without all hope of day!

John Milton, Samson Agonistes

Chapter Thirty-Six

"I wish Set had not insisted that you be seen in front of the camera in the clothes in which you arrived," said Nalini.

"Why?" Kirin asked, tucking her hair under the edge of the veil on her head.

"Typhon has seen you now. His reaction was tangible, as I feared, which is why both Lucien and I have conspired to keep you from his sight."

Kirin stopped and looked at Nalini. "So this is worse than the way Lucien is always so intense, so sure that we should be together, whenever he finds a reason to be near me?"

"Much worse," Nalini said, swinging her feet over the side of the cushion and standing up. "Typhon won't care if he can convince you to accept his advances. It won't even occur to him that your opinion matters."

"What makes you think he will, well, even bother with me?"

Nalini wondered what it must be like to be so blissfully unaware of the danger lurking around every corner. Walking over to stand in front of her, she said, "Kirin, you have got to stop being so naïve. Pay attention to the men around you. You have to if you are to survive here. I just told you. Typhon lusts for you. He wants you, so the way that his mind works the next logical action is to have you. Men are all about action, Kirin. Especially these men. You must always know before they do, what it is they want. Their motivations will alert you to their actions so you can take steps to protect yourself." She realized she would have to be with Kirin at all times in order to keep her safe. Somehow this woman trusted men, apparently. Probably it was those protective brothers. Hadn't it occurred to them to at least alert her to the potential danger of most men?

"You said that you and Lucien had kept me away from him. How did you know he would react like this?"

A quick surge of anger rose in Nalini. It wasn't fair that Set had stolen her mother away from the safe environment this spoiled, naïve princess lived in so blissfully. But then she reminded herself that it wasn't Kirin's fault and that no woman from the western world would understand her position here. It wasn't as if it made sense.

Sighing, Nalini grasped her shoulders and turned her to face the mirror. If anything the black veil only emphasized the creamy complexion and brilliant emerald sparkle of the wide intelligent eyes reflected in the silver-backed glass. Even with her radiant hair covered, she was striking. Amea, thrilled to finally serve a woman who would wear makeup, had taught Kirin to apply knoll to her eyes, which made them appear even bigger and brighter. What man wouldn't be attracted to her, Nalini wondered.

Arai entered. "Typhon wishes to have an interview with the princess. He has sent a guard to escort her to him."

Nalini threw her hands up and rolled her eyes. She looked meaningfully at Kirin. "Tell the guard that she is currently indisposed. She is distraught after speaking to her family via satellite."

Nodding, Arai left to deliver the message.

"Now what?" asked Kirin.

"We wait," Nalini responded with more confidence than she felt. In truth, she wasn't sure. She wanted to wait for her mother to get back.

"Set needs me unharmed to trade for the incantation that can unlock the secret to *The Book of Life*, doesn't he?"

"Why do you ask? Is that what your brother has negotiated? Does he have the incantation?" Nalini asked.

"My mother said they're to do the exchange in Cairo."

Of course, it was perfect, crowded, loud."When?" Nalini asked anxiously.

"In three days."

Was it soon enough to keep her safe? Nalini wondered.

Astarte slipped through the hidden door from the secret passageway. "So you are still here. I am glad," she said.

Nalini glanced at her mother's stomach. Even under the concealment of the flowing robes she wore, the fetus's presence had grown obvious. "You have news, mother?" she asked.

"Yes. It concerns you both." Motioning for them to follow, she moved to the chaise and lay down, putting her feet up. "Ah, much better," she said, smiling.

Nalini handed her a glass of water and set a tray of fruit on the small table beside her. "You are too good to me, Nalini," she said. "Now come close, both of you."

"Yes, the walls, ears, we get it."

"Set has reached an agreement with the Vargas's"

"Yes, Kirin's mother told her. He's not going to do it, is he?"

"No." Nalini glanced at Kirin, deciding how much to tell her.

"What do you mean? He has given his word. The deal has been made," cried Kirin.

Astarte ignored Kirin's questions and instead confirmed Nalini's fears. "He agreed to let Lucien marry Kirin as a reward for bringing back the book as well as Kirin. Also, for rescuing you, but I do not think that was his mission, regardless of how much Set tells me that is why he sent Lucien."

"He can't give Lucien permission to marry me. I will not agree!" Kirin said, passionately. Both women ignored her words. They had already explained that her wishes didn't matter to the men, and she had yet to believe it.

"Typhon was furious. He claims that as first born he should be allowed to have her. They had a terrible fight."

Nalini suddenly noticed that her mother's eyes were puffy. "Have you been crying?" Fear shot up her spine. "What was the outcome of this fight?"

"Set agreed to let Typhon marry you if he manages to get the incantation away from Ljluka. He wants him to try to get Ljluka as well."

"Get Luc? No," Kirin cried. "He has made a bargain, why is he lying? And how can he possibly think he can force us to marry anyone? You are to marry this man you call a monster? Your own brother?"

This time Nalini turned to her, determined to make her understand. "You are no longer in the west, Kirin. You know the cultural norms here. Even in the marketplace in Cairo you must let one of your brothers or some other man bargain for you and make any arrangements. Here it is much worse. Set can kill us, permanently, and no one would even care. We are merely women, property, less valuable than livestock. I should be glad he didn't have me buried alive at birth."

Kirin turned away, but not before Nalini had seen a tear slip down her cheek. She wadded the edge of her veil in her hand and walked to the far side of the room.

Nalini felt a twinge of guilt over the harshness of her response, but she knew she had to make Kirin realize the seriousness of their situation, for all of them. "Her mother. She is speaking to her mother," Nalini said to Astarte, who nodded.

"I have appealed to Set, but I am not able to so strongly influence him in my weak condition. I can still try telling him I will be so distraught I may lose the child if he doesn't call this off," Astarte said.

"No, you will do nothing. Arai told me how you endangered yourself and the child with constant worry when I was kidnapped. It is very possible that Set really did send Lucien to get me, mother. He could not have known Lucien's true agenda."

"You can't marry Typhon, Nalini."

"I have no intention of doing so," she said, fists clenched at her sides. Her bravado was more for her mother than herself. There was no way to fool herself. The shudder of revulsion that shook her core was involuntary. Her fear was an almost tangible thing. Everyone in the palace had heard rumors of Typhon's perversions. All in the harem feared him. Not even Rashid would tell her what he knew, thus magnifying her revulsion and intensifying her fear. She needed time to think, to decide on a plan. But time, she knew, was the one thing she had just run out of.

A soft tap sounded on the door. "Enter," Astarte called.

Rashid walking into the room and headed toward Nalini. He had been quiet since his return. She wondered what the truth was behind his sudden release by none other than Isis herself. He had said very little except that Isis had released him, realizing no one would negotiate for his return.

"Set has sent for you both," he said, his expression sober. He already knew what Astarte had just told her, Nalini guessed.

"Kirin," she said. "Pull yourself together. We cannot so easily defy Set. We must go." She pulled the veil over her face so that only her eyes showed. Then, she moved to do the same for Kirin, reassured by the anger in the woman's emerald eyes, the determined thrust of her chin. "No sense letting the jackals see their prey too soon," she said.

"Wait," said Astarte. She rose, with some difficulty, but then walked to the table across the room. Mixing a fine powder into a cup of tea from a pot on the side bar, she said, "Drink this so that Set cannot read your thoughts." Kirin hesitated, then lifted the veil aside and drank the tea. "Set will think it all your mother's doing, and will not question it."

"Let's get this over with," Nalini urged. "Remember to say nothing unless Set asks you a question. We will deal with this in our own way. And pay attention to what they do not say, their expressions and gestures, the way they stand." She sighed, seeing Kirin's terrified expression. "Okay, just pay attention and I will do any talking," Nalini instructed. She turned and led Kirin out the door and prayed the woman would keep her mouth shut.

"I'm so scared, but at the same time so angry that I should have to be so scared," Kirin confided.

"I know. Welcome to my life," Nalini said softly. "The secret is not to show it. Where there are lambs, wolves descend. Try not to worry. You have family who will do whatever it takes to save you."

"Who will save you, Nalini?" She turned to glance at her, the sincerity in her voice was echoed by the clear concern in her eyes.

Good question, Nalini thought. "I will save myself," she said, with more assurance than she presently felt.

The double doors to the throne room opened and they walked inside. Nalini saw that both Typhon and Lucien were present. Lucien leaned against a pillar, the rigidity of his shoulders betraying the nonchalance he tried to portrait. She paused in front of the dais, waiting for Set to make an appearance.

Typhon surprised her. She had expected to see him grinning like a fool, gloating and attempting to disquiet her with his lewd or suggestive gestures. Instead he was staring at her in a curious way, as if trying to decide something. He noted her choice of clothing. She was covered entirely in black, like a bag of garbage she had joked, which is all she thought would be left if he ever got his hands on her.

Perhaps that was it, she thought, perhaps he was imaging what he would do to her, or what he wanted to do to her. She would kill him first, of course. Curiously, he was paying no attention at all to Kirin, though apparently there had been heated debate. Having got what he thought he had wanted for so long, he must no longer envy his brother's prize.

Lucien, however, had eyes only for Kirin. Nalini had watched as they first walked in and had seen him frown at Kirin's wardrobe, and then scowl at Nalini for a moment, rightly understanding who had influenced the choice.

She glanced back at Typhon, growing disturbed that he was so uncharacteristically silent and pensive. At last the door to the right of the throne opened and Set appeared, followed by his usual entourage. Another surprise though was the appearance of her mother at Set's side. She looked pale. Suddenly stepping forward, she reached to slip her hand through the crook of his arm. Surprised by the public intimacy, he glanced down and was instantly solicitous. Bracing her as she slumped, he yelling out for someone to bring a chair and some water.

Nalini rushed a sidelong glance at Typhon and nearly moved toward him, defensively, so passionate was the look of hatred he directed at her mother, or more precisely, her mother's stomach.

Astarte was quickly seated, and Set himself handed her the goblet of water the young serving girl provided. Then, so quickly she was uncertain she had seen it since she had been focused so intently on her mother, Nalini thought the serving girl darted a conspiratorial look at Typhon.

"Stop," she cried instinctively. Everyone turned to look at her. "I mean, my mother has been so nauseous all day that I think she would benefit more from the herbal tea she herself prepared. Rashid can fetch it."

She stared at her mother who didn't understand why, but knew that Nalini would not have interrupted if it were not important said, "Yes, I really think that would be better."

"Fetch it at once!" bellowed Set. Rashid ran from the room.

Nalini watched the serving girl, who accepted the goblet that Set shoved back onto her tray. She turned and hurried away, her head down, speaking to no one. Nalini looked at Arai and nodded her head slightly. He quietly slipped out behind the girl.

When she glanced again at Typhon, he was grinning stupidly. He licked his lips suggestively, and stared at her as if she were naked. This then was his sheep's clothing, Nalini realized, the horrific implications snaking their way up her spine.

Rashid returned and ran to hand the tea to Set, bowing deeply. Astarte sipped it daintily as he held it against her lips, pretending it was of great help. In truth, Nalini thought the color in her cheeks warmed.

Bending over Astarte, Set placed his hand over her stomach. Apparently the child kicked, for he smiled into her upturned face, well pleased. "Leave us! We will continue at another time," he snapped.

Nalini grabbed Kirin's hand and turned to all but run from the room. She didn't slow until the doors shut behind them in the women's quarters. Moving toward her mother's chamber, she pulled the veil from her head and threw open the door.

"We have been so stupid," she said bitterly. She ran to the side bar and picked up a cup and poured out some tea from the pot. She smelled it, tasted it, and put it down. Then she moved to the table upon which the cup of tea Astarte had been drinking still sat, and held it to her nose. Sticking her finger in the bottom of the cup, she swiped it across and tasted it with the tip of her tongue.

The door to the passageway opened and Set entered, carrying Astarte in his arms. Nalini slipped the cup onto the table, and whispered quickly to Kirin, "Watch it is not disturbed," before she hurried to assist her mother. Shocked at the way Set was personally attending her mother, Nalini wondered vaguely if he really did love her. He had put his hand on her stomach in public. It was unheard of.

"Nalini can help me now, my king. I am so embarrassed to be a burden," said Astarte.

"How can you be a burden to me while you carry the promise of our son in your belly? You must get well. I have let Typhon upset you. I will tell him that he must wait until after the child arrives. It is not worth the risk," he said.

"Thank you, my husband. I am sure I will feel much better by tomorrow. I just need to sleep now." Her pale complexion and drawn brow were not feigned. Nalini hovered, waiting for Set to leave.

"Yes, sleep," he agreed. "Help me get her into bed," he said to Nalini. He did not like even the Eunuchs to touch her. Nalini pulled back the covers and once seated, Astarte's feet were gently lifted by Set. "I will check on you once you have rested. The physician has already been sent for. Have him report to me once he has left you." Set pressed a kiss to her forehead, laid his hand on her stomach and felt what he assumed was movement. "Send for me at once if there is any change," he said to Nalini. He glanced around the room, and said, "Where are her handmaidens? See that the lazy fools are punished. They should be constantly vigilant and at hand to care for her every need!"

She nodded, and then breathed an inward sigh of relief once he was gone. "How bad is it, mother?"

"Better. There were mild contractions, though I dared say nothing in public."

"Kirin," she called. "Bring it to me."

Kirin appeared in the doorway, holding the cup. She approached the bed, looking concerned. Nalini took the cup from her and said, "Smell this," to her mother.

Astarte, confused, inhaled the fragrance, taking time to distinguish the different herbs. She paused, inhaled once more and would have tasted as had Nalini, but Nalini reached out to stop her hand.

"No. You have had enough."

"Who would dare?" Astarte asked.

"Evening primrose oil and black cohosh. Someone is trying to make you miscarry," Nalini said, her fears confirmed by Astarte's nod.

"Either one would have worked," Kirin said. "Together they may have proved deadly."

"I forgot. You're a doctor, aren't you?" Nalini glanced over at her, suddenly seeing potential in her presence.

"Not a practicing one, but yes I have the background and education. I work as a researcher, and have expert knowledge of botanicals," Kirin said. "Do you have any idea how much or for how long your mother has been poisoned with this?"

"Probably at least since I was kidnapped. She was sick then, too."

"Perhaps that just gave them the idea and she truly was sick with the pregnancy at that time. Let's hope so. I don't suppose you have any magnesium sulfate?"

"We could get it, but I don't know how soon. Herbs we have in abundance right here," Nalini said.

"Cramp bark," Astarte suggested.

"Yes, that should work," Kirin agreed.

Nalini hurried to the cupboard her mother indicated. Kirin moved to assist her. "There, that one," Kirin directed, pointing to an herb in the drawer Nalini had just opened. "Do you have tea prepared?"

"Yes, here," Nalini said, walking to the two-burner stove incorporated into a wall bar on the opposite side of the room. "Mother grew the ingredients in her private courtyard, so it should be safe."

Kirin brought the herb and placed the appropriate amount in the cup. Stirring it, she handed it to Nalini who took it to her mother.

"Drink, mother," she said. Astarte quickly drank the entire cup.

Kirin approached the bed, raised her hand toward Astarte and said, "Do you mind?"

"No, please," said Astarte.

Softly probing her stomach, Kirin placed one hand to the top of her stomach and gently moved the other hand across her abdomen, examining the fetus. "How long have you felt the contractions?"

"They started shortly after I drank the tea."

Kirin nodded. "I don't suppose you have any medical equipment, even a stethoscope?" Astarte chuckled. Kirin placed her fingers around Astarte's wrist, glancing at her watch. "I didn't feel any contractions. The fetus is strong and moves often, and does not seem distressed." She released her hand. "Your heartbeat is strong and steady. I think the immediate danger has passed."

Nalini stepped closer to her mother as Kirin moved away. "Now sleep," she said softly. "Everything will work out. I will be right outside and will check on you often. You need only call and I will come quickly."

"I will be fine now, though I do feel tired. Your brother moves often today. Already he fights his enemies," Astarte said with resignation.

Nalini clenched her teeth, then willed herself to relax. "Rest, mother."

She turned and walked out the door with Kirin. Just then a harried man entered, carrying a small bag. "She is already resting, and in her bed. Set wants to see you to find out she is doing much better," Nalini said. The man paused, saw the challenge in her eyes, and wisely decided to do as she commanded. He hurried from the room.

"Quack," Nalini said. She thrust herself into her favorite pillow and pulled her feet up to her chin, circling her legs with her arms.

"Suppose you tell me what exactly is going on, Nalini."

"Look, don't worry about it. You will make it out of this okay." How could she explain the occurrences of millennia in a matter of moments?

"You have done what you could to protect me here. I am grateful. What can I do to help you?"

"You are hardly in a position to help anyone," Nalini said, laughing. "Besides, you helped my mother. It is enough." What she thought was that if not for Kirin's mother, hers would not even be here. Neither of them would. Was it their fault Set was a sadistic rapist? Why sentence them to life with him for eternity, if he was so bad? Didn't that make Kirin's mother as bad as her father?

"I watched the men as you instructed me." Kirin's face reflected her nervous tension, her realization that she had more to lose than her temporary freedom if she was not careful—perhaps even if she was.

"And?" Nalini prompted her, impressed that she had taken her instructions so seriously.

"Typhon's desire is not just lust for your body, though he is so completely repulsive it seems obvious that he would favor that ultimate humiliation. He hates your mother with a great passion. It was he who arranged the poison in Astarte's tea, wasn't it? Is he jealous of the son Astarte carries?"

Nalini, stunned, just looked at her a moment. "You learn quickly. Not until tonight did I myself realize how far he will go. That he would dare to murder my mother or her unborn child...." Perhaps Kirin was not just a spoiled, cosseted woman unable to fend for herself. She was obviously very intelligent. Nalini knew that only wits would save them from the brutality of the men in her family. She had been brutalized enough to know how powerful and cruel they could be. Hopefully Kirin could take her word for it, and would not experience it firsthand.

Nalini let anger dominate her fear. Fear could cause her to hesitate, and the actions that must now be taken required quick thinking as well as courage and determination. Their survival depended on it.

"What if," Astarte said, "what if until now Typhon had not actually started his plan in motion? His slip in revealing his true feelings may be because of arrogance or excitement, as he anticipates its success."

"He is far more dangerous and devious than we have ever given him credit for. We underestimated him—the most avoidable mistake. What arrogance on my part to so easily be convinced that he was nothing more than a bully and a leach." Nalini rubbed her hands over her face, and then returned them to clutch her legs. She remembered the look on his face when he was granted permission to whip her. Resting her chin on her knees, she said, "He hates you as well." Glancing sideways at Kirin, she added. "You resemble your mother, and thus his mother, her twin. He hates her for leaving him, you know."

"He must realize she would have taken him if she could. She still mourns her loss of him, loves him. It is he who refuses to communicate with her." Kirin looked deep in thought, then said, "We all have wondered why he refused to understand that she had to leave his abusive father. From what I've seen, there is no love lost there, either. He really is alone. So do you think that is why he wants to marry you, hating you as he does?"

"No, it's not loneliness that motivates him. I almost wish it were. If I were his wife, he could humiliate me in the most horrific ways and no one would come to my aid. He could even ultimately torture me to death, repeatedly if he chose, with impunity. My greatest fear is that with marriage he would eventually force me to bend to his will. He could not be controlled like Set as he does not care for or about me at all."

Kirin looked at her in shock, as if the quiet simplicity with which Nalini explained it, the resigned way in which she believed and accepted it, were more ghastly than the crimes themselves. Sometimes, Nalini decided, remembering the long walk to be whipped, the fear and contemplation of unknown horrors was every bit as horrifying as the events themselves.

"Which is worse? the wolf who cries before eating the lamb, or the wolf who does not."

Leo Tolstoy

Chapter Thirty-Seven

Sekhmet moved around the counter and held the vial to Luc's nose. "Smell deeply and tell me how it makes you feel," she instructed.

Inhaling, he closed his eyes to better focus on his other senses. "An immediate physical reaction, an adrenaline rush. It makes me feel good, like when we rappel down the mountain or jump from a cliff. My muscles are tense, expectant, like the moment before I freefall from a plane, or during the brief hesitation before I pull the shoot." He inhaled again. "And intensified senses. I can hear the water dripping in the sink in the next room."

She took the vial away. "Now how do you feel?"

"Like a junkie in withdrawal. I want it back, desperately. I am suppressing a desire to open my eyes and take it back from you. My entire focus has shifted."

The vial was under his nose again. "I felt an instant of relief, but almost simultaneously the physical reaction has taken over again."

"What is your impulse? How do you feel you should react to these physical reactions? What is your emotional reaction?"

She pulled back the vial. Luc opened his eyes and looked at her. He swallowed, conquered the desire, then thought for a moment and said, "I guess my response to the physical reaction when I smell it is that I should repress it. It is so overwhelming, it feels like I wouldn't be able to control it if I let it consume me. I think it makes me feel almost angry."

Sekhmet nodded. "It sounds like you are describing fear."

He thought about it. "Fear of losing control."

"So what you need to learn in order to no longer feel afraid is that you can control it."

"That makes sense. Listen, Andrew told me that once when the mortals tried to revolt against Osiris, he sent you as his enforcer and you killed so many men that you were unable to stop until Isis forced you to drink a tonic."

"Andrew does not have the facts right. There was an occasion where the killing got out of hand. What is not well known, however, is why. Set used my DNA in his genetic experiments. You used the word vampiric with me, but you did not know how offensive it truly was."

Luc reached out to put his hand on her shoulder. "I have forgiven you. Surely you can forgive my unfortunate choice of words. It was more than I could process so soon after returning from the Underworld."

"No, no," she said, smiling at him. "I didn't mean to chastise you. What I meant to do was illustrate how offended I was by Set's initial betrayal. He took a strand of my hair, also against my will." She looked away for a moment, as if remembering. Luc gave her a gentle hug.

"Hey, you don't need to tell me everything today. It can wait. What we need to concentrate on is teaching me to control it, this blood lust."

"I'm fine. It's just that I have kept all these things separate from my relationship with you for so long, it seems strange to be able to finally share them openly. Let me finish. You should know, so any future rumors you hear will not bother you. What Set's unscrupulous scientists created in his laboratories were the first vampires. They were well pleased with their creations, until they discovered that they had a very serious problem."

Luc struggled to keep his features expressionless. He had always known Sekhmet had a reaction to blood that made her a lethal force in battle. They all knew. It had not been kept secret, though the cause seemed unknown. The vampire stories his brothers had told him as a boy he had thought as a man to be only stories children made up to scare younger siblings. His use of the word with Sekhmet had been triggered by anger and bitterness. Shaking his head as if to clear it, he asked, "They didn't consider the fact that they were vampires to be a problem?"

"No way, the perfect predator. They were with me in that battle. Set thought of them as the ultimate achievement of his goal. The problem was that the creatures could not be controlled. They nearly wiped out the human race once their bloodlust turned to an actual taste for the pumping crimson. Then, still hungry, they turned on their creators and had to be destroyed. Only one escaped."

"Are you trying to tell me that they really do exist? What have they evolved into?" Luc was stunned by this newest revelation; his gene pool had produced vampires. What new horrors would be revealed?

"The stuff of legends, Ljluka," she said, laughing at the horror in his voice.

"It has gotten to the point that I feel I should believe every myth and legend I have ever heard of, let alone the ones my own actions have generated."

"You don't have to take it that far, though as you know from your own life most legends and myth have some basis in reality, depending on who is defining reality."

"Well, speaking of reality then, why does blood have the effect it does on you and me?" He watched her face closely, anxious to hear her explanation.

She hesitated as if considering her words carefully. Then, said with complete seriousness, "I'm not sure. Kirin has tried to help me discover the source. We have concluded that the cause is a near-primeval reaction to the scent, an instinct for survival, for continued life that blood represents. Consider how the church reveres blood." She studied his face as if gauging his reaction. He was in fact too stunned to react at all. "But come, we need to continue with your training. If you are able to command your instincts, to draw them up when you need them and utilize their true power, you will realize you have nothing to fear."

"While I was in the Underworld, they saved my life," Luc admitted.

"How?" She asked, clearly surprised.

"I let the bloodlust take me. It's how I destroyed this mad creature who called himself Legion."

"You destroyed Legion?" She was intensely interested, and surprised, too. Her head tilted slightly as she studied his face.

"Yes. You know of him?" He already knew that she did, could tell by her intense reaction to his news.

"You may be more powerful than I am," she said, apparently impressed. She grew silent for a moment as she continued to observe him. "It must be Set's amazing strength and power that have influenced your genetic inheritance from me."

He grimaced. "Not what I want to hear, Sekhmet. But what makes you think so?"

"Legion existed at all because I was unable to defeat him." Seeing his raised brow, she repeated, "Yes, unable. I only managed to contain him with the help of Osiris and Horus. Tell me what you did, exactly. I assumed you failed to encounter him to have survived at all. I think we all did."

"There was blood. I let myself feel it. Filled with bloodlust, I no longer fought just to defend myself against him. I became aggressive and attacked, even enjoyed the killing on a primordial level. My senses were off the charts. I could hear better, smell better. I was stronger and faster. I could even see in the dark."

Sekhmet nodded, deep in thought. Then she said, "Is there anything else, any other details you can recall?"

"Only that I inhaled again, letting the bloodlust give me the strength I needed to beat the clock and escape in time."

"Ljluka, you have already learned to summon and control it with the use of stimuli. You just didn't realize that's what you were doing. Desperation made you go against your usual instinct, that one that didn't want to allow you to be different from others. Eventually you will be able to call up your powers without outside stimulus. Before now you were afraid to be what you perceived as strange. You have suppressed your natural power for a long time."

"Yes, when I was very young I first realized I had this reaction to blood. Though it was nowhere as strong then, it frightened me because I didn't understand it and I was afraid to even speak to anyone about it. No one has ever known, not even Andrew."

"And yet, even in a latent state it has been what enabled you to be so good at your job. Do you realize how much you are feared throughout the mortal world? Even a whisper that you will be sent makes them quake. Anubis does not terrify your enemies as much."

"You must surely be a bit prejudice. Andrew is much stronger than I."

"Mortals too can sense the submerged threat within you. Though it's on a subconscious level for most, those who are intuitive would sense your power. Perhaps Anubis is stronger when your power is in a dilatory stage. You have both been trained to watch the eyes and muscle movement of your enemy to detect their next move, but you are always a step ahead of them, sensing what they are going to do before the thought has yet occurred to them. Have you never noticed?"

"No. I probably would have chalked it off to coincidence."

"Yes. That seems likely," she agreed, nodding. "Come. You need to practice. Let's go to the PT center. Anubis is already there with your men."

They turned and walked to the door. Luc grabbed and held it as she passed through. He didn't know if he would ever think of her as his mother. Though he had loved her for his entire life, he wondered if he would ever get past the loving devoted aunt persona in which he, Kirin and Andrew had always viewed her. She herself agreed with Isis and Osiris that he was still their son, that they had effectively adopted him. It was something they had all agreed upon before his birth.

They also all regretted Lucien's fate. Sekhmet admitted that she loved him, too. She could not help loving Luc more, she explained, as she did not know Lucien personally. Isis declared that she felt no maternal emotion toward Lucien—and of course she had never seen him in person either.

He followed her down the corridor to the elevator. They stepped in, laughed at the speed in which it delivered them up three floors, then stepped out and came face to face with Andrew.

"I was just coming to see what was keeping you," he said.

"Great timing, then," said Luc.

"We're all set up," Andrew confirmed.

They followed him across the foyer to a hallway that angled off to the right. A few doors down, they stopped and entered. The room was vaulted and paneled with mirrors. Neat rows of exercise equipment were framed by stands of free weights. Along the far wall, weight benches were positioned in such a way that fitness minded lifters could heft loads while monitoring their form in the mirrors.

Further into the room, the wall by the entrance jogged and a hallway butted against it from the right. They followed the hallway until it opened into another vaulted room, one that would not be found in most gyms. Rather than mirrors, the room's walls were bullet proof. Instead of free weights, the room was bordered with weapons. There was no exercise equipment, only mats like those used by gymnasts.

Standing around the edge of the enormous mat area were the men that had accompanied them, and another dozen from Osiris' personal guard. Luc noted his father standing in the far corner, and wondered if he was planning to participate or observe.

"We may as well begin," Sekhmet said. "Watch carefully first, Ljluka. Then we will discuss what you perceive before you begin."

He nodded.

She walked into the center of the mat, drawing a dagger from a sheath on her belt. The men moved inward, a circle of highly trained combat veterans, cautious because they knew Sekhmet's reputation, but confident because they were used to victory. They were armed with their favorite weapons: knives, swords, or num-chucks, but no artillery.

Sekhmet circled slowly, wary and prepared, trying to maintain a sense of where each man was located. The first man, behind her, moved in to attack, wielding the num-chucks. She twisted around, slid down and outward, sending her foot into his kneecap, and simultaneously grabbing the other end of the numchuck, taking possession of it as he went down. She spun around and used it against another man, about to slice her with a knife. He staggered, went down and fell under the feet of another man who had been about to attack.

She continued her skilled defense and managed to back off over a dozen men single-handedly for nearly twenty minutes, using masterfully applied non-incapacitating blows on potentially lethal or debilitating pressure points. Then, she began to tire, the proof of it illustrated by the blow she sustained in the mouth-- after failing to jerk her head back far enough, in time. Blood trickled down her chin. She wiped at it and then brushed her hand across her nose, savoring the scent. Luc's pulse quickened with only the imagining.

An immediate shift in her energy level and technique became evident. Rather than waiting for the men to attack, she assailed them. Promptly adjusting their strategy as well, the men became more wary, paired up against her. It didn't matter. Within five minutes the entire group had been beaten, holding their hands up in defeat, conceding to her superior force.

Andrew, the last to give up, laughed and offered her a high five, saying, "You win. You came, you saw, you kicked our ass. You're a terror, Aunt Sekhmet. You gonna teach that to this little pipsqueak?"

"Oh, I don't think you want to add anger to the mix, my dear," she said, laughing and accepting the bottle of water one of the men held out to her. "Did you react when I smelled the blood?" she asked Luc.

"Yes. Immediately."

"Good. That is similar to how you bring up the power without outside stimulus. You remember the reaction, imagine how it feels when it occurs." Luc thought about it a moment. It made sense. He nodded.

"That so, little brother? You think I need to worry about making you mad from now on?" Andrew taunted.

Luc grinned and stepped onto the mat, not feeling a need to discuss further when he could experiment instead. "Shall we find out?"

"Sure, but I warn you I'm in a hurry. I'm starving and we were supposed to eat a half-hour ago."

Andrew immediately grabbed Luc and flipped him onto the mat. Luc kipped to his feet and seeing that Andrew had pulled out a knife, reached for the knife in his belt. He angled to the right, noting that the rest of the men had returned for more sport. Like Sekhmet, he managed to fend them off. Two men limped a little and moved off the mat to be replaced by reserves who stood on either side of Osiris.

Andrew came at him again, the blade from their knives clashing over and over as they parried and thrust. Jab. Slice. Twist. Luc spun around and countered an attack from behind and came back again. Andrew was unrelenting in his pursuit. Hand to hand, knives immobilized when each one caught and grasped the other's wrist. Andrew threw up an elbow and caught Luc on the jaw.

Luc dropped and used his body weight to leverage Andrew's larger bulk, twisting to the side and landing Andrew onto the floor. Trying to angle his wrist, Andrew tightened his grip on his blade, but Luc said, "Uh-uh. I wouldn't if I were you."

He glanced down pointedly. Andrew followed his gaze until he realized that Luc's knife was positioned above his genitals.

"Care to turn your head and cough?" Luc asked, grinning. "And I'm not even mad. In fact, I think it's hilariously funny."

"You definitely win, little brother," Andrew said, chuckling.

Luc twisted again, and shoved his knife up to block an oncoming blade. The man parried and came back at him, just as another man ran up behind him. Luc managed to block another thrust, then spun out of the oncoming lunge and tapped the palm of his hand, lightly, into the nose of the man coming from behind.

Blood spurted.

Luc grasped his shirt, pulling him closer. He inhaled the heady aroma and let the bloodlust shoot directly into his veins.

He was unstoppable.

Osiris chose that instant to step forward. He pulled his knife and entered the foray. Andrew, back on his feet, grabbed Luc from behind. Luc bent at the waist, threw him over his head, and shouted, "Not fair!"

Then he turned to dive for the knife of an oncoming assailant and held it to the man's throat until he gave up and moved off. In much less than five minutes the other men, Andrew included, had conceded—Andrew for the second time--until only Osiris remained.

He moved toward Luc and dropped his weapon. Luc followed suit. Osiris rushed to grasp him around the torso, locking his arms against his sides. He dropped to his knees, twisted, threw an elbow into Osiris' stomach and shoved his knee under Osiris' leg and flipped him, pinning his shoulder to the floor.

Laughing, Osiris said, "I'm glad you're on our side. I knew I chose right when I made you our enforcer."

Luc pushed back the adrenaline flow. He battled the yearning. Then he remembered what Sekhmet had taught him and released his hold of the physical reaction. Rather than suppress it, he channeled it to an acute inner strength and uncanny perception.

He let it empower him. Then he stood up and took several long breaths, savoring the feelings he experienced. Still a bit shaky from the hard rush of now smoldering frenzy, he stood and reached down to grasp his father's hand. The contact gave him strength and he pulled him to his feet. He felt very close to his father at that moment, bonding as fighting men do, and sweat or no sweat, he reached to pull him close.

"I would happily die for you, father. I'm proud to be your enforcer."

Osiris hugged him back, and said, "I could never allow you to die for me, my son, but I am very proud to be your father." He slapped him on the back and added, "You make us all proud."

Sekhmet approached with a bottle of water and said, "Well done. Your instincts are incredible, and if anything your natural fighting skills are in themselves nearly impenetrable."

"I have to admit it, little brother, you are one badass dude," said Andrew, strolling over to drop his arm around his shoulders.

"Dude?" Luc asked, raising his eyebrow.

"Andrew? Just consider what you just saw and add motive and anger to that mix," Sekhmet said.

"Yup, total badass. Bring on the bad guys. But wait until after lunch. Let's go."

"Good to see your priorities are in order, son," said Isis.

Luc wondered at her sudden appearance. He knew she had been standing there for a short while to watch her sons fight with their father. She seemed well pleased at their male bonding. But she also seemed troubled, and he realized it must concern Kirin.

The boundaries which divide Life from Death are at best shadowy and vague. Who shall say where the one ends, and where the other begins?

Edgar Allan Poe, The Premature Burial

Chapter Thirty-Eight

Andrew stood beside the desk, shouting into the phone in Italian. "Tell Giovanni I said hello," Luc called out. In response, Andrew turned his back, used a curse Giovanni may have invented, apparently finally got the response he was looking for and switched to another line. This time he spoke charmingly in Swedish, then strung out a line of numbers, waited, named an impressive amount, in Euros, and then another string of numbers, a password for a wire transfer, and waited to hear it repeated back. Satisfied, he hung up and walked over to seat himself beside his brother.

Luc knew Giovanni's fear of doing the wrong thing sometimes resulted in him doing nothing. He was an able and willing worker who needed a bit more guidance. "Listen, why don't we get Claudio to pick up the leadership in that area until this is over. He's a good man, trustworthy, and not afraid to make a decision."

Andrew paused a moment, and then said, "That's a good idea. Depending on how it works out, I think it might have to be permanent. I can't baby-sit Giovanni."

Luc nodded his agreement to Andrew, then signaled the young server who stood at his side with a wine bottle, waited for him to fill the glass, and drew it to his lips. Their father kept the lower floor well stocked.

The working lunch was no surprise. Luc already sensed that Isis had important news to share. They sat at a small oval conference table in Osiris' study, eating from a light buffet that had been provided, waiting for Isis to speak. Luc studied her. She toyed with her food, deep in thought, not looking at anyone present. He realized she was communicating with Kirin.

Mother. I wish to speak with Kirin.

You may speak, Ljluka.

Kirin?

Is it you, Luc? Your brother is incorrigible.

He has not touched you?

No, no, but he wants me to agree to marry him.

Say no.

You need to save Nalini, Luc.

From whom? He asked, knowing enough to ask who and not what. He felt a rush of adrenaline, and then wondered why he cared so much.

Typhon. He scares me. He is more dangerous than them all, combined. If he has his way I don't even want to imagine what he will do to Nalini, and she's been so good to me, even after how I treated her. Did you know it was Typhon who whipped her for not killing you? He enjoyed it, Luc.

Luc's shoulders stiffened at the terror he sensed in his sister, at the obvious perversion of Typhon and how dangerous he was because of it. How bad must it be for her to be so afraid? She was usually so fearless. But he, too, feared what Typhon would do to Nalini. *Tell her to leave, at once. She isn't a prisoner like you, is she?*

No, but she won't. Both her mother and I have urged her to do so. She feels we need her to protect us, so she risks her own life. I must go, someone's coming.

Luc stared at his mother. She refused to meet his eyes. *Tell me, mother. What further secrets do you hide?* When, he wondered, would she finally admit that there was more going on here, that she had something to do with the events that were now playing out.

Concern yourself with saving your sister. If you can, save this woman and her mother.

"Very well, mother. Let's discuss just how we will be doing that."

"Doing what?" asked Andrew.

"Saving our sister and the other women from the maniac's regime."

Isis stared at him silently for a moment, and he sensed that she was reaching a decision about what to tell them and still retain some secret she would not give up unless absolutely necessary. He had to find out what it was, he decided. Refusing to look away from her piercing gaze, she finally revealed at least part of what she knew.

"Set plans to dupe us. He'll be sending Nalini disguised as Kirin to make the switch. He intends to force Kirin to marry Lucien and work for him in his genetics lab."

"He wants Kirin to marry Lucien?" asked Sekhmet.

"Yes, Lucien my brother, who kidnapped Kirin and is trying to force her to enter his bed against her will, Sekhmet. That isn't something you think is a good idea, is it'?"

"Of course not, Ljluka. Has he harmed her?" She said it as if she knew he wouldn't. Luc was incredulous. She hadn't seen him since his birth, how could she presume to know anything about him, he wondered.

"Not yet, but that will be next, won't it?" He grew annoyed at Sekhmet's apparent defense of Lucien's behavior.

"Would you harm her?"

"I assume that's a rhetorical question." He resented her comparing him to Lucien. She seemed unsympathetic to Kirin's plight and unwilling to see the problem with Lucien's behavior.

"Enough," Osiris interjected forcefully. "You speak about my little Kirin as if she were nothing but a pawn in all this. She belongs to no man. It is not for others to decide her fate."

"I think we can all agree on that, father," Luc said, gazing steadily at Sekhmet. He was pleased with his father's defense of Kirin. Osiris had always treated her with tender indulgence, but Kirin had earned his trust. She was an irreplaceable source of unfailing gaiety, kindness and understanding in a family filled with so many testosterone reliant males, a family run without question by an iron-willed female with a matriarchal disposition for whom surrender was not an option.

"I'm going after her," Andrew declared, apparently sharing Luc's growing need to see her home safely.

Luc pressed his hands against the table. He sensed resistance from Isis and before his mother could speak, he said, "Yes, I think that is what needs to be done. Andrew needs to go after Kirin and Nalini's mother." He continued to hold Isis's stare, defying her rising anger. "I will go and get Nalini who you say will be disguised as Kirin in Cairo, so they do not suspect we know."

"What makes you think they don't know, Luc? They know Kirin is talking to us," Osiris questioned.

"Yes, but Set doesn't know his wife Astarte is deceitful, running from him to Kirin and Nalini, telling them all his secrets and plans," Isis interrupted, standing as if her anger propelled her upward.

Luc watched as Osiris turned his head and studied Isis, who openly glared at him. Isis, probably the most jealous woman alive due to several indiscretions on the part of Osiris when he was much younger, just before he moved to the Underworld guardianship, was clearly jealous of Astarte. Luc wondered if Sekhmet could be induced to spill what she knew later on, in private.

He noticed his father glance up and down Isis's frame, his look becoming more heated, if also more guarded. Clearly he still lusted after her. Isis, at the very least was still passionately possessive of him. She had noted his glances too, if the way she lowered her lids and ran her tongue slowly across her full bottom lip were any indication.

"This can only end in a full scale war. Set will never part with Astarte, mother," Luc said, growing impatient with his parents' continued battle of wills. They had all lived with the emotional warfare their entire lives, and he certainly wasn't about to watch them seduce each other as if the rest of them weren't there.

"You are probably right, since she grows large with his son in her belly," replied Isis, but she was still not looking at him. She was watching Osiris' expression, which remained coolly neutral, Luc noticed, quite impressed. There was much more going on than jealousy and seduction, he realized.

"I have already contacted Horus. He will be sending forces and coming to help us end this once and for all," Osiris said, finally turning his attention away from his wife and addressing Anubis.

"We need to discuss the logistics. Obviously Luc needs to take a platoon and arrive early enough in Cairo to take out any snipers or peripheral personnel Set has in place. He needs a plan to get Nalini. Set has no intention of letting us have either Kirin or Nalini."

"They probably think once we learn of the duplicity we'll change tactics and go after Kirin, leaving Nalini as having no further negotiable value," offered Isis.

Luc nodded. "No problem taking her with me unless she herself tries to prevent it. I will get her either way, but it would simplify things if we contact Kirin and tell her the plan."

"It will be done, along with instructions for Kirin and the woman. Now how are you planning to--"

"Anubis will take his men and go for the women," Osiris commanded, with a meaningful look at Isis. "He and I will speak to Kirin and come up with a strategy for getting to them with the least resistance." Isis stiffened with rage, but remained silent, glaring at Osiris, who pretended not to notice.

"I think the real problem is going to be that these two events must take place simultaneously if they are to have the best chance to succeed," Luc said.

"Set will retaliate and go after them the moment he discovers they are gone," Sekhmet said, looking toward Isis. "He will want the woman and unborn child, above all else."

"The army must immediately come between him and what it is he wants," Isis said. "Horus and the rest of our army must be in place."

"They should arrive in small units, disguised at Bedouin," said Anubis.

"Or tourists," Luc remarked, thinking of a way for them to regroup with the rest of their forces. "I have an idea. What if I take Nalini and also the incantation? Let him think it is in our possession and that I have taken her to double-cross him. It's what he understands. He won't question it. But he will also pursue us, and we can lead him straight to the trap." And then he planned to beat the hell out of the bastard for what he did to Nalini, Luc thought.

"If you distract him and lead him into a trap, we will have less interference getting Kirin and the woman out. What's this woman's name, anyway?" Anubis asked.

Luc noticed the glare Isis shot Osiris. He wisely chose to remain silent, looking away and reaching for his glass of wine. "Her name is Astarte," Luc supplied softly, deciding he had discovered the true reason his parents no longer resided in the same domicile.

"Okay," said Osiris, "let's be sure we're all clear on the plan. Ljluka takes a platoon and gets Nalini, keeping the papyrus. It will probably be Typhon who will give chase and Ljluka will lead him straight into the ambush. I think, Anubis, that you will need to take a company of men with you. You will not need them with you in the palace to procure the women, but they will need to run interference while you get away and rejoin the army."

He looked to Sekhmet and said, "The pregnant woman will need to move slowly, so they will require additional time to escape. Set and Lucien will immediately give chase. That means the most logical location for the army will be the Syrian Desert."

"It is the easiest place to cover our activities both from Set and any too observant mortals, especially the Coalition Forces," Sekhmet agreed.

"Very well. Call in the Lieutenants for a briefing. We need to make this happen," confirmed Isis.

There were a lot of pieces to the puzzle, Luc realized. As usual, his was the first strategic move. He just hoped Nalini would cooperate. Too much was at stake for her to fight against him.

"Here thou must all distrust behind thee leave"
Dante Alighieri, *The Divine Comedy*

Chapter Thirty-Nine

"Get out!" Typhon bellowed at Rashid.

When the silent Nubian didn't budge, Typhon reached to his belt for his knife. "Do as he says, Rashid," Nalini commanded. Rashid hesitated and she added, "Do not return until I call for you."

As the Nubian exited, casting a menacing look at her brother, Typhon turned to her and said, "Wise decision."

The backhand he delivered caught her full in the face and she smarted more from her lack of preparation than the blow. "Next time see that you train him to follow my orders. As your husband, he will be my property because you will not have any."

"Rashid is not a slave," Nalini said, running her tongue across the inside of her cheek in an attempt to stem the flow of blood where his hand had slammed it against her teeth. "And don't you need me to be well enough to make the exchange?"

"You will be able to walk. How well doesn't matter," he said, advancing forward. She backed up, her hand going to her waist.

Realizing her intent, he snatched her wrist and threw himself into her with his entire body weight, smashing her to the floor of the tent where her head bounced it hit so hard. Her breath whooshed out of her. Stupid, stupid, she thought as she tried to force air from her lungs so she could suck in a slight breath. His weight was crushing her.

A moment of relief from the slow suffocation on her chest was soon forgotten as she realized he had only lifted up so that he could put his hands in her robes. He was ripping and tearing, searching for weapons, she realized. He threw them aside as he found them, and there were many. Finding a breath at last, she took another shallow gasp. He pulled aside her robes, ripping down the front and exposing the cotton camisole and underwear she had on beneath.

"Fine," she said softly, and in a way she hoped was seductive. "Would you like me to help you?"

Typhon glanced at her face in surprise. Calling her bluff, he smiled and said, "Yes, take your clothes off."

"Get off me. I am unable to do as you command."

"I think not." He sat up, straddling her waist. He let go of her hand and said, "Take off your robe."

Gritting her teeth, she reached down and began to tug on the bottom. "You are sitting on the edge," she said. He reached to pull it free. She tugged it up and over her breasts, exposing them to his greedy stare. He grabbed an edge to help her pull it over her head. Then he reached behind her head and snapped the band that held her hair confined and pulled it forward.

He lifted and moved his leg until he was kneeling beside her and said, "Now the pants."

She made a move to get up and he said, "No, stay here on the ground. Wriggle out of them."

Panic made her movements stiff as she curled her fingers around the waistband. His eyes moved from her breasts to her fingers as they slowly drew the waistband downward. She sighed as if completely bored. His gaze shifted to her face. She kept her expression stoic, barely able to breath past the tension in her chest. Lust, dirty and revolting gleamed from his eyes. She forced herself to meet his look with one of complete indifference rather than the hysteria she truly felt.

He bent down and grabbed her hair, jerking her to her feet with him as he rose. "Did I not tell you what a little whore you are? How many men have you been with?"

"Does it matter?" she asked evenly.

He nearly pulled the chunk of hair he held from her head as he used it like a handle and punched her face with his fist. "You are all whores," he raged. "Your mother, too, nothing but a whore, spreading her legs to get whatever she wants for the two of you. Don't think the rest of us don't know."

Nalini gasped, spitting out blood as she tried to breath. Her nose was completely plugged and blood dripped down her chest. He punched her in the stomach and said, "You could be carrying some bastard child too, for all we know!" She doubled over and fell to her knees thinking, stupid, stupid, why weren't you prepared when you knew how much he hated you?

He kicked her in the side and she rolled away, drawing her knees up and protecting her head with her arms. But he wasn't done yet. She was still alive. He grabbed her arm and jerked her up again. This time she managed to get in a right hook. Surprised, he left himself open to a knee in the groin and it was his turn to go down.

She felt his fingers wrap around her ankle and she lifted her other foot to kick him, but her reflexes were slow, her breathing labored, and she was bleeding all over the place. He pulled her foot out from under her. When she fell, he pressed a blade to her throat and unable to fully straighten his body, he still managed to reach with the other hand and clutch painfully at her breast. "And the biggest whore of all," he screamed, "was the one upon whose breasts I suckled!" He squeezed until she finally cried out in pain.

Then, satisfied, he staggered to his feet. She looked up at him and said, "When you use force on a woman in this way, you create an enemy that is only half conquered, Typhon." She meant the warning to be his last. Nothing he did would save him from her revenge now. He was insane. The loss of his mother had robbed him of all his humanity.

"Get your ass up and dressed. We leave in fifteen minutes. When I have more time, I will conquer the other half. You will be begging me to do whatever I want in order to please me and prevent me from getting angry."

He must die very soon. What she feared most he had just put into words.

She had not yet struggled to her feet when Rashid rushed in. Seeing her, he cursed and bent down. "How badly are you hurt?"

"I'll live," she whispered, but the laugh hurt too much to execute.

"We haven't much time. Please, help me assess the damage."

"Broken ribs, two. Split lip, one. Black eye coming, one. Bruised cheek happening, one. Bloody nose, one, though I don't think it's broken this time. Bruised fingerprints appearing on my arms, possibly my ankle, and my right breast," she said. "Helpful enough?"

"Sorry, little one. I am so very sorry," he said, and she knew he was. "They held me at gunpoint, or I would have returned sooner. As soon as they took me, I knew what he intended all along—but dead, I could not avenge you."

He went away for a moment and came back with a basin of warm water and a soft cloth. She kept her fingers pressed on either side of her nose, stopping the flow. Gentle for such a large man, he cleansed her face, softly dabbing the blood from her nose as she lifted her fingers and discovered the bleeding had stopped. He then washed the blood from her body. Helping her to stand, the huge Nubian acted as her handmaiden, lifting a new camisole over her head, then clean robes, ones no longer covered with blood. His act of kindness was noble and she felt respected and cared for, the violent humiliation of before fading beside his quiet dignity.

"Not much longer, Rashid. Soon we will be free. I can survive any of it knowing that at last there is an end in sight."

He nodded, looking into her eyes, a question being asked without words. "He-he didn't do that," she said. His silent look of relief embarrassed her more than his helping her clean and cover her nakedness. She glanced away and said, "We better go."

Before they left the tent, she pulled the covering over her face. Her quick intake of breath reminded Rashid of her ribs and he lifted the transparent veil over her head that would mask even her eyes. Intended to disguise Nalini's lavender eyes so the Vargas clan would not realize it wasn't Kirin's green eyes staring out at them, it was instead good camouflage for the swelling and bruises.

She moved stiffly to the camel. Rashid helped her mount. A gasp escaped her as the poor beast did only what was natural and stood up like a folding yardstick about to be used.

Glancing at her hand on the saddle, she noted the scrapes and swelling of her knuckles and hoped Typhon's eye was at least a little puffy, and that the saddle rubbed him raw in new and rewarding ways. He was out of control. His violence confirmed the wisdom of her decision to escape with the help of Vargas.

It was her mother's tears that had finally persuaded her to agree. Fearing harm to the child or her mother, she had tried not to think of how angry Vargas must be, how difficult it would be to face him again. He probably blamed her for his death, the kidnapping of his sister. She could still close her eyes and see the blood spreading across his chest, see him toppling over the cliff.

Even Rashid believed he was sincere in his offer to help her escape, however. She had agreed to cooperate, but she would reserve judgment about the honest intentions of the Illuminati's enforcer. Ljluka was far too complex to simply come to her aid. He was no longer a chivalrous medieval knight, a Templar, and he was still a man.

She continued to contemplate that fact for the entire trip. Though it seemed a longer and more uncomfortable ride to Cairo than she had experienced in centuries, she had still not sorted through her feelings about the coming transaction.

Rashid helped her dismount when they neared the *Khan el Khalili* market. They were traveling on foot now to help them remain anonymous in the loud, confusing chaos of the market place. Even more congested than the other impossibly narrow streets of Cairo, with its complete lack of road markings or apparent traffic laws, the market sounded like a playground for insane adults.

The cry of "How can I take your money?" sounded amidst the hawking of stall owners, who normally would have rushed forward to thrust wares in their faces and extol on their virtues.

Apparently the sight of Typhon and entourage intimidated even the most desperate vendors. Rashid, with no more than an occasional sharp stare was able to shield Nalini from any possible jostling. No one wanted to get within reach of her formidable companion. Her severe apparel and subservient position five feet behind Typhon signified his possession of her. Rashid signified his intention to keep her.

She wondered how Typhon could possibly think even a small group of militant and heavily armed soldiers were blending in. His covert operatives were though, slipping here and there throughout the market, looking for Vargas operatives, and drawing nearer and nearer to the target, the *Naguib Mahfouz* coffee shop.

The location was perfect, in the heart of the market with its thousand or so shops and its crowded, constricted streets. One of the noisiest places in the world, she doubted the sound of fighting, even gunfire, would draw much undo attention. The intellectual clientele in the coffee shop named for Egypt's Nobel prize winning author was also a good choice. It would be difficult to openly kill someone inside the more civilized air-conditioned atmosphere of the crowded sandwich and snack shop.

She saw the shop down the road. Typhon stepped up his pace. One of his men appeared just ahead, pretending to look at a brass platter in a stall. Nalini turned her attention and glanced up as she felt a hand on her upper arm, and nearly gasped when his intense blue gaze pierced straight through her veil. She got a fleeting impression of a blue ball cap, its brim shading his face from the hot sun and masking the light blond of his hair before he turned and pulled her with him toward a side street.

Realization lent her feet wings and she raced down the steps, Luc's hand still grasping her arm. This was it. If she didn't escape Typhon now there would be no second chance. She sensed Rashid behind her, but didn't dare turn to look for fear of tripping in the nearly ankle-deep trash that had been swept into the narrow street by stall owners.

Through a stone arch, they ran down another set of steps, speeding dangerously for a shop overcrowded with hundreds of lamps. A lamp over her head shattered. She ducked, and then gasped as her ribs protested. Luc turned and fired back, and then moved his grasp from her arm to her hand. She wondered at his possessive contact. Was he concerned for her safety or taking no chance that she might try to evade him as well as Typhon? She considered the possibility, the probable consequences.

A man who had just entered the shop toppled into a stand of glass lampshades. Luc's bullet had found its target. The owner began cursing in Arabic and rushed forward. They ran out under the archway at the back.

Her chest heaved with the sustained running and she took faster but shallower breaths to ease the agony of her broken ribs. She tried to keep her upper body stationary, but he was grasping her hand tightly and pulling her along in such an urgent way that it caused constant shifting of her ribs until she could barely breathe at all. If only she were not injured. She realized she might not escape Typhon even with help in her current condition. There was little chance she could escape them both, and where would she hide? For now she was stuck with Vargas. Glancing up at him, she noticed a sparkling gleam in his eyes that could only be excitement, a thrill of the danger. She recognized it because she understood that thrill all too well. If not for the agonizing pain, she too would be more excited.

They ducked into a shop, raced through the aisles of colorful Indian saris and Egyptian women's apparel, through the exit where they turned right. She glanced back and thought she saw Typhon, eyes blazing with fury. And then she did feel a spark of excitement. Even more than that. She felt pure joy to be the cause of Typhon's rage, knowing that he could do nothing about it. Nothing at all. She smiled, then grunted as she broke open the cut on her lip.

Coming out to another street, Luc pulled open the door of a battered car and pushed her inside. Rashid raced to the other side. A man she had not previously seen turned and shot behind them, then jumped into the front passenger seat and Luc, sending another bullet behind him, quickly slid in beside her.

Vargas was a huge presence in such a small vehicle, or perhaps it just seemed so to her because he was so close. His left arm pressed up against hers so tightly she could feel his muscles flex as he turned to look out the window. From hip to knee her leg rode intimately against his and unbidden she remembered what it felt like to have her legs wrapped around his waist, his tongue exploring her lips. She sucked in her breath, let it out slowly as her ribs protested.

They sped off among the mass of tooting horns, camels, sheep sandwiched between parked cars, cattle hauling produce, yelling and hand waving gestures that were uniquely and typically Cairo.

Luc shifted in the seat, facing forward to glance at the vehicle's occupants. Nalini slowed her breathing again, and pressed her hands against her midriff. The car was hot and confining, the large men on either side of her now cramping her sides. She tried to inhale, but felt as if the air was too thin to breath. Resting her eyes for a moment, she leaned her head against the solid arm beside her. Luc's muscle flexed slightly at the unfamiliar contact, and then remained still. She still didn't trust him, but she was grateful to be free of Typhon. For now she needed his help.

"Thank you," Nalini said softly.

She rested her eyes for a moment longer, and barely heard something that sounded like a gunshot, but couldn't figure out why she was just now hearing the glass of the lamps shatter. Luc would probably have enough money to pay for it. If not, she would sweep it up when she woke, she thought weakly.

419

When that which is coming comes - and no soul shall then deny its coming - some shall be abased and others exalted.

The Qu'ran, 56:1

Elizabeth Alsobrooks

Chapter Forty

Nalini fell forward and he reached to pull her up. He smelled the blood and stiffened before he saw it on the front of her veil. "Have you been hit?" he cried.

She didn't respond and Rashid leaned down and looked at her. He ripped a piece of his sleeve off and reached under her veil to press it against her nose. "She hit her nose and it is bleeding," he said. "She hates to draw attention."

Luc nodded, and then reached into one of numerous pant pockets to retrieve more bullets and reloaded his gun. Roscoe, in the front, was already firing back. Rolling down his window, Luc let the metallic scent rush through him. He reached up and shot at the roof of a nearby shop and a man holding a rifle rose up at that instant. The man, hit in the forehead, staggered back and disappeared from view.

Turning his attention to Nalini regardless of her dislike of it, he said again, "Are you okay?"

"She has fainted, the heat is all," Rashid assured him.

"Fainted? Is that normal?" She hardly seemed the type to faint from the heat. Hell, she lived in the desert.

Then Rashid nodded, and said, "She is unused to the heavy draping." Now that made sense, he decided, and turned back to look through the newly ventilated back window.

Satisfied that they were not being followed, Luc turned around and tapped the earpiece. "We got her. Didn't even have to enter the restaurant. Some. Oh, they were surprised alright. No, we're just leaving Cairo."

They reached Giza, and their driver sped toward the Nile.

Reaching the landing they sought, Luc opened the door and got out, reaching back for Nalini. Rashid was already helping her out the other side. He stood and looked over the top of the car, frowning as he saw her stumble. Hurrying around the car, he scooped her up and moved toward the boat. Rashid followed behind.

Once on board the barge, Luc carried her into a cabin, kicked the door shut behind him in Rashid's face, and sat her on the edge of a bunk. "What's going on?" he asked, reaching to pull the transparent veil from her face. "Shit." Then cursing loudly, he pulled the entire hijab from her head.

He stared at her, momentarily unable to take it in. Her left eye was green and yellow and nearly swollen shut. Her lip was slit and also swollen. Her nose still had traces of blood in the nostrils and it was bruised. Her cheek had a cut over the bone and that too was horribly discolored. He swallowed. He swallowed again. Steeling his spine, he reached for her hand. Gently he lifted it to his lips and anointed each bloodied knuckle. He was angrier than he had ever been before, but determined not to show it. She might think the anger directed at her and she had obviously had enough of angry men for a lifetime.

Typhon would be dealt with.

Later.

"I hope the shiner I saw on that bastard was from you, scrapper," he said softly. Her lips turned upward slightly, but she grimaced and instinctively reached to press the back of her hand against it. His gut tightened at the gesture, at the pain that crossed her injured face.

"Lean forward," he said. She would have protested, but he insisted. She was too tired, too weak and too sore to put up much of a struggle.

Gingerly, he pulled open her robe. "Nalini, I don't mean to get personal, but I want to wrap your ribs. It's obvious they're broken. You're been hugging them the entire time and I can't believe I didn't realize sooner. If I don't tape them, they may shift and puncture a lung. We really need you to be able to stay conscious for the rest of our trip today."

She nodded, leaning against his chest as he helped her slip down the sleeves of her robe. As she sat up again, he moved to a nearby cupboard and looked around for the medical supplies his men always kept stocked. Finding what he needed, he moved back to the bunk and kneeled down. She had closed her eyes, exhaustion showing in the weary slump of her shoulders.

That was when he noticed the bruises on her chest just above the simple periwinkle ribbon that laced in and out around the top of her camisole. The elongated discolorations crowned the rise of her breast. His lips set in a firm line, he tugged the little bow in the center of her camisole.

"No," she protested softly, raising her hand to cover his.

"Please, Nalini. I need to see." He reached with his other hand and gently pulled her hand away. She dropped it into her lap and looked down as though embarrassed, running her tongue across her swollen lips. If Typhon were within his reach at that moment he would have been dead and diced.

Her camisole separated and he pulled it down and away from her chest, revealing the blackened imprint of Typhon's fingers on her pale skin. His eyes narrowed with the force of his emotional reaction.

"I wasn't prepared. I should have been. It was stupid, my own fault," she said, jerking the undergarment against herself.

"Your fault?" His head snapped up in surprise. "If it's anyone's fault besides that sick bastard's, it's mine. I never should have let them convince me to allow you to come to Cairo alone with him."

"Look, you know I'll be fine in the morning," she said, refusing to look him in the eye.

"The physical scars may be gone, Nalini, but the emotional ones remain."

"He didn't rape me."

At least she had been spared that horror. This time. Typhon needed to die. Leaning his forehead against hers, as the only spot on her face not cut or bruised, he said, "I am so sorry you ever had to suffer at their hands, Nalini." He had promised never to kiss her again unless she asked him to. Until she did, he could never break that promise. Too many promises had been broken to this slight woman before him. Now, though, he wished he hadn't said it. He wanted to softly and gently kiss away every bruise on her body. Not just the physical ones, but the mental ones, the ones with more lasting and damaging scars. He felt an overwhelming need to protect her.

"Can you do me a favor?" he whispered.

"If I can."

"Try not to think of him any more. But if you do think of how cruel and evil he was, of what he did to you, remember that not all men hurt women. Most men do not. And some men wish only to give them pleasure and bring them happiness."

"Which kind of man are you, Luc?" She stared with luminous lavender orbs straight into his heart. It quickened in response.

"Which kind do you think?" He waited anxiously for her response.

She hesitated and then said, "I-I think I am only beginning to realize how different you are from all the men I have known in the past." Her breath came in soft wisps that fanned his face like a caress.

"I will continue to show you then, until you are sure, Nalini. Will you give me a fair chance?" He realized he must prove to her that not all men wished her harm or to use her for their own selfish purposes.

"Yes. That I can promise," she said.

He decided to settle for that.

For now.

The urge to kiss away her pain settled to a dull ache, and he vowed, "I swear to you that while I have breath in my body, I will not let that animal put his hands on you again, Nalini."

She nodded, looking relieved that someone was taking care of her for a change. Unable to resist, he admitted, "I wish I could so easily kiss away your memory of each blow." It looked for a moment as if she was going to ask him to do so. She dropped his gaze and even looked down at his lips, but kept silent.

Knowing the critical timing they were under, he reluctantly looked away and moved to wrap her ribs, tightly, though not too tight. "How's your breathing?" he checked, mindful to quiet his own. Her nearness intoxicated him.

"Better. Thank you."

He dug in the bottom cupboard, pushed aside some scuba gear and pulled out an oxygen mask. Attaching it to a tank he had just noticed fastened to the bulkhead, he pulled the elastic straps around her head and said, "Here, breathe from this for a few minutes. It should make a big difference."

His sudden desire to take a few long dregs of the oxygen himself was delayed by a soft tap on the door. Luc reached to pull up Nalini's robe before he said, "Come."

Rashid entered, looked at Nalini and her oxygen mask and visibly relaxed.

Luc bristled at the way he seemed to be reassuring himself that Luc had not harmed her in some way. The man was alert and cautious. Well he should be, Luc thought, banking his displeasure for Nalini's sake.

He stood to face the stern-faced warrior, moving his gaze up a few inches. His brothers were taller still. Luc was certainly not intimidated, but could sense the suppressed disquiet in the Nubian. Good. His instincts were strong. Rashid sensed the unusual lethal power Luc possessed. He was glad for Nalini's sake that the man seemed so alert, though the hulking guard had already failed her at least once.

"I would appreciate it if in the future should I ask you about Nalini's physical or emotional wellbeing, you give me a truthful answer, Rashid. Unlike the vile pervert you allowed to attack her earlier today, I would never, ever hurt her."

Rashid stiffened at his words, but remained mute, holding his stare with stubborn effort, Luc noted. "She should have been carried. I have no idea how she made it out of the bazaar under her own power. I might have injured her worse by not knowing," he told him. I am going to make Typhon regret he ever put his hands on her, is what he told himself.

He tapped his earpiece and said, "Yes. How long ago? We're on our way. Make sure the plane is there." Opening a small refrigerator, he pulled out a water bottle. "Here," he said, twisting off the cap and holding it out to her. "You want a couple of those?" he asked, pointing to a bottle of aspirin on the counter. They both knew anything stronger would only slow her natural cell regeneration. She nodded and he opened the bottle and shook out three, handing them to her. She put them in her mouth, took a long drink, then grimaced a little and touched her hand to her split lip. Straightening the pillow on the bunk, he suggested, "You have about an hour before we get there, so why don't you get a little sleep? We will keep watch over you."

She turned without argument and let him help her lay down. He pulled a blanket over her, and she was sound asleep almost instantly.

Rashid sat in a chair in the corner, so Luc stepped out to speak to Roscoe.

He found him standing under the shade of a lean-to on the front of the mock house boat, vigilantly scanning the shores. Dressed in khaki shorts and a linen shirt that must have come from the tourist market near the pyramids, he still didn't quite fit the part of a sightseer. He was too alert, too bulky with tensed muscles, looking like he'd be more comfortable in desert camo with dark smudges finger-painted under each eye, bullet belts crossing his back and an automatic weapon clutched at his side.

"The woman is injured." Stated like a known fact. Luc realized Roscoe had quickly assessed the situation, as usual.

"Yes, but she is resting now. She should be able to make the transfer."

"I take it our final A/O will be changing?" It was more a statement than a question and Luc wondered briefly how a man seemingly so devoid of emotions or long-term personal relationships could have such uncanny insight of both.

"What makes you think so?" Luc couldn't resist asking.

Roscoe turned to look at him then, shaking his head. "Not my place to say so, but since you asked, for a man so infrequently wrong about situations, you sure don't seem to be reading the signs between you two very well."

"What are you talking about?" Luc pressed, though he was beginning to wish he'd never asked in the first place.

"Good thing you're actually on the Nile," Roscoe said. "It's not like you. Face it and move on or do something about it. Whatever you decide, we always got your back," he concluded, shrugging.

"Damn. You don't miss much, Roscoe. You're right, our final target has moved. We'll be changing the area of operations, but not until the rabbit's in the snare."

"Figured you'd be needin' payback." Roscoe turned again to scanning the shores, letting Luc keep his thoughts and feelings to himself. He'd said all he intended.

Luc stopped a grin at the idea of Roscoe spouting Socratic wisdom, swiveled on his heels and walked to the other end of the boat.

He noted the covert locations of the Illuminati's Cairo faction. Most were now behind shuttered windows of small cabins that ran the length of the houseboat which boasted a motor a much larger and sleeker craft would have envied. They had arrived both before and after him, separately or in pairs. Those in view around the rails, some with cameras that were secretly used to zoom in like binoculars, were dressed in tourist garb, as was he—which is why Typhon's men had not recognized him, even now that they knew to look for a Lucien look-alike. The ball cap Abdul had once teased him about had probably done the trick.

He moved to the railing, clutching it to still his escalating temper. The more he admitted his feelings for Nalini to himself, the angrier he got about what Typhon had done to her, and not just this time. That he had whipped her for not killing him…. His gaze automatically scanned the shoreline, the passing boats and their occupants. But his mind was on Nalini.

Teeth clenched, he thought of the bruising and abrasions that marred the larger portion of her otherwise smooth and supple skin. He still remembered the way it felt as his fingers glided along it the one time he had actually held her in his arms, and could not imagine why Typhon would want to damage it, to give her so much pain. The man was demented.

Kirin thought Typhon hated her and Astarte. His psychosis ran much deeper than that. *The man has some serious mommy issues*, Luc said to himself. He obviously desired women, but his behavior insinuated that he hated them for that, too, considering his desire to be a weakness that they preyed upon because all women were whores, in his mind. If Nalini had remained in his clutches he would have killed her, over and over again like a blowup doll he could smash down, shove under a bed and take out and inflate again at will. Not even Set made him want a complete genetic transplant more.

Glancing at his hands, he lifted them and realized the metal railing had bent under the force of his grip. So too, he vowed, would Typhon's neck. He was anxious to see how well the bully did against someone of his own gender and physical advantage. It couldn't hurt that his own strength had grown considerably since channeling his powers in a more positive way.

Nalini, despite Typhon's warped reasoning, was not responsible for his mother's leaving. Nephthys had not left Typhon, she had fled in terror from his father, after his father killed Osiris. To kill a member of one's own clan was unheard of, until Set. And now he planned to make another exception, and again because of Set. He knew for a fact Nephthys had tried to contact Typhon and he had continued to curse her and shout such vile things that she had eventually given up.

It was their father who had caused the flight that ravaged Typhon's life. How ironic, Luc thought, that Typhon inherited the very trait that had ruined his chance at a normal life and would ultimately end it.

The terrible bodies of the giants lay crushed beneath their own massive structures and the earth was drenched and soaked with torrents of blood from her sons. Then, they say, she breathed life into this warm blood and, so that the offspring might not be completely forgotten changed it into the shape of men. But the men thus born, no less than the giants, were contemptuous of the gods, violent and cruel, with a lust to kill: It was obvious that they were the children of blood.

Ovid, Metamorphosis

Elizabeth Alsobrooks

Chapter Forty-One

Luc stood on the rung beneath Nalini, his arms on either side of the rope ladder, his torso leaned solidly into her back, to prevent her from slipping. She was little refreshed from the nap, and realized she might not have the strength to hold on without his help. As the ladder neared the hovering helicopter, he lifted her carefully into the arms of Rashid, who hung well over the side to ensure her ribs were not jarred or crushed in the transition.

As Luc climbed into the cargo door, the soldier he called Roscoe slipped a hand under his arm and helped heave him aboard. Nalini had heard Luc tell Roscoe that the hydroplane had been forced by overzealous Egyptian airmen to turn aside from the rendezvous point in the Mediterranean. Though a backup plan, the chopper would get them to Damascus and still bypass Israeli and Lebanese airspace.

They hoped the trouble in Egypt d was a sign that Typhon was hot on their trail and trying to slow them down. Luc moved to stand patiently beside Rashid. It took a moment for the Nubian to realize Luc was waiting for him to vacate his seat next to Nalini which he quickly filled.

Nalini knew better than to assume his infatuation with her was more than lust and admiration. It was no doubt merely momentary fascination. Did he think she would so quickly become comfortable with the idea? His nearness disturbed her. Did he have to be so intense all the time? She closed her eyes to block him from her thoughts so she could get some rest.

His arm brushed against her as he raised it, and she realized he tapped his earpiece. "Yes," he said softly. "So you're sure it was him? Good." He clicked off the satellite feed and she felt his attention on her. She opened her eyes and studied him pensively.

"Something I can answer for you?" he asked.

"Are we still on schedule? We were supposed to be on a plane, right? Won't this slow us down?" She needed to stay on top of Typhon. His death had become a priority for her. Though relieved she was free of him, she would never feel completely safe while he lived. And she knew he would not rest until he killed the child within Astarte's womb. No doubt he would consider his troublesome sister a bonus.

"It might have, but we made better time in the boat than we anticipated, so we will still be arriving as scheduled."

She nodded, relieved.

"No," he said.

"No? We are not on time?" Why was he being so obtuse?

"Yes, we are on time. No, you will not be confronting Typhon."

Why did he always seem to know what she was thinking? It was infuriating. She glanced away. "I was wondering if my mother has been rescued yet and if--""It's no use. In answer to your question, that probably won't be until tomorrow night. We don't expect Typhon to catch up with us until then either. He certainly won't confront us before that time. We have set up roadblocks, because we don't want him to think we aren't trying to escape. All you need to worry about is recovery. I would think it a relief to have someone else responsible for keeping you safe for a little while, Nalini."

She looked into his eyes and said seriously, "It is. I mean, at first I thought Kirin was soft, weak, because she had been so sheltered, because she had all of you looking out for her. But then I realized that it actually made her stronger. It's like you are all a part of who she is. Her self confidence comes from the security of her family's love." Nalini was surprised at her own candor. Until this moment, she had not put her feelings about Kirin into words.

"She is never really alone," she continued. "I don't mean just because your mom, well, you know, can talk to her. It's because she has this incredible sense of belonging, of knowing who she is and who she loves and who she can trust. It must be so freeing, so liberating to feel that way." Noticing his rapt attention, she suddenly felt embarrassed by her honest confidence. Why did this man have the ability to make her reveal so much of herself? No one else had this effect on her. He made her feel hopeful, as if a better future was a certain reality.

"Who do you trust, Nalini?" Why did he care?

She looked immediately at Rashid, and said, "Rashid. I was placed into his hands at birth, and my mother challenged him to protect me with his life. The only emotion I have ever seen him display has been over me." Luc glanced across at Rashid who had never taken his eyes from them. Nalini thought he looked to be reevaluating his impression of the Nubian. "My mother of course," she added. "I trust her."

"No one else?" he prodded.

"Well, sometimes I thought Lucien tried to help me, to protect me from Typhon. We were close when we were children," she said softly, feeling regret that they no longer were.

"Is there no one else that you can trust, Nalini?"

She studied his face silently for a moment, suddenly realizing he wanted her to trust him. What shocked her the most is that she wanted to believe in his sincerity and perhaps already did. Remembering the way Kirin spoke of her brothers, she said truthfully, "I would like to be able to trust you, Ljluka, the way Kirin does."

"I consider it a worthy goal," he vowed. "We will need to be often together in order for you to measure my trustworthiness," he murmured, shifting closer and leaning down to her so that his face was mere inches away. Was it possible that he too felt a need to be near her, to spend time in her company? Or did he feel only desire as she had assumed?

Perhaps his actions were a trick, and his true purpose was revenge on her for the wrongs he imagined she'd done. "Aren't you still angry with me for before, when I escaped."

He reached into his tourist shirt and took a ring from the pocket. Lifting her hand, he slipped it onto her finger. "I have been waiting to return this. You left it with Andrew," he explained, cupping her much smaller hand within his own, though he had no further reason to possess it. "Your message to Rashid, the one he would know came from you."

"Yes," she agreed, gazing down at the ring she had missed. Her thumb, from years of habit, often rubbing against it, seeking to right the slipped face of the too large ring. "My mother gave it to me. She said it was very special and I should never lose it. I rarely take it off. We were both distraught when I remembered where I had left it. Thank you." When she didn't pull away, he laid his other hand over hers.

The vehicle dipped and lowered and they realized it was about to land. "You're welcome," he said simply, though for a moment it seemed he wanted to say much more and she realized he too knew there was much unsaid between them. "We have arrived in Syria," he added, as if to refocus his current purpose, his mission, rather than to reveal their location.

Moments later Roscoe slid the door open. Luc released her hand, and Nalini hoped he didn't notice her involuntary grimace when she stood. He hurried to the door, jumped down and turned back to take her gingerly from Rashid. Careful not to jar her ribs, he carried her to the waiting plane. She enjoyed his solicitous attention, the way he carefully handled her, attempted to safeguard her from painful jars and bumps.

Despite herself, she felt safe and cared for while he looked after her. If she should feel trapped or imprisoned, it was too late to rectify. She slept tucked into his side most of the way.

The cushioned vibrations of the small plane as it landed in the deep desert and bumped to a stop at the top of a wide sand hill woke Nalini. She righted herself and rubbed at her uninjured eye. As the door opened, she stood.

Rashid helped guide her down from the plane, still drowsy, and Luc walked with her to the waiting Land Rover. He settled her into the back and walked around to get into the driver side back seat. Roscoe slipped into the driver's seat and Rashid occupied the passenger side.

Studying his strong jaw line as he gazed out the window, she wondered what Luc was thinking. He was a man his powerful family trusted with their most dangerous high-stakes missions. And yet he was also a man who could gently urge her into the crook of his arm and tell her softly to rest so she could heal, a man who had vowed to keep her safe. Was she just another mission to him, or did he care as much as the concern in his eyes told her? He turned to her at that moment, and she nearly gasped at the intensity of the feelings his stare evoked. Her heart fluttered in her chest and she found it difficult to breath, impossible to look away.

He smiled then, a smile that reached his eyes and made her feel that she was the most important person alive at that moment, at least to him. She was lost, struggling to free herself from the seductive pull of his nearness. He refused to release her, refused to look away. Finally she managed to force her eyelids down, willing her exhaustion to pull her from his dangerous magnetism. It was her only defense, and by morning that too would be gone.

An hour before sunset, they arrived at a small Bedouin encampment. After a quick and necessary pause to use the facilities, the men changed into Bedouin clothing and walked to camels sitting caravan-style in the hot sands behind the camp. Nalini sighed at the sight of the rocking torment, but Luc was quick to reassure her.

"Don't worry. You can ride with me and I will help counter the rocking so your ribs won't be jostled."

Grateful, if nervous to be so intimately against him within the embrace of his arms for so long, she nodded. He hopped into the saddle, tied a bag down and slid back, making room for Rashid to lift her onto the front of the saddle. Her breath caught in her throat when Rashid released her. She held herself stiffly a moment, then relaxed her torso as the pain dissipated.

Once seated, Luc leaned into her so that she would not have to lie backward and strain her ribs in order to gain the stability she would need.

The camel unfolded its legs and stood, and Luc, apparently realizing what she had done said, "Don't hold your breath. Just take shallow, gentle breaths. It will ease once we get going." True to his word, he gently moved against her back, countering the motion of the camel. Comforting in more than a physical sense, she gave herself over to the security of his care, deciding it could do little harm for her to enjoy this one small pleasure. It did not, she told herself, mean that she trusted him.

As their journey progressed he fed her handfuls of nuts and dried fruit stored in the bag dangling from his saddle, and kept her constantly hydrating with ample dregs on his goatskin. The result of his pampering was every bit as relaxing as riding a camel usually was. Her ribs were not strained, her stomach was filled, and she reminded herself that he no doubt had some unrevealed motivation for keeping her healthy and content enough not to escape his supervision. Nevertheless, when her eyes began to flutter downward and became too heavy for her to lift from her cheeks, she again felt safe in his arms as she drifted to sleep.

She stirred briefly as the platoon, now dressed in Bedouin garb along with the true Bedouin warriors who had joined them, passed between the armies of Osiris and Horus to the East and Isis and Anubis to the West. They kept going for another half hour, then stopped to make camp. Nalini was aware, on some level, of their progress, but not until they stopped did she bother to stir herself from her comfortable position between Luc's legs, her back supported by his rigid chest. But then he moved and she allowed him to gently lift her in his arms as he threw his leg over the seated camel and easily landed, moving to kneel down and set her upon a rug tossed on the sand by one of the Bedouin.

Hassidim arrived in a Humvee, and soon made Nalini more comfortable in Luc's tent--at his command. He remained outside speaking to Roscoe and Abdul. As Hassidim began preparing dinner, Luc entered the tent and said softly, "I need to return to the army encampment for a final war conference. Abdul, Roscoe, Rashid and the others will keep you safe until my return. Just relax and continue to rest so that you can heal."

When she responded with only a slight nod of her head, he studied her a moment, his eyes asking a question she wasn't ready to think about, let alone answer. He reached out as if without conscious thought and pushed the veil down from her head. Lifting a stray lock of hair, he smoothed it back, running his hand down the length of it as it cascaded down her back, in a casual but no less erotic caress. More deliberately, as if he needed to touch her but feared rejection, he gently grazed his knuckles across her uninjured cheekbone. Then, without a word he stood up and walked toward the entrance.

Her troubled gaze followed his progress, noting the easy, purposeful long strides, the seemingly effortless military posture, the way his broad shoulders tapered to a narrow waist and hips, and the way his legs took their time reaching calf-high military boots.

She watched as his long fingers reached to lift the tent flap, held her breath as he turned to glance back at her as if reluctant to leave or perhaps wondering if he held her attention, and then exhaled in a sigh as he ducked his head and disappeared. Her aloof feelings for this man, her determined disinterest no longer existed even in self-denial. He was unlike any other man she had ever known. What good did it do to deny the truth of it? She still knew enough about men to know a lie from the truth when she heard it and to understand the difference between hostile brutality and tender kindness. Even if he had ulterior motivation to keep her safe and under his protection it was not necessary for him to see to that care himself, preventing even Rashid from interfering.

She had noticed, too, the way he took any opportunity to touch her, if only to place his hand in the hollow of her back. His touch was possessive, but not in a repressive, subjugating way, more like protective, intimate gestures. Like a lover, she thought suddenly, the idea sending warmth to her cheeks. There was no denying the passionate nature of this man. He no longer made any attempt to disguise his desires. The intensity of his stares were stimulating for her as well, but there was something else there, something more than physical attraction. It was that which frightened her.

Hassidim interrupted her confused thoughts with the more welcome arrival of dinner. Thanking him, she turned her attention to safer thoughts.

His hands tightened on the steering wheel. Luc was trying his best to be patient, to remember the abuse Nalini had suffered at the hands of the male members of her own family. What more, he wondered, could he do to assure her that not all men were like that? He knew in his head that he must let her reach those conclusions in her own time and continue to be unfailingly tender and considerate. But his heart, now awakened, was impatient to requisition reciprocal affection.

Luc arrived at the portable communication headquarters that Roscoe had pointed out as the ant hill on their way past. He ran up the steps and entered the vehicle.

"Everything go okay?" Andrew asked, already knowing the answer as he kept in near constant touch with Luc whenever they were on a mission.

"Yes."

He shifted his weight and ran his hand through his hair, uncomfortable under Andrew's keen scrutiny. "What aren't you saying?" Andrew asked. The other occupants turned to look at Luc. He moved to stand across the table from his mother and father. Horus, like Andrew and Sekhmet was standing. Seeing Nephthys seated across from his mother, he went to stand beside her. She smiled up at him, and pressed her cheek against his shoulder as he leaned down to hug her.

"Yes, what aren't you saying, Ljluka?" Isis demanded.

He frowned at her imperious tone, especially given what he suspected of her. *It is this, mother. Father, you too must know.*

We are with you, Ljluka.

He let them explore his thoughts and opened up about his feelings. He thought of Nalini, gasping in pain, slumping against him, staggering at the car, holding her breathe as she was mounted onto the camel, the look of her battered face, her bruised and beaten body._These things he concentrated on so that his parents would know and understand. Then, the way she took his breath away when she looked up at him from under sooty lashes, the feel of her hand, so tiny within his, as he kissed each knuckle, the way his heart swelled whenever his eyes fell upon her, all these feelings he laid raw to them. After all, he knew it was useless to try to hide the truth, and they should know he intended to keep her safe, which meant away from her family. That left only his family with which she could live.

I must be allowed to kill him. He must never again be allowed to put his hands on her or any other of our women. He is a worse threat than his father.

Isis and Osiris looked across the table at each other. Their presence left his mind and he knew they were speaking privately. No doubt they were also considering Nephthys' feelings. She would not react well, but she must be made to realize the man he had become in no way resembled the boy she was forced to leave behind.

Finally, Osiris said, "You must follow your heart, but Nephthys must be told."

"Told what?" she asked.

Isis glanced at her and Luc could tell that she was conveying all that had occurred. Nephthys stood up. Then she sat down again. She pressed her hands against her eyes and whispered, "My fault. All my fault."

"There is plenty enough blame to go around, Nephthys," said Osiris, looking at Isis. "Now is the time to make things right."

The glory of Him who moveth everything
Doth penetrate the universe, and shine
In one part more and in another less.
Within that heaven which most his light receives
Was I, and things beheld which to repeat
Nor knows, nor can, who from above descends;
Because in drawing near to its desire
Our intellect ingulphs itself so far,
That after it the memory cannot go.
       Dante Alighieri, The Divine Comedy

Chapter Forty-Two

Sidled against his warmth, Nalini lay on her back to protect her ribs. Her hand had slipped casually against his thigh and he wisely decided to let it fall away as he rotated to his side so he could better enjoy the look and feel of her against him in the firelight. Who knew when he would get another chance?

Her breathing was shallow, but not labored. Already the bruises on her face were fading. By morning, as she had said, she would be completely healed. The sleep he had insisted she get during the day had ensured the healing time needed.

The cut on her lip appeared less severe, the swelling already gone. He remembered the taste of her, and reached out to finger a stray strand of hair from her face. She seemed so delicate snuggled up next to him, so innocent in her slumber. Too exhausted to argue, she had allowed him to lie down beside her in the tent Hassidim had miraculously acquired for her. But he had declared that he was not leaving her alone until she was completely restored and her mother and Kirin had arrived to keep her company.

He didn't want her to wake up and be alone and afraid. She would never admit it, but he sensed that she sometimes did. He suspected it was why she slept on the bathing room floor at Kirin's laboratory facility. If he could help it, she would never feel alone or frightened again. He thought being alone must be one of the most horrible feelings anyone could experience. Well, that and not knowing who you were, he reminded himself.

His siblings were such a big part of him, he couldn't imagine life without them. Andrew, who always knew what was going on with Luc, had assured him that even if Nalini had not helped their Kirin, if Luc loved her he would treat her like family. Learning what Nalini's upbringing was like, Luc had made peace with the choices his parents had made. He knew he would never take their love for granted again. Nalini and the life she had led until now would act as a constant reminder of what he himself might have experienced, along with his twin.

He felt a rush of empathy for his unknown sibling, and wondered if there was any way he could help him as they were Nalini. But perhaps he didn't want to be helped, Luc realized.

Nalini sighed and clutched a handful of his shirt.

"Please. Don't hurt her," she said in a quick rush, without waking.

His heart constricted, and he reached to smooth her brow and said softly, "Shush, my little scrapper, you are safe now. No harm will come to you on my watch."

As if she heard and understood, she settled back into a peaceful slumber, her hand dropping to her chest. He buried his nose in the fragrance of her hair and inhaled familiar lilies and bergamot and Nalini, sweet, angry, smiling, fighting, running, cursing Nalini.

Then, finally, he too found peace and slept until the dawn tiptoed quietly past the restless sentries and throughout the sleeping camp.

Nalini stirred in his arms, bringing him quickly back to awareness. Her cheek and right hand rested against his chest and her left leg straddled his. His eyes popped open and he glanced down to see that she was still asleep, though obviously healed.

Her breasts were pressed against his torso and her left arm was flung casually across his stomach, positioning her left hand dangerously close to his now undivided attention.

He inhaled, and then regretted it. The warm scent of her flooded his senses until he nearly groaned aloud. She stirred again, and snuggled closer, forcing him to take a deep, ragged breath.

Her eyes flew open.

He tensed.

She pushed away from him, her left hand brushing for just a moment against his current reason for not breathing. "Sorry," she said, obviously embarrassed.

"Don't go," he whispered. She looked up at him as he turned to his side and gazed down into her face.

"I-I wasn't going anywhere. Where would I go?"

"Wherever you like, as long as you're safe. I was just hoping you'd like to stay here. With me."

She stared at him silently, and he wished he knew what she was thinking. He glanced at her lips, noting that they were again soft and smooth, full and enticing. Her tongue slipped between them and lathered them with a wet sheen. It was her complete lack of artifice that made the movement so seductive. He remembered kissing her before, her inexperienced awareness and natural passion, a heady combination.

Her eyes darkened from lavender to violet to that cerulean blue. The pupils dilated. He leaned forward by a mere few inches and paused. Her cheeks were flushed, and he detected a sudden increase in the rise and fall of her chest. It nearly matched his own. His rigid control had become an almost painful entity.

Unable to resist, he reached out and palmed her cheek, running his thumb across the full suppleness of her bottom lip. A puff of warm breath rushed between her lips and she stared up at him expectantly. He moved his thumb to trace the bow of her upper lip, a trail his tongue had once journeyed. The remembrance of it flickered in her eyes.

Lifting his hand, he ran his finger down the bridge of her nose, now petite and straight once again, with no swelling or bruising. And then he stroked her cheek with his thumb. He leaned closer, gazing into her eyes and said, "Your eyes express every sensation you experience. I want to experience them with you."

She reached up to grab the back of his head and pulled him down until she could capture his lips with hers. He raised his head and took a deep breath.

"Kiss me, Luc. I want you to kiss me," she said.

Not one to argue first thing in the morning, he did as he was told and kissed her long and well and then turned to his back and pulled her with him. Surprised, she moved up and over him, laying across his body as she lowered her mouth to learn more about the taste of his.

"Nalini," he muttered.

"Uh-huh," she breathed, teasing his earlobe with her teeth and his chest with the fullness of her breasts as they pressed against him.

"I want to touch you," he said, reaching his hand to the hem of her long shirt, which is all she wore.

"Yes," she said, her breath hot against his face as she angled her head to slip her tongue into his mouth and find his. He returned her caress and slipped his hand up her leg to her upper thigh, savoring the silky smoothness of it. As his hand scooped the curve of her buttock, he paused, using his hand to both press her closer and caress the firm rise.

Pulling his lips away from hers, he groaned and buried his face in her neck. Raising his head, he said softly into her ear, "Lini, please, if you are going to ask me to stop, let it be now."

She lifted up to look down at him and said, "So no matter what, you would stop if I asked you to?"

Confused, he said, "Of course." Then, realizing why she would ask, he said, "Most men would, love. All real men would."

"But it would be difficult."

"Very. The longer we wait and the more advanced our intimacy, the more difficult it would be for me."

She thought about it a moment and said, "For me, too." Then, she reached out to weave her fingers in his hair and pressed her lips against his. "So don't stop," she murmured before running her tongue across his lips.

He grasped her then, and rolled over, letting her ride with him until he could rise above her. Taking her hand, he held it where earlier she had mistakenly brushed and said, "Be sure. I want you to be sure. It's okay to say no, Lini. We can wait until you're ready. We have eternity."

"Then let's not waste any more if it," she declared.

He let out his breath and reached down to help her pull the shirt over her head. His soon followed. He cupped the fullness of her breast and bent down to flick his tongue against a taunt nipple. Nalini squirmed beneath him, pressing closer, aroused, impatient. Luc captured the pink nub in his mouth and gently suckled, swirling his tongue around and over, taunting her, heightening her desire.

Rigid willpower kept his roving hands gentle as he explored her warm curves. Reaching between them, he used his thumb to circle her swelling womanhood. Her eyes widened, then closed as she bit down on her lower lip, sucking in her breath. He was nearly undone as he felt her body arch against him, and her legs open with an instinctive invitation.

Luc raised his head and moved above her, licking her lips, then slipping his tongue into her mouth as her lips parted to take a deep breath. He had wanted to do this for so long. He would not be rushed. Slowly and tenderly, he taught her to trust him.

He taught her to want him as much as he wanted her.

Another hour passed, the lessons having reached the reciprocal practicing portion that leads inevitably to perfection, and to consummation. Gently, and then without lingering delay that would only prolong her discomfort, Luc brought Nalini from sexual need and satisfaction to full understanding and fulfillment. His own long overdue release was heightened by overwhelming emotions.

Long after she had fallen into a contented sleep, he held her against himself, thoughtful and worried. Then he too sought the soothing mists of sleep.

Luc heard Hassidim outside the tent, through the whirling of the rising winds far above them, which protected them from aircraft or satellite detection.

"I think breakfast is soon to be served," he said.

"Good, I'm starving," Nalini said. She sat up and pulled the blanket over her chest. He tugged it down and slowly ran his hand from her throat to her waist. "He'll be in here soon," she said, chuckling. Then she stopped and stared off at nothing. Her fingers curled into the blanket. She gasped.

He called her name, but she didn't hear him, didn't respond, and she was seeing but not him and not there. "Now. Now. Now. They must go for them now." Back with him, she looked at Luc who sat up in concern and said, "They must get my mother and

Kirin out now. If they wait until this evening it will be too late. Typhon suspects the deception."

"How do you know this, Nalini?"

She shook her head, her eyes wide. "I don't know how. I saw it, as clearly as I see you. I was in the palace, and then I saw Typhon and I-I knew what he was thinking. How can this be? My mother has the sight, but I have never before..." She glanced down at the rumpled blankets and back at Luc. "She never said anything about sight coming to me after, that is, she did once say she had not had it as a child, but...I just don't know how I know. I only know that I do!"

She was clearly shaken by the realization of what had happened to her. Luc wrapped his arms around her and said, "I believe you." He reached under his pillow and pulled out a cell. "Andrew, Nalini has had a vision. You need to get them now or it will be too late. Yes. She's sure." He flipped it shut and reached to wipe the tear from the corner of her eye. Pulling her close against his chest, he kissed the top of her head and said softly, "They're going in now. You will know within the hour, Lini. It's going to be okay. Try not to worry."

She wrapped her arms around him and breathed in his scent. Despite his reassurance, they both knew that the stakes of the coming battle were now much higher than either had expected.

...man can have nothing but what he strives for

The Qu'ran, 53: 39

Chapter Forty-Three

Nalini stepped inside the monstrous, mobile headquarters that didn't even pretend to be an RV with its armored shell and gun ports, satellites littering the roof, levered metal blinds that could instantly flash down over thick, bullet-proof glass. She looked around until she spotted Luc.

"They have them, your mother and Kirin. Set and Lucien are already in pursuit, but the biggest problem we have right now is that we can't locate Typhon," Luc said, trying to sound casual.

He didn't fool her. Her eyes reflected her instinctive panic before she swiftly masked it and said, "We need to find him." She rushed to the row of surveillance screens, looking over the shoulders of the men who were monitoring them.

Walking to the satellite feed she sought, he pointed to the screen and said, "Here, Nalini. This is your mother and Kirin with Andrew and his men." Leaning across the computer tech's shoulder, he said, "Would you zoom in?"

Nalini moved to his side. The feed-out first narrowed, losing clarity and then zoomed in and enlarged its focus area. "Where?" she asked.

He pointed to the slow-moving images on the screen.

"What's that?" she asked, pointing to a blur behind them.

"Cover," he said, pointing over his head.

"Dust storm?"

"Yes. Soon we will lose satellite readout, but we will still be in constant contact."

"There is no way Typhon can be hiding to ambush them?"

"No way at all, Lini. We are certain of that." He touched the screen and said, "Do you see here," he moved his finger and said, "Andrew, his company of soldiers and their charges." He drew a circle around a ball of dust and said, "and there, just in front of the sandstorm, reinforcements." He indicated a point just beyond the scope of the narrowed focus area and said, "They are coming here, to us. Even now Horus and his cavalry are moving to intercept them and add their support to the escort. Once they arrive, the armies of Isis and Osiris will close before us and the actual battle will begin soon after."

"Soon after?" she asked.

"Yes, Set and Lucien did not immediately discover the ruse, so they were given enough of a head start. Typhon arrived and it was then they discovered your mother and Kirin had already fled. Your warning likely saved them all."

She visibly relaxed and said, "So how is it Typhon is unaccounted for?"

"He was seen leaving on horseback with a platoon just before Set and his army headed out after Astarte."

"So he was not in pursuit of them?"

"At first that's what we thought, but then he disappeared. Do you think you might be able to focus on him and find his location?"

"I don't know. It's the first time I ever had a vision. But I can try."

He nodded and led her to a conference table in the back. "Sit here."

She sat down, and he stood silently behind her. Her eyes shut. She breathed deeply a few times. He felt her shoulders relax beneath his hands. Nalini remained that way for several moments. His first indication that something was happening was when she tensed beneath his hands. She didn't say anything, like the first time, but her breathing increased until she sounded as if she had been running. The stiffening of her spine alarmed him, especially when her eyes flew open and he could see that she was no longer in the room with him. Instead she was looking at something distant, whether in time or space, he did not yet know.

He relaxed when she did. Her breathing slowed and he could tell when her sight returned to her present surroundings.

"What did you see?"

Down on his haunches he was eye level with her. She looked afraid. "Typhon. H-he has the book," she said.

She sounded frightened, too, her voice quivering slightly. To clarify her revelation, he said, "Typhon has *The Book of Life*?"

"Yes."

No, it was anger, not fright. She was angry, Luc realized. "The book is worthless to him. He doesn't have the incantation," he said, trying to calm her.

"There's more. He has Nephthys. If not now, then soon."

Luc jumped to his feet. Now he was angry. "He hates her," he said. *Mother!*

I know. We are after them now. Nalini's mother and Kirin should be there within minutes.

"Luc. Nephthys knows the incantation."

Mother.

How do you know?

Nalini had another vision.

We must get her and the book. You will have ninety minutes before Set and Lucien arrive. We have given orders that Lucien is to be captured if possible.

Kirin won't be safe until he is stopped, Luc pointed out.

Prepare for her arrival.

Luc realized he had been dismissed and pulled Nalini to her feet. "Your mother will be here soon," he said, pulling her into his arms.

"What will happen if Isis doesn't get to them in time?" she whispered.

"She will." She must. He was still reeling from the realization that Nephthys had read and memorized the incantation and was now planning to betray them all after everything he had risked to get the incantation in the first place. Luc, from centuries of practice, tempered his anger by distracting himself with positive thoughts. He remembered that the journey to the Underworld had made him whole, a man now comfortable if not thrilled with who and what he was, a man who could love a woman unconditionally.

Having mastered his dark secret, his bloodlust, he was no longer destined to live out his days with only casual and fleeting friendships. And who better for a bloodthirsty assassin like himself with a dark and horrific past to put behind him, he decided, than a woman like Nalini who could see into the future.

The arrival of Humvees sounded. Nalini turned her attention from the screen and ran to throw open the door jump to the ground. Luc followed her, heading toward the vehicle Andrew was driving. The back door opened and Kirin got out and rushed around to the other side. By the time he arrived, Kirin and Nalini were helping an obviously pregnant woman from the back seat. Her hand went to her back, and he shouted for a guard to fetch the doctor.

"I am fine, just tired," he heard her tell Nalini. She looked more like Nalini's sister than her mother, the same eyes and hair, the same petite build. Kirin leaned over to place her hand over Astarte's stomach. She was probably all the doctor the woman needed. It occurred to him then that Astarte was the only mother figure Typhon had with Nephthys gone and Set's second wife long dead by his own hand. His desire for Nalini, Luc speculated, might actually be an unrealizable lust for Astarte, and the fulfillment of an Oedipus complex.

Kirin saw him and would have knocked a weaker man down when she ran to throw herself into his arms. He laughed and hugged her back, kissing her forehead. "Ah, we have missed you, little sister. Andrew is so grouchy and hard to control without you around." Then, stepping back to look her over carefully, he stared more seriously into her eyes and asked softly, "You are really alright? No one has harmed you in any way?"

"I am really alright. I promise you, Luc."

He smiled then, his relief evident in the quick squeeze he gave her.

"Come, I want you to meet Astarte." She grabbed his hand and drew him forward. "Astarte, this is my brother, Luc, the one who looks something like Lucien, but who is nothing at all like Lucien," Kirin said. "Luc, this is Nalini's mother, Astarte, and she has managed to save us all, including Amea, Kazim and Arai."

"A great pleasure," Luc said, tipping his head in response to her gesture. He had nearly given her his hand, but remembered in time that he should not touch her. Perhaps Horus' accusation that he spent too much time in the west was not far from truth. "We thank you from the bottom of our hearts for bringing her back to us. It is a debt we can never repay."

She pressed her cheek to Nalini's and said, "You already have, Ljluka. It is I who should be thanking you."

"You will want to clean up and rest. Let me show you to your tent," Luc said. Astarte nodded gratefully and followed him to her quarters.

He left Nalini with her mother, knowing they had a lot of catching up to do. Walking toward headquarters he ran into Andrew, who was apparently coming to get him.

"We know where he is."

"Typhon?" A shot of adrenaline fired along his spine.

"Yes. He's about twenty miles east of here."

Not too far. They could get him, he thought with excitement. "Is mother there?"

"No. Apparently Nephthys lied to her, whether because Typhon forced her to or she is helping him from a sense of guilt, who can say?"

"She won't know how much he hates her until he wants her to know. By then it will be too late. So where is Isis?"

"On her way back. Set will be here in less than half an hour."

He tempered his disappointment. Typhon would still be there after the battle. The world was not big enough for him to hide from Luc's revenge. "We need to get ready," Luc admitted. His first instinct was to see to Nalini's safety. He turned to glance toward her mother's tent.

"One more thing," Andrew said. "Typhon has telepathic abilities too, like Horus. He just never let anyone know."

"Of course. The firstborn. We should have known. He is more devious than anyone thought, far more dangerous than Set," Luc muttered, marveling again that Nalini had survived in the Usurper's household for so many centuries unscathed. Of course she still had emotional scars that would take time to heal. She was only just beginning to trust him fully.

"And who would have thought it was possible for someone to be more evil than Set?" Andrew marveled.

He was always so straightforward and sincere, Luc thought affectionately. Though his brother could be trusted to keep a secret for eternity, there was no artifice or deceit in even the most private regions of his mind. Andrew's confident outlook was often comforting to Luc, who was forced to spend so much of his life in secret meetings with mysterious people and high stake subterfuges. "You ready to saddle up?" Andrew prodded.

"I just need to speak to Nalini. I'll meet you outside headquarters in five."

Luc hurried back to Astarte's tent. There was now another Nubian standing next to Rashid before the entrance. He scowled as Luc approached. "I hope that's not your I'm happy to see you face," said Luc. "If so, you really need to work on it." When the Nubian failed to respond, Luc turned to Rashid and said, "You going to introduce me to your friend?"

Rashid, without moving said, "This is the one I spoke of."

"I gathered. He has the look of the other fool," the taller Nubian said.

"I see the pleasure is to be all mine. I have work to do. I need to see Nalini. So do you move aside, or must I take the time to move you? Rashid?"

Rashid hesitated, but seeing that Luc was no longer amused, he stepped quickly aside. The other Nubian followed his lead, but moved only slightly so that Luc was forced to step around him in order to enter the tent. He would need to deal with him later, when he had more time, Luc realized.

He entered the tent, and seeing that Nalini was kneeling beside a soft pile of angora pelts upon which her mother was resting, Luc crossed to the middle of the spacious tent. Nodding toward Astarte, he turned to look at Nalini and said, "I am off to the front lines. Could I speak to you for a moment first?"

She quickly stood and came to his side. He noticed that she had changed and said, "Nalini, you must stay here and protect your mother. You cannot fight on the lines."

"I am a warrior, too. This is very much my fight. Arai will stay with my mother, and I know you have an entire company stationed here at headquarters. If we lose, it will not matter where she is, because Set will find her."

Unable to argue with her logic, Luc tried another tactic. "I don't think I would be able to concentrate, knowing you were in danger."

"Look, I've been taking care of myself for a long time. I nearly killed *you*, didn't I?"

"And Typhon nearly beat you to death only yesterday," he countered, frustrated at her stubbornness. "There are worse things than dying, and I couldn't bear it if--"

"Nalini. You never told me that--"

"Are you happy now? Just go. I will fight with someone less insufferable," she snapped, rushing over to reassure her mother.

Sighing, Luc ran his fingers through his hair. Unable to come up with a better solution, he called out, "I would rather have you near me than wonder where you were or what was happening to you."

"I feel the same way about you," she said, returning to his side. She smiled up at him and he was nearly lost, but he grasped her arm and headed her out the tent flap. He hoped for more convincing support from Andrew.

Andrew, for once, didn't respond as Luc assumed. He accepted Nalini as a warrior, having once seen her in battle. At her approach, he ordered another horse to be delivered to the front, and tossed the rifles off one of the back seats and into the space between them. Noting her pistol and knives, he nodded toward the rifle and said, "Want one?"

"Sure. Thanks. Do you have ammunition belts?"

Andrew tapped his earpiece and soon a young Bedouin arrived to deliver them.

She strapped them across her shoulders and drew the scarf across her face. Dressed as she was, unless someone knew they would think her a young boy. Except, Luc thought, for the breathtaking eyes that looked across the seat at him as she slid in and pulled the door shut. He wondered vaguely if his heart would ever stop quickening when she looked up at him that way, and then hoped that it never would.

"Double time," Andrew said and Roscoe backed up the Humvee and spun sand behind them as he headed toward the battlefield. They could not afford to lose, and the enemy had every intention of winning.

Well shalt thou see, if thou arrivest there,
How much the sense deceives itself by distance;
 Therefore a little faster spur thee on."
Then tenderly he took me by the hand,
And said: "Before we farther have advanced,
That the reality may seem to thee
Less strange, know that these are not towers, but giants..."

Dante Alighieri, The Divine Comedy

468

Chapter Forty-Four

"What's the plan?" Nalini asked.

"Stay alive," Luc said. "Andrew and I will be leading our men straight up the center. That's why we're going to wait until Horus has a chance to use some of his heavier artillery. They'll be assaulted from both sides by Isis and Osiris, to keep them channeled toward us. Horus will be closing in behind them and cutting off their supply lines."

"Won't we be attacking?" She sounded disappointed.

"We will attack from the front and effectively cut off any escape. By then we will be on horseback or in hand to hand combat, making machinery and even rifles too difficult to use. It'll be too crowded to get a clean shot and too close to raise it and fire."

"It is what I was trained for."

"I've seen you in action," Luc said dryly.

"And you're about to again," she said, excitement apparent in her voice.

She loves the adrenaline rush as much as I do, Luc thought. Hearing the rocket launchers, he didn't need Andrew's confirmation to know Horus had begun his assault. It continued for around twenty minutes, and then stopped.

It was difficult to see through the dust and swirling sands. Though the sand storm created by the new equipment Horus's scientists had invented was meant for cover and it raged above their heads. The residual debris in the air made it difficult to see. It was like thick fog at dusk. Luc remembered how it looked in the cloud forest. But instead of moist and fresh, the air here was parched and the dust clogged the nostrils and smarted the eyes of those foolish enough not to be wearing goggles and masks. Those native to the desert like Abdul and Nalini had the corner of their *keffiyeh* over their faces.

Abdul rode up leading two spirited Arabian horses. Luc moved to take the reins and nodded to draw Nalini over. "Your ride is here," he said.

She ran over to the sleek black animal and threw her arms around the horse's neck. "Mahdi," she cried.

Nalini looked to Abdul and smiled her thanks, but he said, "You will have to thank the small one, Kazim. It is thanks to him your horse is here, as well as the one of Anubis."

The stallion turned his head to nuzzle her and snorted in disgust when she told him she had no treat today. Laughing, she grabbed a handful of his mane, slipped her booted foot into a stirrup, bent her other knee to spring upward and landed unassisted into the saddle.

Luc jumped into his own saddle and watched her for a moment. She bent down to whisper into the horse's ear and he responded like a long-lost friend, shaking his head in delight and agreement. He was a magnificent animal and Luc was grateful for the added security his familiarity would provide her.

He called her name and tossed her another bag of ammo to tie to her saddle. Riding alongside, he said, "Try to stay near me. We can cover each other," he added diplomatically. "Andrew will be nearby too. It is how we always fight. We try to function as a unit. Our men are well teamed. Roscoe and Abdul will also be near. These men are familiar with one another and we have saved each other on numerous occasions. You can join our team today, and be my partner."

She nodded, noting the men around her, their mounts and apparel so that she would quickly recognize it in her peripheral later. Contemplating her actions, he began to relax. She had been well trained, albeit to kill *him*. Now she was just switching sides. It nagged at him that their enemy would know her fighting style, but then he realized she had probably fought many of these men before and would know their weaknesses too.

They could hear the sound of the battle now, the pain-filled screams of the wounded and the ferocious cries of those attacking. "Get ready, but wait for Andrew's signal," Luc said to Nalini.

She glanced behind her at hundreds of mounted warriors. Ahead of them were Humvees that would move out first, spraying artillery fire to soften the oncoming ranks before falling back so that the cavalry and then the infantry could surge forward. Luc watched her tug at her bottom lip with her teeth. Her eyes sparkled with restrained anticipation. It was hard to believe this savage little warrior could be defeated by any man.

Flaming his own adrenaline, he inhaled and smelled even at this distance the sweat-smudged scent of blood on the battlefield. The Humvees moved forward, the cannon cockers, as Roscoe called them, spraying bullets into the oncoming soldiers. The sound cranked Luc's anticipation up another notch.

The vehicles slowed, then stopped, and Andrew sounded the go. They kicked their horses and charged forward. Luc passed a Humvee and began firing at the attacking warriors. Many were still on horseback, but some were already on foot. He saw Nalini plunge forward into the fray, her gun pumping death into men on either side of her horse. He maneuvered toward her, firing into the oncoming enemy.

The battlefield became crowded and the tight quarters escalated the chaos. As more horses tripped over fallen bodies or ran off without riders, the infantry rushed forward, crying out for blood.

Luc's blood pumped through his veins like a rushing river. His heart beat like a pagan drum. He tossed down his rifle and pulled his sword. The red robes of those who fell beneath this more intimate weapon disguised the flow, but could not mask the salty metallic scent that continued to seep into the sands and waft through the air.

Nalini, no longer on her mount, had a scimitar in one hand and a dagger in the other. She was death, power shopping. He jumped from his mount and slashed his way toward her. She spun and parried. He slashed and jabbed, spun around and ducked. She lunged and killed. Her scimitar nearly severed a man's head. His sword severed a man's arm.

Achieving his goal, they were now back to back, with only a one-eighty to defend. Abdul and Andrew were similarly positioned ahead of him. He noted Roscoe and, of all people, Rashid occupying the same vicinity. All this he saw and still he killed with uninterrupted velocity.

His headgear soaked up his sweat, but he still managed to get salt in his eye. He elbowed an attacking soldier in the face, and swiped his sleeve across his brow. Nalini bumped against his back and he glanced around to see that she had sustained a punch. He looked just long enough to see the man was made to regret it. Then he turned back and used his dagger on the man whose sword he had just parried with the sword in his other hand.

The line of attackers was thinning. They fought a few more minutes and then ran forward, toward the back of the enemy lines where the fighting seemed more congested, more desperate, more exciting.

Hearing him before he actually saw him, Luc angled toward Horus. That's when he realized that Osiris too was engaged in hand to hand combat before he was attacked by three men at once. His sword parried and his knife thrust and he took down two, but they were soon replaced and he realized he was not just another enemy but a particular target.

Once aware of the concentration of warriors, he quickly distanced himself from Nalini, leading the clustering assailants away from her. Now more men joined the fight, and he inhaled the battlefield into his senses and fought on, brutally. Still they came at him.

He glimpsed Andrew at his attackers' backs, trying to thin them out. Nalini too was there, slashing and clashing. Again he was surrounded. He became the offender. They fell before his fury like drunken sailors coming off Cinderella Liberty after months at sea.

Then he saw the reason for the targeted assault.

Lucien.

Two soldiers attacked Lucien. Luc noted that each of his brother's hands bore a sword and each wielded it with equal skill. He made quick work of his adversaries, and then he faced Luc. Thrust. Slice. Clash. Sparks. They met parry for parry. Luc fought for his own life, but not for that of his brother. He couldn't bring himself to kill him. Knocking the sword from one of his brother's hands, he thrust forward, but his brother blocked and countered the jab.

Close enough to deliver a blow, he delivered. Lucien staggered back, but recovered immediately and hefted a dagger from his boot and threw it toward Luc's heart. He spun and turned, catching the camel bone handle in his hand. Flipping it over, he threw it back. It entered where he aimed, his brother's bicep. The sword dropped from Lucien's hand.

"The firstborn too. Sure, why not? You insufferable bastard," Lucien shouted bitterly.

"You would know," Luc countered sadly.

Abdul rushed up to take Lucien captive as Luc looked around, realizing the battle was ending. A few skirmishes remained, those too stupid or too stubborn to surrender. Nalini stood at his side, panting and bloody, but uninjured except a few bruises and scrapes. He dropped his arm around her shoulders. Looking toward his father and Horus who were walking toward them, he called out, "Where is Set?"

"Not here."

Sekhmet ran toward them. As she reached them she too asked, "Set?"

"No."

They looked around. Luc and Andrew talked into their headsets. They both shook their heads. Osiris cursed.

Then Horus said, "He has escaped into the desert. One of Isis's men saw him ride off."

"We need night goggles," said Andrew.

"Let's go," Osiris yelled, running toward a Humvee. They split off and ran toward vehicles or mounts.

Luc noticed Nalini watching intently as Rashid helped Abdul wrestle an angry Lucien toward a Humvee. Nalini glanced toward Luc, and he saw her struggle to push worry for Lucien aside, for now. She whistled and soon her horse appeared. No word was spoken, but she raised her brow at Luc in challenge. He shook his head and grinned. Just then the young Bedouin ran forward leading his horse. Luc hopped up and said, "You coming?"

Laughing, she mounted.

From a bag on his saddle he took out his night goggles. He had not yet learned to pull up his ability to see in the dark without an external trigger like blood. "You have some as well. Check your bag."

Nalini reached around and dug through her saddle bag. Pulling them out, she put them on. Not yet needing them, she flipped them up onto the top of her head. He tapped his earpiece and said, "East? That's the same way Typhon went. Mother? Okay."

Turning to Nalini he said, "Let's go. Isis is in pursuit." They headed out into the open desert along with a full company of Andrew's men. Horus and Osiris had already started out. Luc wanted to hurry and join them.

If Set was meeting up with Typhon, nothing good could come of it. The battle might be over, but as long as those two lived, Luc knew the war was not.

All men's souls are immortal, but the souls of the righteous are immortal and divine.

Socrates

478

Chapter Forty-Five

"Luc!" Nalini called. He was instantly alongside her.

"What is it?" She didn't respond and he reached to lift her goggles. Her eyes were staring off into the night, but not seeing it. He grabbed her horse's reins and drew him to a stop. Andrew stopped beside him and he said, "A vision, I think. Go ahead. We'll catch up in a minute."

"I'll wait, it may be important to our mission."

Luc nodded. Nalini became restless and muttered incoherently. Afraid she would fall off her horse, he reached around her waist and pulled her over to sit in front of him. Andrew rode up and took her horse's reins from him.

He wrapped his arms around her and listened intently to her muttering. This vision was lasting much longer. Finally she came out of it and said, "How did I get here?"

Laughing, he said, "I didn't want you to fall off your horse and ruin your esteemed reputation as an equestrian."

"Oh, thank you," she said, clearly disoriented to be so docile and grateful to him for taking charge of her.

He gently lifted her back onto her own mount and prompted, "What have you seen?"

"I know where they are going."

"Where?"

"To the vault where we first found *The Book of Life*," she said softly. "They have stopped for the night, waiting for Set to catch up with them."

He sensed she was holding something back. "What else do you know, Nalini?" He prodded.

"I know that Nephthys doesn't realize Typhon hates her. He is pretending to be thrilled to be reunited with his mother. He is telling her how much he hates Set and letting her know all the terrible things Set has done to us all. She is most sympathetic and feels terribly guilty." Her anger mounted with her revelations. It was carried in the tone of her voice, which quickened and rose in both tone and volume.

Quickly discerning the purpose of Typhon's deceit, he said, "He plans to kill her, doesn't he?"

"Yes," she said, frustration causing her to gnaw at her bottom lip and focus on something he couldn't see.

"Do we get there in time?" he asked, attempting to nudge her conscious thoughts.

"Yes, in time," she responded, her brow creasing with her painful effort to wring truth from her memories of the future. "I don't know if we will be able to prevent it."

"What else did you see, Nalini?" She was still holding something back from him, and he regretted his inability to read her mind.

He regretted, too, not being able to see her eyes, even with the aid of the night goggles. Her emotions played out in her eyes. If he could only see them, he would know for sure.

"What else, Lini?" he said in a tone that was more like pleading than asking.

"Your mother's secret," she revealed grudgingly, looking up at him in the gathering shadows that cloaked more than the landscape.

"Which is what?" Luc and Andrew said together. Surprised, she turned her head to see Andrew sitting on his horse next to her.

"In all fairness, she doesn't know the answer either, but it is why she kept the book from Osiris."

"What answer? You are speaking in riddles." Luc retorted, his own frustration growing.

"I would rather not say," she muttered. No kidding, he thought with irritation. Then he noticed her slumped shoulders and appreciated her exhaustion. Tapping his headset, he said, "We need to veer off. We know where they're headed."

Why have you stopped, son?

Nalini was having a vision. They're going to the vault, but have stopped for the night.

We will stop for a few hours. The men are exhausted and hungry. Have Andrew call back for supplies.

"Father wants to stop for a few hours. He wants you to call for supplies."

"Yeah, I was in on that one." Andrew grimaced at Luc and yelled out, "Roscoe!" Tapping his earpiece, he said, "Get one of those Humvees over here and have a couple tents thrown up. It's starting to get cold."

Luc dismounted and motioned for Nalini to join him. A Bedouin rode up and jumped down to take their horses and lead them away. Another had already started a fire and thrown down rugs before it for them to sit upon. Nalini's slump was more a collapse, but once down she tucked her feet under her knees, drawing them up to rest her arms upon. Luc sat behind her and stretched his long legs out on either side of her. She shivered and he pulled her back against him, wrapping her in his arms.

Andrew dropped a blanket beside him. Luc picked it up and wrapped it around them. She leaned back into his chest, sighed and rested her head against him. He glanced down and noticed that her eyes were shut. A vibrating hum sounded and he tried to find it among her many layers, but its gyrating caught her attention and she sat up and pulled the cell from a slit pocket cleverly sewn in her sleeve.

"Mother?" She stood up and walked off a way, but he could still hear her conversation. "No, I can actually sense what they are thinking, mother. You've never done that, have you? Well it seems to be accurate so far, but how would I know? I have only had the three. The one I induced, the others were spontaneous. Yes. Yes, I'm fine. Luc would not let me out of his sight, believe me. Rashid had nothing to worry about today."

She wandered a bit further and he had to focus to hear her. He glanced across the fire to where Roscoe was tearing his gun down and cleaning it. His attention snapped back to Nalini when he heard her mention Isis. She had said, "Isis knew?" and then, "both the same day? So you don't know either? Why didn't you…" and now he was unable to make out anything of what she was saying.

Whatever Isis's secret was, he was now certain it involved Astarte. He and Andrew were right. It did have to do with what happened just before the last great battle.

Nalini came back to the fire and sat beside him on the rug. He lifted his arm and extended the blanket toward her. She shimmied over to him, letting him hug her close. The sound of powerful motors approached and they looked up to see a small caravan of supply vehicles. Before long, Hassidim arrived complaining and fussing about the horrors of the night trip, the unavailability of supplies and the outrageous conditions his poor master had to put up with.

Luc grinned, realizing their makeshift accommodations for the next few hours had just gone up a couple of stars. Platters of fruit and nuts were soon joined by endless rice, goat meat, yogurt and cheeses with humus and breads and steaming hot espresso, and a single pot of tea. By the time they were full, Hassidim had miraculously set up their tent—with the help of a dozen browbeaten young Bedouins--and Kazim, who Roscoe claimed was Hassidim's house mouse.

Hassidim bowed in front of him, pressed his hands to his forehead, crossed his arms and pressed them to his chest and said, 'Merciful and longsuffering prince, your most humble and unworthy servant has prepared you a place to rest your deserving head. It is an unforgivably dirty and smelly hovel unworthy of your great presence. Please forgive your lowly slave, oh great exalted one." With a flourish of his arm, he pointed to the large tent in the distance. Rashid already stood before it, and Luc shook his head at the Nubian's tenacity.

"I think you like all that kowtowing, Luc," Andrew called out, laughing at Hassidim's insulted scowl.

Luc grinned and drew Nalini up. "Come, we will be leaving soon enough. If I know Hassidim, I will enjoy the bath and clean clothing." Even in the firelight he could tell her eyes had brightened at the mention of a bath. He reached out to wipe a smudge of dirt, blood and sweat from her cheek.

"Who's first?" he asked, and let her win the short race.

As he had come to expect, Hassidim did not disappoint. Somehow he had maneuvered a collapsible round tub, large enough to sit in, into the corner of the tent, behind a screen, and judging from the steam rising from it, the fire both in front of the tent and inside it had been used to heat buckets of water to which a mild but musky scent arose.

He was delighted to see the effect it had on Nalini. She was nearly naked before she reached the screen. For someone who so often had to hide her gender, she was incredibly comfortable inside her own skin, he thought with admiration. He decided it probably came from spending so much time disciplining and conditioning her body to fight well enough to defeat seasoned warriors. Whatever they did Nalini had to do twice as well to defeat them, if she was to use their size and strength advantages against them.

Slipping down into the tub, she sighed appreciatively. He walked over, pulling off his shirt and knelt beside her. "So, you win this time. But I don't feel very defeated." He plunged his head into the water and she squealed as he came up dripping. Standing up, he turned toward the mirror hanging from the tent post, grabbed his razor and shaving cream, and prepared to shave. It took a little longer than usual, and he managed to nick his chin, but it was worth it. An added benefit to the mirror's position was that he could watch her bathe and guide his razor simultaneously if not safely.

Wiping the last of the gel from his face, he turned to her and said, "Ready to wash that blood out of your hair?"

Surprised, she pulled a rope of it around in front of her and looked down. "Uh, I guess I better," she agreed.

"Let me," he said. He reached for the shampoo Hassidim had provided, not surprised it smelled like what she must use, because to him it smelled like Nalini rather than the other way around. Kneeling beside her again, he shoved her head under the water and it was her turn to come up sputtering. He laughed at her comical attempt to pretend indignation. Squeezing a palm full of the shampoo into his hand, he applied it to her head and began to lather it into her scalp. She leaned her head back and groaned appreciatively.

"Keep that up and you will be left with soap in your hair and a dirty, smelly soldier on top of you."

She chuckled and groaned again. He rewarded her by dumping a bucket of water over her head. As she gasped and smoothed back her hair, he reached for another, but this time helped her work the lather out of her long tresses. Finally she stood, glistening and glorious, to be wrapped into a thick towel Hassidim had laid out on a portable quilt rack next to the fire.

Moving toward the warmth, she picked up a brush and smoothed out her hair, drying it in the heat of the flames. He opted to stand in the tub, dump a bucket over his head, lather with his own soap from head to toe and dump another bucket over his head to rinse. The entire process only took a few moments, but he felt completely revitalized.

He walked over to the fire and watched her look at him while pretending not to, as she continued to dry her hair. Reaching for a towel, he dried himself off, tossed the towel back over the rack, then scooped her into his arms and walked toward the pile of pelts, sheets and blankets Hassidim had provided for their continued pleasure, which is what Luc intended.

"Aren't you exhausted?" she said softly.

"Perhaps some, though the bath and the sight of you naked have revived me in various ways," he said, grinning suggestively.

"Really? What ways might those be? Could you give me a hint?"she teased.

Her soft chuckle did funny things to his heart. His chest tightened with a sudden need of her, and it was more than physical. He felt a desire to freeze the moment in time, to have her always here, beside him, the soft glow of the firelight dancing across the curves and planes of her naked flesh. Her lips curved seductively upward. The promise of paradise sparkled in her eyes.

Unable to restrain himself, he swooped down to capture her lips. His tongue did an age-old dance across her teeth, dipping deeper to caress her tongue and teach it some tantalizing new steps. And then he kissed her lips again, and then her jaw, plunging to her neck to nuzzle the exact spot where her pulse quickened as she sucked in a pleasure-laced breath. He nibbled her ear lobe, and whispered softly, "Never let this moment end. Stay in my arms forever, Lini."

Raising up on his knees, he moved downward, to savor her breasts, pressing gentle slow kisses down her cleavage until she murmured his name, and said, "Please, take me now."

Recently suppressed adrenalin flooded his cells at the way his name sounded as she uttered it in a breathless plea. He raised his head and marveled at the way his heart contracted when he saw her gaze up at him with passion-drugged eyes as she reached behind his neck to pull him toward her. He couldn't resist her request, and didn't truly want to. At that moment, somewhere in the back of his mind he accepted that he would never want to deny her anything again.

His phone rang less than four hours later. He'd only been sleeping for two. Pulling it out from under the pillow, he said, "Yes. Right there."

Nalini was already up. She moved behind the screen, and he stood up and reached for his shirt. When she reappeared, one arm and her head into the top of her camisole, underwear already on, he walked behind the screen and relieved himself before cleaning up and collecting the rest of his clothes.

Dressed and geared, they emerged from the tent and accepted the coffee and sweet rolls Hassidim had placed on a tray. "I hope you were not too terribly uncomfortable in those deplorable conditions so unworthy of your greatness, oh prince, beloved of Rā, son of she who is fair as the moon and he who is mightier than the mountains."

"You are amazing, Hassidim," Nalini enthused. "Everything was perfect, thank you."

He beamed, bowing low and telling her what a beautiful and enchanting princess she was, and how nothing was worthy of her majesty and greatness.

"You have a friend for life," Luc warned her, smiling.

Sobering, he turned toward Osiris who was striding toward them with a purpose. "Your mother has not stopped. She is going to be in danger if we do not hurry. Speak to her, Luc. She favors you, and might listen. See if you can make her wait for us." He spun on his heels and walked away, never noticing Nalini's deep bow. "Stubborn impetuous woman. If she weren't so damned beautiful the stars cry at the sight of her," he muttered, hurrying away.

Mother!

Don't start, Ljluka.

Wait for us. Please. Your secret is already out. Why do you fight against fate?

Who knows? At least she hadn't denied there was a secret.

Nalini had a vision. She senses thoughts as well as seeing events, mother.

Who has she told? She feared his father knowing, he realized with clarity.

Will you wait? You have nothing to gain.

I will wait two hours.

"Andrew! We have only two hours before she starts after them again."

"Mother?"

"Yes, she has given us that much time to catch up." It was so like her to give them a specific timeframe for her patience.

"We can't; she's too far ahead."

Which explained why she so readily agreed, Luc thought, unsurprised by his mother's continued duplicity. "We must," he said.

Andrew got on his phone. A few minutes later, he said, "Father is already after her, but we have a whirlybird coming. We will ride until they reach us, adding distance."

Luc nodded. "Great. It's a go!" The young Bedouin led their horses up and they jumped into their saddles and headed out. This time it was their mother who they must save from herself. She could not catch her past, no matter how fast she chased after it. Instead, her past was just about to catch up with her.

All men by nature desire to know.
                        Aristotle

Chapter Forty-Six

They were far enough ahead of the storm that the helicopter's navigational system had no trouble finding the coordinates Luc provided. The bluff rose from the desert floor precisely as he had said it would. The bird slowed, listed slightly in the strong wind, and lowered onto a wide valley in the shelter of two tall dunes.

Luc jumped out and reached back for Nalini. Andrew, Roscoe, Abdul and Rashid joined them. They ducked, racing toward the opening Nalini had created in the tunnels.

Seeing no one around, they decided Typhon and Set were already inside. Luc wondered why they had returned here. The only purpose he could imagine was that there must be another artifact still hidden within.

Mother?

Luc finished speaking to his mother and turned to Andrew and said, "We have the element of surprise. They aren't here yet."

"We need to take cover."

"Let's move into the tunnels. Mother is ten minutes behind them, and they're ten minutes off."

Without the scaffolding to jump up into the hole, Andrew gave Luc a leg up. Abdul and Roscoe followed. Rashid bent down and cupped his hand for Nalini. As soon as she stepped in, he sprung up and catapulted her toward the opening. Grabbing Luc's extended hand, he added enough velocity to her jump to land her next to him. Roscoe assisted Andrew, and then it took three of the men to lean down and hoist the Nubian upward.

"Should have had them set us down on the other side," Luc said, tugging Rashid through the opening.

"Except that's the direction from which Set and Typhon are coming and they will likely enter there. Nephthys will know the way," Andrew pointed out.

"Right. Since you're the only one who has never been here, we need to make sure you don't make any wrong steps or take any wrong turns. Stick close to us," Luc warned him. "I think I know a good place for an ambush."

"But you don't know for sure what their purpose is here," Nalini reminded him. "Perhaps we should first let them lead the way to whatever it is. They will let no one but their most trusted men accompany them. Attacking them before they leave seems more advisable."

"She makes a logical argument," Andrew agreed.

"Yes. Where do you think we should conceal ourselves?" Luc asked. "You made it far enough into the tunnels to reach the inner chamber."

She thought a moment and said, "There was a false chamber below the actual inner sanctum. We could hide there."

"Show us."

"This way," she said, holding out her halogen flashlight.

Five minutes later, having avoided two traps that Nalini pointed out, one with which they were already familiar, they reached the chamber and Luc was surprised at how large it was. He reached up to brighten the beam of his headlamp and walked the perimeter of the room, reading the cuneiform.

"Are you sure this is a false chamber, Lini?"

"Yes, see here?" She pointed out a panel near the center of the wall. He moved to read it. "That's how I knew the book wasn't here, but above us."

"Yes, the book, but come read this," he said, showing her the panel he had been reading.

"I never got this far before. I was just seeking the book. You don't suppose this is true? I always thought it was just a rumor."

Luc glanced at his watch. "We have to hurry. Andrew, help us." Andrew walked over and he said, "I think we've found what they came here to get. We have to beat them to it or stop them before they can get it."

"What is it?"

"Look. If this is true it's an appendix to the book. It contains the vital information of the first experiments we thought they already had."

"Here," Nalini said, "We must push these two panels simultaneously."

They rushed to assist her. "Luc, you press that one over there on the opposite panel."

"Okay, on three, not after."

"One, two," they pushed on the three.

Stone grated on stone and the panel between them swung inward. Luc stepped through the opening and could see that it had not been disturbed for thousands of years.

"Shine your light on the floor, Nalini. Let's be sure there are no traps."

Andrew walked forward and before they could stop him, he stepped onto a marked stone. Senses screaming, Luc turned, his movement little more than a flash as he reached to grab the spear, interrupting its direct flight to Andrew's chest. It would have stabbed a man of normal height in the head.

"Hey, thanks, little brother."

"No problem. Thanks for helping us find the trap," Luc said sardonically, wondering how Andrew managed to keep from being killed on a daily basis. "Now would you mind standing still and letting us find any others on our own?"

Nalini let the beam of her light fall ahead of them, and said, "There's another one there, to the left and up about three steps. If we avoid them I think we are safe until we reach that altar."

Altar is what it looked like. Carved and covered with cuneiform, the rectangular limestone box was too short for a sarcophagus, and too tall for a funerary table. He moved forward, avoiding the trigger stone and approached the altar. Brushing the dust from the top, he blew across it, trying to clear the cuneiform so he could read. Nalini added her light beam.

She pointed to an indentation and reasoned, "I think this opens, but it must require a key. Do you think Nephthys has one?"

Luc studied it for a moment, reading the inscription. "No," he said. "But I do." Pulling the necklace from inside his shirt, he slipped it over his head. He placed the iconic symbol in the duplicate one carved into the stone, then tugged at the bottom, releasing the knife. Pressing on the ankh at the same time as he thrust the dagger into the indentation, he held still a moment, and then released them as he felt the vibration. He stepped back and watched. Nothing happened.

"There, on the side," Abdul called from the doorway. And added, "They are coming. What would you have me do?"

"How long before they reach this chamber?" Luc asked, looking down to see that a compartment had opened on the side of the altar. The appendix he sought lay within, wrapped in leather bindings. A rush of excitement at the discovery, at beating

Typhon to its acquisition, made Luc pause for a moment, savoring the importance of the antiquity before him.

"Not long, perhaps ten minutes," Abdul was saying.

Reaching to grab the package, Luc laid it reverently on top of the altar. He quickly loosed the leather ties and unwrapped the bindings. A wide though thin book was revealed. It was roughly the size of *The Book of Life*, in dimensions, though much thinner. He gingerly opened the leather-bound cover and unable to discern any script, he realized it too required the incantation.

"That's it," Nalini whispered. "It has to be." Her own excitement and awe was apparent in her soft words, spoken as if she feared breaking the spell cast by the magnitude of their achievement. She slipped her hand around his arm and pressed against his side, wanting to share the moment, however brief it must be.

He smiled down at her, before wrapping it back up. He pulled his necklace from the lid, watched as the drawer disappeared, and said, "Let's go. Up above. We will come back down and trap them inside."

Abdul moved behind them, lightly dusting the area with combed lama wool to disguise their most recent tracks in the thick dust of the floor. Then he too hurried from the chamber.

Nalini took the lead in order to point out several dangerous traps. At one point they had to run and jump across a wide chasm where the floor had fallen away after an earlier mistake. Only quick thinking on the part of Rashid had saved the man from plummeting to his death. He had literally snatched him from the air. Luc forced him to relive his actions when he insisted that Nalini let him launch her across, into the waiting arms of Rashid. No amount of protest that she had obviously successfully spanned the chasm before would dissuade him.

They were further slowed by the tricky passage leading to the inner sanctum, but the stones were still cleared and Nalini led them through, cautioning them to step only where she stepped. Once across, they had only to walk to the doorway, which she quickly opened with a short incantation. They entered the inner sanctum and Luc looked around at the still-colorful murals and intricate decoration in the vaulted chamber.

He wished he had longer to explore, but they had more pressing business this time too. "Where is the access to the chamber below?" he asked.

Nalini motioned for him to follow and they approached a crack between the altar and the floor. "Once they enter, their lights will be visible. We will be able to hear anything they say."

"Assuming they speak aloud," Andrew remarked.

Luc glanced around and said, "We need to extinguish our lights or they will see us here above." They each turned off their lights.

I am here.

We are concealed in the chamber above them. When they enter, we will be able to hear them. We will tell you when we can trap them between us.

Already my men have secured the exits.

They heard movement in the chamber below. "It is there, in that altar," Nephthys said. "You must use your necklace, the ankh and the blade, to reveal the hidden compartment."

"You have been very helpful, mother," Typhon said.

"This does not excuse you making a fool out of me," said Set. "For that you will still pay. Give it to me, Typhon. They will return my true wife if they think I will give them this."

"They will not trust you, Set. They will not give you Astarte against her will. Not a second time." Luc felt Nalini bristle against his side in reaction to Nephthys' revelation. She had once accused Isis of giving her mother to Set. His mother had denied it. Was that too a lie?

A loud slap was heard, and then another. Nephthys cried out, and was struck again. "You can enjoy yourself later, my king. Let's get the prize we came for. Would you like the honor?" Luc grabbed Andrew's arm, to check his rage at Nephthys' treatment. He clamped his teeth together, his own rage caged like a separate entity.

"Yes, give me the necklace. Get off the floor and out of the way, bitch." They heard rustling and a grunt as if someone had been kicked. Luc tightened his grip on Andrew's arm. Even with his night goggles on he could tell Andrew was ready to explode. The last thing they needed was for him to begin swearing at the occupants below as he rushed blindly out of the chamber to seek revenge.

They heard the sound of metal on stone, and then Set screamed. "What are you--"

Clearly there was now fighting. Metal struck metal. "Typhon, you ungrateful little bastard. I should have known you were as deceitful as your whore of a mother!"

Now, mother.

Signaling the others, Luc rushed from the chamber. Once outside, they switched on their lights and quickly but cautiously made their way to the chamber below. They easily eliminated two soldiers in the corridor, and burst into the chamber. Nephthys had just finished saying the incantation over *The Book of Life*, which was laid out upon the altar. Typhon, dagger in hand, was moving behind her.

Luc ran into the room and saw Set on the floor. Their father was dead and probably soon to be dismantled like a jigsaw puzzle with which his children no longer wished to play. Luc felt only relief.

"Stop, Typhon," he called out as Typhon moved closer to Nephthys.

Spinning around in surprise, Typhon turned back to grab Nephthys from behind and wrapped his arm around her neck, dagger at her throat.

"So kill her, your own mother, Typhon. She will soon recover, but you will not be so lucky," Nalini said, advancing.

Luc made no move to stop her. His need for revenge could not equal the centuries of unfulfilled longing for it that she must have experienced. Though he knew on some intellectual level that revenge was a two edged sword, when it came to an immortal bent on never ending torture and mayhem, swift elimination was the only possible solution.

"Come to seek me out so I could finish the job? I know how much you liked it. You were squealing like a little pig. Were you very disappointed that I didn't have time to complete what we started?"

She pulled her pistol from her belt and shot it without so much as a second's hesitation. He twisted and it hit the wall behind him. Luc was already halfway across the room. Nalini's right to revenge or not, he would still Typhon's foul mouth.

Laughing, Typhon said, "Ljluka, enjoying my castoffs? I broke her in for you. She should do whatever you want without argument. Don't you think she has a nice set of--"

The knife Luc threw hit its mark. It shot into Typhon's shoulder, to the left of Nephthys' head. Typhon gasped and looked down. It was all the distraction Luc needed. He was on him, Nephthys pushed aside to safety. A crushing blow to his head and then Luc twisted the blade in his shoulder. He punched his cheek, and then his nose, smiling at the blood that ran down Typhon's face.

Ignoring it, Typhon spun away, and drew his sword, still stained with his father's blood. Luc drew his own and they thrust and parried, and each time Luc found an opening he delivered another blow to match the blows Typhon had given Nalini. The bloodlust Typhon's provided allowed him the pleasure of taking his time with Typhon's punishment. Satisfied at last as he heard the crack of Typhon's ribs, Luc turned to Nalini.

"What would you have me do with him?"

"You arrogant bastard!" Typhon screamed. "Do you think my fate will be decided by the likes of you? You're no better than a vampire, a blood sucking leach."

Nalini drew her scimitar and stepped forward. "And you are soon to be nothing!" Nalini yelled. She stepped forward and sliced downward. He parried and tried to make an offensive attack, but she used her dagger and her scimitar to push him back and back until he was up against the wall. "You are not so arrogant when the odds are more even, are you Typhon?"

"Fuck you, bitch. You only wish you were me, you freakish male wannabe."

She focused her attack until his dagger hit the floor. He held up his sword and thrust at her and she kicked him in the stomach. "There's one Luc didn't know about," she said. He doubled over and she spun around and lifted her scimitar with both hands, severing his head on the downswing. She didn't stop, but continued to slash at him until he lay in a dozen pieces. "And now, you cruel, miserable beast, I will think of you no more!" Nalini shouted, panting and triumphant.

"No!" cried Nephthys.

Nalini turned to look at her. She seemed momentarily surprised that anyone else was present. The demons she was putting to rest had haunted her for far too long. Bloody, her face glistening with sweat, she walked toward Nephthys.

Luc, who had moved to support her after she carried out her decision, held Nalini's gaze steadily. He wished her to know that he accepted her decision as just and one with which he himself agreed. He would not let Nephthys' guilt over her son push guilt onto Nalini.

Nalini stood before Nephthys and grasped her hands. Placing her hands on either side of her face, she said, "See the truth and face it, painful as it may be."

Luc watched as Nephthys gazed into Nalini's eyes. The vacant look in both their eyes told him Nephthys was reading Nalini's thoughts as Nalini remembered more from her past with Typhon than Luc himself could ever bear to know.

Tears streamed down Nephthys' face, and then she sobbed, gasping for air. She reached up to grasp Nalini's hands, pressing them to her lips. "I am so sorry," she said.

Nalini pulled her close. "It was not your fault. You were as much a victim of Set as any of us."

Andrew, who with Roscoe and Rashid had watched the scene unfold with the solemn countenance of judges presiding over a long overdue execution, stepped forward and put his arm around Nephthys. "Mother is approaching. Let me take you to her." They turned and left the chamber.

Luc reached out to pull Nalini into his arms. He kissed the top of her head and said, "You okay?"

She smiled, weakly, and said, "The most empowered I have ever felt. I feel so free, knowing I no longer have to be alone and no longer have to be someone's slave. We make a great team, Luc," she added, pulling back to look toward the altar.

"I couldn't agree more, love." His heart swelled with pride at the strength and capacity for survival in this small warrior at his side. He felt glad to be the recipient of her softer side as well, for she loved, he was discovering, as fiercely as she fought.

Nalini moved to the altar and looked at the book. She turned to him, her eyes confused and questioning. "Set is your father and Sekhmet your mother? That is what he meant about the vampires?"

He nodded, watching her closely, gauging her reaction. When he discerned only mild curiosity, he felt a surge of relief. Turning his attention to the book, he reached to turn the page. Running his finger down it, he stopped when he reached her name, then moved back up an entry.

"Osiris? My father is Osiris," Nalini whispered, as if afraid to say it out loud. Hearing a commotion in the hall, they both turned at once.

"The book is here?" Isis demanded.

"How could you have done such a thing?" Nalini exploded, completely unconcerned with the commanding attitude Isis projected. "Please, tell me how you condemned us to an eternity in hell to quench your thirst for revenge? Does not your husband love you? His passion for you is legendary. Punish them both, yes, but like this? Can you imagine what her life has been like? What my life has been like?"

"This was your doing, mother? You knew Nalini was Osiris' daughter and you sentenced her to be molested and tortured for millenniums because she was your husband's bastard child? How do I reconcile this woman with the one who could so love me, an adopted child you saved from Set's fury?"

"I did not know." She had the decency to look guilty, even frightened. But it wasn't Nalini's anger that disturbed her. She was staring unwaveringly at Luc.

"You suspected," he accused. He watched her struggle to deny it to herself and felt a surge of anger at her continued duplicity.

"It was unlikely. Set took her the same night, and probably every night until the pregnancy was known, so great was his lust for her."

"Was it you who sent him in to her, mother? Did you want to be sure your husband had no bastard children around to embarrass you?"

Nalini gasped. "Surely not. You could not have sent him to rape her?"

Isis now turned her attention to Nalini, clearly angry herself. "No one sends Set to rape any woman. They are all his playthings. He desired her. Envious of all Osiris has ever had, including me, when he discovered that Osiris had been to her bed first, he went mad with rage. No one knew until it was too late. By then she went with him willingly to conceal her shame."

"Which shame?" Nalini demanded. "The adulterous seduction or the rape?"

"Does it matter?" Isis asked coldly. "She went willingly. We had our reasons for not interfering. I see now that I was wrong. It was a mistake, for which others have paid. I am truly sorry for what you have suffered, Nalini."

"Too little, too late," Nalini muttered.

Luc turned and bound the book within its leather casing. He tucked it into his shirt with a defiant look at Isis, then put his arm around Nalini and walked toward the door. "It may take a while to earn forgiveness for this one, mother," he said.

"The book," Isis commanded.

"Has been demanded by the king, who just arrived," Andrew announced from the doorway.

Nalini walked stiffly past Isis. Luc, noticing how she shivered with emotion, drew her against his side and walked with her down the passageway.

But see the angry Victor hath recall'd
His Ministers of vengeance and pursuit
Back to the Gates of Heav'n: The Sulphurous Hail
Shot after us in storm, oreblown hath laid
The fiery Surge, that from the Precipice
Of Heav'n receiv'd us falling, and the Thunder,
Wing'd with red Lightning and impetuous rage,
Perhaps hath spent his shafts, and ceases now
To bellow through the vast and boundless Deep.

Dante Alighieri, The Devine Comedy

Chapter Forty-Seven

They neared the exit before Nalini bolted. Luc caught her swiftly and pulled her against his chest. Lifting her chin, he looked solemnly into her eyes and said softly, "You have slain your dragons, princess. What more can you fear now?"

Only Luc would joke at such a moment, she thought. No wonder she loved him. And she did love him, she realized, passionately and unconditionally. He understood her so well. That he could appreciate the complete emotional upheaval she had suffered in the past few days was a blessing. She didn't need to explain. That would have been even more painful.

So what dragons remained? Nalini thought. How about a father she had never even met officially, a stepmother from hell who had before she was even born plotted to make her life insufferable. And then there was the matter of her being in love with their son, except that he was not their son after all and his father, formerly her father, was dead at the hand of her brother who tried to rape her, except that he wasn't really her brother.... Sighing, Nalini, in a moment of dark humor, thought that writers from daytime television would pay a fortune for her memoirs, and then dismissed the notion as she realized her life was too melodramatic for that venue. To prove it she pulled Luc's head down so he would kiss her.

The quick hot release of stoked passion his immediate response evoked gave her the temporary channel her confused and frustrated senses needed. She gave herself over to the kiss, and he lifted her up against him to more fully capture her lips. Of this one thing she was certain, Luc could go on kissing her forever and she would live a blissful life.

"Not your usual game face, son," Osiris interrupted.

Lowering her to the ground, far too slowly Nalini thought with panic, Luc muttered, "Works for me," and smiled unapologetically.

Horus, who stood beside him, threw his head back and roared with laughter. Nalini wished her sword were in her hand.

Then she glanced from Luc's look of smug satisfaction to Osiris' suppressed amusement, and since she glanced around but couldn't find a convenient chasm to fall into chose to remain mute--though she could feel the color surging into her cheeks. She noticed Andrew, who had gone ahead, standing a little to the left of his father. He shrugged his shoulders and held up his hands as if innocent of at least any intentional wrong doing.

Osiris held out his hand and Luc delivered *The Book of Life*. Then, he reached inside his shirt and pulled out the second leather-wrapped package and held it out.

"What is this?" Osiris asked, turned his hand to view the parcel from all angles.

"The appendix to the book. It contains the notes from the first experiments."

Osiris glanced up, his eyes shining with delight. "Are you sure? Do you know what this could mean?"

"Not as well as Kirin, but I have a good idea. She's going to be excited, too."

"Come, we must look at these. Anubis, take care of the mess, four corners of the globe for the refuse. The same for its sire." Then he turned and hurried toward the exit.

Andrew gave Luc a mock salute as he moved past him, and then they both chuckled at Osiris's continued choice of

Andrew as the one to clean up the messes his brother was always making.

Nalini tried to still her nerves as they followed Horus and Osiris from the tunnel. She was used to being around men who towered above her, but for some reason she felt adrift in a tide of giants. Not yet used to this jocular group of men who could switch so swiftly from laughing to lethal, it was like mental Olympics trying to keep up.

She was used to men who walked warily past each other in the hallways, silent and deadly their hands resting on their weapons. The men in her family had spies who followed and reported on the activities of the entire household as a normal routine. The only secrets in this family were the intimate secrets parents are known to keep from their children, Nalini thought.

"You okay?" Luc asked, and she was again amazed at how sensitive he was to her moods.

"I think I'll live," she said, turning her lips up slightly.

"Yes, but I have a need to keep you pleasured and happy," Luc said, smiling more openly. She couldn't resist a warmer response, her lips moving into a genuine smile.

When they moved to the exit, she recognized the cluster of tents that had been erected, similar to the setup Luc had before. Osiris moved into a large tent and set the parcels on the table in the center. Luc pulled her in front of him and rested his hands on her shoulders. He probably sensed her desire to stand behind him, she thought, watching tensely as Osiris opened the book.

He scanned the first two pages. Finding nothing out of the ordinary, he turned the page. Again, nothing. Nalini gasped, and the men turned to look at her. "Sorry," she said softly. She had been holding her breath and forgot to breath. Now that she remembered it was a struggle to keep her breathing shallow and normal.

Osiris looked back at the book. He read another page, then looked at the one next to it. Then he stopped and looked at Nalini.

"You have read this?"

"Would you rather I had not?"

He gazed at her carefully then, as if he had never really looked at her before. Or, perhaps it was as if he were remembering her mother, since she favored her mother so much. "I wanted to know if I would have to tell you, or just explain."

"Whatever you like," Nalini replied nervously.

Luc's hands tightened on her shoulders as if lending her courage. "She needs to know you don't blame or resent her," Luc explained. How he always knew what she was feeling when it was most important was a constant mystery to her.

"Resent her? *Blame* her?" He reached then, to pick up Nalini's hand. He noticed the ring and examined it carefully. Pressing it to his lips he said, "This once belonged to me. I gave it to a woman who I cared for deeply, genuinely and passionately." Nalini noted that he did not say he loved Astarte. She would not have respected him for that lie. They all knew he loved Isis, then and now. She was willing to believe he had really cared about her mother. No one questioned that he had desired her.

Osiris moved to pull her into his arms then, a real hug, the kind you give someone you love and cherish, Nalini thought. "My dear child, had I but known all these many, many years. To think of you in the clutches of those monsters." He pulled back to look down at her then and said, "But that is over. From now on you will know only security and belonging. You are now my daughter in fact and in my heart. Those who have conspired against you shall be brought to justice," he added, raising his head to look behind her.

Nalini turned and saw Isis enter the tent. "There will be a lot of changes from now on," Osiris said, holding Isis' gaze and then following her movement to the other side of the tent.

He looked back at Nalini and said, "Luc has told me much about you. You will be a great asset to this family. Let us hope we will enrich your life as well. What say you, daughter?"

Nalini felt stunned. He made decisions so swiftly, accepted her without question. Yes, the proof was before him, but after his initial regret at her past, he moved directly forward into the future, as if it could now become suddenly how it should have been all along. "I am overwhelmed just now. I hardly know what to say," she admitted as he continued to wait for her response.

"Of course. You must be overcome. Don't let these Neanderthal brothers intimidate you, either. They are nothing like you are used to, I assure you. I wish I could wipe out the mistakes that were made in the past. Know this, little one, I am delighted to have another daughter. My little Kirin will enjoy having a co-conspirator against her troublesome brothers, though I see you already know well how to get what you want from this one," he said, glancing up at Luc. "I look forward to getting to know you better, daughter. You will be welcomed by all in our family, now and forevermore." The last he said with conviction, an imperious command, and he had stared straight at Isis when he said it. Her expression was unreadable, but she remained silent. Watching, listening, but not participating.

Nalini bowed her head, pressed her hands to her forehead, crossed her wrists and pressed her hands to her heart. She had never done so to Set, but she felt a sudden desire to please and respect this man, this stranger, this anointed king who was now her father.

He nodded, then pulled her to him and kissed her on each cheek and then her forehead. "You are from this day forth Nalini Vargas, princess of the crown, under my protection and those who serve me, blessed by Rā, and a beloved daughter of the true royal bloodline. So is it recorded in *The Book of Life,* by my own witness and so shall it be recorded for all time."

"Thank you," she said simply.

"And now she must rest, and will want to speak to her mother," said Luc.

Osiris nodded, and Luc pulled her with him to the exit. He lifted the tent flap to let her pass, then drew her toward a smaller tent, farther away from the vault. A small fire burned in front and she rubbed her arms against the sudden chill.

Once in the tent, she walked to sit near the fire there, drawing her legs up. Luc handed her a cup of tea from the table and wrapped a blanket around her shoulders. Then, handing her a cell phone, hers, fully charged, he said softly, "I'll be back in a few minutes. I want to grab us something to eat."

Grateful, she realized he knew she would want time to think and to speak to her mother. The phone rang only once before Astarte said, "Nalini?"

"It's over, mother." Or should she have said it was just beginning, because suddenly she felt like she had been reborn. Osiris, Luc, everything was changing. At last she would look forward to each new day rather than dreading her immortality.

"They're both dead?"

At long last, they were both free, Nalini thought, feeling as if she should shout and dance.

Instead she said, "Yes. Are you feeling alright, mother?"

"I feel safe. It's a wonderful relief." So her mother shared her sense of liberation. She had no remorse, it seemed, for the loss of her husband.

"Mother?"

"It's Osiris, isn't it?"

"Yes, my father is Osiris. Did you know?" Should she be angry at her for not telling her the truth all these years?

"I always sensed it, knew it in my heart."

So she had known. "Did you love him, mother?" Nalini asked, trying to understand how her mother could have risked so angering Isis for a night of passion in Osiris' arms.

"How could I not?" she said almost wistfully, as if remembering.

"But knowing that he truly loves Isis, why did you do it? Try to make me understand. Please, I don't want to judge you, but I need to understand."

"I trusted him. I had a vision and I saw Osiris in my bed, and you in my arms. After that, what else could I do? It was my destiny."

"You trusted him, and then you had a vision?"

"My first."

"So it was trust?" Nalini looked into the flames, watching the blues and greens vie for domination with the orange and yellows. She was only able to love Luc after she trusted him. Until she trusted him, she could not fully give her heart to him. He now had it firmly in his hands, she realized. No matter what else happened, as long as they were together it would all be worked out.

"Nalini?"

"Oh, yes, sorry, mother. I was thinking of something."

"I'm sorry I couldn't tell you. It wasn't safe, and there was no sense in getting your hopes up. Isis would not have let us return."

She could imagine how intimidating Isis could have been defending her husband against an adulterous affair and even worse a bastard child. Her mother had little choice, she admitted to herself.

"When are you coming back here and where will we go?" Astarte asked quietly.

"I assume we come back tomorrow, mother. I'm not sure where we go from here, but what matters is that we will be together. There is much to consider."

"Yes. We will talk more when you arrive. Kirin has been hovering over me like a nursemaid. She is such a warm, caring person."

"I get the sense that everyone in her family adores her. Mother?"

"Yes."

"Is it right that I should love Osiris and become the daughter he has decreed me openly to be?" She couldn't help wanting to become a part of Luc's family, despite Isis. Osiris seemed genuinely loving and most willing to get to know her better as his daughter. He made her feel like he was glad she had come into his life, even though he had previously not even known of her existence.

"You are his daughter, Nalini. It is your right to be treated as such." The tremor in her voice alerted Nalini to the fact that the news made her mother emotional. Astarte was pleased to have her belief confirmed as to Nalini's paternity.

"His bastard daughter, mother," she reminded her.

"Has he made you feel that way?"

"No." He had in fact even insinuated that Kirin would be thrilled to accept her as a sister.

"Do they treat your Luc like a bastard child?"

"No, of course not."

"Then I fail to see the problem. You have paid for our sins long enough."

"I will talk to you tomorrow, mother. I love you."

"I love you, too, Nalini."

Nalini snapped her phone shut, considering her mother's advice. Even Astarte felt she should accept being a member of the Vargas family.

Luc returned looking troubled, and Nalini said, "Has something happened?"

"A lot for one day," he said, running his hands through his hair. She had noticed that he did that most often when he was exhausted or frustrated or angry.

"Andrew came back to camp. He said Typhon's body is missing."

Nalini jumped to her feet, dropping her cup.

"Nephthys is missing too."

"After all I showed her? How could she forgive him? She knows he wants to kill her. Will she revive him?"

"She feels it is her fault, not his. There's a note. She takes full responsibility."

"But will she revive him?" she repeated, fear creeping up her spine like a recurring cancer she had hoped cured.

"It seems likely, Lini," he said reluctantly, reaching out to pull her against him. "We will search for them, but she will go underground and not be found any time soon. Until then, we will live our lives as we have always done. They will not be causing havoc any time soon."

Nalini shivered from more than the chill night air. "I told you, love, he will never put his hands on you again," Luc promised. He picked her up and snuggled her, carrying her to the pile of blankets and pillows. Though not as elaborate as Hassidim's provisions, Nalini knew she would feel warm and safe until dawn. Tomorrow was time enough to decide what to do about Typhon.

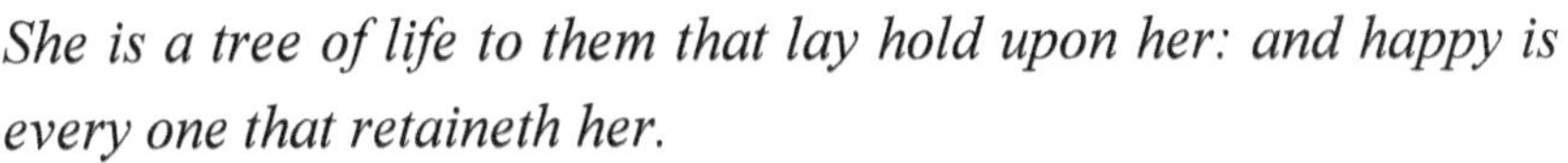

She is a tree of life to them that lay hold upon her: and happy is every one that retaineth her.

Proverbs 3: 18

Chapter Forty-Eight

"A sister, at long last," Kirin said, hugging Nalini to her, another of those true hugs given to someone you really love, Nalini thought.

Nalini hugged her back. She was fast growing used to being loved for her own sake, rather than lusted after or used as a pawn for the selfish pleasures of others.

"Your mother will be glad to see you," Kirin said. "She is feeling much better."

"I'm looking forward to seeing her, too."

Not that lust was necessarily a bad thing, Nalini mused, remembering the previous night. Luc, however, was far from selfish. *Pleasured and happy, my love, I want you constantly pleasured and happy,* he had breathed into her ear in the long warm moments just before daylight. *It's fairly simple to please me, and pleasing you makes me very happy indeed.* He had proved it once more, just so she would be certain, he had assured her.

Nalini walked into her mother's tent and was relieved to see the color back in her cheeks. Kirin was good for her mother, Nalini decided.

"Things are going well with Osiris?"

"Yes. He is most generous. I have funds at my disposal, whatever I desire, wherever I wish to live. Ironic really, when my needs are so meager. Though I will have to buy more western clothing now. Kirin, Luc assured me, will be happy to help."

"Where will you live?"

"With Luc. You will live with us too, of course."

"What about Isis?" Her mother looked worried, her hands pressed against her stomach.

"A helicopter picked her up last night. Osiris had her taken back to the Underworld. He said she would stay with him now, as she was his wife and that's where she belongs. The incredible thing isn't that he put his foot down. The truly incredible thing is that she obeyed."

"She went without a fight?"

"Yes. Luc said it is proof she feels remorse for what she has done and feels she deserves his anger. Also, if she stays in his bed, she will not have to worry about anyone else being there. Luc told me his father stopped his infidelity after the incident with you. I think he felt responsible for what happened to you even then. Luc thinks that's when he finally understood what his wanderlust was doing to Isis. He realized he could never have even a second wife with her as his first."

"In my heart I always knew that," Astarte said softly.

"You don't still love him, do you, mother?"

"After what he allowed to happen to us? Hardly. He chose her over everyone. I can't delude myself that I was more than a passing fancy, from the very beginning. I was under no illusions about that. Naturally I thought I might have more than the one night before our affair would end."

"I believe I could learn to love him, this reformed husband and father. But I too feel hurt and angry about what happened to us. Still, they are all trying to make amends. I would rather be empowered by our new freedom than let our past continue to rule our lives."

"You are right, of course. So where do we go from here?"

"Rome. Luc wants to show me the family business. I am to help run the Illuminati. Kirin returns to Peru to begin work with her new data."

"Yes, she is so excited. She has spoken of little else."

"Soon we shall have a new baby brother to spoil. What will you call him?"

"He has not yet told me his name."

"I see." Nalini placed her hand upon her mother's stomach, already feeling affection for her unborn brother.

She turned as Luc entered. It was his brother too, she realized. Odd that they were not siblings, but they shared a sibling in common. The royal bloodline was strong and did not stray far, which she supposed was understandable when one considered the alternative—having only mortals from which to choose. Most immortals would not even consider the torment of outliving and being forced to bury a spouse in what seemed a very insignificant amount of time when compared to eternity. There were some, however. Children from such unions lived longer than normal mortals, but they too were not immortal. That was another reason, Nalini knew, for the genetic experiments—at least from Kirin's point of view.

Luc nodded to Astarte and smiled. "Osiris requested that I ask your permission for him to visit with you for a moment."

Nalini watched her mother closely, saw her smooth her hand across her stomach and grasp Nalini's hand before she looked toward the entrance.

"May I tell him you will see him?"

"Yes, of course," she murmured.

"Nalini," he said, holding his hand out for her to accompany him so that her parents could speak alone. She glanced anxiously at Astarte, who nodded her reassurance, then moved with Luc toward the doorway. Luc pulled the tent flap back and waited for her to exit. She saw Osiris outside, pacing. He turned as they emerged and looked anxiously at Luc.

He nodded, and Osiris moved forward. Reaching out to pull Nalini into a quick hug, he said, "Good morning, little one. You look well." Kissing her forehead, he turned and ducked into the tent.

"He is nervous," she said, shocked.

"It is difficult for men to beg forgiveness, especially when they should," he said.

"I will remember that," she said teasingly, smiling up at him.

"Let us hope you seldom need to," he said, leaning down to kiss her forehead as well.

"All this happiness and kindness, it is going to make me soft," Nalini complained.

"Oh, I think you will find the family business helps you keep the edge up," Luc said, laughing. "You may not be in the hot sun and desert as often, but you will find there are plenty of scorpions. Come, you are about to receive your first sting, but this venom will protect you—a gift from Osiris."

Curious, Nalini followed him into a tent she had not noticed before. She saw equipment on a table similar to a funerary table, with a man who resembled a high priest standing beside it. Looking up at Luc, she said, "What is all this?"

Rolling up his sleeve, he pointed to the symbol she had often idly traced with her finger. "Usually members of our family receive this mark when they come of age. You know it as the symbol of Rā, but it is recognized by mortals as the symbol of the Illuminati. Once you receive this, you become one of us for all time, a ruling member of the Illuminati's inner circle with equal voting privileges and responsibilities."

"Do I have a choice?"

"There is always choice. The reason they are not here for the ceremony yet is that you are to make that choice. Once you have done so, they will witness the initiation."

"And the one on your back?"

He placed his hand in the small of her back. "Much smaller than mine, Nalini. More appropriate to your size and gender. Designating you as a daughter of the anointed king, the immortal phoenix, rising from the ashes." He placed his hand upon her upper right shoulder. "Rā, here, Like Kirin's," he explained, "the flames encircling your upper arm, the eternal circle."

She nodded, thoughtful. Osiris had truly accepted her, completely and immediately. She was overwhelmed. He barely knew her. How could he already love her? Was it because Luc loved her? But they all seemed so genuine. Looking up into Luc's serious face, she asked, "What would you have me do?"

He made a gesture for the priest to leave, waited silently for a moment and then said softly, "I would have you take your rightful place in our family, Nalini." He pulled her down beside him on a narrow bench so that he could gaze directly into her eyes. Capturing her lips, he gently caressed them with his own. Rising up, he continued, "I would have you as my wife, the mother of our children. It is all for you to decide." Seeing her eyes widen in surprise, he added quickly, "There has been so much happening too quickly for me to burden you with my own desires. First, make the decision Osiris has asked of you."

When she would have spoken, would have told him she wanted the same things, but was confused by the suddenness of everything, he changed his focus, redirecting her attention to Osiris' offer. "If you accept Osiris, you will also be offering him your forgiveness. Isis too."

How well he understood her, as if alert to every expression and seeking the implied meaning of every word. But he truly loved her, wanted her to be the mother of his children. Her heart, so closely guarded for so long seemed overflowing with warm emotion. She was so happy she felt anxious, afraid something would happen to take it all away. Unwilling to consider the possibility in the midst of such happiness, she remembered what Luc had said about Isis. She would need to cross that bridge now.

"Does she ask it? Does she feel regret, remorse?" She did not feel very forgiving of Isis.

"Yes, she has said so. She would not lie about such a thing." Seeing the indignation on her face, he added, "truly, Lini, she is not an evil woman, not like the motivation behind the actions of those in your wrongful family. Astarte was not the first, she was just that last straw. I spoke to Sekhmet about it. She said Isis stopped ignoring father's infidelities. She tried pleading, rages, and threats. Nothing worked. Always he promised to stop, that it meant nothing. And always again his eye would stray. When it appeared that he felt more than the usual passing fancy for Astarte, she went ballistic."

"She sent Set to my mother?" Nalini felt her temper rise, even though she better understood Isis's angry vengeance.

"No, she had nothing to do with that. At least in that regard she did not lie. Not even in anger could Isis set such vengeance upon another woman, Nalini. Do you know that she was so distraught about the entire affair she moved out and has refused to live permanently with Osiris for over three thousand years?"

"The longest separation in the history of the world," Nalini said, amazed.

"If you can call it a true separation considering they are together half the time even now."

"So now he will make her live with him all the time?"

"She's not exactly under house arrest. One doesn't quite tell Isis what she must do. She chose to obey him. But you know, I almost think he may have been angry enough to imprison her if she had refused," he said, glancing away as if considering the possibility. "I think she agreed because we are all angry with her as well as Osiris. She really is trying to make amends, Lini."

"If you say so, I will try to believe it," she said honestly.

"Once you and Astarte have managed to forgive her, and once Osiris believes she is truly contrite and able to accept Astarte's presence in our lives, he will let her return to her former reign. Or, she will think he's taking too long just to keep her with him, get angry, have a fit of rage and leave," he said, grinning.

"Or perhaps he will make her so happy she will not want to leave," she suggested.

"If he is as wise as I have always thought him, that is the tactic he will use," he agreed, laughing.

Luc had already forgiven his tenacious, impetuous mother, Nalini realized. No doubt he was used to doing so, with Isis' legendary temper. "And do you have fits of rage like your parents?" she asked.

He leaned down and captured her lips, pulling her against him. A few moments later, he raised his head and she saw that his eyes were as blue as the Mediterranean at dusk, the pupils dilated, lids heavy with lust. His breathing was shallow but rapid. "I have fits of passion," he whispered, gazing down at her.

"I accept," she said.

He smiled. "You accept what, Osiris' offer?" Seeing her nod, he said, "You will be a great asset to the Illuminati, and to me." She tilted her head back to accept his continued passion as well.

He raised his head again and said, "Let's go tell the family before I grab you and run away to keep you all to myself for a year or two."

Though his second idea held more appeal, she let him lead her from the tent. She glanced up at a distant sand hill. Two lone Bedouin had stopped to adjust their camels' loads.

Seeing the small tent currently housing Lucien as a prisoner directly at the bottom of that hill, she asked, "What's to become of Lucien? He was so reticent when I tried to talk to him. Though he doesn't seem to blame me for his fate, he is angry and frustrated, feeling abandoned, disconnected from us all." If only he could be persuaded to join them, to become a welcome member of this new, loving family, she thought. Surely he didn't miss the constant subterfuge, the evil intent of Typhon, the rages of Set.

"We are still debriefing him. Sekhmet seems to be having a better effect on him than Nephthys had on Typhon. Right now I am not quite sure," Luc said, his voice carrying his own concern about his twin brother's fate.

They turned toward Osiris' tent and neither of them noticed that one of the Bedouin covertly peered through binoculars at the tent in which Lucien still waited to discover his fate. Luc hunched his shoulders and shuddered as if with a sudden chill and rubbed the back of his neck, turning to glance behind them.

Nalini looked up at him questioningly. He turned back and glanced down at her, and then smiled with reassurance and urged her toward the large tent where the family had gathered.

To where their new life would begin.

Just the beginning...

Now that her children have flown from the nest, Elizabeth lives with her newest baby (AKA a precocious Maltese named Hudson), and husband, Kenton, at the foot of the beautiful Catalina Mountain Range in Oro Valley, AZ. She loves to hike the mountain trails, ride her bike, sit on her patio sipping coffee and reading or brainstorming plots and enjoying the grandeur of her breathtaking mountain views.

Elizabeth calls herself a pantser on steroids. Her love of mythology and ancient literature and history were the backbone for her series, and the Sigma Force series by James Rollins inspired the fast-paced adventures.

A friend compared Elizabeth's series to what it would be like if Ford and Jolie stepped through the Stargate, tried to kill each other, and ended up falling into a love as seemingly hopeless as Romeo and Juliet.

Visit her at: www.elizabethalsobrooks.com

529

Tell-Tale Publishing would like to thank you for your purchase. If you enjoyed this story, see what other great reads you can find at:

www.tell-talepublishing.com